MW00584478

MURDER BY LAMPLIGHT

PATRICE McDONOUGH

KENSINGTON
PUBLISHING CORP.

www.kensingtonbooks.com

KENSINGTON BOOKS are published by

Kensington Publishing Corp.
119 West 40th Street
New York, NY 10018

Copyright © 2024 by Patrice McDonough

All Kensington titles, imprints, and distributed lines are available at special quantity discounts for bulk purchases for sales promotion, premiums, fund-raising, educational, or institutional use. Special book excerpts or customized printings can also be created to fit specific needs. For details, write or phone the office of the Kensington Special Sales Manager: Attn. Special Sales Department. Kensington Publishing Corp., 119 West 40th Street, New York, NY 10018. Phone: 1-800-221-2647.

The K with book logo Reg. U.S. Pat. & TM. Off.

Library of Congress Control Number: 2023947406

ISBN: 978-1-4967-4636-8
First Kensington Hardcover Edition: March 2024

ISBN: 978-1-4967-4638-2 (ebook)

10 9 8 7 6 5 4 3 2 1

Printed in the United States of America

For my parents, who always had books beside their reading chairs

He knows a baseness in his blood
At such strange war with something good . . .

—Alfred, Lord Tennyson

PROLOGUE

A clanging jolted little Jacko from his broken sleep.

Under a threadbare blanket, he curled himself against the stinging cold. Shivering, he saw the fog of his breath and felt the gnawing hunger in his stomach.

During his weeks inside the walls, the boy had learned that a workhouse child was an empty belly with hollow eyes and darting hands ready to grab any unguarded crust. The pinch of hunger made thieves of them all. Tired and weak, he had to get up if he wanted to eat. And he'd better be quick, or he'd feel the crack of Matron's hand and would face a day with nothing until dinner.

But when he heard the keys jangle and saw the sliver of light at the bottom of the door, he froze on his cot. Barely breathing, he listened until the lamp moved on and a key scraped at another door.

Relief flooded. Then he buried his face and sobbed.

"Jillie."

CHAPTER 1

November 1866

Julia Lewis edged her way through the gawping crowd. Then a young policeman blocked her way when she finally broke through.

"Sorry, miss." The bobbie pointed his truncheon. "That way will take you to the markets along the Commercial Road."

"Thank you, Constable, but someone else is shopping today. I'm here to examine a corpse."

He stared, opened his mouth, and closed it.

Julia sighed. "Perhaps you'd be kind enough to call your superior officer?" She pulled out a note and checked the signature. "Inspector Richard Tennant?"

"Paddy," he called over his shoulder to a tall, burly copper. "Lady wants to see the guvnor." When he added, "It's about the body," the big man looked at her sharply.

His eyes dropped to her medical bag. "All right, Bert. Find himself and tell him he's wanted." The younger constable walked off, glancing back at her over his shoulder.

The big policeman touched his helmet. "The officer's after

fetching the inspector," he said, the lilt and cadence of Ireland in his voice.

"Thank you, Constable . . ."

"O'Malley."

Julia nodded. "Constable O'Malley."

She dropped her medical bag and looked around. The note had directed her to a construction site, the last unfinished section of London's massive sewer project, but the discovery of a body had halted all work. Pickaxes and shovels leaned against piles of gray stone and dusty brick while idled men puffed on clay pipes, in no hurry to resume their labors. They had pulled down a row of houses to make room for a tunnel, and the void yawned, like a gap-toothed smile, between dilapidated buildings, their pitched roofs and chimneys a jagged line against the sky.

It had rained the night before. Julia glanced up at a pewter sky that threatened another downpour. The murder scene would turn into a bog if the inspector didn't hurry.

Minutes ticked by, and Julia tapped her umbrella against her side. She looked down at the watch hanging on its chain and then up at O'Malley. The constable smoothed the ends of his bushy mustache and turned away, whistling an off-key tune. Finally, a well-tailored man with a military bearing approached and touched the brim of his hat.

"Detective Inspector Tennant," he said in a clipped baritone. He gestured to a short, wiry officer at his elbow. "Detective Sergeant Graves. How may I help you?"

Julia shifted her umbrella and extended her right hand. "Julia Lewis." She nodded to the sergeant. "You sent for my grandfather, Andrew Lewis, but I'm afraid he's unavailable. I assist him in his practice."

"Are you a nurse, Miss Lewis? Because we need a—"

"It's Doctor Lewis."

"Surely you're not proposing to—"

"Indeed, I am, Inspector."

Sergeant Graves had been rocking heel to toe, his thumbs hooked into his pockets, fingers drumming his jacket. He stopped. "Blimey." He looked her up and down. "Never."

Julia smiled. "It's true, Sergeant. I've thought about carrying my medical diploma with me. But even rolled up, it won't fit into my bag."

Reactions like his still galled her, but four years after qualifying, she usually managed to hide her irritation. The sergeant returned her smile, but Tennant did not. She sighed. *No sense of humor.*

"Is the victim over there, Inspector?" She nodded to the line of policemen's helmets and shoulders visible over the edge of a ditch.

Tennant nodded. "But I'm afraid it's not a sight for . . . Doctor Lewis, I don't think — "

"Inspector Tennant, you sent for my grandfather, and I am standing in for him while he convalesces. I am a fully qualified doctor listed on the medical register. Now, shall I proceed with the examination? Full-blown rigor may set in if we dither much longer."

Tennant stepped aside. "Of course, Doctor."

Julia picked up her bag and brushed past him. "I've seen my share of dead bodies."

Sergeant Graves called after her. "Not like this one, you haven't, miss — Doctor."

"A lady doctor," Tennant muttered. "Heaven spare us."

Julia edged down the twenty-foot incline, dislodging a shower of loose pebbles. It ended in a half-completed drainage tunnel. At the bottom of the pit, viscous ochre mud sucked at her boots. She skirted around piles of bricks and ducked under a web of oak scaffolding.

Sergeant Graves scrambled into the pit after her, Tennant trailing a few paces behind. He struggled to navigate the slope —

surprising, Julia thought, for a man who looked to be in his mid-thirties.

The lower half of a man's body, propped on its left side, extended from the end of the brick tunnel. His upper torso, shoulders, and head were thrown into shadow. His trousers and underdrawers had been yanked to his ankles, forming a tangled mass around his boots. His right hand covered his genitals. *Was it placed there after death?* Julia thought it probable. Traces of blood stained the soil under his fingers.

Julia took a breath. *Steady on*, she thought. *You've done this before.* Still, she'd never examined a murder victim, and she'd be damned if she let the policemen see her hand shake.

She pulled a vulcanized rubber glove from her medical bag and crouched in front of the corpse. One of the constables groaned when she exposed the gory mess hidden there. He reached reflexively to cover his crotch.

Julia looked over her shoulder at Tennant. "Have your officers searched the area carefully, Inspector?"

"Of course."

"I should have them look again. The killer may have discarded the man's—" The stricken expression on a young constable's face stopped her. "You may find the victim's member somewhere nearby."

They'll probably never find it, Julia thought. *Carried off by feral cats, most likely.* And rats had been busy with the fingertips and earlobes.

She stood up. "Not as much blood as one might expect; the mutilation must have happened postmortem." She walked around the body. "Sodomized as well, it seems."

For a big man, Constable O'Malley moved quickly and deftly. He looked around, pulled a handkerchief from his pocket, and straightened up with a broken stick in his hand. "With this, Doctor? Looks to be blood on it."

"Possibly." She stashed the evidence in a cloth bag. "Well spotted, Constable. Thank you."

A chipped front tooth slightly marred O'Malley's friendly smile. While he had the open countenance of an easygoing man, the broken nose on his round, amiable face told another story perhaps. The right hand that offered Julia the stick had several sunken knuckles and misaligned fingers. *Metacarpal fractures—quick with his fists? And with his wits*, she thought. He'd watched every move she'd made.

Tennant had said nothing since he'd entered the trench. Julia noticed his slight pallor. Despite the morning's chill, a layer of sweat covered his forehead.

"Shall we shift the body forward, Inspector?"

Tennant turned away abruptly. With his back to the mouth of the gaping tunnel, he nodded. "Perhaps you'll be good enough to have your report on my desk tomorrow morning?"

"Of course."

Tennant scrambled awkwardly up the graveled incline, leaving Sergeant Graves to oversee the removal of the body. *The help will do the cleanup work*, she thought.

"Carefully, now," Julia said to the constables as they moved into place.

When the victim's head and shoulders cleared the end of the tunnel, a bobbie muttered, "Bloody hell. It's the Saint of Spitalfields."

He watched the coppers perform on his stage.

The first scene the night before had been so easy. Would the clergyman come? There was a boy who needed help. Of course, he would. He'd aided so many boys over the years, hadn't he? The "Saint" had followed the messenger into the fog-shrouded night, probably thinking Providence and his collar protected him. But when the messenger breathed a name and place in the old cleric's ear, the man froze as if an icy shard had pierced his heart.

With a blade at his throat, the clergyman had listened to what would happen next.

He'd gathered his cast, observing them like a director surveying the stage. *Right on cue.* The inspector and his crew couldn't drag their eyes away.

Look at me. Look what I have wrought, he wanted to crow.

No, he'd stay quiet, behind the fourth wall, invisible. It was still early in the first act, and he'd planned an open-ended run.

He watched them wince and cringe, relishing the final shock as the scene ended. And that woman—an unexpected addition to his ensemble—he'd add her to the script. Why not?

Doctors. They're just as guilty.

The following day, Julia's grandfather struggled down the back staircase to her office on the first floor. Dr. Lewis leaned his shoulder against the doorframe, stopping to catch his breath. He watched his granddaughter, her head down, absorbed in a document.

"I saw your last patient leave by the side gate, Julie. I wanted to catch you before you left for the clinic."

Julia looked up. "You didn't have long to wait." She picked up a list and waved it at him. "Only three of your patients have agreed to see me. I suppose the rest have gone to Uncle Max?"

"I'm sorry, Julie."

In the half-light of the shadowy hallway, his gray hair looked darker than it was. Then, when he moved into the room, stooped, stiff-gated, and supported by a cane, her heart caught. Within a month, he had become an old man. He was no longer the grandfather who had taught her to swim, raced her across the pond, and hiked the cliffs of Dover. Julia noticed he'd missed the third button on his waistcoat.

"How did the police take to the substitute Doctor Lewis?"

"About as you'd expect. Consternation all around, although Inspector Tennant tried to swallow it. More or less."

He cleared his throat. "Julie, I should like to talk to you about—"

"Can it wait, Grandpa?" She tapped the document on her desk. "I have to finish this medical report for Scotland Yard, and I'll be late for the clinic before I'm done."

"Julia."

There was something in his tone, and he'd used her proper name instead of his usual Julie.

"You can't keep up this pace, my girl. Hurling yourself back and forth from your practice to the clinic—it's punishing. Surely you see it's not good for you or your patients. You've looked exceedingly tired of late."

"Grandfather . . ."

"Have you been home in time for dinner one night this week?"

Julia rounded her desk, slipped her hands inside his jacket, and pushed the forgotten button through its slot. Then she kissed him on the cheek. When she stepped back, her right hand came away with his watch.

"I'd make an excellent pickpocket. It's my deft doctor's touch." She smiled and showed him the face. "You see? I'm going to be very late."

He didn't return her smile. Instead, he retrieved his watch and tucked it away, frowning.

"Last night at the dinner table, you barely kept your eyes open. No, don't shake your head at me. By heaven, I'm a doctor, too, or have you forgotten? I know a case of exhaustion when I see one."

"I'm as strong as a cart horse." Julia smiled again. "And you're a fine one to talk. Why are you fully dressed and taking the stairs? You should be resting until luncheon."

His attack had come as a shock to them both. Four weeks earlier, her grandfather had been changing for dinner when he felt an intense tightness in his chest, and his knees gave way. Julia knew diseases of the heart were always unpredictable. A second attack could come at any time, or it could be years away.

Her grandfather sighed, searching her face. "Julie. Listen to me, my dear. You must know there aren't enough hours in the day or days in the year to wash it all away. Until you forgive yourself—or, better yet, understand it wasn't your fault—you'll stay trapped in the prison you've made."

All this exaggerated concern, she thought. *Would you say this to me if I were a grandson?*

Julia had begun to doubt that she'd ever win the professional respect that was automatic for men who earned a medical degree. Now it was her grandfather. The one man who'd always encouraged her worried she wasn't up to the job's rigors. *I'll just have to work harder. Harder than any man.*

And she could see no other way to silence the voice except by filling her days with work. But, tired as she was, on many nights, sleep eluded her. One face haunted her; one voice returned in her dreams.

She jumped, Julia.

Constable O'Malley elbowed Jonathan Graves outside the inspector's office and tipped the post so the sergeant could see it. Graves read the direction on the envelope: "To Inspector Tennant of the Yard," written in a florid hand in purple ink.

"What are you thinking, Sarge—a love letter for himself?"

Graves took the post and added it to Dr. Lewis's report. "Don't know, mate. But I'll wager a pint he won't turn a hair when he sees it." He nodded at the medical report. "Lady doctors—what next?"

"She's a cool one, now," O'Malley said. "Never a blink, even after she spied the clergyman's knob went missing. Knows her stuff and all. And she's thorough. Looked over every inch of the ground around the corpse. Most docs only have eyes in their heads for the body."

Graves grunted. "Coppers in skirts before we know it, Paddy."

When the inspector waved them in, Graves handed him the post and the medical report. "You sent for us, guv?"

Tennant didn't answer. He was staring at the top letter. As the silence stretched out, the officers exchanged glances.

Graves shifted his weight and cleared his throat. "Sir?"

The inspector looked up from the envelope. "Why isn't Higgins in a holding cell? What are you waiting for, Sergeant? He'll be outside the Blind Beggar, thirsty for his first pint of the day."

"Thought that, with the Atwater case, we were handing Higgins off."

Tennant fixed his stare on Graves.

"Right, guv. We'll get on it."

"Take the constable with you."

Outside, at the end of the hallway, O'Malley said, "What's with himself? The frost's on him, sure. Still, that letter gave him a turn, so you're owing me one, Sarge."

Graves eased his collar. "I could do with a pint right now."

After the officers left, Tennant looked at the calendar and flinched: November 14. Two years earlier, he had celebrated his greatest success, the arrest of the infamous "Railway Murderer." The hunt for the man who bludgeoned a respectable banker in his first-class carriage had left the city on edge, assaulting English ideas of security and propriety. Such horrors were confined to the unsavory corners of the capital, or so people thought.

Fear made good press, and the swift arrest of Franz Meyer made Tennant's career. The inspector's star had risen along with newspaper circulation. Ridership on the North London Line returned once the killer was behind bars. Then, a year earlier, on the first anniversary of Meyer's execution, Tennant received the first letter written in purple ink. A prank, he thought at the time, dismissing it.

But the same message had arrived in his post that morning—a single, livid line scratched across creamy writing paper.

You hanged the wrong man.

A messenger from the chief inspector's office stuck his head around Tennant's door just before noon.

"The chief sends his compliments, Inspector. He'd like to hear your report by the end of the day."

Tennant thanked the man but doubted the preamble of politeness came from Chief Inspector Clark. He tried to put the blasted letter out of his mind and opened the medical report, flipping to the signature page at the back.

"Julia R. Lewis, M.D.," he muttered. *A lady doctor—that will put the chief's knickers in a twist.*

He paged back to the beginning and started reading, wondering how much irrelevant nonsense he'd have to wade through before she got down to the facts. But the report surprised him. Dr. Lewis had done a thorough job: It was clear, comprehensive, but concise. "Cause of death," he read, "a knife wound to the chest, a slim-bladed weapon plunged directly into the heart. Time of death: based on an examination of the body, sometime between eight p.m. and four a.m. Based on the condition of the ground, probably sometime before midnight."

Dr. Lewis noted that the ground was damp, but the area under the body was dry. That night, the rain had begun shortly after twelve. The timing was consistent with the evidence of their only witness, a night watchman who'd seen the victim.

That narrows it down. The doctor seems to know her stuff. Tennant set the medical evidence aside and picked up the police report.

A letter in the victim's pocket had confirmed his identity. The constable had been right, although Tennant had little reason to doubt him. The mane of snowy hair, the broken, gold-framed glasses found at his side, and the clergyman's "dog collar" told their story. It made the mutilation of the body all the more shocking. The "Saint of Spitalfields," the Reverend Mr. Tobias Atwater, was the rector of St. Edmund's Church on Commercial Street. A tireless champion of the downtrodden, the sainted clergyman was dead, and Tennant hadn't a clue about the killer's identity or the motive.

They'd found a gold pocket watch and three pounds in paper and silver on his person, so robbery hadn't been the motive. Then there was the mutilation, which made it hardly a run-of-the-mill crime. And the killer had stuffed something odd into the slit of the man's waistcoat pocket: a popped balloon, a child's plaything.

But why pick it up? Why hold on to it?

Next he reviewed the stack of witness interviews. Neither the clergyman's housekeeper nor his part-time curate could explain what had brought Atwater to the site. The sewer under construction, soon to be part of the vast, citywide system, would carry its waste away from the eyes and nostrils of its East End residents. But the murder scene was a mile from Atwater's rectory.

What was he doing there in the middle of the night?

A small army of coppers had conducted house-to-house and shop-to-shop interviews. Only one person said he'd seen the victim that night. Around 11:30, the witness spotted Mr. Atwater on Commercial Street near Christ Church, about a half mile from the murder scene. The man, a night watchman at the church, knew the clergyman by sight. He said Atwater was walking with someone he took to be a prostitute. According to the report, "Mister Atwater handed the streetwalker something the witness believed was a handful of coins. They parted, walking in opposite directions. The witness described the woman as 'ginger-haired.'"

A henna-haired prostitute—wonderful, Tennant thought. There were hundreds in East London alone, and not one would talk to the police. He dropped the report on his desk and swiveled to look out his window. The leaden sky and curling chimney smoke failed to inspire. He tipped his chair back and stared at the web of cracks in the ceiling paint. *The crime scene—something's wrong there.* Something about the position of Atwater's body nagged at him.

Why take the time to drag it halfway into the pipe? Why not leave it out in the open? If concealment was the aim, why not shove it all the way in?

Tennant brought his chair down to the floor with a jolt. Had the killer's placement of the corpse been staged to produce a series of shocks? First, he had exposed the clergyman's naked lower body for the world to see. Then, when Dr. Lewis moved Atwater's hand, the mutilation appeared. Finally, the last surprise: the victim's face and identity. Had the killer thought it all out?

What kind of sick, calculating monster is this?

Tennant drummed his fingers on the medical report and opened it again.

The doctor's cover letter listed two addresses: her practice at 17 Finsbury Circus and the Whitechapel Clinic in the East End on Fieldgate Street. Her clinic hours there were listed as noon to six.

He checked his pocket watch.

Tennant set out under a gray and lowering sky. He hopped off an omnibus and turned right on Fieldgate Street, the lane curving away from the noise of Whitechapel Road. As he walked on, the clatter and squeak of hooves and wheels on cobblestones faded.

Once, the neighborhood's soot-blackened tenements must have been brick red and the trim freshly whitewashed. Now paint on the doorframes and lintels peeled away in curling strips. Up and down the road, ragged clothing drooped from lines and railings. When Tennant passed a row of shops, he pulled back as a butcher's boy hurled a bucket of pink, frothy water into the street. By a grocer's half-price barrow, he turned his head away from the sour smell of spoiling cabbage.

Then, at the bend where the lane met Plummer's Row, the silvery tones of a set of handbells stopped him. Someone sounded the scale from behind an open window, sliding into a familiar melody: the chimes of Westminster. Tennant stepped back and looked up. A plaque over the door read WHITECHAPEL BELL FOUNDRY: ESTABLISHED A.D. 1570. A smaller sign in the window announced BELL-FOUNDERS OF BIG BEN AND THE LIBERTY BELL.

When the long-threatened storm finally broke, Tennant ran the last thirty yards to the corner of Fieldgate and New streets. He ducked into the doorway of the Whitechapel Clinic, shook out his rain-splattered hat, and waited for the ache in his left leg to ease.

The clinic surprised him. He'd imagined a charity facility located in one of London's most impoverished districts would be a ramshackle affair.

Inside the front door, a wheeled invalid's chair waited for a patient. In the wide corridor that ended at an office door, oak benches, deserted at the moment, lined the walls. Tennant's steps slowed. He glimpsed two wards, one for men and the other for women, each lit by rows of oil lamps. On sunny days, natural light would stream through the large windows and brighten the space. Shelving at the far ends of the rooms held piles of snowy towels, lines of green and brown bottles, rolls of bandages, and sundry tools of the medical arts. Eight beds lined the walls of each ward, most of them filled. Tennant breathed in the sharp, clean, leathery scent of carbolic soap. His footfalls had clicked sharply against the stone floor, but the two nurses who ministered to the patients trod silently on cork-soled boots.

Julia spotted the inspector and waved him into her office.

"Is this a good time, Doctor Lewis? I have a few questions about your report."

"Of course." Julia gestured to a chair facing her desk.

"You seem well set up here, Doctor."

"Supported by ill-gotten gains, I'm afraid." At his raised eyebrow, she smiled. "Oh, nothing you can arrest us for—now. A century ago, my great-great-grandfather marched off to India with General Clive. He left England a humble lieutenant and returned with a cache of jewels and an eye-popping bank balance."

"The fortunes of war?"

"Indeed, literally. *Filthy* rich, I suppose you'd call the Lewis family. I should think it unlikely he amassed that money in a strictly legal way."

He nodded, unsmiling. "You have several open beds. After the past few months, is that a hopeful sign?"

Since the summer, cholera had been burning through the district. All autumn, London Hospital, "the London," as the locals called it, had been swamped by the sick and dying.

"I think we're finally on the other side of the outbreak. The number of deaths has fallen three weeks in a row." Her eyes dropped to her desk clock.

"I shan't take up much of your time, Doctor. I have only a few questions. Your report was comprehensive, but . . ."

Julia raised her eyebrows. "But, Inspector?"

"Sometimes valuable impressions or intuitions don't make it into a clinical report."

She smiled and shook her head. He looked at her curiously.

"Forgive me, Inspector. I remembered a professor from my medical school days. 'Facts,' he insisted. 'Facts and observations—I want no flights of female fancy in your case notes.' And here you are, asking me to speculate in an official report."

He looked at the framed medical school diploma on the wall

behind her. "I see you traveled all the way to America to qualify as a doctor."

"No college in Britain admits women into their medical programs. Several do in the States."

"And yet you are permitted to practice medicine here?"

"Pure accident, I assure you. I came in through the back door, the happy result of unintended consequences."

"Oh?"

"Eight years ago, Parliament passed the Medical Act to weed out the charlatans in the profession."

"Are there many?"

"I regret to say they are legion. Still, the new law keeps out the worst of the quacks. Now doctors must present their credentials to the General Medical Council before they're added to the registry. But here's the loophole: Parliament added a clause to the act recognizing the degrees granted by foreign medical schools. The act included students who'd begun their studies as well."

"So someone with a degree from"—he looked up at the diploma—"from the Female Medical College of Pennsylvania had to be added to the list."

"Exactly. Women who had foreign degrees or had commenced their studies by 1858 *had* to be admitted to the medical roll, the last thing anyone wanted or expected."

"There can't be many of you."

"No. But a year after the law passed, the registry recorded its first female physician, Doctor Elizabeth Blackwell. I'd already sailed for Philadelphia to begin my medical studies, so I slipped in under the act's provisions."

"I imagine medical school was only the first of your hurdles."

"In four years of practice, I've heard it all—every joke, every condescending remark disguised as a compliment, every professional snub." She shrugged. "Any woman who chooses to leave the domestic sphere for a more public life has to develop a second skin, a hide of iron." Julia folded her hands and leaned forward, her forearms on the desk. "Now, Inspector, how can I help you?"

She wore a third skin as well, Tennant thought. Her tailored wool jacket and skirt mimicked the male uniform of the professional class. She pulled her chestnut hair back from a face that was not conventionally beautiful but striking all the same, with high cheekbones and a generous mouth. Her dark eyes flashed when she was amused—and probably when she was angry, he suspected. There was no nonsense about her. He had better get down to business.

"Two things, Doctor. The cause of death was a stab wound to the heart, but you mentioned cut marks on the right side of the neck. Can we assume the killer is left-handed?"

"Not necessarily. The marks were slightly toward the back, as if the killer held the blade against him from behind."

"But you can't be sure?"

"No doctor could be." She eyed him coolly. "But get a second opinion, if you feel you must. And your other question, Inspector?"

He looked away from her. "It's about the mutilation. I wondered if you had any impressions beyond the obvious."

"Such as?"

"Did the amputation display any specialized knowledge, reveal the application of some particular skill? Or was it just a crude hacking off of the man's member by a deranged assailant?"

Julia leaned back. She picked up a pencil and spun it between her forefinger and thumb.

"I have no reason to think a medical man carried out the act," she said, "if that's what you're asking. Nor can I discount the possibility. But neither do I detect the hand of a frenzied maniac in the attack. To be frank, Inspector, all that was required was a steady hand and a sharp knife."

"And a good deal of anger?"

"Perhaps. It certainly seems quite . . . personal." Again, he observed that amused glint. "I suppose that's an absurd understatement. What could be more so than such an intimate attack?"

"Indeed. I have one last question. Did you find any evidence that the victim was assaulted—I mean raped—by his assailant?"

"I would have included it in my report if I had. Still, I can't rule it out. He may have sodomized the deceased with that stick after the act." She stood. "Again, you may submit my findings to another doctor's scrutiny, if you like, but I think you'll find my conclusions are sound."

Tennant stood, a little off-balance. "Of course, Doctor. I think there's no need to—"

"Entirely your decision, Inspector."

"Well, should you think of anything else . . ." After a moment's hesitation, he offered his hand, as he would at the end of any interview with a professional male.

Her handshake was firm, cool, and brief. "Good luck with your investigation."

Tennant walked to the corner of Whitechapel Road and Commercial Street to catch an omnibus heading north to St. Edmund's Rectory.

The inspector usually felt he had the upper hand in an interview. As the 'bus jolted along, Tennant tried to figure out why he felt like a schoolboy called on the headmaster's carpet. *Headmistress's carpet.* Dr. Lewis had bristled every time he probed her conclusions. *It's my job to ask questions, damn it.* He'd have done the same with any doctor, male or female. *Touchy*, he thought, *like most women.* Still, if she wanted to bat in the pitch with the men, she'd better get used to some rough and tumble.

Her manner was off-putting, too—not mannish, exactly, but oddly direct for a woman. The way she met his gaze; it was unsettling in a lady. And she discussed the unsavory medical details without batting an eye. "Strong-minded" was the term people used for such unwomanly females. But she wasn't that, not exactly. Still, she probably had a chip the size of a plank on her shoulder. Out to right all the wrongs visited on womanhood, he didn't doubt.

Still, Dr. Lewis was right about the murder. Tennant felt it in his bones. It *was* personal, and the answer was hiding somewhere in the life of the Reverend Mr. Atwater.

But interviews with his housekeeper and assistant curate provided nothing useful. The murder had shocked them both; neither could supply a motive. Tennant left the rectory and found that the sun was out at last. Still, the inspector was as much in the dark as ever. Tobias Atwater, unmarried and living alone, was an enigma.

The nature of the crime was suggestive: That specific amputation and the assault with the stick opened a possible line of inquiry. There were plenty of "sodomite rows" around the city; the south side of St. James's Park and the Royal Exchange were examples. But Thrawl Street, where the body was found, was not known as a place where men sought out other men. And as far as the inspector knew, there were no "molly houses," where such men gathered, in the immediate area.

So far, no suggestion of sexual scandal had surfaced about the clergyman—no rumors of any kind, no motive for murder.

Nothing.

He thought about the letter he would send.

He pictured it burning Tennant's hand like a spill of corrosive acid. No, exploding like a bomb. Tennant wouldn't be able to ignore it, not like the others.

He kneeled in front of the fire grate, poking at the glowing coals. Flames flared, licking around the black pile, throwing enough light into the room for him to find the edge of the loose floorboard. He set it aside and peered into the space between the joists. He wondered, *Which one?*

Idly, he turned over his treasures; his collection was growing. Touching the tip of the diamond stickpin, he flinched, drawing blood. He fingered the small pile of brightly colored balloons, separating one from the rest of the pack.

"Yes," he murmured, selecting a red one, finding the stickpin again, its tip flashing silver in the coal light, laughing as the pin ripped through the rubber. *The cat will be among the pigeons now.*

He pulled a sheet of paper toward him, dipped his pen in the bottle of purple ink, and wrote. *Poor Meyer. You should have believed him, dear Inspector. Pop.* He folded the balloon into the letter and stopped. He picked up his pen and added one more line.

That's the way the money goes.

Tennant found the envelope with the rest of the morning post and opened it. A punctured balloon like the one in Atwater's pocket fell on his desk. He read the message inked in purple.

Poor Meyer. You should have believed him . . .

For all his ambition, and to his credit, it wasn't professional embarrassment or the threat to his advancement that made Tennant's stomach turn, made him send Sergeant Graves to the evidence locker to retrieve the boxes from the railway murder case.

The horror was that he may have sent an innocent man to the gallows.

The following day, Sergeant Graves handed Tennant the sickening news. He and O'Malley had reexamined the evidence from the railway murder case. The constable had found something overlooked in the original inventory—a popped balloon. Why someone missed it was anyone's guess.

When Tennant reported the discovery to Chief Inspector Clark, he expected to be relieved of duty. Instead, the chief delivered a command and a warning.

"Find the links," he said. "Something must connect the banker to the clergyman. Find them fast, by God, or we may need fresh eyes on the case."

Tennant remained the lead investigator—for the moment. The reopened railway case would remain an internal matter with no public announcement yet. At least for a while, he wouldn't have to deal with the hounding press.

But the inspector knew his reprieve was temporary, his head close to the chopping block.

CHAPTER 2

For weeks, he'd shadowed his prey.

Child's play, really; the company director was a man of clockwork habits. Once or twice a week, he followed him from his office to his club. The only surprise was how the fellow spent some Saturday evenings, the naughty old bugger.

The lamplighters made their way along Pall Mall. One by one, the lamps blinked on, but the creamy light from their glowing centers did little to penetrate the street's shadowy corners. It was easy to stay hidden in the darkness.

As the evening deepened, the clop and bustle of carriage and foot traffic on cobblestones died away. Even the street-crossing lads had given up; there was no one left to guide one across the dung-splattered roadway. Brooms strapped to their backs, torches doused, the sweepers melted away, each boy clinking his hoard of ha'pennies. Only the club's doorman remained, flapping his arms across his chest, stealing the occasional nip from a flask hidden in his pocket.

Tonight, the watcher decided. The reckoning was overdue.

The night was raw, but he barely registered the cold stinging his nose and ears. Anticipation had warmed him at his core. He relished the hours, savored the minutes before the last act: his quickening pulse, the pleasurable tingle in his groin, the victim's belated shock of recognition, and his final flash of terror, the glint and thrust of the blade. Then, in a spasm, it was over. It always ended too soon. Still, the waiting was all pleasure, and he didn't feel the cold.

His mark would take another twenty minutes to finish his meal. Then he would emerge from his club, pause in the portico to light a cigar, the glow from the gaslight staining his face and his shirtfront yellow. He would wave away the doorman's offer of a cab and walk beyond the lamplight's hazy glow. Then, in a black cape and hat, he'd vanish into the darkness, only to reappear when the corner lamplight found him. And where Pall Mall met Waterloo Place, his first surprise would be waiting for him.

He smiled at the aptness of the name: *Waterloo*. Before the night was over, the director's first surprise would end with his last.

Three days after the killer's letter upended the murder investigation, Tennant stood over a body found in a Whitechapel bathhouse.

The victim was on his back, fully clothed, tucked inside a "slipper bath," one of the shoe-shaped tubs rented by the half hour for a penny. He was dressed in formal evening attire and out of place in a public bathhouse catering to the working poor. The killer had tossed a piece of soap on his chest. The fingers of his right hand were wrapped around a bath sponge, and a white towel covered his face.

Tennant pointed. "Remove it, Constable."

O'Malley crossed himself, pulled the cloth away, and gagged. A foul mixture oozed from the man's mouth—excrement, by the look and smell of it.

While there were no signs of mutilation, blood from a single wound in the dead man's chest had stained his white shirtfront crimson. It had spattered across the porcelain surface of the iron bathtub as well. Tennant stared at the scene. There was something theatrical about the victim's placement, something staged. Something macabre, too, a sick joke.

Look what I've done, the killer seemed to say.

He's enjoying this. Playing with us, Tennant thought, *like Atwater, again.*

The inspector reached inside the victim's trouser pockets and pulled out a set of keys, a matchbox, and a silver money clip stamped with a coat of arms. He handed the clip to Graves, who pulled out the banknotes and counted.

"Eight pounds," the sergeant said. "Not robbery, then."

In the victim's right breast pocket, Tennant found a leather case holding two cigars. The inspector patted the front of the man's waistcoat. Inside the left pocket, his fingers closed around something. Withdrawing his hand, he opened it and stared at the object on his palm.

He hesitated. *Hell and damnation.* But Tennant had to call her in; he would need the same doctor who'd examined Atwater. *Sod it.*

"Sergeant, go to the Whitechapel Clinic on the corner of Fieldgate and New streets. If Doctor Lewis is there, give her my compliments. Ask her to return with you to the baths."

Sergeant Graves craned his neck, looking down Whitechapel Road for an omnibus. On the corner where they waited, Julia watched the boisterous crowd that had gathered in an empty lot and the speaker who commanded their attention.

He prowled across a ten-foot platform like a great jungle cat. Squarely built, his muscular frame strained against the seams of his coat. The red-faced speaker punched the air with one fist and rested the other on his hip with his jacket pushed back. Behind him, a banner displayed the Union Jack with lightning bolts bookmarking Britain's national flag. Across the top, a scroll framed the letters BP.

"A *Great* Britain can and must be great again," the speaker shouted. He opened his clenched hand and sketched an imaginary map above their heads. "From the South Atlantic to the South Seas, from the Khyber Pass to the Cape of Good Hope, an expanding British Empire has room for all your sons. Spare them from the factory floor and backbreaking docks, sweating their lives away for a few shillings a week. A bugle calls them to grander destinies."

A swell of assent answered him.

Julia said, "Who's the speaker, Sergeant? Do you know?"

"That's Sir Harry Jackson."

"*Sir* Harry Jackson?" Although expensively tailored, the man had the pronounced working-class accent of East London.

"Self-made bloke—owns the Black Falcon Brewery off Brick Lane in Spitalfields. Started life in the workhouse, or so I heard." Graves shrugged. "They say there's always room at the top. Likely they're right."

"Is he running for Parliament?"

"Starting a new party, or trying to." Graves nodded at the banner. "The BP stands for the Britannia Party. They'll be plenty of new votes to be found in this neighborhood."

"Indeed, should the Reform Bill pass next year, and it certainly looks like it will. The law will add lots of working-class voters to the lists—*male* voters, that is."

"Looks like the blighter's not done yet, Doc. Like most politicians, he's all rabbit and pork, in love with the sound of his yammering."

Julia smiled at the sergeant's cockney rhyming slang. "Yes, they do like to talk."

Jackson used the speaker's trick of lowering his voice to quell the raucous throng. The crowd quieted down for him.

"Make no mistake, my friends. While Britain's rebirth is in our reach, a glittering prize for our taking, threats remain for our island and our empire." He paused for the rumbling crowd to subside. "Across the sea, America, with its teeming millions, is taking our trade. Nearer to home, a rising German empire makes war on its neighbors and gathers strength. And just outside your doors, in the houses along your streets, a gibbering rabble grows, speaking strange tongues, worshipping unknown gods."

"Chinamen, peddling their opium," someone yelled.

"Jews and bloody Eye-ties, stealing our jobs."

"Send them back to the holes they crawled from. We don't want 'em here. They're filthy. Diseased."

A chorus of approval followed the final shout: "*They* brought the cholera, like as not. *They're* spreading it around."

The speaker raked his eyes across the crowd. He raised his hands to settle them down.

"You've been betrayed, my friends. The Conservatives? The Tories don't give a toss for your troubles. And as for the so-called Liberals in Parliament, dining in their fancy clubs, swilling brandy and champagne, *talking* reform. They do nothing while . . . *you . . . all . . . rot.*"

He reached into his breast pocket and withdrew a slim volume. "And as for the so-called *manifesto* of Professor Karl Marx and his friend Mister Engels . . ." Jackson dripped scorn over the word and the names. He held a corner of the book, dangling it between his thumb and forefinger before tossing it aside like a diseased thing. "They say all power, all property, goes to the *government*." He lifted his chin, his lip curled in contempt. "You know what that means. Instead of a thousand bosses, the workingmen of East London will have just one— Whitehall. Politicians with their pig snouts in the public trough, giving damn-all about you, as usual."

A man shouted from the back. "Too right, mate. Sod 'em all."

Judging his moment, the speaker raised his fist. "The time for Britannia to arise is now!"

He began to sing, borrowing the words from a well-known music-hall song. His powerful baritone carried to the back of the crowd. "When we draw the sword, a victory we will forge/With the battle cry of Britons, 'Old England and Saint George!'"

The crowd sang a thundering refrain: "We don't want to fight, but by jingo when we do/We've got the ships, we've got the men, and we've got the money too!"

Sir Harry jumped down from the platform. The audience at the front surged forward, extending their hands. The speaker shook all those he could reach. Finally, the crowd began to disperse. Then a man holding a stack of circulars rushed up to Sir Harry, offering him one. He looked at it, crumpled it into a ball, and tossed it aside. Jackson poked the man repeatedly in the chest, said something to him, and stalked off. The man looked down at the pile in his hands. Then he dumped the papers into a rubbish bin.

"A demanding boss, Sir Harry," Julia said.

"Pays well, though. Highest workingman's wages in the district, I hear."

A voice behind them drawled, "Sounds like he's won your vote, Sergeant."

A tall, cadaverous man—his red-and-black checkered tie loose at his neck, his bowler hat tipped back on his head—pulled his shoulders away from a lamppost and walked over to Graves. He stood a foot taller than the bantam sergeant.

Graves grunted. "Here to do the hatchet job you call journalism—on Sir Harry this time?" He turned to Julia. "This is Mister Osborne, Doctor Lewis. He reports for the *Illustrated London* so-called *News*. Don't credit a word he writes."

The reporter's brows shot up. "*Doctor* Lewis? Now that's what I call a story." He made a show of righting his tie and tipping his hat. "Johnny Osborne, at your service, Doctor." He handed her his card. "Care to sit for an interview sometime?"

"Don't be taken in by this penny-a-liner, Doc. He'll write anything to swell his pay packet. Once he's done, you won't recognize yourself in the story."

Osborne shook his head. "Rank ingratitude, I must say. And speaking of rank, I see it's still *Sergeant* Graves." He sighed. "I tried so hard to be helpful. I was sure my reporting would kick you up a rung to inspector. And how is dear Inspector Tennant, by the way? I've missed the good old days, hunting down the railway killer."

The sergeant rocked forward on his toes, jutting his face as close to the tall reporter's as he could. "I'll give the guvnor your love, Mister Osborne."

"How about giving me a tip on the Atwater murder instead? I heard a rumor that some of the details were unsavory. Just my stock-in-trade."

"No comment. The guv would have my head if I talked to you. You know the inspector plays it by the book."

The reporter smiled. "He'd have to, wouldn't he, with his history?"

Julia waited for Osborne to say more, but the sergeant took her by the elbow and steered her away. "Here's our 'bus, Doc."

Osborne called after them. "Come on, Graves. We all profited from the Meyer story." In a few loping strides, he caught up with them as they waited to board the omnibus. "A foreign fiend nabbed, the German behind bars, then swinging from the gallows, the railways safe for travelers once again—fame for Tennant, a massive circulation boost for the *Illustrated London News*." Osborne laughed. "And best of all, a rise in salary for yours truly. Think about it, Graves; we could slay it with the 'Saint of Spitalfields' murder."

The conductor hopped down from the rear running board to help Julia up the steps. Graves followed her. At the top, he turned. "Bugger off, Osborne."

After two raps of the conductor's knuckles, the omnibus juddered to a start. For a few paces, the reporter jogged alongside. Finally, he gave up and yelled, "Murder pays," as the 'bus rumbled away. Graves flashed the cockney's two-fingered insult and ducked inside.

After they'd taken their seats, Julia said, "*Could* Sir Harry win your vote, Sergeant?"

"Probably just another lying bast—" he grinned. "Sorry, Doc, just another lying bloke, like all politicians."

"Not God's gift to the workingman, despite the high wages he pays?"

"Like I said, too fond of the sound of his voice. Bit of a performer, Sir Harry; he'd make a good music-hall chairman, barking out the acts."

The sergeant's a shrewd one, Julia thought. And she agreed with him: there was something too practiced, too staged about Sir Harry's performance to be genuine.

She turned on the bench and looked squarely at Graves. "I didn't expect to find you on my doorstep today, or any day, for that matter. To put it mildly, I'm surprised the inspector wants to avail himself of my professional services. So tell me. Why has he asked for me, particularly? Do you know?"

"He wants the same doctor who examined Mister Atwater to have a squint at this body."

"Because?"

"Because he found a popped balloon tucked away in the victim's pocket. Same pocket as Atwater's, as it happens."

Julia was late for the dinner party and grateful that Kate was waiting to help her into her evening clothes. After the maid slipped the final fastener in place, she turned her attention to Julia's hair. As best she could, she tried to pin it into something presentable.

"Well?" Julia said, looking at her reflection in the full-length glass.

Kate smiled at her in the mirror. "You'll do, Doctor Julie. Just."

As she hurried down the staircase, Julia remembered she'd meant to ask Kate about her grandfather's guests for the evening. Uncle Max and Aunt Ellen. And Aunt Caroline, thank God.

The Franklins and her great-aunt always dined with them on Wednesdays. Aunt Caroline, Lady Aldridge, was her grandfather's sister, the widow of a baronet. On dinner-party evenings, Julia tried to be home on time, but her aunt stepped in as hostess when she was late. The Franklins weren't really Julia's aunt and uncle. Max Franklin was her grandfather's oldest friend from their medical school days at the University of Edinburgh.

Julia paused inside the drawing room entrance and caught her grandfather's eye. He winked and tipped his head in the direction of Aunt Caroline. It was the second Wednesday in a row that Julia hadn't been home in time to greet the guests.

She smoothed her skirts and took a deep breath. "Good evening, everyone. Please forgive me for being late."

She touched hands with the circle of guests, greeted the Franklins with kisses on both cheeks, smiled apologies to Bishop Kincaid and his wife, and thanked her aunt.

"You look tired, Julia. Are you getting enough sleep?"

"You say that every time you see me, Aunt."

"Because every time I see you, it's true."

Julia turned and greeted the last gentleman of the party. Surprised, she offered her hand to Sir Harry Jackson just as Mrs. Ogilvie, their housekeeper, announced that dinner was served.

*   *   *

At the table, Sir Harry, seated on her right, asked Julia about her medical training in the United States.

"My grandmother was born in Philadelphia," she said. "I have relatives there, so the medical school for women was a good fit."

"I've long had an interest in that country and its people. As a race, are they very different from us, the Americans?"

"Yes, but it's hard to explain. Differences among social groups seem . . . *less* there, somehow."

Sir Harry frowned. "And how is that, Doctor?"

"Oh, it's not that the very poor are any happier—of course not. But it seemed to me there were fewer of them. And, in America, there is a great mass in the middle, of men who show little deference to the gradations of rank we bow to here."

"What?" Dr. Franklin said in mock surprise. "No crawling and scraping, no doffing of caps before their betters? Shocking."

Julia smiled. "Very little, Uncle Max." To Sir Harry, she said, "You'd have a difficult time in 'Philly' convincing any man that he wasn't as good as the next fellow. Somehow, the American in the middle breathes easier than a workingman here. He fills his chest with freer air." Julia looked at her grandfather. "I think it took my living in Philadelphia to understand my free-spirited grandmother."

He raised his glass. "I toast your sentiments, Julie, but what of the Irish immigrants? Have they found free air and a welcome in America?"

Julia shook her head.

"Come now, Andrew," Dr. Franklin said. "We English haven't laid out a welcome mat for them either."

"True, Max, but what about the American Negro? Britain outlawed slavery decades ago."

"Only after centuries of profiting from the trade, my friend," Dr. Franklin said.

Dr. Lewis looked at his granddaughter. "Even after emancipation, do the freed slaves breathe free air?"

"No." Julia looked down at her plate. "And the death of President Lincoln was a blow." Then she looked up. Her lips twitched. "But you forget the most oppressed group of all, Grandfather, in America and every other country on earth—the half of humanity that is female."

"Forget? My dear Julie, you'd never permit that."

After dinner in the drawing room, Julia observed Sir Harry standing a little apart from the other guests. He had his back to the fireplace and looked down at his feet, jangling the coins in his pocket. Aunt Caroline's glance and nod telegraphed a message, so Julia walked over to him.

"By a strange coincidence, I found myself on Whitechapel Road this afternoon and heard you address a crowd."

"Is that so, Doctor Lewis?"

She hesitated. "You are a very effective speaker. Passionate. And you certainly struck a nerve with your audience when you mentioned all the newcomers who've arrived in the East End of late."

He nodded. "The English workingman feels besieged in his homeland, and our politicians ignore their plight. Too many men are fighting for a slice of less and less, clawing for survival."

"You make them sound almost bestial. Is that how you see them?"

"Aren't men only animals, Doctor? Mister Darwin tells us so. And only those species that are suited to their surroundings thrive, or so he says."

"I'm not sure he was talking about people, Sir Harry."

"But doesn't the same principle apply? Your grandfather

mentioned groups who haven't done well in their American surroundings. Perhaps it's because the Irishman and the Negro belong to subject races, fit only for lesser roles in the world. They may never thrive in the 'freer air' of the America you described."

His sentiments didn't surprise her. Julia had heard them before, but it was shocking to listen to them aired in her grandfather's drawing room.

Dr. Franklin joined the conversation. "Man is fundamentally a *rational* animal, Sir Harry. As such, he can make choices. Change. Adapt to his environment in ways that a finch or an earthworm cannot."

Julia's grandfather nodded. *Hurrah for the scientists*, she thought.

Bishop Kincaid shook his head. "Man is a *spiritual* animal, a being of faith, of soul. Altruistic. He is the only creature capable of deep devotion to others, not captive to his self-interest alone."

"But what of the faithfulness of dogs, Bishop," Julia said. "Pilot, for instance?" Pilot was their black Labrador. "Devotedly, he sits by Grandfather's door, waiting for his last patient to leave. And when I tickle him under his chin, he looks at me with such *soulful* eyes."

The bishop raised his hands in surrender.

"Man is the tool-making animal," Sir Harry said. "He's the only being who can bend nature to his will."

The clergyman, the two doctors, and the businessman—each saw the world through the prism of his experience; each had a different definition of man's essential self. Julia opened her mouth to ask what kind of animal *woman* was, but she looked over at her aunt Caroline and held her tongue. *Late two weeks in a row*, she thought, *I've annoyed her enough for one evening*.

Dr. Franklin lifted his brandy. "Well, here's to the one altruistic *and* rational *and* tool-making man in London. Let's drink to him."

"Oh?" Dr. Lewis said. "What paragon encompasses all our definitions, Max?"

"The engineer who finally came forward and admitted what happened. For months last summer, his company, the East London Waterworks, had released unfiltered water from the River Lea into the system, despite their denials."

"The source of the cholera outbreak, undoubtedly," Bishop Kincaid said. "All those poor souls."

Dr. Franklin nodded. "Unconscionable—over four thousand dead. Whitechapel, the only district not linked to the sewer system, was a charnel house. Its drinking water teems with filth."

"Surely that settles the debate," Julia said. "It proves, once and for all, that water, not air, is the source of the cholera poison," Julia said. "The doubters will have to concede. After all, the same winds that blow through Whitechapel and Spitalfields reach Bishopsgate and Hackney. Thousands didn't die there."

"By God," Jackson rasped. "Someone has to pay."

"Assuredly, Sir Harry. Perhaps someone already has," Julia said.

Her grandfather looked at her. "What do you mean, my dear?"

"This afternoon, I examined the body of Sir Maxwell Ball, the chairman of the East London Waterworks Company." She paused. "Someone had stabbed him through the heart." She looked around the circle of shocked faces. "That's why I was late."

Sir Harry was the last to leave. With one foot on the first step of the portico, he stopped and turned.

"Doctor Lewis, I'm thinking about setting up a medical clinic at my brewery for the workers and their families. May I visit you at yours and consult you about what's needed to set it in motion? Or could you visit my brewery and assess the project on the spot? That might serve better, I'm thinking."

"Of course, Sir Harry."

He wrote the address in his agenda, tore it out for her, and then wished her good night.

As she closed the door behind him, Julia thought, *Maybe he isn't such a bad sort, after all.*

She looked for her grandfather and found him in the library, brooding in front of the fireplace. Julia crossed the room and sat in the armchair next to his.

"So, you're consulting for the Metropolitan Police again," he said.

"Inspector Tennant sent for me. He wanted the same doctor who examined Mister Atwater to look at the new victim."

"Linked?"

"Probably."

"What's he like, this inspector?"

Julia settled back in her chair. "Dour, no sense of humor. He smiles rarely, and when he does, he looks as if it pains him. He strikes me as intelligent, though."

"Ah, that's something, at any rate."

"He has surprisingly polished manners. Rather a fish out of water at the Met, I expect. He's guarded. Something there, I think, but I'm not sure what. He has a slight limp that he hides rather well; he's not one to show vulnerability. Not an easy man to know—or like. He just about manages to tolerate me."

"And yet he called you in again."

"Only because I'd examined the first body. He made that clear enough to me."

He nodded, staring into the fire.

"What is it, Grandpa?"

"This epidemic. I was wrong, Julie, too slow to change. Back in '49, when John Snow came to me . . ." His chin dropped to his chest. "I thought he was mistaken."

Julia reached for his hand. "Most agreed with you, Grandpa. Nearly everyone thought it was carried in the air. People understood the evidence of their noses; it was difficult to believe in something they couldn't taste or see."

"But John Snow . . ."

"Doctor Snow hadn't gathered any real evidence—not until the outbreak in '54."

Her grandfather sighed. "All the sick and the dead . . . traced to that one contaminated pump."

"When he finally made his case, you supported him. Others doubted his conclusions. Many still do."

Her grandfather picked up his brandy and stared into the amber. "So many lives, Julie, four thousand dead this year. More, probably."

She squeezed his hand. "You're always telling *me* not to dwell on the past, not to hold myself accountable for events beyond my control."

He shook his head. "But Joseph Bazalgette was ready. The engineer had all his plans drawn up. His sewer project could have started years earlier—would have been finished by now—if only I had listened to John Snow."

Jump, Julie . . .

It began as the happy dream for a change: Julia on the sun-streaked July morning of her tenth birthday. When she woke, she knew that, if she stayed still, if she didn't open her eyes, she could recapture every detail.

"Jump," her dream grandfather had urged her, just as her real one had on that long-ago morning. "Jump, Julie—I'll catch you."

Julia remembered it so clearly. She'd hung back, her brave

mask slipping a little. Finally, she'd edged her way cautiously to the end of the log, rough bark scraping at the soles of her feet. Still, she wasn't eager to give up her solid perch. From a platform twice as high as her height, she looked down at the black surface of the pond. Her grandfather opened his arms. She shut her eyes and leaped, plunging into the dark water, sinking to her shoulders, gasping at the cold but held safe in his strong embrace.

Julia remembered the shock of the water and shivered under her blanket.

"That's my brave girl," her grandfather had said, pushing his way to the pond's bank. "But never dive in until you know what's lurking below." He looked down at her and smiled. "Unless a tiger is chasing you. That changes the calculus."

"Not many tigers are running around Surrey, Grandpa."

He lifted her onto the grass and hauled himself up beside her. "Oh, I don't know. There's a circus in town. I saw the sign last week." He made a low growl in the back of his throat. "Wild things hate cages." Then he extended his hand. "Come, my girl. Find your clothes and change. I've got three tickets to the show. A birthday treat, so look surprised when your grand-mother tells you. Then we'll see if all the beasts are secure in their pens."

Julia stretched beneath her blanket and smiled. Yes, she'd jumped—and, ten years later, she did it again.

"It's quite a leap, Julie, across the Atlantic to Philadelphia," her grandfather had said. "But it must be done if you want to be a doctor."

"You know I do, Grandpa."

"I'll have a new shingle made," he said. "We'll hang it out-side the town house, ready for your return." He sketched an imaginary sign in the air. "Andrew Lewis and Julia Lewis, Doc-tors of Medicine." He put his hands on her shoulder. "That ought to shake up the profession."

It completed the circle, Julia thought. A quarter-century earlier, after her father's death, her grandfather had taken down the brass plate that read ANDREW LEWIS AND WILLIAM LEWIS, DOCTORS OF MEDICINE. It still hung in his office.

Jump, Julie, her grandfather had said. Still, she did it to live *her* dream, not to honor a dead father's life.

But the dream had shifted in time and space, as dreams often did. A figure appeared at her dormitory door, tear-stained, strangle-voiced.

"She jumped, Julia."

CHAPTER 3

Julia decided to deliver the medical report on the death of Sir Maxwell Ball to Scotland Yard. She'd never visited the headquarters of the Metropolitan Police and was curious to see it.

London's nickname for its constables was common knowledge; "bobbies" were named for the founder of the Met, Sir Robert Peel. But, that morning, Julia discovered the origin of the force's unusual name when a constable directed her to the back entrance. While the front of the building faced Whitehall Place, the rear entry opened onto a backstreet called Great Scotland Yard.

The duty sergeant at the front desk informed her that Inspector Tennant was in, so Julia gave him her card to send up and waited. He appeared a few minutes later, glanced at the cover sheet of the medical report she handed him, and looked up.

"Do you have time to give me a summary, Doctor? And to answer a few questions?"

"Of course."

"This way." As Tennant led her up a staircase, again she noticed his slight limp. Inside his office, he offered her a chair and took his seat behind the desk, leaving his door ajar. Amused, Julia wondered if the open door was a gesture to propriety.

Her report wasn't complicated. A single, clean thrust to the heart by a thin-bladed knife was the cause of death. The time of death: probably sometime between eight at night and six in the morning. The body wasn't discovered until noon. On Mondays and Wednesdays, the baths opened later, at midday.

He dropped the report on his desk. "Could Mister Atwater and Sir Maxwell have been killed with the same knife?"

"Very possibly. The wounds appear to be about the same size."

"Both victims were stabbed in the chest, but you found no injuries to the neck this time, or any other mutilations. If not for the other thing . . ."

"Finding the balloons," Julia said.

"They link Sir Maxwell's death to the Atwater murder definitively. But a clergyman and an industrialist—are the men connected in some way we don't understand? Mister Atwater's life seemed blameless. But as far as Sir Maxwell is concerned, there's the public outrage over the water company to consider."

"Someone avenging the death of a loved one? But how does that involve Mister Atwater?"

"We found his body in a sewer pipe. It's suggestive, Doctor."

"If the motive is connected to the cholera outbreak, that leaves you with thousands of possible suspects."

He grimaced. "Tens of thousands, if we reach back to the earlier epidemics."

"I don't envy you your task."

He pushed his chair back and stood. "And there may be no link at all. My team may waste hundreds of hours chasing down a phantom connection that doesn't exist. The victims may be arbitrary, the random choices of a madman." He ran his hand through his dark hair and looked at her. "Does medicine have anything useful to tell us about criminal lunacy, Doctor?"

Julia shook her head. "The mind remains a great mystery. Where is the seat of mental disease? We have no idea, really. Is someone born with a malformation in the brain? Or is it a physiological process, a sickness that develops from some chemical disturbance? Doctors once thought an imbalance of bodily fluids caused all diseases."

"Yes, the Greeks," he said. "The four humors—blood, two forms of bile, and phlegm. I remember that from school."

"Perhaps it's not physical at all. Perhaps it's experience, an illness of the spirit arising from some lacerating tragedy. Something that deranges the mind and distorts the capacity for moral decision-making, something that shadows one through life." She looked away. "I know my grandfather is haunted at the moment."

"How so?"

"After the cholera outbreak of '49, my grandfather sat on the sanitary commission that investigated the epidemic. They concluded that the disease spread through the air."

"The miasma theory."

"Yes. Nearly everyone thought so at the time. They recommended slum clearing, to rid the worst of London's rookeries of their bad air."

"Yes," said Tennant. "I've heard talk about that for years, but that's all it is."

"The commission considered the water theory but rejected it as unproven; that's the difficult part for my grandfather. Five years later, the 1854 outbreak settled the matter, at least for those willing to look at the evidence."

"Fifty-four—"

He swung around and stared out his window. It was a rare sunny morning, the first in days. Slanting sunlight lit up the side of his face, but it failed to warm his granite expression. The silence stretched out between them. Julia was about to stand and leave when he spoke.

"I shipped out for the Crimea in 1854. But I couldn't out-pace the illness." He turned and faced her. "By the time I reached Turkey, cholera was burning through the military barracks. Hundreds of sick and dying soldiers filled every ward of the military hospital at Scutari. It was a broiling, fetid death pit."

"I remember reading the stories in the *Times* about the conditions there before Florence Nightingale arrived."

He sat down. "A year later, I found myself back at Scutari, recovering from injuries. But it was a different hospital. Miss Nightingale's reforms had transformed the place."

"Good nursing works wonders."

Julia wanted to ask him about the wounds that had sent him to the hospital, but she sensed he wasn't a man who invited sympathy. *What makes him so self-contained, so guarded? Being a policeman?* Then she remembered the sunny, inappropriately named Sergeant Graves. *Something else, then.*

"What changed your grandfather's mind about the epidemic?"

"Doctor John Snow. And ale, as it happens." Julia smiled. "Brewery workers gave Doctor Snow his first clue. They drink ale, not water, all day long. Their neighbors sickened and died, but the brewery men stayed as strong and healthy as their dray horses. Quite inconvenient for the temperance folk—so much for 'demon drink.'"

She waited for a smile. He merely nodded.

"Well. In the 1854 outbreak, Doctor Snow traced every house and place of business where someone had died of cholera and plotted it on a map. The dots had one thing in common: the water from Broad Street pump. When Snow convinced the authorities to remove the handle, the deaths stopped."

"And your grandfather blames himself for all of it?"

"By 1849, Doctor Snow already doubted the miasma theory. He sought out my grandfather and tried to persuade him and others that the real culprit was East London's drinking water." She sighed. "Fifteen thousand people died of cholera that year. In 1854, thousands more."

There was a knock at the open door. Sergeant Graves stood in the doorway.

"Sorry, Doctor. The chief asked to see you, guv. Looks a bit put out." The sergeant grinned. "More peevish than usual."

Julia looked down at the watch pinned to her jacket and stood. "I must be off anyway. I'm late as it is." It would mean another long evening for her at the clinic.

Tennant stood. "Will you escort Doctor Lewis to the lobby, Sergeant?"

"I can find my way—down the corridor, the first staircase on the left? I won't get lost."

At the door, Julia turned. "She's not right all the time, you know. Miss Nightingale, I mean."

"Hmm?"

"She's a great believer in the miasma theory. For her, it's all about the air. Nothing will budge her. Even your celebrated 'Lady of the Lamp' has her blind spots."

"You doctors have your microscopes, yet what have you seen?" He shrugged. "Have any of you actually found the cholera germ in the water?"

"Well . . . no."

"Miss Nightingale threw open all the windows in the ward at Scutari. The stench disappeared, and so did the sickness. There's something in that."

"I think you'll find there's nothing in that, Inspector, where cholera is concerned."

Tennant sat back against the edge of his desk and folded his arms. "Are you so sure you're right? The disease could be carried by water *and* air. Surely it would be smarter to hedge your bets."

"On this point, I'm quite sure. Hedging bets isn't smarter. It's a waste of time." She lifted her chin. "This is science, Inspector, not dog racing." Julia turned on her heel and walked out the door.

Tennant slammed it behind her. *Bloody woman. She speaks to me as if I'm an imbecile.* And the chief inspector—*what does that pillock want?*

Hell and damnation.

Tennant returned to his office after the chief inspector's grilling and loosened his tie.

Clark had been withering about the mistakes and lack of progress in the case. *Still, the bastard is enjoying himself*, Tennant thought. *Watching me twist in the wind.*

Experience had made Richard Tennant cynical about institutions and those who ran them. Banking, the military, the law—they were all the same: filled with well-connected men contaminated by arrogance, entitlement, and incompetence. He had hoped the Metropolitan Police would be different, mainly recruiting on merit within the ranks. In the past, the Met had shunned clubbable "old boys" from the right schools—men, in fact, like him. Tennant represented a new breed of policeman. Recruited from the professional classes and the army, the "new men" of the Yard were resented by the older generation of working-class coppers.

All detectives felt the pressure to deliver results, but Tennant felt it more acutely than most. Word had gotten around that the commissioner of Scotland Yard, Sir Richard Mayne, was his godfather and namesake. And, on top of it all, he was *that* Tennant, the son of the "swindler," William Tennant. Sir Richard's patronage was a great advantage, but his father's disgrace was a weight hanging around his neck, his millstone.

Ten years ago—it seemed like yesterday and a lifetime.

A few months after he'd returned home from the Crimean War on medical leave, the news broke. John Sadleir, the director of the Tipperary Bank, had been arrested for embezzlement. A million pounds was missing, and thousands of his clients faced bankruptcy in the massive fraud. Having handled the bank's legal affairs, William Tennant was dragged into the scandal. In the end, the investigation found him innocent of wrongdoing but guilty of being a gullible fool. His father had been cleared before the bar, but not in the capital's barrooms and clubrooms.

The scandal ended his son's career as well.

The colonel called him in for an interview. "Given your circumstances, and with hostilities winding down, perhaps it's an opportune time to take half-pay leave." He didn't have to say the words *for the honor of the regiment*. They hung in the air between them. The next day, Captain Richard Tennant spurned the face-saving offer of temporary demobilization and resigned his commission.

It had taken him six long months to recover from the physical injuries he'd sustained in the Crimea. He carried other wounds—the sweat-inducing nightmares and the suffocating terror that seized him whenever he found himself in a dark, confined space.

Still, to speed his return to active duty, he'd struggled to regain his strength. He'd spent hundreds of agonizing hours working to erase the traces of a limp, and he'd learned the tricks of concealing his invisible scars. None of it mattered; his military career was over. In a matter of weeks, the war hero had become damaged goods. *Six months of work for nothing*, he'd thought at the time.

A year later, he suffered an additional sting, overlooked when the first Victoria Crosses were awarded for valor. But for the scandal, his actions at the Battle of Balaclava, as one of the officers who led "the thin red line," would have won him the medal.

Then, at his lowest point, Sir Richard had stepped in and offered his godson a lifeline: a fresh start with the Metropolitan Police. Tennant's hard work had paid off, after all; any visible disability would have barred him from the Met.

He'd paid a personal price for the scandal, as well, in the person of Isobel.

After the story exploded across the newspapers, he felt a chill settle in with every visit to his fiancée's house. Isobel grew distant, her father more formal, and he had forgotten the last time her mother received him when he called. One morning, not long after his separation from the army, a letter from Isobel's father arrived in the post.

He wrote: "It is only fitting and prudent for a father to solicit an accounting of his prospective son-in-law's finances. In light of your changed circumstances, how, exactly, do you intend to support my daughter?"

Tennant's plan to join the Metropolitan Police failed to impress him. And as for Isobel—

"Scotland Yard?" She'd laughed, but there wasn't a trace of amusement in the sound. "Surely, you're joking, Richard."

He tried to make light of it. " 'For richer, for poorer,' darling; those are the words of the marriage vow." But the joke was on him. She broke the engagement by letter within a week.

He ought to have expected it; his mother had reacted in much the same way, making no attempt to hide her disdain. Icily, she'd told him he was a fool to give up his rank and the army's offer of half-pay.

"At least you'd salvage something of your life," she'd said. "It would keep you from sinking into the tawdry world of police work."

"I'm sorry your only child is such a disappointment, Mother."
He'd turned on his heels and left. He didn't see her again until the
reading of his father's will five years later.

Both she and his fiancée cut their losses and moved on.
Within a year, his mother was living apart from his father. Isobel had married a fellow officer in the Grenadier Guards, the
younger son of an earl.

Life was unfair, and Clark was a bastard, but Tennant had a
job to do. *Begin at the beginning.* He heaved the railway murder box from the floor, pulled out the bundle of witness statements, and began reading.

The following day, Tennant poked his head out of his office.
"Constable, where is Sergeant Graves?"

"I don't know, sir. The chief's after sending for him an hour
past."

"I want to see him as soon as he reports in."

Tennant flung himself into his chair and pulled at his tie.
He'd spent another frustrating morning with little to show
for it.

At nine, he'd had a tense, unpleasant meeting with the railway victim's two sons and the dead banker's private secretary.
More than two years after the murder, they were shocked to
learn that the wrong man had been hanged and furious that
their father's killer was still at large. The swift arrest, trial, and
execution of Franz Meyer had made it unnecessary to look
closely at Thomas Rigby's life. Tennant asked the sons and secretary to search their memories, comb through any remaining
letters or documents for evidence of someone with a vendetta
against the banker. But it was long after the fact.

Then, shortly before noon, he'd presented himself at the offices of Sir Maxwell Ball. The headquarters of the East London
Waterworks were located on a pleasant square in Bishopsgate,
far from the stinking filth of the company's pumping stations

on the River Lea. A clerk led him down a long hallway where thick carpets cushioned and quieted their steps. From the comfort of a deep leather chair, the inspector waited for Sir Maxwell's private secretary.

A gold-framed panorama in oils faced him on the wall behind the desk, a rendering of the company's plans for a new facility along the Thames. He rose to take a closer view. White, cottony clouds dotted a perfect sky. The river water flowed clear and blue, spilling into a series of filtering ponds ringed by promenades where ladies with parasols folded gloved hands under gentlemen's arms. There wasn't an engine, pump, or outflow pipe in sight, and the artist had erased the filthy sewer water from view.

He turned away from the picture when he heard the door open. A short, middle-aged man in a gray suit with a black armband pinned to his sleeve entered the room. With a hint of uncertainty in his voice, he asked, "Inspector Tennant?"

He nodded.

After a fractional hesitation, as if calculating what degree of politeness was due to a copper in a Savile Row suit, the secretary offered his hand.

The inspector shook it. "Mister Jenkins, I believe? You were Sir Maxwell's private secretary?"

"Yes, that is correct, for nearly twenty of his thirty-five years as company director. Won't you sit down?" He gestured to a seat and settled behind the desk. "This is a shocking business, Inspector. Appalling. How can I help you?"

Tennant asked about Sir Maxwell's personal life, daily habits, and movements on the last evening of his life, eliciting mainly unhelpful answers. As far as Jenkins knew, the director had left that evening for his club.

"When in town, Sir Maxwell always stayed in his apartments there."

"Not at his house?"

"After his wife died and his only daughter moved to India with her husband, Sir Maxwell had little use for a house in town and sold the lease. That was ten years ago. He has—had—a country house, of course, in Surrey. The rooms at his club were more convenient for his working week."

"And the name of this establishment, Mister Jenkins?"

"The Carlton," he said, naming one of London's most venerable gentleman's clubs.

"I know it—on Pall Mall. Did he have a manservant to whom I might speak, a regular valet at his club?"

"That would be Haskell, Inspector. Thomas Haskell looked after Sir Maxwell's personal needs."

"Your employer's body was found at the Goulston Square baths. Did the company supply their water?"

Jenkins shook his head. "The baths are not a company customer. I cannot imagine what would take Sir Maxwell there."

"As Sir Maxwell's private secretary, you open all his mail. Is that correct?"

"Everything that arrives at the office."

"Did Sir Maxwell receive threats in the post?"

"Well . . ."

"I should like an answer to my question, Mister Jenkins. Was he threatened in connection to the recent revelations about the company? That the East London Waterworks had dumped unfiltered water into the system, effectively poisoning its customers."

Jenkins squirmed. "Yes, Inspector."

"Did Sir Maxwell file a police report about the threats?"

The secretary shook his head.

"And why not?"

"I believe Sir Maxwell thought little could be done to trace the source of the letters."

"And the less said, the better? I wish to speak to the engineer who exposed the company's actions—Stanley Hughes, I believe. Does he have an office in this building?"

"I'm afraid Mister Hughes no longer works for the company."

"I see. Shown the door for telling the truth?"

"I believe—that is to say . . ." He looked down at his desk.

"Yes, Mister Jenkins?"

"Sir Maxwell felt the revelation could have been handled more . . . adroitly."

"Papered over, you mean. Did Sir Maxwell fire Hughes himself?"

Again Jenkins hesitated. "Yes, he did."

"I'll have the engineer's address."

Tennant heard muffled voices outside his door.

About time, he thought. "Sergeant Graves?"

"We've got another one, guv—a third victim. Fourth, if we're counting Thomas Rigby."

"Hell and damnation." Tennant swept some papers into his top desk drawer and jammed his pen into its holder. "Where the devil is O'Malley, and where are we heading?"

The constable walked in behind Graves. "There's no call to be rushing, sir," he said. "They're after finding the body nearly two months past, behind a house off the City Road."

"I just got back from H-Division headquarters," Graves said. "Coppers there confirmed it."

"And there's this." O'Malley reached into his pocket for a letter. "The mail clerk has sharp eyes on him. He spied the purple ink and brought this to the chief direct." He handed the letter to the inspector.

Tennant unfolded the letter.

My dear Inspector,

Can an artist ever allow a masterpiece to be overlooked? For weeks, I've waited patiently for the police to recognize Bertie

Parker as my handiwork. The local coppers found him where I left him—in an alley near the Eagle Tavern, just off the City Road.

The last line of the letter chilled him.

Keep on your mettle, Inspector. Every night when I go out . . . I feel it growing inside me.

CHAPTER 4

"Got another victim on our hands, Doc."

Sergeant Graves sat in a chair opposite Julia's desk and handed her a medical report. "The guv asked if you'd have a butcher's hook at this, give him your impressions."

Julia scanned the cover page. "Does the inspector want me to view the body as well?"

"Can't be done. It's a ripe one—over six weeks old. Burial's done and dusted."

Graves drummed his fingers on the arms of his chair while Julia read the report. The victim, Bertie Parker, had been found in a back alley off the City Road, stabbed through the heart with a thin-bladed knife. This time, the victim's genitals were smashed rather than severed, probably crushed by one of the cobblestones found at his side. A punctured balloon had been pulled from the dead man's mouth.

She looked up at Graves. "He left his calling card again."

"A green one this time."

She put the report aside and sat back in her chair, tapping a pencil against her palm. "What do you make of the balloons, Sergeant?"

"Beats me, Doc. We've faffed away hours talking about it. Maybe the blighter just wants to waste our time."

"But to carry them to a murder scene. To take the time to place them on the bodies . . . They must mean something to the killer."

"Birthday parties? Kiddies playing in the park on a sunny summer day?"

"So, happy associations. But a *punctured* balloon—why that? An end of innocence, of happy times, perhaps?"

"Maybe. Or something we can't even guess at."

"Yes, it's a bleak thought." Julia tapped the report with the blunt end of her pencil. "How did this older case come to light?"

"A letter from our killer. I got the lowdown from an old friend at H Division, a copper who walks a Hackney beat along the City Road. He found the body and remembered the balloon."

"Why was Parker's case never referred to the detective bureau for investigation?"

"Local coppers handled it. Bloke was a music-hall performer." The sergeant's face colored. "A sodomite, too. He sang in a drag number at the Eagle Tavern's theater."

"A drag number?"

"Theatrical slang, Doc—men who perform dressed up like women. Coppers figured it was just a quarrel between queers and not worth the bureau's time."

"So, the queen's justice isn't for everyone," Julia said.

"Not for *that* old queen. You can bank on it. Still, it's not why I joined the coppers, but there you are. Kill a clergyman or a company director, and you'll turn the Yard upside down. Kill some old molly . . ."

"And no one cares." Julia tipped her head. "Why *did* you join the police, Sergeant?"

"Wanted to ever since I was a kid. Thought I could do a bit of good in the world, put away some dodgy buggers." Graves shrugged. "Still, it's the way the world works. Justice for some. Coppers wouldn't get very far anyway. Sodomites don't give the police the time of day."

"Well, I don't have much to tell the Inspector either, at least nothing he doesn't know already."

"How about you, Doc? What made you go into medicine? Most folks must think it's pretty daft for a woman."

"You're right about that. Like you, I thought I could do a bit of good in the world."

The sergeant picked up a wooden object from her desk and looked at it. "I guess I thought I'd be like Gabriel. Sounding a trumpet on Judgment Day." He blew into it. "That's not much of a horn you've got there, Doc."

Julia smiled. "It's called a stethoscope. It's used for listening to the heart and the lungs. That's the first one my grandfather owned—an antique." She leaned over and pulled something from her medical bag. "Try this. Stick the ends of the tubes into your ears and hold the metal part over your heart."

He followed her directions, and his eyes widened. "Blimey— I can hear it thumping away." He handed the instrument back to her. "I'd like to take that to the barmaid at my local, give *her* a listen to my ticker." He grinned. "She says I haven't got one."

Julia stowed the stethoscope away and pulled the report toward her again.

"I might have a word with the doctor who examined the body." Julia flipped through the pages to check the signature and sighed. "That old fossil won't want to talk to me. I could ask my grandfather to speak to him instead."

"The guv won't say it, but I will. Anything you can do, Doc, we'd be grateful. We're getting nowhere fast."

*   *   *

Tennant spotted the book in the corner of Julia's desk and flipped idly through the pages while he waited for her. She had sent a note asking him to see her.

"You're welcome to it, Inspector," Julia said from the doorway. "I was about to consign it to the fire."

He got up from his chair. "Not your cup of tea? The title is quite a mouthful—*Principles of Education Drawn from Nature and Applied to Female Education in the Upper Classes.*"

"The most *unnatural* pack of nonsense I've ever read. A relative from Philadelphia sent it—to annoy me, I'm sure. My cousin Matthew and I sparred over the topic on more than one occasion."

Tennant handed it to her. "An American book, then?"

"Published first in Britain; somehow I missed it. This is the American edition. My cousin kindly bookmarked some passages for me."

She flipped through the pages.

"Listen to this: 'The aim of education is to fit children for their position in life. Girls are to dwell in quiet homes, to exercise noiseless influence, to be submissive and retiring. Her health will break down under the effort of a male education. She will probably develop some disease, which, if not fatal, will be an injury to her for life.'"

Julia tossed the book aside. "Well, Inspector?"

"You look no worse to me for your studies, but I'm not a medical man."

"Neither is the author."

"Still," Tennant said, "men and women have natural affinities for study and work that set them on separate life courses." He shrugged. "The patterns are plain to see."

"You think so? Men are generally hopeless with a needle and thread. But if they worked at it for hours a day from an early age, they'd embroider pillows and screens as well as their sisters."

"That's a very narrow skill, Doctor. It's hardly a good argument for—"

"My grandparents educated me as if I were a grandson. I daresay that I would have found medical school beyond my capacities if I had had a string of governesses who taught me nothing but embroidery and the piano."

He shook his head. "You're guilty of embracing a common fallacy, Doctor—the hasty generalization drawn from an insufficient sample. You may be an exception to the rule that men excel in demanding professions, while women do not."

She gave him a tight smile. "And you've accepted the fallacy of questionable cause and effect. You've concluded that men excel because they are male. But, by all means, let a 'sufficient sample' emerge. Let's give girls and boys the same education. Then we'll see what women can do."

"That's rather unlikely, so I suppose we're at an impasse."

She seemed on the point of saying something else, then sat back on the edge of her desk and looked down at the floor. Seconds ticked by, and Tennant's fingers itched to pull out his pocket watch. He had a pile of reports sitting on his desk.

The inspector cleared his throat. "Did your grandfather speak to the doctor who examined the body? Had he anything to add to his report?"

Julia shook her head. "No—I mean, yes, my grandfather spoke with him, but he had nothing useful to say."

Tennant shifted his weight from his left leg to his right. "Then . . ."

"Sergeant Graves told me one line of your investigation was difficult for you to pursue, certain witnesses who are reluctant to speak to the police." Julia held his eye. "Men who consort with other men, I mean." She paused. "I believe I can help you there, Inspector."

He raised an eyebrow. "Indeed, Doctor. How so?"

"I know a man, a quartermaster-sergeant retired from the Royal Marines named John Bingham. He operates a sporting club during the day and a night refuge that opens its doors to boys who . . ." Julia lifted her chin. "Young men who sell themselves to other men."

He met her gaze and nodded.

"It's not far, Inspector, a few streets away. Quartermaster Sergeant Bingham—his friends call him Q—first came to my clinic about a year ago. A boy had been badly beaten and needed my help. Yesterday, I went to see him—Q, that is—to ask if he'd be willing to talk to you. He agreed."

"I see."

"I'm not sure you do. He was reluctant at first. He's afraid you'll frighten the boys away. Q said they'd 'spot a copper in civvies in two seconds flat.' I assured him you didn't look like a policeman." Julia smiled. "Forgive me, but I described you as quite presentable. The boys would say you dressed like a 'toff.'"

He grasped the lapels of his coat. "The fraying relics of an earlier life."

"Have you time to come with me now? This afternoon?"

"Well . . . I suppose so." *Useless waste of an afternoon*, he thought.

Julia stiffened. "Of course, if you think it's not worth your time . . ."

Tennant sighed. "I'm here. Shall we go?"

As they walked along Whitechapel Road, the inspector asked about Q and his work.

"The boys come to his club for recreation or a meal and a bed. His goal is to help them change the direction of their lives and find them other work."

"Is he successful?"

"Sometimes. But all too often, these 'rent boys,' as they're called, go back on the streets. Some appear healthy but are quite ill—in the first stage of syphilis or in the latent phase that follows it. I try to do what I can for them, but medicine has little to offer the sufferers. There's no cure for syphilis."

"I thought mercury—"

"'A night with Venus, a lifetime with Mercury?' I'm afraid that old saw is misleading. Mercury can alleviate the early symptoms of the disease, but it's useless against the wasting and paralysis or the dementia and hallucinations of late-stage syphilis."

"What a dark world you see here in Whitechapel, Doctor."

Julia stopped and turned. "Surely you don't think it's only here? The disease washes up at my respectable doorstep on Finsbury Circus, a flood of misery. I see it all the time in my consulting room."

"Surely men with this malady don't seek treatment from you. A young woman."

"Not men. Wives."

"Wives?"

Julia looked at him. "Yes, Inspector, wives who have been infected by their husbands, of course."

He gritted his teeth. She sounded irritated—and condescending.

"These women come to me, confused by their symptoms. They leave devastated. You see, their trusted family doctors rarely tell them the truth. That would betray their husbands' secrets, and it's the gentlemen of the household who pay the fees. And then there are the daughters."

She broke off, a catch in her voice.

"Last week, a lovely young woman and her mother faced me in my office. The daughter, married for five years, had suffered three miscarriages. As soon as she opened her mouth, I understood. I saw the half-moon notches in the tips of her front teeth. Medicine has only recently recognized this telltale sign of congenital syphilis. Most likely, her father had passed it to his wife, then the mother to the daughter when she was born. A terrible family legacy."

"The mother didn't know?"

"The disease can have long latent periods. Now she understands her history of ill health." Julia shrugged. "Her husband is dead—for *him*, perhaps it's for the best. *He'll* never know he infected his daughter and caused the stillborn births of his grandchildren. If he understood the reason for his wife's poor health, *she* will never know."

"A distressing conversation to have with a mother and daughter."

Julia looked at him. "Quite." She dug her hand into the pocket of her coat and walked on. "Men," she said coldly. "They take their pleasures where they find them, giving no thought to those they claim to love."

Julia stopped beneath a streetlamp and nodded at the sagging row of dilapidated terrace houses facing them.

"We're certain we know what goes on behind *those* doors and windows. The vice, the filth, and the disease endemic in the East End. All the things that horrify us, all the things we do nothing about. They're here, we think, far from our doorsteps. But consider the elegant town houses in neighborhoods like mine, the respectable residences that ring Finsbury Circus."

When Tennant said nothing, Julia resumed walking.

"London is filled with brothels; you know that as well as I, Inspector. They infest the city. And everywhere, streetwalkers and rent boys wait for their customers in dark corners, thousands of them, most of them diseased."

Julia stopped and faced him. She was a tall woman, the top of her head just an inch or two below his line of sight. Evening was falling fast, but the lamplight caught the anger kindling her eyes.

"Tell me, Inspector. Who are their clients? Some are the charming young men dressed in fine suits and snowy shirtfronts who ask for my hand at a ball."

The owner of the George Street Sporting Club looked the inspector up and down. "I've seen enough brutality against these lads to last a lifetime, Mister Tennant."

John Bingham wasn't a tall man, but he was powerfully built. He had a boxer's muscled neck and shoulders and filled the space of his small office.

Julia said, "I asked Q not to use your police rank in front of the boys."

Tennant nodded. "Doctor Lewis told me about your work with these boys, that you provide them with healthy recreation and give them a place to stay. Life on the streets is a dangerous way to survive."

Bingham jerked his head at the window. "Out there, a pugilist's skills help to even the score. I'm happy to teach them what I know, Mister Tennant."

After Julia left to check on two ailing inmates in the dormitory, the quartermaster offered to take the inspector on a tour of the sporting facility.

Once a sizable silk-making factory, the building had a former work floor that provided ample room for the young boxers. Whitewash on the walls brightened the space, and at the far end, oak benches supported a variety of barbells and hand weights. Scuffed leather gloves tied in pairs hung by their laces from hooks.

"I see you've joined the crusade against bare-knuckle boxing, Quartermaster."

"Call me Q—everyone does. Bare-fisted boxing will be a

thing of the past. A draft set of rules has been sent to London's sporting clubs. They propose three-minute rounds, a ten-count by a referee when a boxer is down, and boxing gloves. So we've got an early start on them."

An oak beam suspended from the ceiling secured a row of leather punching bags. A solitary boxer, a slight, straw-haired lad, kept one of the bags in constant motion, his arms moving like pistons, punching to a rhythm.

"It must take intense concentration to maintain that pace," Tennant said.

"Aye. And Jackie Archer's got that in spades. But I wish he'd join in with the other lads more." Q nodded at the platform in the middle of the room.

Two young men stripped to their waists stood in the center "scratch," trading punches in the roped-off ring. A cheering section of equally bare-chested boys surrounded the platform, whistling and calling out a mix of encouragements and insults. Tennant looked back at Jackie Archer, his shirt buttoned tightly at the chin and wrists.

When a drayman called Q away to sign for a delivery, the inspector wandered over to a wall of framed posters featuring boxing legends. It was a revealing collection, outsiders all of them.

First on the wall, "Dutch Sam" Elias stared at the viewer, stripped to the waist, his powerful arms folded across his chest. The "Man with the Iron Hand," the "Terrible Jew," was an imposing presence. Next to Elias, on a poster from the "Famous Fights" series, "Gypsy" Jack Cooper stood triumphant in victory, looming over the prone, defeated figure of "Strong Arm Cabbage." Finally, there was Tom Molineaux, the "Black Ajax," bare-chested, bare-fisted, his raised hands clenched in a classic boxing pose.

"All the greats were showmen," Q said over Tennant's

shoulder. "The boxing ring's a stage, just like a music hall. He was robbed, you know, the Black Ajax."

Tennant glanced at Q. "Robbed? How?"

"Back in 1810, the heavyweight title should have been his. He flattened Tom Cribb, scrambled his brains with a mighty blow. But the crowd couldn't stomach a black champion and stormed the ring, disrupting the match. Under the rules of the day, Cribb had just thirty seconds to crawl back to the center. Without that delay, he never would have made it back inside the scratch in time. Bastards."

The quartermaster spit out the last word. "But Tom Molineaux finds justice on my wall."

The inspector looked from Q back to the poster. The event was old news, a half century in the past, well before Q's time. Tennant quoted a maxim of the law: "Let right be done though the heavens fall."

"Let right be done." Q's eyes narrowed. "Is justice possible under our laws?" He swept his arm across the boxing ring. "For these lads?"

Tennant said nothing. He'd learned the value of quiet, how silence drew out unintended revelations from a suspect. *Suspect—why that word? I'm here to interview a source.*

Still, Tennant wondered about the quartermaster. Impatient with the law's plodding pace, with its uncertainties and blind spots, was Q the kind of man who might take justice into his own hands?

"Let's go back to my office, Mister Tennant." He dropped his voice. "We can talk there without the lads overhearing."

Inside the cramped room, Q removed a pile of papers from a chair and pulled it forward for Tennant. He sat behind his desk. "What do you want to know?"

"We have a string of murders on our hands. The details suggest a motive connected to sexual revenge. I'd like to know if your boys know anything about Tobias Atwater—"

"The clergyman?"

"Yes. Or Bertie Parker, the music-hall performer."

Q swiveled back and forth in his chair. "Never heard a squeak about Atwater other than all the good he did. As far as Parker goes, music halls are prime places where boys find customers, men in their cups looking for a fumble in an alley." Q nodded to the training room. "These lads know it, so they hang around when the performances let out."

Tennant glanced back into the room. He spotted Julia talking to Jackie Archer. She put her hand on his shoulder and tipped her head to catch the boy's eye, seeming to wait for his response. After a moment, Jackie nodded, and Julia smiled when he shook her offered hand. Then she patted his shoulder and headed back to the office.

Q said, "I'll ask the boys if they've heard any talk, Mister Tennant. I'll pass along anything they tell me."

Before they left, Julia exchanged a few words with the quartermaster. Then, opening her medical bag, she removed a blue bottle and placed it on his desk. The label read, "Mercury bichloride, quarter-grain tablets."

Outside, Tennant asked, "Mercury for one of the boys? Jackie Archer?"

"No. Two other lads. Blisters are forming on their palms and backs; mercury might help control the rash."

"A lifetime with mercury . . . for as long as their lifetimes last."

"These boys are already pariahs, Inspector. Then blisters appear like the mark of Cain." Julia shook her head. "But under it all, you can see the children, the pretty little boys they were. Once upon a time."

"Tell me about Jackie."

Julia eyed him. For a moment, Tennant thought she wasn't going to answer.

"He was the boy who brought me to Q's refuge in the first

place. He'd had a tooth knocked out and needed a few stitches to his upper lip. Lacerations covered his back, shoulders, and upper arms, wounds caused by a thick, buckled strap—his father's belt."

"Good God."

"After the beating, the man threw his child to the gutter, shouting he wouldn't have 'some Nancy boy' for a son."

"Scars from the lacerations," Tennant nodded. "That explains the shirt."

"Scars inside and out." Julia bit her lip. "I have no idea, Inspector—none—what it must feel like to suffer a parent's rejection and contempt."

Tennant walked beside her in silence. When he looked up from his boot tips, he found she'd halted a few paces behind him.

"We can slip through here, Inspector. It's a shortcut to Whitechapel Road."

She stood at the entrance of a narrow alley that sliced between two dilapidated dwellings. Overhead, washing lines crossed the gap between the buildings. Bed linens and clothing, tattered and dun-colored, hung suspended in the gloom, line after line, receding into the darkness. Somewhere beyond Tennant's sight, the creak of a turning pulley meant someone was taking in the washing for the night.

He felt his throat tighten, and a rush of blood pulsed in his ears. When he hesitated, Julia looked at him curiously.

"Inspector?"

Tennant nodded. "Right behind you, Doctor." *Blast the bloody woman.*

He followed her into the alley, working to control his breathing and tamp down his panic. Finally, after several agonizing minutes, her dim silhouette became a sharper outline against the brightness ahead of them. The iron band across his chest eased.

When they reached Whitechapel Road, Tennant stopped to take a few deep breaths. Then he turned abruptly, putting several paces between them. Julia followed him.

They hadn't gone far when he halted. "Damn it to hell!"

"Inspector?"

He nodded. "Over there."

A man wearing a sandwich board was hawking the latest edition of the *Illustrated London News*. "Railway Murder Reopened," he shouted, as if the screaming, three-inch headline wasn't enough to get a customer's attention. In smaller type, an editor had fun with a play on words: MIS-"CARRIAGE" OF JUSTICE IN A FIRST-CLASS CARRIAGE?

Tennant handed the man a coin and scanned the opening paragraphs. "That hack, Osborne—why am I not surprised."

"What does he say?"

"He can't decide. Either the police are bungling fools, or we deliberately framed an innocent man." Tennant crumpled up the journal and dropped it in a rubbish bin. " 'Justice'? That's a joke coming from him. Osborne's screeds whipped up a frenzy of blood lust, and not only against Meyer."

"What do you mean?"

"In all his articles, Osborne referred to Meyer as 'the Jew.' As it happens, Franz Meyer was a German Catholic. But so many tailors and clothing peddlers in East London *are* Jews. They seem to have cornered the market, and anger is spilling over."

"I hear it all the time, in the complaints of some of my patients."

"After the tailor's arrest, a mob broke shop windows all along Petticoat Lane. They carried out a rash of assaults against Jewish second-hand clothing merchants, all of it thanks to that gentleman of the press and his ilk."

"It's not only journalists. Last week, Sergeant Graves and I heard Sir Harry Jackson inflame a crowd."

"One accusation is off the mark: Foreigners aren't the 'criminal contagion' so many claim. As a policeman, I can attest to that. It takes a lot to leave your home. To start life over in a new place requires courage. It takes energy and ambition."

Julia nodded. "I barely have time to treat the foreign speakers who come to my clinic before they hurry off to a second job."

"Criminals are a lazy lot. They're more likely to be homegrown wastrels, not foreigners."

"What will this headline mean for your investigation, Inspector?"

His jaw tightened. "I'm afraid it means a circus, Doctor. With my head on a pike as the sideshow."

Tennant woke in a sweat, tearing at the collar of his nightshirt, yanking off the smothering bedsheet that had trapped him in its folds.

He knew what had triggered it—*that blasted alley*. Often, some dark passageway he'd traveled during the day or a blinding fog that swallowed him at night tunneled him back into a suffocating dream.

On those nights, the Crimean War raged again. The Russian attack came from nowhere, the advancing army moving through a shroud of dense fog. In his sleep, he heard concussive blasts as the battery collapsed around him, crushing him beneath sandbags and splintered timbers, trapping him in midnight. He gasped for breath. Overhead, atop the wreckage, the Russian guns pounded away. Soldiers in close combat cursed and grunted. Inside a shared tomb, he heard his dying sergeant keening, calling for his mother.

For twenty-four hours, he had endured the darkness. Entombed, he'd waited for the truce that would send rescue parties scrambling across the blasted landscape to seek out the wounded and carry away the dead. Finally, someone heard his muffled shouts and freed him from his premature grave. His visible wounds were serious enough, but not life-threatening. His left leg was broken in two places. A deep, slashing wound had sliced into his thigh, and he had torn tendons and ligaments around his knee. The damage meant he'd never walk comfortably again. Then there were his invisible injuries.

Ten years after the war's end, they haunted him still.

CHAPTER 5

Johnny Osborne had the good reporter's knack for being at the right place at the right time. He had an hour to spare, just enough time for an interview, and he'd spotted Julia waiting to cross Whitechapel Road.

"Allow me, Doctor."

Osborne inserted two fingers into his mouth and let loose a piercing whistle that got the attention of a pair of sweepers. Two young boys wearing soft caps, woolen mufflers wound around their necks, and ragged jackets that fell below their knees trotted over to the reporter.

Osborne introduced the boy in charge. "Doctor Lewis, this is Joe. He tells me what's what around the neighborhood. Keeps his ears to the ground for me, right, mate?"

The boy nodded to Julia and jerked a thumb in the direction of his friend. "This here is Billy. Happens he's helping me out today. Pitch him a brown or two, Mister Osborne, and we'll lead you and the lady across the road."

The reporter held up his empty palms for Billy to see. Then, reaching behind his ear, he plucked three copper "browns" out of nowhere. One by one, Osborne tossed the pennies in the air, juggling the coins before snatching them up in his fist. When he opened his hand, it was empty. He reached again behind the boy's ear, and the coins reappeared. Osborne dropped one in Billy's hand and tousled his hair. He tossed another one to Joe.

Billy got to work, sweeping a clear lane through the muck while Joe held a burning torch high against the foggy gloom. They cleared a path through the horse manure and mud, pushing aside the piles of dung and the rotting garbage that had fallen from passing wagons. In minutes, they had Julia and the reporter on the other side of the road with their boots reasonably clean. Then Joe spotted another stranded pedestrian under the streetlamp. The boys ran off, hopping over piles of mud and muck.

"Where did you learn that trick, Mister Osborne?"

He tapped the side of his nose in confidential cockney fashion. "My misspent youth, Doctor."

"Is this a chance meeting?"

"Yes, as it happens. But I'm a great believer in seizing an opportunity; it's the secret of my success at the *Illustrated*."

"I haven't time for an interview today." Julia turned right at the top of Fieldgate Street.

"An hour . . . thirty minutes, Doctor," he said, trailing after her. "That's all I ask."

"We don't have an empty bed in either of our wards, and I'm late for my rounds. So I'll say good day to you."

Osborne passed her with long, loping strides and continued with his questions, walking backward.

"Surely King Cholera's reign is at an end, Doctor. Isn't the epidemic over?"

"A more plebeian plague is filling us up," she said dryly. "Influenza is back, and it's just getting started."

"Why do these blights keep washing up on our shores? Our 'Sceptered Isle,' as Shakespeare calls it, seems no bastion against contamination. Our island kingdom ought to be safe from these waves of infection that begin far from our homeland."

"Are you practicing lines for your next article, Mister Osborne?"

He fell in beside her again. "These streets already teem with poverty and vice. You know it well, Doctor. Must our slums be filled with foreign diseases, too?"

"Illness spares no nationality or class, as even Her Majesty knows. If you recall, Prince Albert fell victim to a fever only a few years ago."

"Yes, but *some* neighborhoods, some people more than others, crawl with contagion. I walked through the old-clothes market on Petticoat Lane with my face in a handkerchief. Every long-curled, be-hatted Jew hawking his wares from a clothing barrow was hacking his lungs out."

Julia could see where this interview was going. "Much as I'd like to help elevate your stories in the *Illustrated*, I have no time right now. If you'd like to come back another day and write a piece about the challenges of a small clinic like mine, I would be happy to oblige you. But if you aim to stir up hatred and fear, sensationalize . . ."

"The public loves being frightened, Doctor. A ghoulish headline in the *Illustrated* and the cover of a penny dreadful novel on a night table—they're the same. They crack open our orderly world to reveal the darkness churning below, unseen."

"But in a novel, the villain is always unmasked. Right is done. Do your articles do justice to the people you write about?"

"My dear doctor, that is for the public to decide. Still, it's not the ethics of journalism but rather our recent epidemic of murders that I want to discuss with you. I believe you were the medical examiner in the last cases. And it seems an *old* crime has come back to haunt the intrepid Inspector Tennant."

"I've read your articles, Mister Osborne. You called the recent murders 'un-English.' What's the basis of your claim?"

Osborne smiled. "The thin stiletto blade, Doctor; it has the whiff of something foreign about it. It's a dago's weapon, not an English one at all. A homegrown, beef-eating 'John Bull' would bash his victim over the head with a solid British brick."

"Are you reporting facts or manufacturing a case of your own invention?"

"Ah," he wagged his finger, "you've read my articles. Didn't you notice the sentinel words, the bodyguard phrases surrounding my speculations in print? I wrote 'perhaps' and 'maybe' and 'it might be the case.' *Caveat lector*, dear Doctor. Let the reader beware."

"Your coverage will have the public baying for foreign blood."

He shrugged. "I only report. The reader reaches his own conclusion."

They'd arrived at the door of her clinic. "You Fleet Street journalists have much to answer for, Mister Osborne. I'll say good day to you."

He slipped between her and the door. "Before you go, Doctor, think of that name. Fleet Street—a metonym that's a metaphor if I ever heard one. The Fleet River christened our humble byway. It gave our profession its nickname—a stream so fetid, so malodorous, so teeming with putrefaction that the city fathers covered it with a road. You can't see the river now. But it's still there, running under our feet, its toxins merely out of sight."

"Should you be compounding the misery, adding to the poison?"

"We newspapermen know the world is a sewer, and we write whatever sells." He tipped his hat. "Goodbye . . . for now, Doctor Lewis."

He's enjoying this, Julia thought, as she watched him saunter down the street. Was there something more malignant festering there, something his acid jokes masked?

To chase a sensational story, how far was Johnny Osborne willing to go?

Tennant returned from his interview with Chief Inspector Clark, his gray eyes as hard as granite. Graves and O'Malley exchanged glances.

Meetings with the chief rarely raised even a hairline crack in Tennant's reserve. But that morning, dusky smudges under his eyes hinted at sleepless nights, and the lines around the inspector's mouth etched deep into his cheeks.

He said wearily, "We've got ground to cover, and the chief's patience is paper-thin. You both know that. Find something solid, something that will move this investigation forward. We've got the music hall and the engineer, Stanley Hughes."

"I'll tackle the water company bloke," Graves said.

Tennant nodded. "I have the man's address. Use your charms on his landlady and any female servants at his lodging house. You know the drill."

The inspector often made good use of the sergeant's fair hair and blue eyes. Over cups of tea, motherly cooks and doe-eyed maids usually told Graves what he wanted to know.

"Right, guv. I'm on it."

"Constable, that leaves you to follow up on the music-hall connections at the Eagle. Meanwhile, I'll interview Sir Maxwell's manservant at the Carlton Club." The inspector pulled out his pocket watch. "I'll expect your reports by four o'clock."

It was a short walk from the Yard's headquarters on Whitehall Place to the Carlton Club's address on Pall Mall. But for Richard Tennant, the route was a jarring journey into the past. He passed the Horse Guards Parade and thought, *ten years.* That was the last time he'd marched with the Grenadier Guards,

"Trooping the Color," wave after wave of black caps and scarlet tunics marching before the queen, rifles shouldered, bayonets flashing silver in the sunlight. *A lifetime ago.*

Tennant dodged the carriage traffic clattering along Pall Mall, darting between two hansom cabs, wincing as he regained the pavement. He looked up at number 94, admiring its symmetrical rows of Romanesque arches. The Carlton Club's creamy limestone façade shimmered in the afternoon sunlight. In the evenings, the lamplights atop the club's balustrade lit a line of iridescent halos that glowed in the darkness. In the daytime, the lamps stood like sentinels, guarding the building from the sidewalk's throngs.

Most coppers at the Met would have taken a deep breath and straightened their ties before mounting the Carlton's portico steps. Such clubs held no fears for the inspector. Before he fell from grace, his father had been a longtime member of the Reform Club. Tennant had dined countless times in the club's "coffee room" and wished he had a pound for every fiver he'd lost at the billiard tables. Thinking of bets, he eyed the front door. He wagered the Carlton's secretary would greet him frostily and expect him to use the tradesman entrance around back. Tennant was willing to make one concession. For his interview with Sir Maxwell's valet, the inspector would not insist on a room in the club. Instead, he'd suggest a pub or a bench in the park.

When Tennant gave his name and rank, the doorman didn't blink. He'd mastered the art of never betraying anything so vulgar as surprise. Still, the inspector saw the man's gaze drop, just for an instant, a flicker that registered Tennant's red-and-blue regimental tie.

The Carlton's secretary was not what he expected—not some rusty old boy hanging on from the days of Victoria's coronation. Instead, Mr. Clifford was a pleasant, sandy-haired man in early middle age and eager to be helpful. He waved away

Tennant's offer to interview the valet away from the premises and suggested his office.

"For the next hour," he said, "I'll be in the cellars supervising a shipment of claret, so you're welcome to my study. I'm sorry I can't be of much help to you, Inspector. I was here, of course, the last evening Sir Maxwell dined at the club. But so was the prime minister, and the Earl of Darby's party included Mister Disraeli."

At the mention of that flamboyant politician's name, Tennant smiled. "I understand. You had your plate full that evening."

"Indeed. Will you follow me, Inspector?"

They crossed a central hall dominated by an ornate, curving staircase that extended three stories high, its gleaming mahogany handrail rubbed to a high polish. Tennant slowed his pace to admire it.

"A boy's dream, Inspector," the secretary said over his shoulder. "It's the perfect banister for a slide-down, although I've never had the nerve to try."

Mr. Clifford reached for a door handle and pushed it open. Bookcases lined the walls, and club chairs flanked the fireplace. Tennant breathed in the clean, familiar scents of fine leather and beeswax polish.

"Here we are. I've sent for Thomas Haskell, Sir Maxwell's valet—and for William Rivers, as well. He served Sir Maxwell at table that last evening."

"Before you go, may I ask a few questions about Sir Maxwell?"

"Certainly, Inspector."

"Did he stay at the club often?"

"Oh, yes. Sir Maxwell used his suite of rooms as his address in town."

"He was a widower, I understand. He never remarried? No . . . romantic entanglements?"

Clifford smiled. "Sir Maxwell, like many successful businessmen, seemed married to his work."

"One last question, if I may. What was your opinion of
the man?"

The secretary sighed. "If you'd asked me that question two
months ago, I would have said Sir Maxwell was the very best
Britain had to offer. A model industrialist—upright, civic-
minded. But after the revelations . . ."

Tennant let the silence play out.

"It's one thing to make a mistake and want to hide it from
public view. But to keep on making it, to lie about it for
months, when all the while . . ."

"When all the while, people were dying in the thousands."

"It offends the conscience."

When the door closed behind the secretary, Tennant thought,
that will teach me. A good copper never assumes.

Thomas Haskell had nothing to offer that the inspector
didn't already know. Sir Maxwell left the Carlton after dinner, but his valet had no idea where he went or with whom he
met. But the waiter, William Rivers, added something new to
the inquiry.

"At the end of the meal, I asked Sir Maxwell if he required
anything else. He shook his head. He'd taken a note from his
breast pocket, and I . . ."

"Yes, Mister Rivers?"

"I wouldn't want you to think I was looking on purpose, sir."

"What did you see?"

"When I stood behind Sir Maxwell to pull out his chair, I
caught a glimpse of the letter. It looked like instructions written under a sketch of a map."

"Did you recognize the location?"

The waiter shook his head. Tennant thanked Rivers and dismissed him.

That was how the killer lured Sir Maxwell to the baths. It was an easy matter, after the killing, to retrieve the letter and destroy it. *Clever.*

A question remained: How did Sir Maxwell make his last journey? Pall Mall was less than two miles from Goulston Square, but the Carlton was a world away from the public baths where the body was found. A vigorous man on a warm night might easily make the walk. But the evening had been raw, and a stretch of rough neighborhood separated the club and the baths. Had Sir Maxwell taken a carriage?

Tennant looked for the doorman on the way out and spotted him at his post by the entrance portico. "Were you on duty the night Sir Maxwell was murdered?"

The doorman nodded. "I was, sir."

"Did he ask you to call a cab for him?"

"He left on foot. Walked east, and . . ." His eyes widened. "Good Lord, I've just remembered. At the corner of Waterloo Place, he hailed a carriage. Stood aside to let someone get in ahead of him."

"Did you get a look at him?"

The doorman shook his head. "It was just starting to drizzle, and the open door blocked my view. The figure, someone on the smallish side, was wearing some kind of long, hooded cape against the weather. But . . ."

Tennant swore under his breath. "Out with it, man."

"I thought it was a woman."

Jonathan Graves whistled. "A woman? Not possible, guv."

Tennant leaned back in his chair until his head and shoulders touched the wall. "I'm inclined to agree with you. But tell me your reasons, Sergeant."

"It's the nature of the killings. They're too . . . too physical; they needed too much strength. Now, a spot of poison in a teacup, that's a female weapon. But a knife in the chest? A smash across the groin with a heavy cobblestone? It's just not on, guv."

"It might explain why the victims were taken by surprise. In her medical reports, Doctor Lewis described a 'thin, sharp blade.' It wouldn't take much strength, I suppose, to drive a knife like that home. Still, I don't see a woman wielding that sort of weapon either."

"Let's not forget that Sir Maxwell was a big blighter." Graves rounded his arms and blew out his cheeks. "He weighed sixteen stone, at least. A woman couldn't do it. I'd struggle to get him into that tub. My money's still on some Nancy boy."

"But there was nothing about Sir Maxwell's body to indicate—"

"Maybe something spooked the killer before the puff got a chance to slice and dice him. Didn't you say Ball never remarried? A rich bloke in the prime of life—strange he never replaced his trouble and strife."

"Back to the question. A woman might have *coaxed* the victim into that tub. Gotten him in on his back and finished him off with the blade. Some men like unusual places for their amorous encounters."

"No. A woman couldn't do it. And what about the railway murder, guv? The killer threw the victim off the bloody train. The carriage was a gory mess; he put up a struggle, that banker. No. A woman couldn't do it."

"On the other hand, Thomas Rigby was an older man. The banker was in his sixties. Our killer is a strong, *young* woman, perhaps? And let's not forget those letters. The handwriting looks feminine to me, not masculine."

Tennant righted his chair and pulled a file toward him. He leaned over the last letter from the killer. "What do we make of that line—*That's the way the money goes?*" He looked up. "Any theories?"

"Some quarrel with the banker about a loan gone sour? Did

his sons ever get back to you with anything useful?" The inspector shook his head. "Too bad. A foreclosure on a sodding great loan with some threatening letters would come in handy about now."

The life of Thomas Rigby seemed frustratingly ordinary. The banker had been a man of sober habits, lived a life as regular as clockwork, every day taking the same train at the same time, back and forth, to and from the city. Only his murder had ripped a jagged tear through his seamless life.

Tennant leaned back in his chair and gazed at the ceiling. "We may have to reconsider the testimony of the witness who saw Mr. Atwater in the company of a prostitute—the night watchman at Christ Church. We assumed she had nothing to do with the case. But the evidence puts both the clergyman and Sir Maxwell in the company of unidentified women on the evenings they were killed—in theory."

"How sure was the doorman, guv? Was his identification solid?"

"Not solid at all. He *thought* he saw a woman. Still, it's a reminder to us, Sergeant, to interrogate our assumptions. All we can be sure of is that the murders are the work of the same killer."

"Those ruddy balloons," Graves muttered. "Without them, we'd never connect the crimes. One man with his Johnny crushed, the other bloke had it sliced off, and two men with their knobs all safe and snug inside their drawers. He—"

Tennant raised an eyebrow.

"Come on, guv. You don't really believe it was a woman either. He—or she—is all over the map."

"Does the geography of the murders tell us anything?" Tennant swung his chair around to face the ordnance survey map of East London. "The last three . . ." He stood and tapped the circles he'd drawn on the map. "All are in striking distance of High Street and Whitechapel Road, the heart of East London—

all but the banker. His body was found miles away along railway tracks in North London."

"Looks like the killer hunted the banker down, but the waiter said . . ."

"Yes. Given what the waiter told me, the killer lured his last victim to Whitechapel. Caught him in a trap. Perhaps he drew maps to lead all of them to their deaths."

Graves grinned. "He?"

"Let's agree to 'he' for convenience while keeping an open mind."

With his right index finger, the sergeant circled all of Whitechapel. "Looks like he's settled on his hunting grounds."

"A predator who blends in, prowls his jungle, knows every inch of his habitat." Tennant lifted an eyebrow. "Any naturalist will tell you that, for some species, the female is the deadlier."

"All right, guv. Have it your own way."

"Tell me what you discovered about the engineer, Stanley Hughes—a dead end?"

"Bit of a letdown. Hughes wasn't out of a job for long. Joseph Bazalgette hired him. He's working for the great engineer on the last leg of the sewer project. The bloke's landed in a tub of butter."

"A cushioned fall; that certainly drops Mister Hughes down the suspect list," Tennant said.

"His landlady said he's working at the pumping station at Abbey Mills."

Tennant found the location on the ordnance map. "I'll track him down. Someone else at the company might have nursed a grudge against Sir Maxwell. Perhaps Hughes can suggest a name."

Graves pulled out his pocket watch. "O'Malley's bloody well taking his time."

"You passed on the music-hall assignment, Sergeant. Now I'm wondering if it answers our question about the doorman's evidence."

"How do you reckon?"

"On that raw evening, did the doorman see a man or a woman? Have you considered a third possibility? Perhaps he saw both." Tennant saw the flicker in his sergeant's eye; the penny had dropped.

"One of the drag queens from the music hall."

The inspector nodded. "Or someone else dressed as a woman."

When Tennant knocked on Julia's office door, she called out a distracted "Come in. Come in."

She stood at a table spread with instruments, collar undone, her jacket thrown carelessly across a side chair. She looked away from a bottle she was holding to the light. CHLORO-FORM—Tennant read the label from across the room. Waves of her chestnut hair had escaped their pins. When she raised her hand to push them away, Tennant noticed bloodstains on the sleeve of her blouse.

What a way for a woman to spend her days, he thought. "Some new information has come to light." Tennant explained the doorman's evidence.

"A woman?" Julia put the bottle down.

"The witness wasn't sure. Still, I think it's unlikely."

"Why? It's certainly possible. A sharp knife doesn't need much force behind it to drive the blade home. And there was no evidence the killer dragged the bodies; it would be difficult for a woman, in the case of Sir Maxwell, less so for the clergy-man. For both, a firm push might have landed the bodies about where you found them."

"I suppose the same could be said for Bertie Parker," Tennant said slowly. "He—or she—attacked the performer in a dark alley, then melted away into the night. Still, a woman wouldn't have the strength to carry it off. That cobblestone the assailant used was heavy."

"Many women, most outside the middle classes, work at

grinding manual labor every day. And working-class women are much stronger than you think."

"Perhaps."

"An angry, vengeful woman would fit the bill equally well. You may have drawn the wrong conclusion about the sexual nature of the mutilations."

"I've drawn no conclusions yet, Doctor."

She smiled faintly. "I wonder. Shall we sit?" Julia gestured to the pair of armchairs by her fire grate.

He stood in front of one of them, waiting for her to take a seat. Suddenly, she placed the flat of both hands on his chest and shoved. He toppled backward into the chair.

"The element of surprise. That's how a woman might have gotten the upper hand, Inspector."

He scrambled to his feet and pulled at his coat sleeves and cuffs. "Understood, Doctor," he said icily.

Julia walked back to her instruments table. "I saw the calloused hands and muscled arms of a skivvy this morning, but her life of toil hadn't hardened her enough to survive." Julia picked up a scalpel and tested the point. "Given a chance, would she have taken a knife to the man who wronged her? I wonder."

She set the scalpel down and picked up an instrument with curving blades. It opened like a long, dull scissor. Julia read the question on Tennant's face.

"Forceps, Inspector. Used by doctors to assist in difficult deliveries."

"You attended such a birth today?"

Julia said nothing at first. Dully, with her back to him, she said, "A servant girl—the skivvy I mentioned. She'd kept her pregnancy hidden, although I suspect the parlormaid with whom she shared a room knew. Others, as well, perhaps."

"It must have been difficult to hide."

"Possible, Inspector, by lacing one's corset as tightly as one can stand." Julia turned away from the table and dropped the forceps on her desk. "And imperative. If a servant girl 'loses her character,' she's flung out of the household to live on the streets." She sat down and looked away. "Even those closest to a desperate girl can be fooled. Family, friends, even doctors."

"Can you tell me what happened?"

He saw her throat constrict. "They found her before breakfast on the floor of the back-garden privy. The house, of course, was equipped with water closets for the family. But servants still relieved themselves outdoors, dumping their chamber pots in the morning. The girl had been on the floor for hours, and it was many hours, still, before the lady of the house sent for me. The girl was bleeding heavily, unable to deliver the child."

Julia dropped her head, her hair falling like a curtain across her face. Her grip tightened on the handle of the forceps. Then she pushed the instrument away.

Tennant hesitated. "And the girl?"

"I was too late. She'd lost too much blood and hadn't any strength left to push." She nodded at the forceps. "I used those to deliver her stillborn baby. She was hardly more than a child herself. Dead, and not yet sixteen."

"Good God," he said.

Julia looked up. "As to the father of the child, who can say? But the son of the household appeared, half-dressed, wild-eyed, asking if it were true, sobbing out her Christian name. Mary." Her lips twisted. "A fine time to care about Mary, now that she was dead."

"I'm sorry. That was a shattering experience."

"His mother appeared, furious and cold-eyed. Told her son to control himself, ordered him back to his room. Then she handed me four five-pound notes, buying my silence, I suppose. I gave the money and my card to the weeping parlormaid. Told her to get away from that house and find another situation."

Julia picked up the forceps and brought them back to the table. After a brief silence, the inspector stood. He offered his hand and held hers until she met his eye.

"Forgive me for giving advice to a physician, but you look all in. I hope your day is over." He glanced out the window at the falling light. "It's getting late. May I find you a cab or escort you to an omnibus stop?"

"Thank you, Inspector. I'm nearly done for the day but not quite ready to leave. Fred, our porter, will fetch me a cab from the stand on Whitechapel Road."

He regarded her gravely. "Very well, Doctor."

That night, the dream returned.

"She jumped, Julia."

The nightmare voice grew louder, insistent, repeating over and over until she jolted from her sleep, her heart pounding.

"Helen," Julia sobbed, burying her face in her pillow.

CHAPTER 6

Tennant arrived early at the Abbey Mills pumping station for his meeting with the water engineer.

Mr. Stanley Hughes—fired by Sir Maxwell Ball, hired by Joseph Bazalgette, the maestro of the metropolitan sewer system—wasn't high on his list of suspects. Still, the man might have a story to tell. Tennant waited uneasily for the engineer to appear, hoping he wouldn't have to navigate any tight underground spaces.

Hughes arrived on the dot. He was a small man, neatly dressed in a brown tweed suit, his fair, thinning hair parted precisely down the middle. A brief exchange between the engineer and his assistant showed him to be a meticulous, soft-spoken individual. But Tennant knew that finding a quiet man's consuming passion could make the words flow. For Stanley Hughes, the subject was sewers.

Hughes insisted on showing him the wonders of the pumping station. After some deft questioning about their destination, Tennant followed the engineer down a series of iron staircases. The engineer had assured him they led to a vast, open chamber built to house pumping machines not yet installed. He looked down, trying not to think about the climb up.

Along the way, the inspector listened to a disquisition on the history of sanitation, beginning with the Old Testament. Moses, it seemed, on the journey to the Promised Land, had advised the Israelites to "carry a stick" and "dig a hole" so they could bury their waste. Tennant answered "no" when Hughes asked if he knew that the first evidence of indoor lavatories dated to the Babylonians. After brief visits to Egypt and India, Hughes arrived at those wizards of waste removal: the Romans. He quoted an obscure ancient historian who claimed that drains were among Rome's three greatest achievements. When the inspector pressed the man to name the other two, Hughes said he'd forgotten what they were.

Tennant winced when his left boot finally hit the bottom. They'd arrived at their destination, deep in the bowels of the pumping station.

"By the time we're done, this empty chamber will be filled with machines taller than the four-story mansions that line Belgravia." The engineer pointed to the mouth of a gaping tunnel. "There it is, Inspector Tennant, the end of the Northern Highline Sewer."

Behind his steel-framed glasses, the engineer's eyes glittered. He spoke the tunnel's name as a sculptor would the Pietà or a violinist, a Stradivarius. Tennant positioned himself to view the gaping void obliquely.

"What do you notice, Inspector?"

"Well . . . the color of bricks at the bottom third of the channel. They're a dazzling blue. Beautiful but invisible; almost no one will see them."

The engineer nodded. "Staffordshire blues, bricks especially fired to be watertight. A thousand years from now, this tunnel will hold its flow. What else do you see?"

"The diameter of the tunnel. It's much larger than I'd expect."

Hughes flushed a happy pink, looking as pleased as a school-master whose favorite pupil had run the table on Prize Day.

"Very good, Inspector. Full marks to you. Mister Bazalgette estimated London's population at the end of the century. Then he doubled the figure and designed his tunnels accordingly. It's an honor to work for a man who is a visionary."

Tennant saw his opening. "Unlike Sir Maxwell Ball?"

"The man was a criminal. Do you know he trained as an engineer? I can hardly believe it. He disgraced a noble profession." His shoulders sagged. "But I blame myself. I should have spoken up sooner."

"Who else might blame Sir Maxwell? Someone killed him."

"Surely you don't think . . ." He drew himself up to his full five feet, four inches. "Inspector, I have a better position working for a great man on a project that matters to people's lives. Why would I kill him?"

"Someone else, then, someone at the company with a motive for murder. Sir Maxwell's death followed so soon after the story hit the newspapers. The timing seems too suggestive to be mere coincidence."

Hughes thought a minute. "I'm the only one who lost his job. As employers go, I suppose he wasn't a bad fellow, until that last disastrous decision to release the unfiltered water. No, Inspector. If the scandal drove someone to murder, I don't think you'll find your man at the company. You need to look at the cholera victims' families."

Tennant feared he might be right, and they numbered in the thousands.

The engineer led him back up the winding staircase. Tennant reached the top and leaned his weight against the railing, easing the pressure on his left leg. Then he dug into his pocket and handed Hughes his card. "If you think of anything else that can assist us in our investigations."

The engineer tapped it against his palm, his brows knitted.

"Mister Hughes?"

"As it happens . . . but it couldn't possibly be relevant."

"Allow me to be the judge of that, sir."

"Well, Sir Maxwell had only planned to give me a dressing down. His private secretary told me—to soften the blow, I suppose. One of the principal shareholders in the company pressured him to cut me loose."

Tennant asked sharply, "Who was that person? Do you know?"

"It was Sir Harry Jackson, the owner of the Black Falcon Brewery."

An hour later, a stony-eyed Tennant faced Sir Maxwell Ball's secretary.

"Mister Jenkins, at our last interview, I asked you if anyone connected to Sir Maxwell and the company was angry about the water scandal. Not from you, I have learned that Sir Harry Jackson was furious. I know he had the water engineer fired."

"But . . ."

"You've wasted a considerable amount of police time, sir. Your actions could be construed as obstructing an official investigation."

Jenkins bristled. "It's absurd. To think a man like Sir Harry would resort to murder over a business dispute? He never crossed my mind as a possible suspect."

"You are not paid to make such judgments, Mister Jenkins. I am. I want to know all about Sir Harry Jackson and his relationship with Sir Maxwell and the company."

The secretary said nothing. With steel in his voice, Tennant said, "Don't tempt me to continue this interview in official surroundings—at Scotland Yard."

Jenkins sighed. "Sir Harry is a principal shareholder in the company. He's also an important customer. As you can imagine, it takes a lot of water to manufacture ale."

"Did the company pump a contaminated supply to the Black Falcon Brewery?"

Jenkins shook his head. "Spitalfields is connected to the sewer system. The water supplied to the Black Falcon comes from a different pumping station where the river water is filtered. But . . ."

"Yes, Mister Jenkins?"

"Some of the brewery's workers live in Whitechapel." The secretary looked away. "While none of Sir Harry's employees became ill, several of their family members . . . succumbed to the disease."

" 'Died' is the word, Mister Jenkins. Some would say 'murdered.' "

The secretary's face turned a mottled red. He opened his mouth and closed it again.

"Sir Harry believed your employer was responsible for the deaths?"

Jenkins nodded. "He said Sir Maxwell's chairmanship was hanging by a thread. He threatened to lead a shareholders' revolt unless the company cleaned house."

"What did he demand?"

"That the water-filtration system be engineered to conform to legal standards and that the engineer be fired."

"Why? Surely the man performed a heroic deed at great risk to himself."

Jenkins smiled thinly. "Sir Harry is a principal investor in the company. The price of the company's shares has yet to recover, Inspector. 'I want the bastard fired.' His words. He was adamant about it, said a company required absolute loyalty from its workers."

"So his outrage was more financial than moral?"

The secretary narrowed his eyes. "I'd say equal parts. His voice shook when he spoke about cholera and the families of his workers. About the company, his tone was icy, his demeanor controlled."

"Since the murder, have you had any communication from Sir Harry?"

"Apart from a conventional note of condolence, no. He offered to assist in the transition to new management."

Tennant got up and held the secretary's eye. "Have you told me everything, Mister Jenkins?"

"I have. He's a complicated man, Sir Harry Jackson."

At Scotland Yard, Julia watched Constable O'Malley and the duty sergeant roast Jonathan Graves over his purchase of a new suit.

O'Malley brushed some imaginary lint from the sergeant's shoulder. "Sure you're looking a right Beau Brummel, Sarge."

"He's joined the carriage class," the duty sergeant said. "Too good for the likes of us."

Graves adjusted his sleeves. "That's right. If you see me in the street, just keep walking."

O'Malley spotted Julia standing inside the doorway. "What d'you think of himself's new glad rags, Doctor?"

Julia circled Sergeant Graves. Leaning forward, she inspected the details of the tailoring. She straightened, tapped her finger to her chin, and considered. The sergeant reddened.

Finally, she said, "Very smart."

He smirked at his fellow coppers. "Thanks, Doc."

"Harris Tweed?" Julia said.

O'Malley guffawed. "Sure, I knew it. 'Tis a right *cappietalist* our sergeant is, wearing his profits on his back."

"Profits? My Aunt Fanny. After paying the rent collector *and* the roofer *and* the glazier, I never had enough brass left over to replace me old boots until this year." He waggled a foot.

"Wish *I'd* be having an old uncle who'd up and die," O'Malley said. "Leave *me* a house. Heard the sergeant screws every last farthing out of his tenants."

"Don't know how he sleeps at night," the duty sergeant said.

"I couldn't; that was the problem," Graves said. "Moved out

after three months, I did. Those walls were so thin you could hear an ant sneeze, not to mention a lot of other things. But I'll spare your blushes, Doc."

"Thank you for that, Sergeant."

"The place was rubbish when I took possession. For five years, it bled me dry. This year, I had a few quid left over after the rent collector took his fee, tucked away a bit of sausage and mash and bought me this suit." Sergeant Graves straightened his coat jacket and adjusted his tie. "First new one since I joined the Met. Honest, Doc."

Julia nodded. "A sound investment, Sergeant."

He flashed a grin, quick and cocky. "Speaking of glad rags, Doc, you're a picture in blue this morning." He clasped his hands to his chest and sang, "'I lost my heart and my senses too/To a dark-haired girl dressed in blue.'"

Without missing a beat, Julia sang back. "'So all you young men—take care what you do/When you meet a strange lady, a girl dressed in blue.' She stole five pounds from him, if I remember, that girl in the song."

Graves widened his eyes. "You'd be liking the music halls, Doc?"

Few well-to-do people thought them a respectable form of entertainment, especially for young ladies.

"I can't count the number of times my grandmother and I sat upstairs at the Canterbury on ladies' night. From the boxes, you can watch two shows—the acts on stage and the antics of the audience. "

O'Malley whistled. "You and your granny, now. Didn't you both do the nobby; those seats cost nine pence."

"Comic songs were her favorite, Constable. She was an American and knew all the lyrics to Robert Glindon's 'Yankee Wonders.' She loved the way he mocked her countrymen's tendency to exaggerate everything. Do you know that one?"

In a wobbly, off-key baritone, O'Malley sang, "'There once

was a woman as large as a tree/Can't say where they found her/But setting off one morning fast from her knee/ Took me a week to get around her.' "

Hands over his ears, the desk sergeant howled, "Stop. That's enough, Paddy. No wonder Glindon sang 'No Irish Need Apply.' "

"Who would have guessed Scotland Yard was a locus of popular entertainment?"

The drawled question came from Johnny Osborne in the doorway. With his bowler hat pushed forward over his eyes, the reporter lounged with studied nonchalance.

"I'll write a review for the *Illustrated*—'Coppers on Parade.' "

Tennant's arrival, hard on the heels of the reporter, broke up the party. The inspector had wasted his morning chasing down a phantom connection to the water engineer, and his interview with Sir Maxwell's secretary hadn't improved his mood. O'Malley took one look at his boss's face, clapped on his helmet, and disappeared through the rear entrance of the Yard. Graves gave the duty sergeant, suddenly busy at his desk, a wink and hurried off.

The inspector certainly knows how to empty a room, Julia thought.

Tennant asked, "Is there some way I can help you, Mister Osborne?" not sounding helpful at all.

"A quote on the record would be nice. Have the police made any progress? Are you any closer to catching the killer terrorizing our fair city?"

"The police investigation continues. I have nothing to add at this time."

Osborne scribbled in his notebook and read back his copy. "When questioned by this reporter, Inspector Tennant said, quote, 'I have nothing.' " He flipped his pad shut. "That's about the size of it, isn't it, Inspector?"

Tennant turned to Julia. "Are you here to see me?"

She nodded.

As they walked away, Osborne called after them. "Will the Yard apologize to Franz Meyer's mother? *She*, at least, is still alive, and living in Bavaria, I believe."

At the top of the staircase, Julia said, "He really is insufferable."

"Insufferable but not inaccurate, unfortunately. Osborne is right. I have nothing."

In his office, Julia sat at his offer of a chair, peeled off her gloves, and removed a book from her medical bag.

"The other day, you asked me whether medicine had anything to say about criminal lunacy. My grandfather gave me this from his library."

Julia handed Tennant a slim volume covered in brown, hand-tooled leather. He opened it to the title page and read. "*Unsoundness of Mind in Relation to Criminal Acts* by John Charles Bucknill, M.D., Fellow of University College."

"You can read the entire monograph in an evening. It's only a hundred pages or so. I've bookmarked some of the most relevant passages—definitions of insanity. 'Moral insanity' as opposed to the loss of reason. A discussion of criminal lunacy begins on page eighty."

"Moral insanity," Tennant said, shaking his head. "When one appears perfectly rational but can't distinguish right from wrong."

"Judge Parke agrees with you. He's having none of it, either. Doctor Bucknill quotes him on page eighty-two. The judge calls the doctrine of moral insanity 'a dangerous innovation coming in with the present century.'"

"The present century. Does that imply that every age produces its own variety of lunacy?"

"Perhaps, just as every era introduces new diseases of the body. Before 1830, cholera was unknown in Europe. Now steamships carry infected passengers from the world's ports. And in our crowded cities, pestilence festers and spreads easily from person to person."

"But why should madness change over time?"

Julia shrugged. "Maybe something about modern life—its fast pace, its incessant demands, its people thrown together in close quarters. Perhaps it breeds new forms of mental instability."

Tennant sighed. "The average juryman looking at a man in the dock understands a raving, wild-eyed lunatic, someone beyond reason. But a quiet, well-spoken fellow who calmly explains how he picked up a hatchet and chopped up his wife? How does one decide what to do with him? Is he insane, or is he evil? Should we confine him for life in Broadmoor Lunatic Asylum or send him to Newgate Prison to be hanged?"

"I don't know, Inspector. Perhaps the unknowable should make us cautious. Hanging is so permanent."

Tennant opened the book to the first page and found a verse at the top. "He knows a baseness in his blood/At such strange war with something good/He may not do the thing he would."

"'The Two Voices,' by Tennyson."

"A baseness in the blood—where does it come from, Doctor?"

"At the top of page eighty-three, Doctor Bucknill says the only source of mental disease is the emotive part of our nature."

He flipped to the bookmarked page and read. "It may be truly said that every crime is the result of an uncontrollable emotion; that is, of passion and desire stronger under the circumstances than the intelligent will."

"But he says something more." Julia extended her hand for the book. "May I?"

He gave her the volume.

She leafed forward a few pages. "Doctor Bucknill says acts of homicidal lunacy are never the result of an impulse. They are events of long standing. The early stages of mental disease are"—Julia read from the text—"unobserved by others and unacknowledged by the patient." She looked up. "He describes them as 'morbid desires' that fester unseen." Julia handed back the book.

"Morbid desires that are unseen and unobserved—they're not very helpful to an investigator." Tennant put the book down and drummed his fingertips on the cover. "I don't know, Doctor. Old-fashioned police work, boots on the ground, not books on a shelf—that's what usually works in the end."

"Have boots on the ground been working for you, Inspector? And does this strike you as a usual case?"

"Points taken, Doctor."

"Surely one approach doesn't have to exclude the other? You can follow all the practical clues while being open-minded about how they may be connected to some trauma from the past. She bit her lip. "There must be something, some clue to the simmering tempest that set these murders in motion."

"Police investigations generally work the other way around, starting with the patient accumulation of evidence. When we find our man, the motive will become clear."

"What of the balloons, Inspector? They're evidence, too. They link all the crimes and must mean something to the killer. Granted, they're not bloody footprints leading you to the killer's door. Still, he's trying to tell you something."

"Obviously, Doctor, but what?"

"It's a child's plaything. Might it point to some early, terrible event—a twisted souvenir of some searing experience early in life?"

Tennant sighed. "Perhaps. Still, that hardly narrows it down for us in a hellish place like Whitechapel."

Julia stared at him coldly. *I've wasted my time.*

Tennant stood and held up the volume. "Still, I thank you for this, Doctor." He added it to the piles of documents on his desk. "I'll read it carefully."

"Will you?" Julia doubted he'd bother. *I thought he had more imagination.*

"Yes, Doctor." Then Tennant smiled. It reached his eyes, warming their icy gray. "On second thought, I'd enjoy telling the chief that a book written by a university fellow was the key to solving the case."

On her way back to the clinic, Julia thought, *Why did I bother?*

For an intelligent man, Tennant could be infuriatingly obtuse. And she suspected he barely tolerated her. Still, Julia thought she knew the answer to her question. *A good sparring match is stimulating.*

She hailed a hansom and settled back into her seat. *He should smile more often . . .*

Whenever Julia pondered the state of affairs between the sexes, she found them wanting. The arrangement of society and the straitjacket of propriety that regulated relationships made it almost impossible for men and women to converse in meaningful ways. Stilted chatter in a drawing room, superficial conversation in a ballroom, all under the watchful eyes of chaperones—it was a miracle that men and women of her class ever got to know one another well enough for friendship, let alone marriage. Perhaps that explained all the miserable ones she'd seen. And there was no chart at all for navigating the unfamiliar waters of a professional association.

Was he interested in her ideas, or had she wasted her time? *To be listened to—that's what any intelligent woman really wants*, Julia thought. *Deep down.* She wanted to be heard, not merely seen.

Even at medical school in Philadelphia, there had been an air of condescension in the instruction. Students were led away from challenging specialties in surgery or neurology and directed down the more "appropriate" paths of gynecology and obstetrics. The case had reminded Julia of that.

After earning her medical degree, she'd wanted to train for a year at the Pennsylvania Asylum for the Insane, famous for its innovative methods of treating mental illness. Her advisor barely listened to her reasons for wanting the assignment. She remembered his thin smile, his murmured "tut-tuts," and the shake of his head before handing her a letter of recommendation for the Children's Hospital of Philadelphia. "This is a more appropriate place for you, my dear," he'd said.

Had she trained at the Asylum for the Insane, Julia thought she might be better prepared to understand the deviant desires that drove the murderer. She was well aware that the normal ones were strong enough. She remembered that night in the library with Matthew, her distant cousin on her grandmother's side. The flickering firelight, his proximity to her on the sofa, and their unexpected aloneness after his family said goodnight had charged the air between them and made it feel alive. A rippling sensation traveled along her skin; the breaths she drew became shallow and quick. When Matthew leaned in to kiss her, Julia met his lips eagerly, followed them as he drew his head away. Ardent young men had embraced her before. Until that evening, she'd never felt the urgent desire that demanded more.

Something made her pull back from the brink. Had she not, Julia sometimes wondered what her fate would have been: an honorable proposal from Matthew the next morning, or their parting, followed by an unexpected pregnancy? Either was possible; either would have been a disaster for her.

In the cool, gray light of a misty spring morning, and after an awkward greeting at her great-aunt's breakfast table, Julia was relieved that sense had prevailed over sensation. As charming as he was and as much as she liked him, Matthew Rush was not her future. Her passion for her profession, her desire for a career would always be a mystery to him. He saw it as an oddity, not the thing that was as natural and needful to her as the air she breathed.

In the end, no hearts were broken or lives upended. When Julia left Philadelphia, they parted as friends. Each knew they weren't necessary for the other's happiness.

Still, she remembered the power of those feelings, a force that switched off sense, shook the pillars of propriety, and unraveled a lifetime's lessons in self-control ... nearly. *Festering, deviant desires must be overwhelming*, she thought. Hidden and morbid, they gathered strength in the dark corners of the heart until the compulsion to act was uncontrollable.

A young man and a note waited for Julia at the Whitechapel Clinic. The message was an invitation from Sir Harry Jackson; the young man was Jackie Archer, the solitary boxer from Q's sporting club.

Julia had offered Jackie a porter's job, and he was there to discuss wages and hours. He'd work a few daytime shifts and three evenings a week, giving Fred, her full-time porter, some time away from the clinic.

The boy had smoothed down his spikey, straw-colored hair. His shirtfront shone white from a fresh laundering. He'd rolled his cloth cap, clutching it between his fists, his wrists and hands jumping on his restless knee. Julia heard the drum of his boot heel against the stone floor. Throughout the interview, Jackie struggled to look Julia in the eye. He would set his jaw and drag his gaze from her desktop, working to return his attention to her. It pained her to watch the battle.

At the end of their talk, Jackie said, "Thank you, Doctor Lewis, for giving me this chance. It will be an honor to work for you." His sliding glance took in the open medical bag on her desk, the anatomy posters on her walls, and the instruments gleaming on the table by the window. "It must be wonderful to work in a place of"—his eyes dropped again—"a place of healing."

Julia listened to his halting speech and remembered the livid wounds across his back and the scars he carried inside and out. She felt a catch in her throat.

She smiled and extended her hand. "It is, Jackie. I hope you will find it so as well. Now come along. I'll introduce you to the staff." She took his arm and steered him to the door. "Nurse Clemmie oversees the wards, so you'll work directly under her." She glanced at the watch pinned to her blouse. "Right now, she's on home visits to patients who've been treated and discharged. She'll be back soon. So, we'll find Fred; he'll give you the grand tour and explain your duties."

As she handed Jackie off to the porter, Julia said, "It's late in the day. Officially, you don't start until tomorrow. Still, if you have the time, I've got a job for you."

"Whatever you say, Doctor."

"Do you know the Black Falcon Brewery?"

"Off Brick Lane in Spitalfields?"

"That's the one. Come back to my office after you're finished with Fred. I'll give you a note to deliver, the omnibus fare, and a tip for your trouble."

Silently, stealthily, he watched her.

He kept pace with her as she headed toward Whitechapel Road, matching footfall for footfall. She jumped at the clang of a rubbish lid crashing to the ground and froze at the scuttling noise behind the bins. A feral cat, the source of the racket, darted through a pool of gaslight. He saw her shake her head, straighten her shoulders, and lengthen her stride.

After a few steps, she slowed and glanced over her shoulder. He kept carefully to the shadows, dodging the faint glow from the lamplights, hiding in the inky darkness. Had she sensed him? Had she felt a frisson ripple down her spine? Had the fine hairs at the back of her neck signaled he was close?

He saw her shift her medical bag to her left hand and pull the collar of her wool cape tight to her chin. She gathered her skirts away from her boots and picked up her pace, hurrying through the lengthy shadows, the scant circles of lamplight, and the dead quiet of the deserted backstreet.

When she reached the lights of Whitechapel Road, he melted away under a starless sky. He passed doorways and dank alleys and stepped around mounds of ragged, clustering bundles. Only muffled coughs and shushed cries tagged them as human. He ignored them as he did the calls of "Hey, mister" coming from loitering streetwalkers and bold rent boys who spread a different plague in the cholera-stricken city. Contagion was everywhere. The cleaning out, the reckoning, was long overdue.

Softly, he whistled the music-hall song from his childhood, from the time before the darkness swallowed him. The tune reminded him. They were Little Jacko and Jillie, child stars of the stage, lit by the limelight's glow. Night after night, costumed, painted, transformed—before everything changed.

Not tonight, Julia. Soon.

CHAPTER 7

The delay in reporting Bertie Parker's murder to the detective bureau meant Tennant had to pick up the scent of a cold trail. Nearly two months had passed since his body had been found in an alley near the Eagle Tavern's music hall.

The inspector looked around Parker's old dressing room. The entertainer's star turn had been a parody of the popular song "Champagne Charlie." Next to a dressing table, someone had tacked a poster to the wall. Bertie, dressed as "Champagne Charlotte" in a form-hugging gown and a flame-red wig, winked at the audience from beneath a fringed parasol. Strands of paste diamonds draped across a generously padded bosom.

Tennant picked up a copy of the sheet music from the dressing-room floor.

Behind him from the doorway, someone sang, "Champagne Charlotte, that's my name. Granting . . . favors is my game. Are you man enough to tame? Champagne Charlotte—try your aim. Champagne Charlotte, I've got class. Never need a looking glass. Know I'll knock you on your . . . reel you in—a tasty bass."

Tennant turned. A slim young man in a dove-gray suit lounged against the doorframe. There was something vulpine in the slant of his brows, and his long nose, ginger hair, and pointed beard added to the effect.

He nodded to the sheet music in Tennant's hand. "The audience filled in the missing words. Champagne Charlotte supplied the leering innuendo."

"Leaving little to the imagination."

"Willie Lomax is doing the number now. He and Bertie Parker go way back, to when the Eagle was just a 'free-and-easy.' No music hall, no tickets on sale, just ale and alcohol. Amateurs did the singing with a few pros like Willie and Bertie thrown into the mix." The young man looked up at the poster. "Willie's all right when he can keep it together. But Bertie killed it."

"Until someone killed him."

The man's anger flashed and vanished, replaced by a thin smile. "Scotland Yard, I presume? I heard there were police on the premises." He dropped his eyes to Tennant's frame and looked up. "I wouldn't have guessed."

"And you are?"

The man offered his hand. "Roland Jakeways, at your service—Rollie, to my friends."

"Detective Inspector Tennant. You played Lord Molliecoddle to Bertie's Charlotte in the Eagle's skits, I believe."

"Only on the stage, I assure you. Florid, old queens are not my taste." He tilted his head and eyed Tennant through slanting lids. "You are well informed, Inspector. Of course—I forgot. The charming Constable O'Malley. We had a friendly chat the other day when he interviewed the troupe."

Tennant picked up a picture postcard from the dressing table. A smiling girl with fair, cascading curls stood on tiptoe. She wore ballet slippers, lace-trimmed panties that stopped at her upper thigh, and a low-cut, sleeveless bodice.

"Sold for tuppence to Lulu's many admirers, Inspector. She's our aerial act. Oh, how the dockers and brewers whistle and stomp, leering up at their 'little French piece' as she soars above their craning necks. If only they knew—Lulu is really Sam Wasgate, born in Brighton." His smile vanished. "Can you imagine their revulsion?"

Tennant held up a padded gown thrown across a chair. "But here nothing is what it seems."

"Very little, Inspector. You might want to talk to Sam. He was something of a protégé of old Bertie's. He's here this morning, rehearsing his act. Willie Lomax should be here, too, if you can get any sense out of him." Jakeways tapped his temple. "Going a little ga-ga, our Willie. Shall I lead the way?"

He escorted Tennant along a corridor. "The stage is this way. The Eagle's owner built the Grecian Theater behind the tavern; it seats two thousand."

"You referred to Sam Wasgate as Bertie Parker's protégé. Do you mean to imply something more, Mister Jakeways?"

He stopped and looked Tennant up and down. "You can hardly expect me to answer that question. It may be a decade since they hanged you for sodomy, but a buggery conviction would get Sam ten years to life."

They walked on.

"Did Mister Parker employ a regular dresser?"

Jakeways shook his head. "Bertie liked to do his own makeup, and the costumes mistress looked after his gowns, laundered them, patched them up for him. And Bertie would ask a stagehand to button up the back of his dress before curtain."

"A pity," Tennant said.

"You're right, Inspector. Valets and dressers see their gentlemen 'with their pants down,' so to speak. Or, in Bertie's case, with his corset unhooked."

At the end of the hallway, Rollie threw open a door.

"Voilà. Here's where the magic happens." At the front of the stage, the red velvet curtains opened on a cavernous auditorium. "Looks like we're just in time for the finale of Lulu's act."

Lulu swung across the stage, executed a somersault, and grabbed the center trapeze. From the floor, her assistant hurled a drum followed by two sticks. She caught them and slipped the belt of the instrument around her waist. Then, arching her back, Lulu suspended herself by her neck from the trapeze bar, all while beating in rhythm with the orchestra playing in the pit. She tossed the sticks aside, gripped the bar, and vaulted from the lowered trapeze, landing on her feet at center stage. Her act ended with a demure curtsey to an absent audience.

"The fellow's lucky he hasn't broken his neck," Tennant muttered.

"The applause, the limelight's glow—they're as addictive as opium, Inspector."

Jakeways introduced the performer. Lulu—Sam Wasgate—was a vacuous young man. He scratched his head in answer to the Inspector's question about Parker.

"Can't think who'd want to kill Bertie. He was a harmless old duffer."

Next Tennant questioned the stagehands, but none had anything informative to say. Then he asked to see the other performers in Bertie's drag skits. One by one, they told him little of interest. Bertie had been friendly enough, but he "kept himself to himself." He shared an occasional pint with Willie Lomax. But, generally, once he wiped his face clean of stage makeup and left for the night, no one had any idea where he went—or they wouldn't say.

For a moment, Tennant thought Willie Lomax, the man who took over Bertie's role, had given him a lead.

"Bit of a set-to, one night," Lomax said. "Between Bertie and—what's his name, Rollie?"

"George Leybourne."

"That's the chappie. Leybourne sings over at the Collins Theater. Threatened to sue Bertie for stealing his song, 'Champagne Charlie.'" Lomax shrugged. "Tempest in a teapot."

Jakeways said, "Or, in this case, a champagne bottle. The suit would have come to nothing. Same melody, different lyrics; in the theater, parody is fair play. But I wouldn't waste your time looking into Leybourne, Inspector; he's been touring in America for the last six months."

Tennant emerged from the dark theater blinking in the sunshine of the City Road at noon. *A morning wasted*, he thought, with no new light, no new leads on the case. He'd send O'Malley to check on George Leybourne's whereabouts, but Jakeways was too smart to lie about something so easy to disprove. And he'd just missed the omnibus, *damn it.* He saw it disappear around the corner.

Hell and damnation.

The same afternoon, a mile away, Julia tapped the roof of the hansom cab with the point of her umbrella to get the driver's attention.

They'd come to a standstill two crossroads from the Black Falcon Brewery. At the corner of Brick Lane and Princes Street, an omnibus, its top benches filled with angry, frustrated men, blocked their way. In front of the 'bus, two black-plumed undertakers had steered their hearse to a dead stop, making it impossible for anyone to move. A brewery drayman reined in his horses and shouted, "Move that bleedin' corpse out of the way." So Julia paid her cabbie and proceeded on foot, peering over the crowd's shoulders for Carter Street.

When she turned right, she saw the logic of its name; more carts than she could count lined the road that ran beside a row of warehouses. Platforms like drawbridges suspended from chains jutted from every upper-story window. Men swung barrels secured by ropes out the warehouse windows and into the hands of the carters below. Then they loaded the massive kegs onto drays and clopped off to keep the ale flowing in the public houses of London.

Julia approached a group of brewers resting on barrels. She recognized them by their gaiters and long leather aprons. When she asked for directions, one man put away his clay pipe and slid off his keg. He pointed out the offices of the Black Falcon Brewery.

"You'll find Sir Harry's secretary there, miss. He'll help you. Like as not, the master will be somewhere in the brewery or inside one of the warehouses."

In fact, the secretary said, Sir Harry was waiting for her at his residence. "I'll escort you, Doctor Lewis. His house is at the east end of the brewery grounds, a five-minute walk."

"Really? Sir Harry lives on the premises?" He was a wealthy man, knighted by the queen for his contributions to British industry, and could live anywhere. Yet he chose to live next to his factory in Spitalfields.

"He likes to keep his eye on things," the secretary said. "And the house Sir Harry built for himself would be out of place in Belgravia or Grosvenor Square."

He was right about that. When they passed the last of the warehouses and rounded the corner, Julia stopped. Her eyes widened at the four-story mansion. The first three levels were conventional enough—a Georgian-style building clad in red brick, although the entrance portico was unusual for a private residence. Where one expected white pillars of concrete or marble, visitors passed through an entryway supported by square, cast-iron columns with wrought-iron embellishments. But it was the fourth story of the building that arrested the visitor, a structure made wholly of iron and glass.

"It looks exactly like the Crystal Palace," Julia said.

"And so it should."

The brewery magnate stood in the portico doorway, his feet planted apart, hands on his hips, smiling. He descended the steps to greet her.

"Sir Joseph Paxton designed the house for me," he said, naming the celebrated architect of the Great Exhibition's famous hall. Sir Harry nodded a dismissal to his secretary and gestured to the entryway. "Welcome to Falcon House, Doctor Lewis."

"Thank you." She took a last look at the top story. "My grandparents and I were at the Crystal Palace when the Queen and Prince Albert opened the Exhibition. It looked like a fairy palace, a magic wonderland to my twelve-year-old eyes."

"But one built of iron and glass."

Sir Harry stood aside to let Julia enter first. The front door opened into a cavernous, circular hall. Three doors set into the curving walls led to other rooms. The inside mimicked the outside, its embellishments made of iron and steel rather than marble and oak. But it was the diameter of the space that awed.

"The open hall takes one's breath away," Julia said. "What keeps it from crashing down?"

Sir Harry pointed to the ceiling. "Steel beams and trusses can support a broad open space."

"And those doors?"

"The dining room is on the left, the kitchens beyond. Two drawing rooms are on the right. Bedchambers are on the second floor, servants' quarters on the third, and—" Sir Harry smiled. "Do you have the energy for a climb, Doctor? My library and offices are on the fourth floor. I promise you, the views are worth the exercise."

He led her up a winding, wrought-iron staircase. "Behind all the exterior brick, the structure is supported by iron beams. Each floor is a grid of closely spaced steel ribs finished with kiln-fired floor tiles."

Between breaths, Julia said, "Your house is a marvel. I've

seen railway stations built in this style, but never a private residence." By the time they reached the third-floor landing, she was happy to let him do the talking.

"Cotton mills were the first to experiment with iron constructions. They're practically fireproof, you see. When a blaze starts in a mill, it spreads quickly. A cotton warehouse will go up like a match." He looked back at her. "I'm confident Falcon House could withstand even a second Great Fire of London." Sir Harry pushed open the doors to the top floor and stood back.

Books filled the north and south walls of the room, hardly surprising in a library. But along the east and west walls, rows of windows held in place by iron frames spanned the length of the house. Curtains, pushed back, reached from the ceiling to the floor. Sir Harry tugged one pair a little farther apart.

"Your views are incomparable. But without those," Julia nodded to the draperies, "it would be a little like living in a fishbowl."

"That it would, Doctor, but I like what I see. The west windows show me where I am today." Sir Harry pointed to the complex of brewery buildings and warehouses below. He tipped his head toward the other end of the library. "And the east windows remind me of where I've been, my past. Come," he said. "Let me show you that view."

Julia traced the curving path of the Thames River all the way to Westminster and the Houses of Parliament. *Perhaps he sees where he's headed, as well*, she thought.

They moved to the windows on the other side of the room, and the brewer swept his arm across the view. "Look east, Doctor—the London of my youth."

"You are a Spitalfields native?" Julia leaned forward, looking at the streets at their feet.

"Born and bred." He lifted the end of a telescope resting on a tripod and presented it to her. Julia looked through the eyepiece at the streets below. "Raise your sights a little higher, Doctor." Then, shoulder to shoulder, he pointed to something in the distance. "Can you see—six, no, seven streets beyond? That structure built in the shape of an H?"

"Yes. Whitechapel Workhouse."

She adjusted the focus. The curving, white cornice over the entrance sprang sharply into view. The heavy oak doors and high brick walls made it look more like a prison than a refuge for the desperate. She remembered Sergeant Graves telling her Sir Harry was a workhouse boy.

"They separate you; did you know that, Doctor?" Julia took her eye away from the glass. "They send the men to one wing, the women to another. Children are taken from their parents to live in a separate dormitory. Two weeks after my father died, we walked through the gates of that workhouse. We had nowhere else to go. My mother never walked out. She kissed me goodbye, and they took her away. It was the last time I saw her. In under a week, she sickened and died in the infirmary." His voice turned husky. "Thirty-four years ago; I'd just turned ten."

Julia did know—not the details of his history but that workhouses were miserable places by design. The Poor Laws were written to make the lives of those sent there as uncomfortable as possible. Local ratepayers paid the costs and insisted they be kept low. Liberality would attract the lazy indigent. Preferring a life of ease, they would become permanent charges on the public purse, or so the thinking went. Life in a workhouse was meant to be a purgatory, a place you fled as soon as you could, the last resort of the desperate.

"They're aptly named. Workhouses," Sir Harry said. "Even the youngest children are expected to work—outside the walls when you are old enough. Depending on the season, I shivered or sweated in a rag seller's warehouse. I worked the dustheaps, too, sorting through piles of ash, looking for unburned bits of coal to toss in a basket. My luck changed—the most important day of my life—when the Whitechapel guardians farmed me out to the Whitbread Brewery. They didn't know they were doing me a kindness, but everything worth knowing, I learned there."

Conventional expressions of sympathy seemed out of place, so Julia just listened.

"I don't tell you these things to ask for your pity or to shock you, Doctor Lewis. You've worked four years in Whitechapel, so I doubt I could. You're no fine lady—meaning no disrespect, mind you. I admire you all the more for it. Well, I'm no fine gentleman, either, despite the title and fancy suit. I tell you these things because I know, firsthand, the problems of the workingman, and I need your advice to build my clinic."

"Of course."

"Understand one thing. I'm no saint—far from it. Here at the Black Falcon, I run a canteen for my men. For ten pence a week, they get a good meal every day. Why? When men eat hearty, they work hard. I want a clinic at my brewery. Why? When men are healthy, they work productively. I'm a businessman, Doctor. That's who I am. And a clinic is what I want."

Julia placed her bag on the conference table, opened it, and pulled out a stack of folders. "Well, then, let's get down to business. I'll tell you everything I can."

At the end of an hour, he said, "I don't suppose you'd like to run my clinic for me?" Julia shook her head. "I didn't think so. Do you know of any others who might—lady doctors like yourself?" Julia raised her eyebrow. "I'm thinking women doctors probably find it hard to secure employment in the medical field."

"You're right about that, Sir Harry. But I'm not sure your brewery men would like to . . ."

"Drop their drawers for you." He blinked. "That's to say . . ."

Julia laughed. "I know exactly what you mean, and you're right. The men who come to my clinic would rather I was male, but they have no other choice, so they swallow their embarrassment."

Rather than take a cab or omnibus home, she accepted the offer of his carriage. And he wished to thank her in another way.

"The theater? Or a musical evening with you and your grandfather as my guests?" He hesitated. "Perhaps the opera?"

"You're fond of Verdi?"

"Well . . ."

She smiled. "May I suggest an evening's entertainment at a music hall—say, the Grecian Theater at the Eagle? It's one of our favorites."

On the ride home in Sir Harry's carriage and all evening long, Julia thought about the things he'd told her.

Thirty-four years ago. She did the subtraction: 1832, the year of London's first great cholera epidemic. Both his mother and father had died within weeks of one another. *Was it possible? Yes.* Cholera had burned through Whitechapel and Spitalfields that year. *And that evening in our drawing room.* She remembered what he said when her uncle Max had turned the conversation to the company's release of unfiltered water.

"Someone has to pay."

She'd say this for Sir Harry: he'd been willing to hire a female doctor for his clinic. Never once had he questioned a woman's professional competence. He merely regretted that his men wouldn't like being treated by a female. *Maybe it was just the businessman in him, calculating he could hire a "lady doctor" at half pay.*

Tennant, on the other hand . . . he wishes he'd sent me packing the first day. Continuity required the same set of medical eyes on the case, so he was stuck with her. Julia expected that, any day, he'd get over that scruple and call in some male doctor. Before he had the chance, she'd show him that a woman could detect as well as any man.

Still, the next day, when Julia faced a stony-eyed Inspector Tennant from across his desk, she felt her confidence collapse like a leaky balloon. Her theory had seemed so promising the night before; it sounded thin and unconvincing in the morning.

She cleared her throat and jumped in. "Last week, you and I talked about a lacerating experience from childhood. Sir Harry's loss of two parents to cholera, a life of misery in the workhouse qualifies."

"But he survived those tragedies and triumphed."

"It may have left its scars."

"That provides a motive to murder Sir Maxwell Ball but not Mister Atwater and Bertie Parker. So how do the cleric and the music-hall performer fit your theory?"

Julia lifted her chin. "We know they must from the evidence at the scene."

"Those blasted balloons," Tennant muttered.

"Sir Harry invited my grandfather and me to the theater. When I suggested the Grecian at the Eagle Tavern, he didn't turn a hair. At the music hall, I'll find a way to turn the conversation to Bertie Parker and his murder."

Tennant stood. "Doctor Lewis, I value your medical insights. When it comes to pursuing possible suspects . . ."

"I'm doing nothing of the kind." Julia picked up her bag. "I'm just a loyal subject of the queen providing information to one of Her Majesty's civil servants, if he cares to listen." She walked out.

Tennant called after her. "The dilettante detective is the creation of the fiction writer, Doctor."

She stopped at the sergeant's desk and raised her voice. "I have Mister Hayward's *Revelations of a Lady Detective* on my night table right now. I'm picking up tips from his famous sleuth, Mrs. Paschal. I'll lend it to you when I'm finished. You may find some inspiration in its pages."

Sergeant Graves looked up from his file and cupped a hand to his ear. "I can hear him from here, Doc. Grinding his teeth."

Julia winked as she passed him.

Blast the woman. Tennant wished he'd never called her in for that second consultation. Still, she was on to something, although he wouldn't tell her that. The water engineer's testimony had moved Sir Harry into the orbit of his interest. Julia had given him a new idea—the workhouse guardians.

Their role in securing Jackson's first job in the brewery business made him wonder: Who were the men who sat on the workhouse board? He might find a link between them, the victims, and the killer.

Ratepayers elected men of standing to serve as guardians on the workhouse boards. *Pillars of the community*, he thought, *but men with secrets to hide?* Tennant wondered if Sir Maxwell Ball might have been among them. Had he sent little Harry Jackson to the dustheaps? Was he nursing more than one grudge against the company director?

Ball's secretary said Sir Maxwell had been chairman of the water company for thirty-five years. *The timing fits.* Maybe he was clutching at a wispy straw, but Tennant was desperate to find an additional link, a new lead to follow. Tomorrow, he'd send O'Malley to the records office to hunt down two pieces of information. He wanted the names of the guardians who sat on the Whitechapel Workhouse board in 1832, and he wanted to know what killed Sir Harry's mother.

And there was something else, something Julia hadn't noticed on her visit to Falcon House. Tennant swung around to the ordnance map and located the brewery. He was right. From his fourth-story aerie, Sir Harry could see another local landmark: St. Edmund's. Mr. Atwater's church stood only a few streets west of the Black Falcon Brewery. *I wonder if Sir Harry is a parishioner.* If he could link Jackson with two victims, he would be getting somewhere.

Tennant grabbed his hat and headed for the door. It was time for a talk with Sir Harry Jackson.

The brewer faced Tennant from behind an elaborately carved mahogany desk. Floor-to-ceiling windows framed by maroon velvet curtains did little to brighten the room on a gray afternoon.

"I met Mister Atwater a number of times," Sir Harry said, "but I didn't know him well. My mother was chapel, not Church of England. I pray with the Methodists on Brick Lane. Still, he was well known in Spitalfields by one and all."

"And Sir Maxwell Ball, chairman of the East London Water Company, I believe you knew him as well."

Sir Harry looked up sharply. "He was a business associate."

"I understand that you were quite angry with the man."

"You understand right, Inspector. The bastard cost me a fortune when the company's shares took a dive. But if you think I killed him . . ." He smiled without a trace of amusement. "No, Inspector, I'd rather have ruined him. His days as company director were numbered. Next shareholder's meeting, Sir Maxwell would have had a nasty shock; I'd lined up a voting majority to give him the sack. Someone spared me the trouble."

"I understand cholera struck close to home."

"What d'you mean by that?"

"Some of your workers—"

"Oh. Yes. Three men from Whitechapel lost wives and children. Good men."

"A senseless tragedy."

Sir Harry's eyes narrowed. "Why are you asking me about Atwater and Ball? The newspapers haven't linked their deaths. Are they connected?"

"Perhaps, but we're not making that public. I'm sure I can

rely on your discretion, Sir Harry. We'd prefer to keep it out of reporters' hands—at least, for now."

"Those buggers; they'll hear damn all from me."

"Don't politicians need to keep in the good books of the press?"

"I'm not a politician. I'm a businessman."

Tennant's eyes dropped to the BP pin on Jackson's lapel. "Am I misinformed? I thought you were one of the founders of the Britannia Party."

"That's right, Inspector. But we have no power—yet."

"Do you really think a third party has any chance in Britain?"

"Oh, yes. It's inevitable. The Liberals and the Conservatives? Neither party works for the interests of the common man. There's only one question. Will it be a socialist party that fills workingmen's heads with a pack of nonsense? Or will it be a new party? Ours offers the 'have-nots' their slice of the pie that capitalism and empire made. Not a handout, mind you. Something real they can earn. Once the workingmen of Britain have the vote, it will be at the cost of the Liberal Party, I guarantee it."

"So political upheaval is inevitable?"

Sir Harry looked Tennant up and down. "Mind, I mean no offense to you, personally. But for too long, men of your class have had a stranglehold on this country. Men like me, we're the exception. In Britain, we piss away the talents of three-quarters of our population. Like a steam engine working on quarter capacity, it's a criminal waste of energy."

"Certainly industrialists such as Sir Maxwell Ball show scant concern for the masses," Tennant said. "What sort of remedies do we have when businessmen—"

"They should be hanged. Our laws should treat company directors who kill their customers as harshly as any rough who splits a man's skull and steals his pocket watch."

"Don't our laws hold such men accountable?"

"You know the answer to that one." Sir Harry's eyes bore into Tennant's. "What's this about, Inspector? Why are you here?"

"I'll be frank with you. We've exhausted our obvious leads and are casting a wider net. With your endorsement, I'd like to speak with your foreman. Ask him if he's heard any talk among the men."

"What d'you expect him to tell you?"

"Mister Atwater was a prominent local clergyman. Some of your men may have been his parishioners. Have any of them heard anything about his death? Many of your workers live in neighboring Whitechapel. Is anyone aware of any threats against Sir Maxwell? Someone may have agreed with you—viewed his actions as criminal negligence that demanded summary punishment."

Sir Harry glared. Tennant returned his gaze. Finally, the brewer stood and opened his pocket watch. He snapped it shut and stuffed the ornate case back into his pocket.

"My foreman will be on the loading dock. Follow me."

But the man had nothing useful to tell Tennant. Still, the inspector went through the motions of an interview. Having taken the measure of Sir Harry Jackson, he felt his morning hadn't been wasted. He'd learned that the brewer was a determined man of fixed convictions. No respecter of the legal system, he was a successful businessman whose will was law within his empire. But was he a killer? Had the tragedies of his early life seeded an infection that had festered and grown into an obsession for revenge?

Not far from the Black Falcon Brewery, Tennant stood at the corner of Fournier Street and Brick Lane, looking up at the Wesleyan Chapel. At the back, he found a gate that opened into a small memorial garden and cemetery. On a gray afternoon in late November, it was desolate. Dry leaves carried by the wind clustered at the bases of weathered headstones. A marble plaque

at the entrance announced a dedication: TO THE MEMORY OF
MARIA JACKSON. MAY SHE REST IN PEACE.

Tennant scanned the headstones but found no trace of her
grave. The Methodist chaplain wasn't in residence, and no one
else was around to ask.

The final resting place of Sir Harry's mother remained a
mystery.

That night, Tennant's dream led him into another dark alley.
His heart raced with desire rather than fear.

He followed the woman deep into the shadows, her head
turning to be sure he was there. She stopped, leaned against a
brick wall, and waited for him. Above her head, a sliver of
lamplight slipped through parted curtains, slicing her face into
halves of shadow and bright. He caught her by the arms and
pinned them over her head, pushing her roughly against the
wall. She pulled an arm away and lifted her dress. She pressed
against him, naked underneath her skirts, and bit him on the
neck.

He woke groaning, his blanket and sheets a tangled heap on
the floor. He tore off his nightshirt, tossed it into the hamper,
and stumbled over to his shaving stand, staring at his reflection
in the mirror.

He hadn't bought sex since the drunken evening he'd won
his commission as a first lieutenant. Even then, he hadn't paid
for it. His fellow officers thought he deserved a night to remember. He knew he had gambled with disease and possibly
death, a loaded revolver whose barrel he'd spun and held to his
head for a thrill. *Click.* He'd been lucky, but he wouldn't risk it
again.

Besides, there were other, safer ways.

He'd met her at a country house party, their affair more
transactional than transporting. Still, for nearly ten years, it
suited them both. Her husband, she'd told him, preferred the

attentions of their footman to her conjugal embraces. They'd produced the necessary heir and spare and felt free to go their separate ways. It had been over a year since she'd moved on from Tennant; his long work hours had made adultery inconvenient.

Before she left, she gave him some advice.

"My dear, find someone fun to be around, someone alive. Isobel was a beautiful bore." She smiled. "Not so beautiful anymore, as it happens; I saw her last week at the derby. You had a lucky escape, Richard, although I'm sure it didn't feel that way at the time. Find someone who won't drop you like a bad penny when you need her most." She pulled on her gloves and patted him on the cheek. "And when you do, invite me to the wedding—to remind me of what I'll be missing."

He turned from the mirror and dropped onto a chair. He touched his neck, almost expecting to feel blood on his fingers from a bite. On the table next to him was Julia's book about criminal lunacy. He picked it up and flipped the pages before tossing it aside. *This damnable case*—He'd waded deep into a cesspool and felt out of his depth.

What darkness drove the killer? What thread linked the victims? He'd gone over it again and again. At first, he'd wondered if a vendetta against pillars of the establishment formed the pattern. Banking, the Church, industry—in some eyes, they all might seem guilty of crimes that demanded punishment. But Bertie Parker didn't fit that mold. Maybe he was trying to construct a template that didn't exist. Perhaps the killer chose his victims at random.

"Sod it," Tennant muttered as he dressed.

His long day would start with a meeting with Chief Inspector Clark. And he'd asked Sergeant Graves to carry a note to Julia Lewis, asking her to meet him at the Yard. She wouldn't like what he had to say.

*   *   *

I wonder if the inspector misses me. I've been thoughtless. Out of touch.

He drew a sheet of paper toward him, opened the bottle, and dipped his pen into the purple.

I must give the poor man something new to think about. He's been going 'round and 'round and getting nowhere. And detectives need their clues.

He thought for a minute. Then he wrote.

The banker, the preacher, the bugger, the faker . . . the butcher, the baker, the candlestick maker—who will be next?

He sat back and tapped the pen against his lower lip. He added the last line.

Everyone is on the table, my dear Inspector Tennant, even the monkey.

He chose a yellow balloon and sealed the envelope.

The angry voice thundered down the second-floor hallway at Scotland Yard.

"So we've got to wait. Is that what you're telling me, Tennant? Wait for this sick bastard to slice up his next victim? By God, that's not bloody good enough. And don't think either Sir Richard or that regimental tie will help you."

Julia raised an eyebrow at Graves from her seat next to the sergeant's desk.

"Chief Inspector Clark. Another letter came this morning." He gathered up some papers. "Time to retreat." He winked and turned left, away from the shouting—and his boss walking down the hallway.

Tennant stood back for Julia, gesturing to his office door. He didn't seem overly ruffled, but she thought he looked a little pale. As she passed him, she said, "You look tired, Inspector. Are you getting enough sleep? If not, I could help you with that."

He opened his mouth and closed it.

She settled into her chair. "A sleeping draught, perhaps?"

"Thank you, no."

Nodding at the receptacle next to his desk, Julia said, "You can kick your rubbish bin if you like. Pretend it's your chief. It might do you some good."

"Is that a prescription?"

"Can't hurt, unless you whack it *too* hard." Julia hesitated. "May I ask, who is the 'Sir Richard' who won't help you?"

"Sir Richard Mayne is the Commissioner of Scotland Yard—and my godfather."

"Ah. That makes you the golden boy born with a silver spoon. I see."

"I believe you do, Doctor. We both have our professional crosses to bear."

"Which do you think the chief inspector resents more—Sir Richard or that tie?" She let a few seconds tick by. "My money's on the tie."

Tennant smiled. *I'm making progress*, Julia thought.

He adjusted his red and blue neckwear. "Do you know, I hardly ever wore the thing until I noticed he couldn't take his eyes off it. Now I trot it out several times a week."

"Fly your colors. Why not?"

"I think it's my middle name that gets his goat. It's Wellesley."

"Richard Wellesley Tennant—very distinguished." Her eyes widened. "Wait a tick. Not as in *Arthur* Wellesley? The Duke of Wellington?"

He nodded. "The hero of Waterloo is a distant relation on my mother's side."

"Ah-ha. Now I understand the military career. It's in your blood. And that steely resolve—a gift from the Iron Duke?"

"You've dissected me, Doctor. I have no mysteries left."

Julia doubted it. *Women cleverer than I have tried to fathom you.* She said, "Sergeant Graves told me another letter arrived."

He handed it to her.

The killer's flippant tone and implicit threat chilled her. *The monkey's on the table . . .* There was something about that, but Julia couldn't pin it down.

"He's enjoying this." She handed the letter back to him. "Is that what you wanted to see me about?"

"No." He frowned. "I wanted to inform you that I interviewed Sir Harry Jackson yesterday."

"I see. So, when I meet him on Saturday, you'd like me to follow up on some line of inquiry you've begun?"

"No, Doctor. That's exactly what I don't want."

"I didn't think so." *He's not used to having his leg pulled. Not by a woman, at any rate*, Julia thought.

"At our last meeting, you made a joke about amateur investigations. But you know as well as I that this killer is dangerous. Unpredictable. There's no telling what might set him off."

"He enjoys baiting *you*, Inspector. He addresses his letters to 'Tennant of the Yard,' not to the police in general."

"Yes." He ran his hand through his dark hair. "And I don't want him to turn his attention to anyone . . . peripherally involved in this case. And as for Sir Harry, I assure you. We are looking at him."

"I see. So you want me to 'hop it,' as the East Enders say."

Tennant's jaw tightened. He rose from his chair. Arms crossed, he looked down at her. "Doctor Lewis . . ."

Julia stood as well. *Two can play this game.* "Surely, you don't think I'm in any danger. All his victims have been men."

"Can we be sure that will continue? We've talked about a pattern to these crimes. I believe there is one, but can we be certain of anything?"

"You don't really think he kills by chance?"

"I don't want this hunter setting his sights on you. Leave the investigating to the Yard."

"Do you think I'm an idiot, or a child that needs a lecture?

I'm not a blundering fool, someone who will put myself or your investigation at risk."

Tennant turned his back. By the time he looked around, she was gone.

"Bloody hell." He dropped to his seat, put his heel to the base of the desk, and shoved himself backward, slamming his chair into the wall. He eyed the rubbish bin and applied his boot, sending it flying across the room.

Sergeant Graves walked into the office and righted the can. "O'Malley's back. Do you want to hear his report?"

"What is he waiting for? Send him in."

O'Malley came in, took a seat, and flipped open his notebook.

Graves, drumming his right heel, said, "Well, Constable, is it good news?"

" 'Tis and 'tisn't. Took a while to locate the old lists of workhouse guardians; they're after being something of a surprise." He paused, flexing the fingers of his right hand.

Graves looked at him. "Come on, mate. Will you stop cracking those bleeding knuckles and get on with it?"

"Don't make a meal of it, Constable," Tennant said.

"Yes, sir. Back in 1832, sure there were no elected guardians. Happens it all changed with the reform of the Poor Laws two years later. Before that, local parishes ran the workhouses. Sir Maxwell Ball wasn't to be found on the parish list, but . . ." The constable smiled broadly. "Who d'ye think I found on the parish board? Mister Atwater. And himself was serving as workhouse chaplain in '32."

Sergeant Graves whistled. "That's a right turnup, one for the books."

"Well, well," Tennant said. "So he was the chaplain when Sir Harry entered the workhouse. Jackson failed to mention that detail when I asked if he knew the rector."

Graves grinned. "Just slipped his mind, I suppose. Funny, that."

"And Maria Jackson?"

"They had no trouble digging out the record of her death; the clerk put his hand on the file right away. He remembered Sir Harry asking for the same information some years back. Died of a fever, the records say. Not that they fretted much about the cause of death, in the clerk's telling of it. Could have been the cholera, says he. Likely, in '32."

"Damn it," Tennant said. "Likely isn't good enough."

"One other thing. They never buried his mam in the workhouse graveyard. With no family to claim the body, they're after selling her off to a medical college. Cutting her up for lessons, I'm thinking." O'Malley shook his head. "Spitting mad about it, Sir Harry—Clark's own words."

"Good Lord," Tennant muttered.

"Wouldn't have happened a year or two earlier," O'Malley said. "The selling of his mam's body, that is. Parliament passed a new law in '32—the Anatomy Act—the same year the Jacksons showed up at the workhouse door. They're still doing it, so says the clerk. Selling off their dead to this day, the workhouses and prisons."

"Right, all in the name of medical science," Graves said. "Bollocks. Saving the ratepayers a few quid in burial expenses."

Tennant ticked off the list. "The workhouse staff, its directors, Parliament, and the medical establishment—they all played their part in Maria Jackson's tragedy."

"But is it enough, I'm thinking?" O'Malley said. "Sir Harry's workhouse days are long past. Why go on a murderous rampage now?"

"*He knows a baseness in his blood . . .*"

"What's that, sir?"

"Nothing, Constable. Timing and motive—perhaps the revelation of the water contamination triggered his belated revenge? Someone, finally, who could pay for the crime of his mother's death?"

Tennant knew the deaths would continue; the latest letter

made that clear. *He has a list. More reckonings, other bills to be paid.*

The inspector pushed his chair back. "Anything else, Constable?"

"Found the name of the doctor who treated workhouse patients back in '32. Sure, he may be dead, but maybe not."

Hell and damnation. Tennant gritted his teeth and gave the order.

"Check the medical registry, Constable. If you don't find his name, ask Doctor Lewis. Perhaps her grandfather might recognize it."

CHAPTER 8

At the end of two solid hours of work, Julia looked up to find only two people left on her hallway benches. Jimmy Donohue, ten years old, waited to see his mother; next to him sat a bareheaded Constable O'Malley. His policeman's helmet covered the lad's head and half his face.

Julia told Jimmy, "You can visit with your mam for ten minutes, but we mustn't tire her."

The boy slid off the bench and got halfway to the ward door before he stopped in his tracks. He removed the helmet and returned it to O'Malley with a grin.

"You've been making friends, Constable." Julia gestured to the door of her office and followed him inside. Julia sat, and O'Malley took the chair across from her desk.

"We discovered shared roots in the soil of County Wicklow. We're both of us sons of younger sons, cast off. Two more of Ireland's wild geese set loose on the winds."

Julia wondered: *Does every Irishman have a touch of the poet in him?*

"How 'cast off,' Constable?"

"A small Irish holding barely supports one family, and that'll be the eldest son. So when Granddad died, it was time for Da to be off."

"To England?"

"To Dublin. He found work on the quays of the River Liffey, and there he met Mam, God rest her soul. The fever took her in Black '47, the worst year of the hunger. She left four children behind—my sister, two brothers, and myself, the eldest at fourteen."

"How did your family come to live in England?"

"The hunger sent us across the sea, first to Liverpool and then to London. 'Twas a brutal time after the potato crop failed. Dublin was awash with waves of specters and skeletons—the near-dead, staggering in from the starving countryside. Da lost his job shoveling coal on the quays, the cough that would take him already rattling in his chest."

"So, at fourteen . . ."

The constable nodded. "Head of the family. I was a big lad for my age, and I'd taken up boxing, although Mam didn't like it and Dublin purses were small. So, after Da passed, like many an Irishman before me, I sought my fortune on these shores, where the boxing prizes were bigger and there was food to be found."

O'Malley undid the middle two buttons on his tunic and removed a slip of paper from an inner pocket. Again, Julia noticed the ruined right hand.

"So that explains your broken knuckles. I'd thought, perhaps, a fight on the force."

O'Malley flexed his fingers and grinned. "Bare-knuckle boxing. Won enough to keep a roof over our heads and food on the table. My married sister returns the favor now. I board with her. Still, you can't box forever. 'Tis lucky I am that the Met took me on."

Julia smiled. "They're the fortunate ones, I think. Now, Constable, what can I do for you?"

O'Malley handed her the paper.

"The name's come up in our investigation, but he's not to be found on the medical registry. The inspector is wondering if your grandfather might recall the man."

Julia raised an eyebrow. "I see." She tucked the slip under the edge of her blotter. "You may tell Inspector Tennant that my grandfather—and I—will be happy to assist him."

"Doctor?" Nurse Clemmie was at the door. "A message just arrived for you."

Julia followed the written directions sent by Whitechapel's Inspector of Nuisances. Behind her, Jackie Archer maneuvered a two-wheeled ambulance cart through the neighborhood's narrow streets.

To anyone unfamiliar with East London, Charlotte Court sounded like an elegant address. But Julia had worked in Whitechapel long enough to know that a "court" was a sunless, airless, claustrophobic lane of ramshackle houses jammed behind a street of the same name. She walked two blocks from her clinic to Charlotte Street, then turned left into a narrow alley that ended at the court. There she found an angry crowd blocking the advance of the Inspector of Nuisances and his two assistants, the public disinfectors.

A report of death from fever at the address had sent them to 27 Charlotte Court. The public disinfectors, dressed in their leggings and blouse-like jackets of heavy white cotton, were in no hurry for the confrontation to conclude. They leaned idly against the two-wheeled sanitary cart, drawing on their clay pipes while the top-hatted Inspector of Nuisances pushed his way to the front door. He hammered at number 27. The louder he knocked, the angrier the crowd became.

Julia said to Jackie, "Push the ambulance behind the sanitary cart and follow me with the stretcher." She was about to plunge into the crowd when she felt a restraining hand on her arm.

"You may want to wait until the inspector surrenders, Doctor Lewis."

She looked up at the reporter for the *Illustrated London News* and down at his hand on her sleeve. Johnny Osborne removed it and jerked his thumb at the milling crowd.

"If you want to do some good today, keep your distance from the Inspector of Nuisances."

"Why? He asked for my help."

"My dear Doctor, the reason is simple. East Enders think the Inspector of Nuisances is the most aptly named public official in London. He's a pest whose job is to make their lives even more miserable than they are. Trust me. You don't want to be seen as his lackey."

The reporter dropped his cigar and ground it with his boot. "What sickens me most is how they wear their middle-class piety like a blindfold. Despite everything they see, they blame the poor for the filth and disease they're condemned to live with every day."

Julia thought, *What's happened to the careless cynic?* She said, "It's an unpleasant job, Mister Osborne, but the inspector—"

"Mister bloody nuisance should try keeping clean in a court where water is only pumped into the neighborhood three days a week. He should try hauling it by hand from several streets away. You watch, Doctor. He'll eject those people from their houses and tell them to keep away for twenty-four hours."

Julia nodded at the stretcher. "The trouble is there's been one death already, and we must collect the body. It's typhoid, most likely. I'm praying it's not cholera again. Unless the flat is disinfected, others may die."

"Where will they go? It's late November. That family will
huddle and shiver on the street all night long. And what will they
find when they return home? The public disinfectors will have
hauled away most of what they own. Half of it won't return;
they'll be told it 'disintegrated' in the disinfecting ovens. Well,
Doctor? Should they open their door? Do you wonder they'd
rather risk infection than endure the cure?"

Julia said nothing.

The reporter looked over Julia's shoulder and laughed. Like
a performer slipping on a mask, the old Osborne was back.

"Well, well, the nuisance has given up. Someone's toppled
his top hat. He's searching for it on the ground. Oh, he's found
it; I see it moving away, bobbing through a sea of soft caps and
angry faces. I'll intercept him, shall I? Ask him a question or
two? That might give you time to accomplish some good."

Julia narrowed her eyes. "All right." She motioned to Jackie
to follow her. "Thank you, Mister Osborne. Will you ask the
inspector to wait while I try my luck at the door?"

He smiled mockingly. "I'll be waiting, too, Doctor. I have a
few questions for you as well."

She followed his thin frame as he slipped deftly through
the crowd. He caught up to the inspector and led him away by
the arm.

Julia scanned the throng. She spotted several familiar faces,
caught their eyes, and smiled. As her name rippled from person to person, the anger of the bystanders ebbed. The crowd
parted, allowing her to pass, and Jackie followed with the
stretcher.

She knocked and called out her name. She heard movement
inside, and whispering. A minute passed, and the door opened.
A thin woman in a tattered apron, her graying hair falling from
its pins, stepped aside and let Julia and Jackie into the house.

Ten minutes later, the door opened again. Julia called out to a man whose broken wrist she'd splinted a year earlier. He bounded up the steps.

"How is the hand, Mister Cooper? Well enough for some stretcher work?"

He nodded and followed her inside. Then, with Cooper in the lead and Jackie at the other end, they moved a shrouded corpse through the crowd and to the ambulance cart. Men doffed their caps, women lowered their heads, and a scattered few crossed themselves as the body passed.

Julia supported a trembling woman by her shoulders, steering her down the steps. Two boys carrying baskets of clothing followed them into the street. She whispered some directions to the lads, and they put down their burdens and waited with their mother. After Julia exchanged a few words with the inspector, he nodded. The boys and their mother could leave with their baskets. As the crowd dispersed, the public disinfectors wheeled their sanitary wagon to the door and entered the house without further trouble.

Osborne waited in the cold, stamping his feet, slapping his gloved hands against his upper arms. "Good work, Doctor. Do you have time for a few questions?"

Julia looked him up and down. "Do you want to know about the rising incidence of typhoid fever in this neighborhood? Is that the story you're planning to write?"

"Alas, no. It's not a subject my editor at the *Illustrated* thinks will . . ."

"Sell many copies?"

"Precisely. Doctor, you've hit the proverbial nail squarely on the head."

Julia sighed. "Just what is it you want to know?"

"It's about these murders. Three men stabbed and mutilated—"

"Not . . ." She stopped herself in time. She was about to say not all of them were mutilated. "Assuming you are correct, how do you come by your information?"

"Coppers are only human. Stand them a pint of ale in their local, commiserate with their frustrations—about their bosses or the public—and they'll tell you a thing or two. They're made of flesh and blood." He smiled. "All except our intrepid Inspector Tennant. That chap has ice water in his veins. Maybe you've been able to thaw him out a little? I envy him the privilege."

"Mister Osborne, I'm busy. What is it you want to know? Then I can tell you—or not—and be on my way."

"The truth about these murders, Doctor. Are they connected? If they are, I believe the people of East London have the right to know there's a maniac in their midst. You don't serve the public by shielding the police."

"I serve the public by attending to their medical needs. When you get around to writing about that, I'll be happy to talk to you."

It had started to drizzle. Julia drew an oiled canvas tarp over the shrouded corpse and nodded to Jackie to follow her.

The reporter called after her. "Doctor, just one more question. What's all this about *balloons*?"

Julia kept walking. How did Osborne know the most closely held detail of the case? What officer would risk his career by leaking that to the press? *He really is the most insufferable, arrogant, smug. . . .* Julia stopped.

Jackie Archer lowered the handles of the ambulance cart and looked at her. She shook her head and walked on. Of all the people she'd encountered on the case, Johnny Osborne sounded most like the killer. She could picture his malicious grin, his glee as he composed the notes.

Back at her desk, Julia spun a pencil between her thumb and forefinger. *How could Osborne possibly know about the bal-*

loons? She exchanged it for a pen and smiled. *The inspector will be delighted to hear from me again, I'm sure.* She wrote a few quick lines to Tennant at Scotland Yard.

Sir Harry was curious. "What does a typical day at your clinic look like, Doctor?"

They were waiting in the library for her grandfather to join them. Julia poured him a whiskey and handed him the glass.

"A typical day? I'm not sure there is such a thing."

He nodded. "It's the same in business. Five cartloads of hops running late from the warehouse, and the day's gone to blazes."

"A clinic's day is even more unpredictable. You can plan your schedule. We never know who—or what—will come through our doors."

"There's something to that and all. So tell me, Doctor. Who or what came through your doors today?"

"The Inspector of Nuisances for Whitechapel—at least, a boy carrying a note from him came to my door."

"What did *he* want, my dear?" Dr. Lewis shook hands with Sir Harry, kissed Julia on the cheek, and accepted the glass of whiskey she offered him. "Well, Julie? What variety of nuisance was the inspector investigating today?"

"Typhoid. A woman's elderly father had died in the night. He'd worked for the railways from the time the first line was laid out of London. But his small pension died with him, leaving his daughter in dire straits. She's a widow, trying to keep her boys in school for as long as she can."

"That will be difficult with no income," Dr. Lewis said.

"They're bright lads, she told me. But, at twelve and thirteen, they'll have to find work if the family is to survive. It took some convincing to get her to allow me into the house."

"Sooner or later, she'd have to let the authorities in," Sir Harry said. "If only to collect the body."

"The problem was her baskets. To earn some money, she'd taken in two baskets of piecemeal sewing. If the public disinfectors took them away to be sanitized, and they never came back—"

"It will ruin her." Her grandfather nodded. "She'd lose the fee for her stitching and have to make good the losses to her customers. What did you do, Julie?"

"I told the inspector she could boil her linens at the clinic laundry. He agreed. Jackie Archer made up beds for the boys, and my nurse took charge of the mother. They'll be able to return to their home tomorrow."

"*Brava*, my girl." Her grandfather kissed her hand.

Julie frowned. "But not every problem in Whitechapel can be solved in my laundry."

"You must learn to celebrate your small victories, my dear."

After a moment, Julia looked away. "Of course, Grandfather."

"Not every problem can be solved in my brewery," Sir Harry said. "But two bright lads, you say? I think I can find room for them."

He reached into his breast pocket and extracted a silver pencil and a card. He scribbled on the back and handed it to her. "Tell the mother to send her boys to see my foreman on Monday morning."

"Thank you, Sir Harry. It's very generous of you. If you'll allow me, I'll tell the mother and the boys your story—how your start in life began in a brewery."

He nodded.

Julia thought, more amused than guilty, *And here I am, hoping to catch him out as a killer.* Still, she remembered Hamlet's line: *One may smile, and smile, and be a villain.*

The chimes of the library clock reminded them it was time to go. In the foyer, Kate helped Julia with her wrap, and the gentlemen retrieved their top hats, capes, and canes. They left in Sir Harry's carriage for an evening's entertainment at the Eagle Tavern's music hall.

An usher led them to a center box along the theater's right balcony. He handed Sir Harry three programs, bowed, and withdrew. The red velvet door swung shut behind him with a muted swish as Julia settled into the middle seat between the two men. She drew off her gloves, folded them over the armrest, and paged through the program, scanning the acts for the one she wanted. She found it listed after the first intermission: "Champagne Charlotte," starring Willie Lomax. As the ushers dimmed the houselights and the spotlights roamed the stage— finding the chairman in the center, at last—Julia plotted her strategy.

In the end, the evening was a disappointment. She knew her grandfather felt it, too. While they waited outside the theater for Sir Harry to return with the carriage, Julia gripped her grandfather's arm a little tighter.

"When Granny was alive," she said, "the jokes seemed funnier and the songs a little sillier."

"Yes, indeed. No one could match your grandmother's full-throated amusement. It was infectious and made the evening sing."

Julia had another disappointment: The conversation she'd so carefully orchestrated had fallen flat. When she pointed out Willie Lomax's name in the program and mentioned Bertie Parker's murder, Sir Harry's comment—"Oh, really?"— couldn't have been blander.

What did I expect him to do? Turn pale? Tug guiltily at his necktie and look away from me, shifty-eyed?

They left the theater in a downpour. The rain began as a steady drumbeat on the roof of their carriage, making it difficult to converse. By the time they reached number 17 Finsbury Circus, the storm sounded like an entire percussion section.

Good old Mrs. Ogilvie. Julia spotted her standing inside the door holding two umbrellas. Sir Harry declined an invitation to come in for a nightcap. He reached under his cape and into his breast pocket, pulled out a small packet, and presented it to Julia.

"A souvenir of the evening—picture postcards of the leading acts."

Julia smiled and thanked him. Then Sir Harry tipped his hat and drove off in his carriage.

Julia hunched under her umbrella and followed her grandfather and Mrs. Ogilvie through the front door and into the library. The housekeeper took her grandfather's soggy cape and folded it over her arm.

"Shall I send Kate down, Doctor Julie?"

"Don't bother her. I can manage." Julia unhooked her evening wrap and draped it over the fire screen, moving it from the side of the fireplace to the front of the grate.

The housekeeper wished them a good night.

When her grandfather held up the brandy decanter, Julia shook her head and sat next to him on the sofa. Idly, she looked at the top photograph in the pack of postcards. Signed "Lulu," it showed the famed aerialist's show-stopping stunt—hanging from the trapeze by the back of her neck while beating her drum. Julia dropped the pack on the cushion beside her and slumped in her seat. She had nothing to tell Inspector Tennant about Sir Harry.

Her grandfather cleared his throat. Then, as if reading her mind, he said, "Perhaps I misjudged Sir Harry. I suppose he's not such a bad chap after all." Julia nodded absently. He took a sip of his brandy and watched her over the rim of his glass. "It was a generous gesture, offering to help those lads."

Julia sat up straight. "So he has the makings of a good grandson-in-law, you think?" She laughed when he blinked and hemmed and said nothing. "Don't worry, Grandpa. I don't like him very much either."

"I'm relieved, my dear. I've been looking through a selection of his political tracts. They don't make for edifying reading. And some of his statements at dinner that evening—" He blew the air out of his cheeks. "Does he really believe the things he says? Or is he just an opportunist, a demagogue casting around for a set of grievances to exploit?"

"God knows. I can't figure him out. He tried hard to convince me that his canteen at the brewery and the clinic he's planning are only matters of business."

"Jackson's a complicated chap. We all are. That's one thing I've learned in seven decades."

"Hmm . . . yes. Did you notice that orange peddler standing on the corner? Sir Harry turned his shoulder away from us and handed her a pocketful of change."

"He remembers where he came from, unlike some self-made men. Still, there's something about the fellow."

Julia looked at her grandfather. "I never asked—why did you invite him to dinner in the first place?"

"Your uncle Max persuaded me. I believe he intends to invite him to join the hospital board. He's cultivating some deep-pocketed donors for the new surgical wing at the London."

Julia picked up her damp wrap and dropped a kiss on his head. "Sleep well, Grandpa. I've done all the *cultivating* of Sir Harry Jackson I intend to do."

Monday dawned with no letup from the rain. Mrs. Ogilvie brought three things to the breakfast table: a steaming pot of tea, the news that water was leaking into the basement, and a pack of picture postcards.

"Emma found these on the settee in the library."

She offered them to Julia, but Dr. Lewis said, "May I have a look at them?" He untied the ribbon and flipped through the pictures, laughing at the last photograph. "They must need a winch to squeeze Willie Lomax into his corset."

He held up the card; Julia stared. She replaced her teacup in its saucer with a crash, slopping some of the liquid onto the tablecloth. Willie had signed the photograph on a bold diagonal that slashed across the picture.

The signature "Champagne Charlotte" was written in purple ink.

On Monday morning, Tennant dumped his broken umbrella into the stand. On rainy days, his leg ached, and the letter he spotted on his desk didn't improve his sour mood. He recognized the handwriting. He slit it open and read Julia's note about Johnny Osborne and the balloons. In a postscript, she'd added that the doctor Constable O'Malley had asked about was dead. He swore under his breath, balled it up, and tossed it into his rubbish bin.

"Graves!"

The sergeant came running.

"I want you to round up every copper over at G Division who did a door-to-door or interviewed a witness in this case. Tell them this: if I catch anyone giving Johnny Osborne even the time of day, I'll have him sacked."

"Right, guv."

Graves bumped shoulders with O'Malley in the hallway. "Dirty weather, mate. And I don't mean outside." He jerked his head at Tennant's door.

O'Malley walked in and handed the inspector a packet. "It's from Doctor Lewis, sir, marked urgent. Her coachman just left it with the duty sergeant."

"Hell and damnation. Is Doctor Lewis the only person working this bloody case?" He snapped the string. A pasteboard card slipped from the letter and landed face up on his desk. It sent Tennant, O'Malley, and two other constables racing to the theater.

Tennant stood in the shambles of Willie Lomax's dressing room, holding a bottle of purple ink. They'd turned out every trunk and drawer and emptied the wardrobes. Then, with his boot tip, he flipped a discarded corset and kicked it away. Other than the ink, Willie's red wigs and a telltale tube of dried-up mercury ointment were the only revealing things they unearthed.

The inspector left the bobbies to finish the search and walked in on O'Malley's interview with the theater's manager.

"Willie moved a year ago," the man said. "Keeps his new digs under his hat."

O'Malley cocked an eyebrow. "You don't keep a record of your performers' addresses? Suppose you need to get in touch with them—for a canceled performance, let's say?"

The manager shrugged. "They'll show up, turn around, and go home. I'm their employer, not their bleedin' nanny."

"Sure you must be having some idea—a street or a neighborhood."

"All I know is Willie boasted that some fancy man with connections was paying his rent."

O'Malley looked up from his pad. "And what connections would they be, now?"

"I thought he was talking bollocks. What would a bloke like that want with an old queen like Willie? Mind you, he was quite the lad . . . in his day."

"But that day was decades ago," Rollie Jakeways drawled. He'd followed Tennant into the manager's office.

"Mister Jakeways. You're here early on a Monday morning."

The actor lifted his slanting eyebrows and smiled. "How fraught you make it sound, Inspector. Is waking with the birds incriminating?"

"No—useful. Can you tell me when you last saw Willie Lomax?"

"Sunday night. We left the theater together but parted company on Shepherdess Walk. He turned south toward the City Road."

"Have you Lomax's address?"

"Alas, no, Inspector. Somewhere off the City Road, I suppose. And I would so enjoy being of assistance to the police."

"In that case, perhaps you'll be good enough to sit with my constable. He's drawing up a list of Willie's known associates and their addresses. We also want to know all the places he frequents—public houses and local merchants, for example."

"Sit with Constable O'Malley? My pleasure."

As far as Tennant could determine, the last time anyone at the theater saw Willie Lomax was after Sunday night's performance. He'd left the Eagle shortly after midnight in the pouring rain. And as far as Jakeways or anyone else knew, he was heading home—wherever that was. "Somewhere off the City Road" left a lot of ground to cover.

But O'Malley's question about Willie's address had pulled Tennant up short. The Eagle's manager wasn't the only one who had no idea where his work colleagues lived. Tennant had only a vague sense of his constable's living arrangements. *Somewhere in Stepney*, he thought. *Boarding with his brother—or was it his sister?*

The inspector had never been the sort to share a pint with the boys at the local, and he doubted they'd welcome it. Still, that was no excuse for his complete indifference to their lives. Tennant recalled Julia's word for him. *Steely.* For a decade, he'd allowed a shell to harden around him.

Tennant headed back to the Yard. He'd left word for Sergeant Graves to join the search for Willie. A quick arrest looked doubtful. Grinding, slogging police work—boot leather on the ground, knocks on countless doors—would ferret Willie out sooner or later. Tennant would put Graves in charge of the neighborhood search; three constables were already fanning out, looking for leads to the performer's whereabouts.

He ran to catch the omnibus on the City Road and felt the bottle in his coat pocket thump against his hip bone. When he gained his seat, he eased his leg and pulled out the ink. Purple was an unusual color. He'd send O'Malley to check at stationery shops around the Eagle to see what he could turn up.

It's not the only bottle of purple ink in London, but it was the first tangible link between a suspect and the murders.

He'd waited in the empty flat, waited for the two clerks to leave for their offices in the city. They wouldn't be long. He leaned his shoulder against the door and listened in the silence. It wasn't supposed to end this way, but every great performance needed a little improvisation or some rewriting of the script. He felt the pleasurable tingle start in his groin and ripple up his frame, accelerating the rise and fall of his chest.

After the second pair of boots clattered and scraped their way down the stairwell, the house fell silent again. Slowly, quietly, he turned the doorknob and emerged from his hiding place. He stood for a moment, listening. Then he smiled.

Curtain time.

Carefully, he slid the latch across the door to the street. For the next twenty minutes, he didn't want to be disturbed.

Treading quietly, he approached the rear flat, put his ear to the door, and knocked. *Nothing.* It would take a while for the man to drag himself from his bed at that early hour. He rapped more loudly. Still quiet. Balling his hand into a fist, he pounded, calling out a name. Finally, he heard a muffled curse and the rattling release of a chain. A bleary-eyed man in a tattered red dressing gown opened the door.

"What the bloody hell—oh. It's you." He stepped back to let the visitor in. "You're up with the ruddy birds. A chap needs his beauty sleep," he grumbled. "Come in."

The visitor swung his cudgel, striking the sleepy man across his cheekbone and temple, and shut the door behind him.

CHAPTER 9

Julia spent a distracted Monday and Tuesday at the clinic, wondering if they'd questioned Willie Lomax, expecting to read news of his arrest in the morning paper.

A photograph signed in purple ink—maybe it wasn't enough to charge Willie with the crimes. But with a suspect, surely Tennant and his men would uncover enough evidence to link Lomax to the murders, if he were guilty.

Julia stared out the rain-splattered window at the gray morning. Despite the dreary view, she smiled. The inspector had ordered her to stay the hell away from the murder investigation—if not in so many words. In under a week, she'd implicated no fewer than three men, starting with Sir Harry Jackson. Julia had followed up with the tip about Johnny Osborne and the balloons. Finally, she'd sent the inspector a note with Willie's postcard on Monday.

I've set a record for accusations—three suspects in as many days.

Still, the postcard was something different. Julia thought the inspector would probably be equal parts relieved to have a solid suspect and annoyed that she had uncovered him.

But late on Wednesday morning, a long line of patients drove thoughts of murder from her mind. Few people turned up at Julia's clinic with minor ailments. It took something extremely painful or potentially life-threatening for a working-man or woman to forego a half day's wages to sit in her waiting room. The wet weather produced its predictable caseload: accidents brought her several broken bones to set and two severe lacerations that required stitches. Hours later, after seeing her last patient, Julia gratefully accepted a cup of tea from Nurse Emily. The doctor sipped and glanced at the clock, wondering what was going on at Scotland Yard.

Then another note from the Inspector of Nuisances drove all thoughts of the case from her mind. After a month of quiet, a suspected cholera outbreak had erupted in a cluster of row houses along Dorset Street and New Court in Spitalfields.

Dear God, not again.

Julia grabbed her medical bag and umbrella and ran to catch a hansom at the cabstand on Whitechapel Road.

When Julia arrived at the scene, the masked Inspector of Nuisances and his disinfectors were escorting residents from two buildings. She noted their face coverings. They wouldn't protect the men from cholera, but the masks would filter some of the stench from the fetid air.

The inspector directed her to the passageway, where she would find the first victim. When she finished, she'd need to return to Dorset Street to examine four others who had died inside their dwellings.

Julia found the dead man in the alley leading to New Court, sleeping rough by the look of it. His blanket, a tin cup, and a sack stuffed with a few ragged scraps of clothing were beside him. The cause of his death wasn't hard for her to figure out. His blue face, sunken cheekbones, and the frothy, white effluvia around his mouth told their story. Cholera had killed him.

The whole area stank like an open privy, hardly surprising

after the recent heavy rains. Much of Whitechapel smelled like a sewer. On her way to Dorset Street, Julia had stepped over streams of befouled water flowing through the gutters. Rainwater had overwhelmed many of the cesspools that remained. They flooded the dank cellars and spilled into the byways of the district. While affluent areas of the city had converted to water closets, most residents of Whitechapel still relieved themselves in back-garden shacks built over pits of human waste.

When Julia returned to Dorset Street, she moved from house to house, donning and removing pairs of vulcanized rubber gloves. At four deathbeds, she declared the causes of death as cholera. Two other souls were in the final throes of the disease. Outside, stunned family members lined the street. Among the survivors, Julia identified a woman and two children who looked pale and feverish, sending them to a waiting ambulance for transport to London Hospital. It wouldn't take long to know if they'd contracted the sickness. Cholera spoke its name with terrifying speed.

Back in the alley, Julia picked up the first victim's tin cup. She looked around for the Inspector of Nuisances. He was picking his way toward her through a collection of smashed crates, building rubble, and decrepit barrows. Julia asked him if he'd heard reports of other cases.

"The ambulance driver said he knew of no others."

"Then it may be a localized outbreak." She looked down at the cup in her hand.

"Do you suspect the water, Doctor?"

"All these houses are built over cesspits or have open privies in their back gardens. Any one of them may have leaked its contents into a faulty water pipe."

Julia braced for an argument. His mask made her assume he was firmly in the miasma camp. She felt relief when he nodded.

"Doctor Snow traced the last outbreak to a local pump," he

said. "We should certainly try to locate the source of this contamination."

A boy pointed them to the standpipe and public sink at the end of Dorset Street. They followed a stinking stream of rainwater running along the gutter. When they arrived at their destination, they found filthy water pooling around the pump.

"All that's required are some cracks in the underground pipes," Julia said.

"I'll post one of my men here and find someone with a wrench to remove the pump handle. People will have to find another standpipe for their water—an inconvenience, but a small price to pay."

With one problem solved, Julia faced another with no obvious solution. Only houses cleared of their residents could be disinfected. On a late afternoon in early December, forty-odd people with nowhere to go faced a cold, rainy night on the street. Her clinic was too small to shelter everyone. She considered and rejected a plan to take in the children for the night. Even that idea wouldn't work.

"What can we do for them, Inspector?"

Instead of answering her question with an indifferent shrug, his shoulders slumped. "I don't know."

"Doctor?"

She turned. A man wearing the black coat, hat, and the side curls of an observant Jew had addressed her.

"Our school is just around the corner." He pointed down Dorset Street. "If they turn left on Bell Lane, they'll find it just after White's Row. They are welcome to stay the night and shelter from the cold."

Julia resisted the urge to hug the self-contained man, who looked away from her as he made his offer. In a neighborhood stalked by disease and drowning in despair, she felt a moment of grace.

*   *   *

In Hackney, a mile north of the cholera outbreak, Sergeant Graves directed a team of sodden constables through the maze of streets off the City Road.

For a third day, Willie Lomax had eluded them. By Wednesday evening, Graves was back at the Yard, reporting his lack of progress to his frustrated superior. Although Willie was a familiar figure in the neighborhood, he'd vanished. Neither the barman at his local nor the tobacconist clerk had seen him in days. All along the High Street, shopkeepers shook their heads.

"Everyone knows him, guv, but nobody knows a thing," Graves shook his head. "Don't know how he's managed to duck and dive all this time. His tailor expected him on Tuesday, but he never showed."

"What about an address? He must bill for his services."

"Lomax pays on the head in bangers and hash. The tailor says he never runs a tab."

"The trail's gone cold on us," O'Malley said. "And we've got effing all from the local public houses; the regulars haven't had eyes on him for a while. But a barkeep at the Britannia Tavern remembered seeing him two weeks ago. On a night when the theater was dark, he'd been in for a knees-up with some mates. Stumbled off in his cups at closing time and went arseways outside the door."

Tennant asked, "Did anyone whistle up a cab for him?"

"No. He righted himself and left on foot."

"If he left drunk and unsteady, he probably lives within walking distance."

Graves shook his head. "Maybe not, guv. There's a cabstand and an omnibus stop close to the Britannia. It runs 'buses along the City Road until midnight."

"Be sure to add the local cabbies and drivers to your list of interviews, Sergeant. Maybe one of them remembers an address, or at least a corner, where Willie might have gotten off."

O'Malley cleared his throat. "I'd be thinking, sir . . ."

"What is it, Constable?"

"Theaters let out just before the pubs close. Can't see these music-hall blokes trotting home to the wife and kiddies. I reckon they do their drinking in some offy, Willie included."

"See what you can find out."

At first, the local coppers were reluctant to talk about the off-license establishments that served alcohol after hours. But O'Malley promised to ask no awkward questions about why they were allowed to operate. After that, the G-Division constables whispered some names and addresses. So, on Thursday, O'Malley handed Tennant a list.

"Shall we pay them a visit, Constable?"

The inspector offered the off-license operators a choice: Answer his questions, or he'd padlock their premises. If they persisted in their silence, he'd charge them with failing to assist the police in their inquiries.

The threats loosened their tongues, but after four interrogations, Tennant and his constable still had nothing to go on. With two more addresses left on their list—and running out of leads—they pressed on.

Smart of O'Malley to think of the offys. Tennant had registered the solid work the constable had turned in since the start of the case.

"Here's Chambers Street, sir."

When they turned left, the inspector tossed a mental coin— *his sister or his brother?*

"You lodge with your sister, am I right, Paddy?"

"That I do. Going on three years now."

"How's that working out?"

"Close quarters sometimes, but we get on all right. I grew up with two brothers and a sister in a two-room flat. But on a copper's pay . . ."

"It's difficult to find a place."

"One you'd want to live in." O'Malley grinned. "And I'm not fussy. Still, when I find my own place, I'll probably miss my nephews and the unholy racket they make. We kick a football around the park on the odd Sunday." He patted his stomach. "And I'll miss my sister's cooking. 'Tis a grand shepherd's pie Maggie makes, and that's a fact."

"You sound happy where you are. Are you sure you want to make a change?"

"A fella's got to move on sooner or later, hasn't he, sir? Get on with things."

Tennant nodded. When they found their man, he'd put the constable's name forward for promotion. Then, on a detective sergeant's salary, he'd be able to afford a flat, and maybe support a wife.

When they found their man. And it was a question of when. East London was a honeycomb of alleys and courts, a hive of nearly a million people, but it wasn't a place where a wanted man could hide for long. Willie Lomax had gone to ground. Sooner or later, they'd flush him out.

"Mother of God, it reeks around here. The rain's been bucketing down for days." O'Malley stretched a leg across a gutter to avoid befouling his boots. "The minute you turn off the City Road, it's like an open privy." The constable stopped at a featureless brick house and flipped through his notebook. Then he stuffed it into his back pocket. "This is the address."

It looked deserted. The front entrance faced Chambers Street, but patrons would know to use the discreet side door. After midnight, the ale would flow, and the offy would come alive as pints clinked, darts thudded, and the door slammed behind surly drunks who'd been tossed into the alley.

The inspector's knock roused the manager. Dan Murphy, a ginger-haired man with woolly muttonchops and a shifty eye, opened the street door and quickly shut the inner one behind him. When Tennant asked if he knew Willie Lomax, the man crossed his arms and said nothing.

Tennant sighed. "Don't tempt me to charge you, Mister Murphy. If you want to avoid being shuttered and paying a stiff fine, impress me with your spirit of cooperation."

"Come on, boy-o," O'Malley said, tapping his truncheon against his left palm with his big, misshapen fist. "You'll not be wanting to see your Irish arse hauled in front of an English judge. The inspector asked a simple question—do you know Willie Lomax?"

The manager grunted. "I know him."

"See?" O'Malley nodded. " 'Twasn't hard. What can you tell us about him?"

"Has a pint from time to time. What of it?"

"You'll be knowing his address?"

"That I don't," Murphy said. "And I haven't seen him in donkey's years. Heard the creature's gone daft."

Tennant held the man's eye. "You're telling me you have no idea where he might be holed up?"

He looked away. "Honest, I haven't a clue."

The inspector rarely believed statements that began with that word. He waited. The silence stretched out. The manager scratched at his bushy sideburns and fiddled with the ties of his bar apron.

"You might . . ." he cleared his throat. "You might try a place 'round the corner from St. Leonard's—27 Collingwood Street."

"What will I find at that address?"

"Mind you, I know nothing about it. But the word is . . . it's a molly house."

He dipped his pen in purple ink and paused, thinking.

"Words, the right words," he murmured. "So important."

He placed the tip to paper and wrote.

So frustrating for you, dear Inspector—all those soggy coppers wasting precious time looking up and down the City Road in the rain. But don't despair. Keep going 'round and 'round. I must be somewhere.

I'm enclosing my usual souvenir.

Pop.

He placed a punctured blue balloon inside the envelope. Before he sealed it, he added a postscript.

I'm afraid I've been a bad boy again. I took a stick and knocked him off.

The letter in the chief inspector's hand shook with his rage.

"This bugger is walking free, posting love notes to you? And you can't find him?" Clark tossed the letter on his desk. "It's been five days of damn all!"

Tennant retrieved the letter, folded it, and slipped it into his breast pocket. "This evening, sir, we'll be acting on information received. A raid on the molly house I mentioned in my report."

Clark glared at him. "Mark you, Tennant, I'll not give you another five days. Find him, or I'll find someone who can."

The inspector left, looking calmer than he felt. His military training had schooled him in stoicism; he could stand up to a dressing down without flinching. He knew his composure provoked Clark, but he didn't care. Nothing mattered except results. The chief's ire would evaporate with an arrest.

Where in hell is the man?

Tennant and O'Malley stamped their feet and swung their arms against the cold. It didn't do much to warm them as they waited in the shadowy portico of St. Leonard's Church. Six constables from G Division and Sergeant Graves were late for the raid at the Collingwood molly house.

Tennant counted the last of eleven tolls. *Where the hell is Graves?*

"The bells at Shoreditch," O'Malley said.

"What's that?"

"The bells of St. Leonard's—at Shoreditch. You know, the nursery tune. 'When will you pay me? say the bells at Old Bailey. When I grow rich, say the bells at Shoreditch.' Never understood the last lines—creepy-like, for a kiddies' song."

"'Here comes a candle to light you to bed. Here comes a chopper to chop off your head.' Yes," Tennant said. "Strange."

The squeak of an iron gate and the scuff of boot leather on the church steps signaled the arrival of Graves and the constables.

"You're late."

"Sorry, guv, bit of a mix-up at the division. The desk sergeant refused to release the men without an order from his chief. Took a while to roust him out."

Tennant signaled them to follow him around to the back of the church. He stopped at the corner of Old Castle Street. He pointed down the road. "Four of you will cut through the alley that takes you to Newcastle Lane. Cover the two exits from the rear of number twenty-seven."

"Right, guv," Graves said. "I'll take that detail."

"It's the last house on the right. Detain anyone who tries to leave through the back door." The inspector nodded to the remaining officers. "You gentlemen, come with Constable O'Malley and me."

They crossed the cobbled road and turned left into Collingwood Street. At the front door, Tennant said, "Stand back out of the light. When they open up, follow me in at speed."

The men stepped out of the pool of light into the shadows.

Tennant, dressed in a top hat and evening cape, knocked and waited. When the door opened a crack, he acted like a nervous customer, glancing from side to side. The chain rattled as it released, and the door swung open. The constables rushed forward and pushed their way into the hallway.

"What the hell—"

O'Malley stuck his truncheon under the man's chin. "Shut your gob."

Tennant said in a low voice, "If you want this to end well, I advise you to pay attention to what I say."

Muffled conversation and laughter drifted down the hallway. The man looked over his shoulder.

"Officers are posted at the back," Tennant said. "If anyone tries to run, he'll be arrested. My constable will guard your front door. Understood?"

O'Malley blocked the exit with his bulk. He tapped his truncheon against his palm. "I'm all for peace," he said quietly. "So listen to the inspector, and don't try anything funny."

The man swallowed hard and nodded.

Tennant asked, "Is the proprietor on the premises?"

"Madame . . ." He coughed. "Mister Ames is in the drawing room."

"Provided they answer my questions, I intend to leave the clients alone. Do we understand one another?"

"Yes," the man rasped.

"Good. Now open the door and announce those facts to the gentlemen inside. After that, you will empty the rooms upstairs and send everyone down to me. My constables will assist you."

Two men tried to flee through velvet curtains at the back of the lounge. Six others sat frozen in the chairs and settees scattered around the salon. "Madame" Ames, the establishment's owner, was easy to spot. Rouged, bewigged, and dressed in drag, he held two glasses of port suspended in the act of handing them to his clients.

Footfalls on the stairs preceded the arrival of four frightened men who entered the room holding up their trousers. Their partners, men dressed in petticoats and loosened corsets, followed them.

The inspector had raided a molly house or two in his time. But that night, one thing surprised him—a face he recognized, a major he knew from his time in the Grenadier Guards.

Tennant called the proprietor out of the room. "Do you have an office I can use for my interviews?" The man pointed to a door. "I'll interview your clients . . ."

"Guests, Inspector. This isn't a brothel. It's a social club for like-minded members."

Tennant raised his eyebrows. "No one is paid, Mister Ames?"

"Well, I collect a fee for managing the establishment. And some of the waiters may accept . . . tips for special services."

"I'll interview your guests one at a time, starting with the gentleman sitting in the Morocco chair by the fireplace. And I'll have a copy of your membership ledger." Ames hesitated. "Now, if you please."

The manager removed a picture from the wall behind his desk. Then, with a few twists of the dial, he opened a safe. Wordlessly, Ames handed over the record book and left the office.

Tennant fanned the ledger, waiting for his first interview. "Good evening, Charles," he said when the man entered. "Sit down, please."

The major slumped in the chair and ran fingers through his thinning hair. Then, leaning forward, elbows on his knees, he dropped his face in his hands.

Not long after Isobel had broken off with him, Tennant had read a notice of the man's wedding in the *Times.* His bride, the Honorable Eugenia Beaufort, had been a friend of Isobel's. He might have been a guest at the major's wedding, if he and Isobel had still been engaged.

"I meant what I said to the doorman, Charles. This isn't a typical raid. There's no police wagon waiting outside to haul you to the local gaol. It's information I'm after, not your arrest."

Dully, the major asked, "What do you want to know?"

"Anything you can tell me about Willie Lomax."

The major admitted he knew the man but couldn't give Tennant the intelligence he most wanted—Willie's address. Lomax was a fixture at the club, but the officer had no idea where he lived.

"Have you told me everything?"

The major hesitated. "One thing about old Willie—I've heard he likes to watch. When he's flush, he'll hire two of the serving lads to go at it. You might ask the waiters; they may know more about him." He looked away. "May I go now?"

Tennant nodded.

At the doorway, the major stopped. "Our names—will they be recorded?"

"Yes. But they'll be buried in a large case file. No charges will be brought."

The major rested his forehead against the frame. "Christ," he whispered. He moved to leave and stopped again. "All we want is to live our lives without fear or harassment. You . . ." He swept his arm and dropped it at his side. "The police and the world make that impossible."

Two young men on the serving staff were Tennant's last interviews. After some prodding, they confirmed the major's statement.

"Willie told us what to do, what he wanted to see." One of the waiters shrugged. "He'd dress up in a ratty petticoat and fumble with himself while he watched. Made us call him the chairman. Said *he* wanted to call the tune for a change."

His partner chimed in. "Willie said it was his turn to be the organ grinder. He'd been a performing monkey all his life."

The inspector stiffened, remembering a line from the letters. *The monkey's on the table.* He looked from one boy to the other. "Lomax used that word to describe himself—monkey? You're sure?"

They both nodded.

With his eye on the door, the bolder of the two asked, "Is that it, sir? Can we leave now?"

"A few more questions and you can go. First, do either of you know where Willie lives?"

They shook their heads.

"Did he ever behave oddly? Do anything that frightened you?"

They exchanged glances. Tennant waited.

"Well . . . it didn't frighten us, exactly, but it was strange-like."

The other boy said, "He liked to cut himself."

"Explain yourself."

"He had this thin knife, see, with a pearl handle."

"And? Come on—out with it, unless you want to be charged."

"While he watched us, he'd touch the tip of the blade to his skin and draw blood."

CHAPTER 10

A week after Julia sent Willie's postcard to the Yard, Q showed up at her clinic.

"How is Jackie working out, Doctor?"

"Very well indeed. The men prefer Jackie to our nurses; it's less embarrassing for them. He's learned some basics—changing bandages, that sort of thing. And he's patient with the men, which is not always easy. He has the makings of an excellent medical orderly."

"All his life, Jackie's father used him as a punching bag, so it will be news to him that someone values him. I thank you for that, Doctor."

"Jackie's a good boy. He's lucky he found your sporting club—and you."

"I've had no son of my own, but fathers who toss their children out like yesterday's rubbish—it's criminal." Q spit out the word. "I'd like to thrash them." The knuckles of his clenched hands showed white.

Time to lighten the atmosphere, Julia thought. "I think *you'd* make a wonderful father." She let a moment pass. "Mind you, that's not a proposal."

He threw his head back and laughed. "*Your* father and mother must be cracking, Doctor, to have a daughter like you."

"I barely remember them. They vanished when I was three." She answered his surprised look. "They were passengers on the last voyage of the *President*."

"I remember it. Back in '41, wasn't it? We were patrolling the Atlantic, looking for slavers. Kept a weather eye out for months, hoping her steam engines had failed her, that we'd find her adrift somewhere."

"For a long time, my grandparents hoped so, too. It was terrible for them, not knowing, only guessing what had happened. Their son—their only child—gone without a trace, along with their daughter-in-law."

"But they had you."

"My mother didn't want to leave me behind, but a winter voyage with a young child on board? My grandmother convinced her I should stay in London."

"A lucky decision."

"Chance." Julia shook her head. "At a dinner party in Philadelphia, someone told my mother that the cabins on the *President* were fitted up like rooms in the finest hotels. In her last letter, she wrote to say my father had canceled their booking on the *Great Western*. They would sail home aboard the *President* instead."

"I lost my parents at a young age, too," Q said. "But when I turned sixteen, I took the queen's shilling and joined the Royal Marines. The navy was the making of me."

A few moments of silence stretched out. Julia didn't want to hurry him, but winter Mondays always produced more than their share of respiratory ailments. For many, Sundays spent indoors huddled around coal fires went right to their lungs. That morning was no different—Julia heard a cacophony of hacking coughs coming from her waiting room—and she had three dressings to change. She looked at the quartermaster sergeant expectantly.

Q said, "Have you seen Inspector Tennant lately?"

Ah, she thought. *We may be getting around to it.* "No. I think they've been busy pursuing some new leads."

"I hear they're after Willie Lomax. Checking on all his haunts." Julia's surprise showed on her face. "Between bouts at the ring, the lads were talking. The molly-house story impressed them."

"The molly house?"

He looked at her. "That's a place where men—"

"I know what they are, Q. What about them?"

"The inspector raided a house in Shoreditch, hoping to find Willie or learn of his whereabouts. But he made no arrests, and that surprised the lads. Tennant promised to let everyone go for information received. And he kept his word. That got the boys' attention."

"What's on your mind, Q? You're making a meal of it, you know."

He grinned. "You're right, Doctor. Heavy weather is what I'm making. It's about Lomax. The word from the lads is that the inspector is steaming up the wrong channel. I think he needs to know that."

"What makes them think so?"

"Some years back, a few of the lads worked at that molly. They knew Willie. They say he's a harmless old duffer—likes dressing up but wouldn't hurt a fly."

"Well . . . I'm not sure what the boys told you is evidence. People can change or appear to be different to different people, but I'll pass it along."

"That's not the only thing. The day we first met, Inspector Tennant asked me about the clergyman, Mister Atwater. One of the lads lived in the rector's parish in Spitalfields and said he was a regular at that molly house. He left his collar at home and showed up in civvies. But the boy knew him, no mistake."

Julia's eyes widened. "Yes, I think the inspector would find that very interesting."

* * *

Tennant knew about the clergyman.

He'd come across Tobias Atwater's name in the molly-house ledger, his dues paid through December. What he hadn't found was the whereabouts of Willie Lomax. In Hackney, Sergeant Graves and his team of constables had cast a wide net. For an eighth day, their catch eluded them.

They'd knocked on every door, but no one had seen Lomax in over a week. At one point, someone reported a sighting of Willie at a local boardinghouse. They scrambled a team to the address, but a room-by-room search turned up nothing. It was just another waste of police time. And despite the killer's claim in his last letter—that he'd "taken a stick and knocked him off"—no new victim had turned up.

Back at the Yard, Graves and Tennant tested the case against Willie Lomax while O'Malley listened.

"So, Sergeant, what do we make of the serving boy's statement that Willie used the word 'monkey'? A coincidence?"

"I don't believe in them." Graves had been jangling the coins in his pocket. He pulled out a shilling and tossed it. He showed Tennant the face of the queen. "If I turned up heads every time, you'd be right to think the fix was in."

"Fair enough, Sergeant. What about the wording of the letters? Does that get us anywhere? He sounds like an educated man. Willie Lomax is East London, born and bred."

"Our lad is a bit of a poser, isn't he? Wouldn't be hard to talk like a toff; they all sound alike." The sergeant grinned. "No offense, guv."

"None taken." Tennant eyed a silent O'Malley, who was popping his knuckles and chewing on the inside of his cheek. "What's on your mind, Constable?"

"It's Lomax, sir. We're after interviewing people who know him well, and I'm bothered. 'Tisn't adding up."

"Explain yourself."

"Nearly everyone we've talked to calls him 'old' Willie, like it's part of his name. To me, our killer is reading like a younger man. And we keep hearing that Lomax has gone a bit daft; some screws have come loose. I'm not sure Willie could pull off these murders."

"The killer seems deranged. If Lomax is insane . . ."

"But it's not like that, sir. Willie's no murderous lunatic. He sounds more like a doddering old uncle who forgets to button his trousers."

Tennant said nothing, but the same doubts had been nagging at him.

"What about the ink in his dressing room?" Graves said. "And Willie knew two of the victims—Bertie Parker and Atwater. What are the odds of that? Another coincidence?"

"I'm just not convinced he's our man, Sarge. That's all I'm saying."

"Paddy, there's no sense being Irish if you can't be stubborn. If Willie's not the killer, why has he gone to ground? That's the mark of a guilty man."

"We'll probably find he's buggered off to Brighton on holiday," O'Malley grumbled.

"In December?" Julia asked from the doorway. "Then he *must* be mad."

The men rose from their chairs. Graves swiped at his seat with his hat. "Sit here, Doc. Nestle your bustle."

Julia shook her head. "Thank you, Sergeant, but I'm meeting my grandfather around the corner at the Athenaeum and am here to pass along some information." When Tennant raised an eyebrow, Julia said, "Meeting him in front of the club, Inspector. We'll be dining elsewhere, of course."

"Ladies not being permitted within the sacred precincts. Some information, did you say, Doctor?"

"Yes, from Q—really, from the boys at his sporting club."

When she finished, Graves jumped in. "The lads were right about the clergyman, Doc. We found his name in the molly-house ledger." Tennant shot a warning look the sergeant missed. "Maybe they're right about Willie, too, that he's nothing but a harmless old bugger."

"Thank you, Sergeant. We won't delay the doctor." Tennant glanced up at the clock. "I have a question or two. May I walk with you?"

The blustery wind hit them as they exited the Yard. When a gust lifted Tennant's hat, he barely managed to catch it by the brim. A leaden sky had turned the late morning into twilight. At the corner, he hesitated. What was the etiquette when a colleague was female? He decided to offer Julia his arm as he would any lady. She took it without hesitation, dropping it when they reached the other side of the street.

"At least the rain has finally stopped. Snow before Christmas? What do you reckon, Inspector?"

"It's turned cold enough." He'd almost forgotten the holiday was only two weeks away.

"Never mind." Julia pointed. "Mister Ogilvie is just ahead with our carriage. Let's get in and out of the cold."

After they settled inside the empty coach, Tennant asked her about the mercury ointment he'd found in Willie's dressing room. Julia had mentioned it was prescribed at the onset of syphilis symptoms.

"The tube seemed old, dried up," he said. "Does that mean Lomax has entered the last stage of the disease when such treatments are useless?"

"Perhaps. But syphilis can go into a long latent period—"

The door of the carriage had opened. "I beg your pardon," her grandfather said, shutting it abruptly.

A moment passed. Tennant looked at Julia, opening his mouth and shutting it again. She reached across and opened the door.

"Grandfather." She waved him back to the carriage. Warily, his head appeared at the door.

"This is . . ." Julia took a breath, but she couldn't keep the laughter out of her voice. "Grandfather, may I introduce Detective Inspector Richard Tennant? Inspector Tennant—my grandfather, Doctor Andrew Lewis. The inspector has a few questions for me about the phases of syphilis—for his investigation."

"Oh. That's all right, then." Her grandfather climbed into the coach and sat next to him. "I thought my carriage was a strange place for a medical consultation. But, then again, my granddaughter can be somewhat unconventional."

"Somewhat, Doctor Lewis." Tennant offered his hand. "It's a pleasure to meet you, sir. I won't keep you, but I have one or two questions, if I may."

"Fire away, young man," he said, settling back into his seat. "Now you have two doctors for the price of one."

Tennant turned to Julia. "About the last stage of syphilis— you mentioned hallucinations. What form do they take?"

She thought a moment. "Auditory hallucinations are the most common, but visual delusions are not unknown. Would you agree, Grandfather?" He nodded. "Often, sufferers experience ringing in the ear or hear music."

"Some hear voices," the older Doctor Lewis said. "But that is somewhat less common."

"One last question, if I may. At any stage of the disease, do sufferers become violent? Would a murderous rampage be a possible consequence of the malady?"

"Hmm." Julia narrowed her eyes. "You've dealt with many more cases than I, Grandfather. What do you think?"

"In decades of practice, I've not seen it."

"Thank you, Doctors." He climbed out of the carriage and tipped his hat. "You've given me several things to weigh."

After the door closed, her grandfather craned his neck and watched Tennant walk away. He turned back. "Not your run-of-the-mill copper, is he, my dear? Perhaps we should have asked him to lunch." He rapped his cane on the roof, and the coach juddered forward.

"Too clubbable for his own good, Grandpa. It gives him trouble at the Yard."

"So the Met doesn't care for the trim of his jib. Well, if he gets the right man, it will be smooth sailing. None of that will matter."

"Or if he gets the right woman."

"Oh?" He smiled. "Stands the wind in that quarter? He's a handsome chap, I'll grant you."

"I meant the killer, Grandfather. You assume he's a man. There are some indications the murderer could be a woman."

He patted her hand. "Well, my dear, all I can say is this—I'd prefer your inspector infinitely to Sir Harry Jackson."

Two days earlier, an upstairs tenant in a flat on Cowper Street had lodged the first complaint. On Monday evening, the rent man had gotten an earful when he arrived at the house in Hoxton.

"Every day, it's worse," the man said.

The collector shrugged. "Probably something in the cellar."

The rent man smelled the odor, too. He wasn't surprised: much of the neighborhood had reeked for days. Night-soil men had emptied the old cesspit years ago when water closets replaced the privies. Still, he checked the cellar anyway and found nothing that explained the smell. The collector returned to the flat to make his report.

"Must be overflow from a neighboring privy," he said. "With the rains finally over, it will probably be gone in a day or so."

"Then come back in a day or two for your money. You'll get nothing out of me until that stench is sorted." The tenant slammed his door.

But by Wednesday morning, the smell had gotten worse, so the two upstairs tenants searched for its source. The first-floor flat that opened to the street had been empty for over a year. They wondered if some animal had gained entry and died there. But the stench that lingered seemed fainter near its door. Outside, they peered through the windows and saw nothing amiss. But as they reentered the house and walked down the hallway to the back flat, the odor grew stronger. At the door, it was over-powering. The tenants exchanged glances.

"The old chap who lives here—have you spotted him lately?"

The second man shrugged. "Works nights. He's never around." He rattled the knob, but the door was locked. "Try over the lintel."

The first tenant reached up, felt along the ledge, and found a key. He opened the door, and a malodorous wave drove them back.

Choking, the man with the key said, "Looked like a body on the floor of the back bedroom. We'd better get the rozzers in."

The police court was just around the corner on Worship Street. The second tenant ran.

The police who were first on the scene left the windows and door open to the December cold. The smell of human decay had seeped into every inch of the place. When Tennant and O'Malley arrived an hour later, the odor forced them to retreat, gasping for fresh air. They spent ten minutes searching the premises with two-minute breaks to clear their nostrils and lungs.

The G-Division coppers had interviewed the men who found the body, but neither could name the deceased. Still, one thing about his identity was certain: he was the killer's latest victim. The man had been discovered on the floor, stripped, with his penis sliced off. The body was taken to the Yard for medical examination.

When their search of the sitting room turned up little of in-terest, Tennant and O'Malley took deep breaths, reentered the flat, and began their inspection of the rear bedroom.

At first, they thought a woman lived with the victim. Bottles and jars of perfumes and creams littered the dressing table. Silk scarves draped the mirror. Shirts and trousers hung from pegs on the wall, while evening gowns, petticoats, and corsets filled the wardrobe. Three flaming heads of hair lined the top shelf, propped on their cork and canvas wig blocks.

The inspector and his constable made simultaneous discoveries. Tennant slipped a gown off its hanger and found it thickly padded at the hips and bust. A quick examination of the other dresses revealed the same alterations. O'Malley pulled out a stack of picture postcards from a drawer in the dressing table—all of the same image, half of them signed in purple ink.

"Sir?" O'Malley held up a photograph of Willie Lomax dressed as Champagne Charlotte. "There's a stack of them." He reached back into the drawer; his hand came away with a bottle. He held up the purple ink.

Tennant shuffled through the hanging gowns and found an emerald dress at the back. He laid it out on the bed. O'Malley dropped a postcard next to it. The gown was identical to the one in the black-and-white photograph.

"That about tears it, sir."

"Yes. We're not going to need the sergeant's report."

Graves had volunteered to interview the rent collector, hoping to discover the tenant's name. Willie Lomax wasn't the killer; he was his latest victim. For ten days, they'd been searching for a dead man.

Tennant dodged Chief Inspector Clark and headed down the staircase to meet Julia in the basement morgue. He wanted to hear her findings before reporting to the chief, and he needed to buy some time to collect his thoughts. He felt the wall of self-control he'd built crumbling.

The gloom of the low-ceilinged passageway wasn't helping him. It was cold in the summer and freezing in December. Even so, he felt a film of clammy sweat on his forehead. He fumbled for a handkerchief, swiping at his face. The uneven tap-tap of his footsteps faltered. He stopped before the turn into the morgue corridor, his shoulders falling back against the tiled wall. The only sound left in the echoing hallway was his labored breathing.

Commanding his body to relax rarely worked. Over the years, Tennant had found something that did. He closed his eyes and thought about the house in Kent, the country home sold years before to settle his father's debts. He pictured the lake at the end of the meadow, felt the stillness of an August afternoon, heard the low hum of unseen insects, and followed the graceful arc of his fishing line as it sailed across the azure water.

When his breathing resumed a normal rhythm, Tennant rounded the corner. A young woman sitting on a bench stared in his direction. For a moment, they looked at each other. Then the girl scrambled to her feet.

"I'm waiting for Doctor Lewis, sir. She sent for a change of clothes." A carpetbag rested on the floor by the bench.

The inspector nodded and peered through the window of the examining room. Julia had covered the remains of Willie Lomax with a sheet and was washing her hands at a basin. He looked back at the girl. "The doctor is nearly finished."

Tennant pushed open the swinging door, but a miasma of foul decay drove him back. Julia looked up and signaled for him to wait. He gagged a second time when she opened the door, and the stink exited the room with her.

"This is Kate Connolly, Inspector. She's brought a few things for me. Inspector Tennant is the officer in charge of the investigation, Kate."

"A pleasure, Miss Connolly."

Julia pushed her hair back from her forehead with her wrist and blew the breath from her cheeks. "Willie Lomax can be handed over to the coroner for the inquest. But after ten days of decay, viewing his body will be an ordeal for the jurymen."

"Mother of God," Kate whispered, crossing herself. "Are you ready for your clean things?"

"Better keep your distance, Kate. Just shove that case over to me. I can manage."

"Permit me." Tennant moved the carpetbag to within a few steps of Julia.

The girl hesitated. "You look knackered, Doctor Julie. Let me help you."

"No, it's all right. Wait in the carriage with Mister Ogilvie. I'll be there in twenty minutes or so."

The girl retreated down the hallway, looking back over her shoulder.

Julia picked up her bag. "I'll use the storeroom."

While she changed, she left the door open a crack and began her report. Tennant stood with his back to the door, listening to her findings. In the brief silences between the details of the postmortem, he heard faint rustlings. It suddenly occurred to him why Julia moved about so freely in contrast with other women. He hadn't thought of it before. He pictured her bending over the bathhouse tub to examine Sir Maxwell, kneeling beside the corpse of Mr. Atwater, rising to her feet with ease.

She doesn't wear a corset.

"Good old Kate," Tennant heard Julia say. "She remembered the toilet water." The door swung open. "That's better. Although my carpetbag may never recover."

The inspector cleared his throat. "Were you able to determine the cause of death? Or is Willie too far gone to tell?"

"I found a narrow stab wound to the chest, like the others. But the state of decay made it difficult to assess if there were other assaults to the body."

"Aside from the usual genital amputation."

"Yes. The murderer sodomized him using a thin-bladed knife with a pearl handle. He left it in the body. And this time, he gouged out the victim's eyes."

"That fits." When Julia raised her eyebrows, he said, "Our information is he paid young men to let him watch them in the act."

"Good Lord."

He felt dizzy and was impatient to end the conversation. Beads of sweat trickled down his temples. He registered Julia's narrowed eyes searching his face. *Blast the woman.*

"Are you feeling well, Inspector?"

"Quite well."

She didn't look like she believed him. "You look feverish."

He flinched when she put her hand to his forehead, but he didn't pull away. Before she could say anything else, he asked, "Did you find a balloon?"

"Yellow. Pierced by the weapon I extracted from his anus. It was wrapped around the blade and hilt."

"So there's no doubt?"

"I'm afraid not, Inspector. The killer murdered Willie Lomax along with the others."

O'Malley leaned forward in his chair, head down, hands hanging between his knees. Graves stared out the inspector's grime-smeared window. Neither man said a word as Julia summarized her medical report.

"I'm sorry, gentlemen, but there it is. Willie Lomax is the latest victim."

After the doctor left, Graves yanked at the window shade. "Bloody hell. All this time, we've had our heads up our arses."

O'Malley, skeptical about Lomax from the start, didn't gloat. "Seemed reasonable, Sarge. He knew Bertie Parker and Atwater—what are the odds?"

"The odds? They're more stacked than you think, Constable." Johnny Osborne slouched against Tennant's doorframe, arms folded, his hat tipped forward.

O'Malley cocked his thumb at the reporter. "Will ye look at what the cat dragged in. How did the creature slink past the duty sergeant?"

Osborne tapped the side of his nose. "I never divulge trade

secrets." He looked around the circle of faces. "Well, well. The whole team is assembled, and I just passed Doctor Lewis in the hallway. Any surprises in the medical report?" Uninvited, he sat in the chair Julia had vacated. "I am interrupting? I sincerely hope so."

Tennant removed the bowler from the reporter's head and dropped it on his desk.

"How can I help you, Mister Osborne?"

"It's more a case of our helping each other, Inspector."

O'Malley snorted. "Bollocks."

Tennant eyed the reporter, but Osborne was one of the few people who could wait out the inspector's silence. "You have my attention," he finally said.

The reporter opened his notebook and flipped to a page. "Tomorrow's headline in the *Illustrated*." Dropping his voice from baritone to base, he read, "MUSIC-HALL MURDERER STRIKES AGAIN."

"Christ," O'Malley muttered.

"Our sketch artist is working up an illustration—bobbies in a circle scratching their heads. The big fellow with an Irish mug looks a little like you, Constable. 'Killer leads Police on a Merry Chase' is the caption."

Livid color surged into O'Malley's cheeks. He sprung from his chair and loomed over the seated reporter. "That's helping us? Giving the killer a fecking nickname? Making coppers look like a thick pack of eejits?"

The reporter turned to Tennant. "I seem to have gotten your constable's Irish up. Can you bring your setter to heel, Inspector?"

"Constable O'Malley makes a good point. Neither the headline nor the illustration helps our investigation. Have you something to offer the police, aside from childish taunts? If not, you're wasting our time."

"Information, Inspector. Information you missed." Osborne pocketed his notebook and rose. "Of course, if you're not interested—"

"It's an offense to withhold evidence from the police." There was a vein of iron in Tennant's even voice. "I never make idle threats, Mister Osborne. Don't tempt me to charge you."

For a moment, the reporter stood his ground. Then he shrugged and resumed his seat.

"Another of your victims is linked to the Eagle's music hall." Again, he flipped open his notebook. "This item will appear in tomorrow's issue. Shall I read my copy?"

Tennant nodded.

Osborne cleared his throat. "In an exclusive, the *Illustrated* interviewed the Eagle's popular songstress, Miss Lillie La Rue, whose rendition of 'She's No Better than She Should Be' captivates theater patrons night after night. She recounted with horror the mounting toll of murder victims linked to the music hall. 'I knew all three of them,' Miss La Rue confided to this reporter, her lovely eyes wide with fear."

"Three, Mister Osborne?"

"Wait for it, Inspector. 'He'd come regular on a Saturday night,' Miss La Rue explained. 'Take me out for a bite after the show. Such lovely manners he had, and ever so generous,' she said, turning her head to the light, flashing the last present he gave her: a pair of diamond earrings."

Tennant said, "And his name? Out with it, man."

Osborne smiled the grin of a contented cat. He closed his notebook, unfolded his lanky frame from the chair, and retrieved his hat.

"The lady's admirer was the late Sir Maxwell Ball. Remember who tipped you off, gents."

O'Malley's hand tightened around the grip of his truncheon. "I'll be remembering you, boy-o."

Pushing back his hat brim with a poke of his finger, the reporter dropped his card on Tennant's desk and sauntered down the hall.

Graves spread his hands. "How the hell did he twig that Ball was shagging the showgirl?"

"A fair question," Tennant said. "Whatever his methods, Osborne's done us a favor. He's given us time to get in front of the story." He pulled out his pocket watch. "We've got five hours to drop a report on the chief's desk before he leaves for the day."

The Carlton Club's doorman confirmed the reporter's story.

"Maybe two Saturdays a month, at 7:30 sharp, he'd pick up a hansom at the corner."

In time for the eight o'clock curtain, Tennant thought. "Why wouldn't he ask you to call a cab? It's part of your job, after all."

"It's not my job to ask questions. Gentlemen like to keep themselves to themselves."

"Do you think he wanted to prevent you from hearing the address?"

"I'm not paid to think."

He wasn't paid to do a lot of things, Tennant thought. *He wasn't paid to think, see, or hear anything that might embarrass the club or its members.*

In her dressing room at the Eagle Tavern, Miss Lillie La Rue agreed to answer Constable O'Malley's questions. He reminded her there was little to be lost. "After all, Sir Maxwell's dead. Sure, you're not doing the man any harm."

"For ever so long, I didn't know who he was. 'Call me Max,' he told me. So I did."

"You never asked him his full name?"

Lillie raised a shrewd, plucked eyebrow and opened her jewelry case, nodding at the contents. "If she wants to keep this lot coming, a smart girl learns to keep her pie hole shut."

"But a smart girl, now, she's no pushover. How did you winkle the name out of him?"

"Dropped an envelope one night, didn't he? Sir Maxwell Ball, the Carlton Club, Pall Mall, London. Fell out of his coat."

"It fell out?"

She winked. "All's fair in love and war, or so they say."

"What about that reporter fella? Johnny Osborne. A particular friend of yours, is he?"

"Nah, never clapped eyes on him afore yesterday. Gave me a fiver."

"To part with Sir Maxwell's name?"

"Didn't have to. He knew it. Wanted to 'confirm his sources,' he said. Fine by me. I was five quid richer, just for nodding me head."

Graves carried two pints of ale to a distant table, where a constable waited for him. He handed the bobbie a glass.

"Cheers, Sarge." The copper sank a third of his pint, then wiped the foam from his mustache.

"How long have you walked the Fleet Street beat, Constable?"

"Coming up ten years now."

"You must know all the newspapermen pretty well. How about Johnny Osborne over at the *Illustrated*. Know him?"

"Well enough to pass the time of day."

"Anything dodgy about him?"

The constable drained another third of his glass and considered the question.

"He's well-liked in these parts. Generous. This pub's his local; he'll stand the crowd a round when he's flush. Has a small army of sweepers and bootblacks who keep him informed. Looks after them when they get into trouble."

Graves raised an eyebrow. "Likes young boys, does he?"

The constable slapped his hand on the table and snorted. "Not bloody likely—you should see his wife. If Osborne's a fairy, my Aunt Fanny's the queen of England."

*   *   *

By five o'clock, the team had assembled a report for Chief Inspector Clark.

"Some new developments, sir." Tennant handed him the document. The chief grunted as he headed out the door.

The next day, when the story hit the newsstands, at least Clark couldn't complain he was the last to know.

CHAPTER 11

Sergeant Graves held up his copy of the *Illustrated London News*, giving Constable O'Malley a full view of the front page.

In the center of the circle of confused coppers, the illustrator had drawn a familiar caricature of an Irishman. The low forehead and protruding upper lip gave an ape-like cast to his countenance. The tip of his constable's truncheon and the neck of a whiskey bottle poked out of his bulging pocket.

"Osborne pulled your leg, Paddy. The bloke looks nothing like you."

O'Malley grunted. "Small comfort. When the chief sees it, we're in for a bollocking."

"The guv's with him now."

A constable stuck his head around the corner. "You're wanted, Sarge."

"In Clark's office?"

He cocked his thumb at the ceiling. "Upstairs. The commissioner wants to see you and Constable O'Malley. The chief and your guvnor are waiting in his office."

Graves smoothed his hair and straightened his tie, while O'Malley buttoned the top of his tunic.

"What are you thinking, Sarge? Will the commissioner be handing off the investigation to another team?"

"Like as not, Paddy."

Sir Richard Mayne had a copy of the *Illustrated London News* on the conference table at his left elbow. But three other documents in front of him had eclipsed its headline. All had arrived in the morning post; all were written in purple ink. One by one, the commissioner read them out.

"My dear Commissioner,
It's not Richard's fault. Truly. Every investigation will have its up and down. I do hope you are not losing faith in your godson. He's gotten so close to me—very close. You have my word on it. And no one knows the in and out of it like Inspector Tennant.
My money's on him, but that's the way the money goes, sometimes.

Chief Inspector Clark,
It would take a weasel like you to pass the buck—blaming coppers for your failures. It would upset me dreadfully if you replaced Inspector Tennant. You may not think he's worth half a pound of tuppenny rice, but the inspector is closer than you know. Meanwhile, remember this: every neighborhood on your pitch is my playground. You wouldn't want to put me in a temper, would you?

My dear Inspector Tennant,
Willie seemed like a harmless old bugger, as buggers go. But go they must—all of them.

*Keep at it, Inspector. Don't let them make a monkey out of
you. So many dark alleys to explore, so many frustrations, but
that's the way it goes, sometimes. Mustn't grumble—shoulder to
the wheel.*

Pop. You're nearer than you think."

Red-faced, Chief Inspector Clark slammed the table with his
fist. "By God, Tennant, the man is playing with you. He's
making a mockery of the investigation *and* the Met. Give me
one good reason—just one—why we shouldn't take you and
your team off this case."

"I direct the investigation at your discretion, Chief Inspector—and Sir Richard's. The work my team and I have done
speaks for itself. If we've fallen short, it's not because of their
efforts. They've served under my direction, and no pair of officers has worked harder than Sergeant Graves and Constable
O'Malley."

Graves cleared his throat. "If you would permit an observa-
tion, Sir Richard?" The commissioner nodded. "The killer is
baiting us. That's clear as daylight. To change horses in the
middle of the race . . . Do we want to play his game?"

The commissioner picked up the note addressed to him and
scanned it. "I think the sergeant has a point. And whether or
not the killer expects us to take him at his word, he may be
telling the truth—that Inspector Tennant *is* closer than we
know. He's someone you've run across. Perhaps someone
you've interviewed."

A tap at the door interrupted them. A secretary murmured
something in the commissioner's ear, handed him a slim packet,
and withdrew.

The commissioner looked up. "It's marked urgent and addressed to you, Richard. Doctor Lewis sent it by messenger."

The inspector broke open the wax seal and separated a covering note from an envelope addressed in purple ink. He read

Julia's opening lines. "This arrived on our doorstep in Finsbury Circus. I am sending it to you unopened."

He looked at the direction. The unstamped envelope was addressed to Dr. Julia Lewis at her Finsbury Circus address. He handed it to Graves, who held it up to the light, turning it over to examine both sides. Nothing other than Julia's name and address was visible on the outside. The sergeant slit the envelope open with his penknife and handed the letter to Tennant.

"My dear Doctor Lewis," he read. "I understand I have you to thank. Your eagle eye spotted Willie's purple ink. Not a little birdie, but some loose talk among coppers in the pubs along the City Road alerted me to the role you played. Well spotted, Julia. I'm afraid that—pop!—just like one of my burst balloons, Willie had to be disposed of earlier than I planned. Well, he had to be dispatched sooner or later."

When he finished reading, Tennant placed the letter on the table next to the others. He felt a vein throb at his temple. His hand shook as he put the letter down, so he thrust his hand into his pocket before anyone could notice.

"Damn it to hell!" Clark said. "Who will the bastard be writing to next? The press? That's all we'll need." He shoved the copy of the *Illustrated London News* across the table at Tennant. "The next sodding thing you know, he'll be writing to Johnny fecking Osborne and—"

"Sirs?" Constable O'Malley was leaning over the table, pushing the letters around to reorder them. "Will ye take a look at this now."

He moved Julia's letter next to Sir Richard's and read some of the words and phrases.

"'Up and down the City Road' and ''Round and 'round the Eagle.'" He pointed at Tennant's letter. "'That's the way the . . . goes.' The word 'money' is in the chief's letter—'That's the way the money goes.'" The constable looked up. "The words 'weasel' in the chief's letter and 'half a pound of tuppenny rice.' And 'pop' is in the doctor's note."

Graves named it. "Pop Goes the Weasel."

Chief Inspector Clark dropped his bulk into a chair. "Bloody hell. The blighter is sending us ruddy children's songs? This is a nightmare."

Tennant tipped Julia's cover letter so Graves could read it, pointing to the second paragraph. He muttered some instructions.

"With your permission, Sir Richard, I've asked Sergeant Graves to attend to an unrelated matter at the request of Doctor Lewis."

While the chief inspector glared, the commissioner nodded. Graves slipped out the door.

Sir Richard picked up the copy of the *Illustrated*. "Osborne's story claims that Sir Maxwell Ball had an association with the La Rue woman. Coupled with the Eagle Tavern reference in the killer's notes, that points to the music hall. I'd redouble your efforts there, Richard." The commissioner said to O'Malley, "Well spotted, Constable," and handed him the letters. Then he said, "Chief Inspector, a word, if you please."

When the commissioner's door closed behind him, O'Malley pulled a handkerchief from his trouser pocket and wiped his forehead. " 'Twas a close one, that. Sure, I thought we were getting the sack."

Tennant nodded. "We live to fight another day—no small thanks to you, Paddy. That was quick thinking."

" 'Twasn't my face the chief was breathing fire over."

"Distractions," Tennant said. "Is it sleight of hand—the letters pointing us to the Eagle? Or is our killer someone attached to the music hall? Someone arrogant enough to draw us in, to toy with us, a cat who likes his mouse in paw's reach?"

"What about Rollie Jakeways? He's a cocky one, but gutless, I'm thinking."

"How much courage would it take? So far, he's killed an old banker, two aging transvestites, a frail clergyman, and Sir Maxwell Ball, who wouldn't be difficult to dispatch. A swift thrust of the knife and a push to topple him into that tub."

Back at his office, Tennant spread the earlier letters across his desk.

"Look, sir," O'Malley said. "In almost all of them—'that's the way the money goes' and 'the monkey's on the table.'" He picked up the letter that had arrived the week before. "Here's 'pop' and 'I took a stick and knocked him off.'"

"Look in at some music shops, Constable, see if you can find the sheet music for 'Pop Goes the Weasel.' I want to read all the lyrics."

"I'll see to it, sir." He started to strap on his helmet, then remembered. "What errand is it the sarge is doing for Doctor Lewis?"

Tennant handed him Julia's note. "The second paragraph."

"Q has been arrested for an assault on Jackie Archer's father and taken to the Whitechapel police station. I know this is an imposition, but can you find out what's happened to him?"

"I sent Sergeant Graves over to H-Division headquarters to make inquiries."

Julia's clinic, usually a calm oasis in its chaotic neighborhood, was in an uproar.

The inspector and his sergeant arrived in the middle of bedlam with Q in tow. An omnibus had collided with a barrel-laden dray, spilling the passengers from its rooftop benches. Dr. Lewis and her porters were nowhere in sight, leaving the clinic's ward nurses to bandage up six bruised and bleeding patients. On top of that, they had a distraught mother and a raving man in the throes of alcoholic delirium on their hands.

The frantic, sobbing woman begged to see her son. It took Tennant a minute to realize she was Jackie Archer's mother.

When Nurse Clemmie explained he wasn't there, that he'd gone to the London Hospital with Dr. Lewis, the woman moaned and cried out, "He's killed him at last. His own son."

"No, no, Mrs. Archer. Jackie is fine," the nurse said. "Truly he is. He's helping Doctor Lewis transport a patient from the London to the clinic. That's all." The nurse patted her shoulder. "Now come along and sit down. We'll make you a cup of tea." She looked at the watch pinned to her blouse. "Jackie should be back any minute, and you can see him yourself."

Across the hall in the men's ward, shouting and a trail of blood led Tennant and the others to Nurse Emily and a man with an open leg wound. He was thrashing in his cot, shouting, "They're all over me, I tell you. Get 'em off me," he cried, writhing in response to an unseen torment. The nurse struggled to quiet him, but when Emily tried to remove his boots, he kicked out at her, knocking her backward. Then he rolled on his back and bolted upright in the bed.

"They're eating me alive," he cried in a strangled voice.

While Tennant helped the nurse to her feet, Q leaned over the man and forced his shoulders back against the mattress. "We'll get rid of them for you, mate. The nurse will help you. Just try to relax." The quartermaster nodded to her.

Nurse Emily measured a dose of white powder and added it to a glass of water. When Q lifted the man by his shoulders, she got him to drink most of the mixture. It took a few minutes to take effect. Then, slowly, his agitation eased, and he drifted to sleep.

Q found the nurse's cap on the floor and handed it to her.

"Thank you for your help, Mister—"

"Call me Q. Everyone does." Nodding at the dregs in the glass, "What was in that magic potion?"

Nurse Emily smiled. "Potassium bromide. He'll sleep for hours, long enough for me to attend to his leg."

"Pity it can't help his D.T.'s."

"Nothing will do that until he gets off this." The nurse held up a stoppered bottle from the man's trouser pocket. She pulled the cork and sniffed. "Gin."

Tennant left the ward to look for Nurse Clemmie and spotted her signing off on a delivery at the front door. He passed a calmer Mrs. Archer sitting hunched on a bench, cupping her tea.

He spoke quietly to the nurse so Jackie's mother couldn't hear him. "Is the boy all right?"

"His injury looked worse than it was. He suffered a gash to his head, but even superficial head wounds bleed profusely. A few stitches and Doctor Lewis had it closed up."

"Do you expect her back soon? There is one pressing question I need to ask her."

"I thought she'd be back by now, Inspector. The battle must have taken longer than she anticipated."

"Battle?"

"With the powers-that-be at the London. Fred, our porter—" The rattling halt of a carriage at the door interrupted her. "That must be the doctor now."

The front doors banged open. Jackie Archer dashed in, grabbed the invalid's chair, and wheeled it out the door. A minute later, the doors swung wide again. Jackie propped them open and rolled a patient into the hallway. Fred followed, carrying a cap and a jacket folded over his arm.

As Jackie wheeled the injured man past Graves and Q, he said, "Can you give me a hand? I need to get him into a bed without jolting him."

They followed Jackie into the ward. The patient's arm was in a sling and bound snugly to his chest to immobilize the limb. The three of them managed to transfer the injured man from the wheelchair to a bed without doing any more damage.

Tennant walked to the front door, looking for Julia. She was speaking to someone through a carriage window. When the coach pulled away, he caught a glimpse of Sir Harry Jackson.

Julia nodded to Tennant as she hurried past him. He followed her down the hallway and into her office. She tossed her jacket and hat aside, rolled up the sleeves of her blouse, and began washing her hands at a basin.

"I see the moment is inopportune," Tennant said, "but may I ask you one question?"

Julia nodded as she dried her hands.

"The envelope you sent had no stamp on it. How was it delivered?"

"A boy brought it. Sandy-haired, about twelve, our maid said. I'm sorry, Inspector, she didn't recognize him." She grabbed her bag. At the door, she stopped. "Emma said he had a broom strapped to his back. Joe is the crossing sweeper on the corner of Whitechapel Road and Commercial Street. He might know something."

"I'll send Sergeant Graves to speak with him. May I wait for you?"

"I'll need to change the patient's bandages and inspect the splinting. Half an hour, and I'll be with you."

Graves and Q nodded to Julia as she passed them in the hallway. She spoke quietly to Jackie and sent him over to his mother.

Q tipped his head at the pair. "Jackie says she's left his father. Moved in with her sister. I'll see that she gets there safe and sound." He extended his hand. "Thank you, Inspector."

Tennant took it. "There are men who deserve a good beating. Joe Archer is probably one of them. But . . ."

"You're right, Inspector. Signal received."

After Q exited with Mrs. Archer, Tennant and his sergeant helped Fred move a partition around the patient's bed. Julia nodded her thanks and disappeared behind it.

"It's Fred's nephew," Graves said. "Injured on the docks, and they wanted to take his arm off at the London. Jackie said

Doctor Lewis would have none of it. Kicked up a fuss with some old battle-ax of a nurse and had him sprung." He chuckled. "Like to have been the fly on that wall."

Tennant explained the delivery of Julia's note. "See if you can find a sweeper named Joe at the corner of Whitechapel and Commercial Street."

"Right, guv."

"Check with the other lads along the road. After that, go home. It's been a hell of a day."

When Joe put two fingers in his mouth and let out a piercing whistle at the request of Sergeant Graves, a squad of sweepers jogged to the boy's corner. None had carried a message to the doctor that morning.

An hour later, Julia stood back from the bed of her patient. She wrapped up the discarded bandages and signaled Tennant to follow her.

"I gave him some chloroform to ease the pain of resetting his splint," she said. "And I've administered a sedative. Freddie will sleep for hours now. Best thing for him."

"Will he recover?"

She began washing her hands at the basin. "It's a bad break, but he'll keep that arm with attentive care. Good nursing—"

"Works wonders. I remember your telling me that. Your nurse said something about a 'battle.' What happened at the London?"

Julia dried her hands and buttoned the sleeves of her blouse. She dropped into her chair, gesturing to the inspector to sit across from her. It was nearly six o'clock, the end of a typically long day. Still, to Tennant's eyes, Julia looked more than usually drained. Dark smudges stained the skin under her eyes, and she looked thinner in the face. The lamplight caught the sharp angles of her high cheekbones.

"I'd rather scrub a surgery floor than deal with stubborn, of-ficious, bloody-minded . . ."

It was unusual for a lady of Julia's class to use that word. Tennant asked, "Whose mind was especially sanguinary?"

"The nurse supervising Freddie's ward at the London. She refused to release him into my care, even though it was what he wanted. He's twenty-five—of age—and had every right to re-fuse treatment." Julia shook her head. "For a dockworker like Freddie to lose his arm, it would be the end for him."

"Yes. I see that."

"Pity she couldn't—Nurse *Patience* Milhous. She's anything but." Julia struck the top of her desk with the flat of her hand, rattling the pencils in a cup. "There was no rush to remove that arm. We'll watch for any sign of infection and amputate as a last resort. But I don't think it will come to that."

"Why should she object? In a busy hospital like the London, that's one less patient."

"She bristled at me from the moment I entered her ward. Usually, nurses are so deferential to doctors—*male* doctors, that is." Then, without a trace of amusement in her smile, she said, "But I had an ace up my sleeve. My grandfather's oldest friend is on the hospital's board of directors. All I had to say was the magic name—Doctor Maximilian Franklin—and her resistance collapsed."

Remembering the carriage, Tennant asked, "And Sir Harry Jackson, how does he come into it?"

"Uncle Max invited him to join the hospital board; they're building a new surgical wing, and Sir Harry was there for the announcement. My grandfather told me he gave a packet for its construction. I ran into him in the lobby, and he kindly offered to drive us back to the clinic."

Very obliging of him, Tennant thought.

Julia grimaced. "Reporters were there to cover the story, Johnny Osborne included."

"That gentleman of the press seems to be everywhere these days."

"Yes, on my clinic's doorstep as well. He's been badgering me for an interview."

After a pause, Tennant said, "You've had a long day, but I stayed to tell you two things. First, Q was released with a caution."

"I forgot all about him. Thank you for taking the trouble."

"It didn't require much persuasion to have the quartermaster released. Joe Archer is well known to the H-Division officers. In their view, his beating was overdue."

"Q feels deeply about his boys. It's from his experience of loss, I expect. Not long ago, he told me his parents died when he was young. The navy was his salvation, he said. I think that's why he tries so hard to be a refuge for forsaken lads."

Tennant nodded. "And, of course, there's the letter you sent on to the Yard."

"What did it say?"

He removed the note from his coat's inner pocket and held it out to her. When Julia tried to take it, he wouldn't release it until she looked up.

"Yours was one of four that arrived today—the only one hand-delivered."

After she finished reading, Julia shrugged. "It looks like the usual thing. Nothing new."

"Yes and no. It was O'Malley who saw it. All the letters quote 'Pop Goes the Weasel.' 'Up and down the City Road, 'round and 'round the Eagle. That's the way the money goes: pop goes the weasel.' We checked the earlier letters; all but one of them included snatches of the song."

Julia reread her note. "Good Lord. Now, 'pop' jumps out. And 'Eagle'—a reference to the music hall?" She handed the letter back to him. "Who else got them?"

"I did, of course. He never forgets me. And he sent one to

my chief and another to the commissioner, Sir Richard Mayne."

"Heavens. It's some sort of perverse game with him, isn't it? It's . . . unsettling."

Tennant set his jaw. "That he's written to *you* unsettles me. It unsettles me more that he delivered it to your doorstep. And this jumps out." Tennant leaned over the desk and pointed to the last word in the first paragraph. The killer had used her Christian name.

Julia said nothing. Absently, she plucked a pencil from the cup on her desk and began rolling it back and forth across the blotter, frowning down at it. Tennant reached across and took the pencil away from her, shoving it back into the holder. She looked up.

"Listen to me. A while ago, you dismissed my concern about your involvement in the case. But this man is dangerous—do I have to tell you that? Now we know he has his eye on you, as well. For God's sake, he called you Julia. Are you hearing me?"

"I can hardly avoid hearing you, can I?"

He held her gaze. "The letters sent to us at the Met mean nothing. We are professional policemen; this is our job, and we can take care of ourselves. You are a woman and a civilian. You cannot."

Julia glared at him. "I'm a big girl, Inspector. Women are perfectly capable of—"

"Sir Maxwell Ball was a 'big boy,'" Tennant snapped. "Look what happened to him." He stood, looming over her desk. "Why do you insist on making this an issue of men versus women? Male victim or female, this man is a killer. Damn it to hell, Julia, will you take this seriously? Watch yourself?"

She sat back in her chair and folded her arms. "Very well."

He looked out her window. "It's been dark for nearly an hour now. I'll walk you to a cabstand. No arguments."

*   *   *

I am invisible. Invincible.

Waiting on a busy railway platform, lurking on a White-chapel side street, or rounding the elegant circuit of Finsbury Circus, he had the actor's knack for blending in. No one glanced at him: not top-hatted gentlemen, fur-muffed ladies, or distracted nursery maids hurrying after their unruly charges.

He crossed the deserted cricket pitch in the center of the cir-cus and headed for the trees. Hidden in the shadows, he looked up at number 17. Its limestone façade shimmered golden in the last slanting sunlight of late afternoon. Soon darkness began to fall. One by one, lights blinked on in the windows of the town house as some unseen servant went from room to room, light-ing the lamps.

He murmured, "The grandfather or the girl?"

Just after the stroke of seven, a hansom cab pulled up to the house. A woman got out, handed the cabbie his fare, and hur-ried up the steps. She shifted her medical bag to her left hand and reached for the doorknob just as an older gentleman with a mane of snowy hair opened the door.

The girl, I think.

The following morning, Constable O'Malley spread four copies of sheet music across Inspector Tennant's desk.

"There are variations in each version," O'Malley said. He picked out the second sheet in the lineup. "But the lyrics in this one include all the references in the letters."

> *Half a pound of tuppenny rice,*
> *Half a pound of treacle.*
> *That's the way the money goes,*
> *Pop goes the weasel.*
> *Up and down the City Road*
> *In and out the Eagle.*

That's the way the money goes:
Pop goes the weasel.
Every night when I go out
The monkey's on the table.
Take a stick and knock it off:
Pop goes the weasel.
All around the cobbler's bench
The monkey chased the people.
The donkey thought 'twas all in fun:
Pop goes the weasel.

O'Malley handed Tennant the sheet. "I've read it twenty times, and it still makes no sense."

"*Nothing* makes any bloody sense with this blighter," Graves muttered.

"And yet he chose *this* song, Sergeant," Tennant said, holding up the music. "He takes the trouble to weave words and phrases from *this* one into his letters. Why?"

"Just some random ditty, I'm thinking," O'Malley said. "Making sport of us, he is. Like the end of the song—'the donkey thought 'twas all in fun.'"

"This is getting us nowhere." Tennant swept the sheets into a pile and stuffed them into his top drawer. "Let's move on, beginning with a return to the music hall."

"You and Paddy have that beat covered, guv," Graves said. "I was thinking about something else. That sweeper, the one who carried the letter to Doctor Lewis. It put me in mind of our favorite reporter. Remember what that copper told me? That Osborne has a small army of street lads who keep him informed?"

"That sweeper boy is the only one who's had eyes on the killer," O'Malley said.

Graves slid off the edge of the desk. "I'll pay the lads along

Fleet Street a visit. Ask 'em a few questions about Johnny bloody Osborne."

Tennant nodded. "After that, interview all the sweepers along the City Road between Willie's lodgings on Cowper Street and the Eagle. Take two constables with you." He clicked open his pocket watch. "We'll meet back here at four o'clock."

Tennant eyed the long line snaking away from the Eagle's ticketing office. A quarter of the customers were reading the latest issue of the *Illustrated London News.* The "music-hall murderer" story was good box office.

Nodding at the line, O'Malley said, "They have Osborne's story to thank for that crowd. 'Tis a share of the till they ought to be giving him."

Inside, Tennant kept it simple for the manager of the Eagle. "Cooperate with the police, and we'll minimize the disruption to the music hall's schedule. Obstruct, and I'll order a thorough search of the premises that will require a postponement of this evening's performance. A pity—it looks as if you have a full house tonight."

The manager scrambled to make an interview room available for Tennant's use. Then he sent an errand boy to round up the persons the inspector wanted to see. At the top of the list, Rollie Jakeways.

The actor entered and settled himself in a seat facing the inspector. Jakeways tugged at the silk sleeves of his paisley dressing gown, crossed slim, well-tailored legs, and smiled at his interrogators.

"Well. Here we are again, gentlemen. Although I am at a loss to know how I can help you."

Tennant wondered what it would take to throw him off-balance—perhaps a statement that was just short of an accusation? "The last to see a victim alive is always a person of interest to the police. You, Mister Jakeways."

"Surely that person is the killer."

"Just so."

Jakeways leaned his elbow on the chair's arm and rested a cheek on his palm. Unperturbed, he looked from Tennant to O'Malley and back again.

"Sir Maxwell Ball seems to have been a regular patron at the Eagle," Tennant said. "He occupied a box two Saturday evenings a month, always when Miss LaRue performed. Do you recall seeing him in the theater?"

"Our lovely Lillie has many admirers, but I confess . . ." He smiled at his use of the word. "I confess I have little interest in them."

"Is that a 'no,' Mister Jakeways?"

"Yes—and by that, I mean no, Inspector. I had no knowledge of Sir Maxwell Ball's comings and goings. I'd never heard of the man until his name appeared in the newspapers."

"I have a question for you, Mister Jakeways," O'Malley said. "The Inspector and I paced the distance from Willie's flat on Cowper Street to the Eagle. It's not a long walk, only seven short cross streets. It seems strange that no one at the Eagle knew where to find him."

The actor looked at O'Malley through lowered lids. "You know where to find me, Constable. I gave you my address, so you know that Willie and I walked in opposite directions. On the rare occasions when the two of us left together, we parted company outside the theater. I hadn't a clue where he lodged, but I can't answer for others at the Eagle."

O'Malley said, "Performing is thirsty work. After the curtain comes down, sure you must go out for a pint now and again."

Jakeways sighed. "Lomax began every other sentence with 'Did I ever tell you about?' The answer was always yes—ten times." He shrugged. "Even the old-timers who 'knew him when' had started to give Willie a wide berth."

"I'll have the names of these old-timers, if you please, Mister Jakeways," Tennant said.

While O'Malley made a note of three longtime stagehands, the inspector allowed the silence to stretch out. Jakeways merely wriggled more comfortably into his seat and suppressed an ostentatious yawn.

Finally, Tennant said, "That will be all . . . for now, Mister Jakeways."

The actor tipped the inspector a two-fingered salute and sauntered out the room. "Happy hunting, gents."

"A nervy bugger, that one," O'Malley said after the door closed behind Rollie. "Too cool and collected by half."

"Much like our killer. See if you can find Sergeant Graves somewhere along the City Road. I want him to extend his search. Ask him to interview all the sweepers north of the Eagle as far as Islington High Street. Maybe Jakeways tipped one of them to deliver a letter to Doctor Lewis."

"Right, sir." O'Malley strapped on his helmet.

"Nose around Jakeways's neighborhood. Drop in at the local pubs. I'd like to know a little more about the man's background. And on your way out, send those old stagehands to the head of the queue."

By four o'clock, Tennant and his team had a stack of interviews to add to the case file but little else. In the inspector's office, Graves extended his legs and eased his feet inside his boots.

"You're looking knackered, Sarge," O'Malley said.

"I jingled a pocketful of coins across half of East London. Not a single sweeper took the bait."

"And Jakeways, Constable?" Tennant said. "Did you turn up anything interesting about him?"

"Popular with his landlady—a 'charmer,' she calls him.

Hanging around music halls all his life. Headliners at the Canterbury in Lambeth, his mam and da; performed with them, he did, in their variety act."

Tennant said, "The old stagehands I talked to had nothing useful to say about him, other than the obvious. 'Fancies himself,' they agreed. They said he could get 'a bit shirty' if something went wrong backstage. But he'll stand them a pint in the local, so all's forgiven, as far as they're concerned."

A message boy interrupted them with a tap on Tennant's door. He waved him in.

"Someone's downstairs to see Sergeant Graves, sir. Funny old cove—name of Benny Kane."

Graves slid out of his seat. "He's the rent collector for Willie's flat. Maybe he's remembered something." The sergeant clapped his hand on the messenger lad's shoulder and followed him out the door.

"Osborne's got those sweeper boys tucked away in his pocket. Sure he could be our man," O'Malley said.

"Yes, and doubtless they've told him we're asking questions about him."

"There's something dodgy about the creature, sir. I'm feeling it."

Tennant smiled. "Your feel for the case has impressed the commissioner, Paddy, and not just your performance yesterday in his office. Credit where it's due, I told Sir Richard you put us onto the off-license pubs that led us to the molly house. Sir Richard said, 'We'll have stripes on his tunic soon.' Detective Sergeant O'Malley—it has a nice ring to it."

The constable looked down at his boots. "I'm chuffed and no mistake. Thank you, sir."

Graves returned and dumped the evening newspapers on Tennant's desk. All of them had picked up Osborne's nickname for the killer: the music-hall murderer.

O'Malley eyed the headlines and grunted. "Bloody hell."

"Kane wanted to know if he could get the cleaners in to sort out Willie's rooms. He's eager to get the place on his books and find a new tenant." Graves grimaced. "Good luck to him. Ghouls like to hang about at a murder scene, but they're not eager to move into a butcher's den. He'll be a long time renting that flat. I told Kane I'd get back to him."

"Tell him to go ahead," Tennant said. "We're done with Willie's lodgings. They've told us everything they can."

CHAPTER 12

Her annoyance dissolved. Unease replaced it.

At first, she thought, *a prank*; someone had called her to a phantom address. But the deeper she plunged into the inky maze of back-alley courts, the more menacing the summons seemed to her. She gripped her medical bag's handle, looked over her shoulder, and picked up her pace. But the moonless evening and scattered gas lamps forced her to step carefully. In the middle of December, darkness blanketed East London early, and she'd miscalculated the hours of daylight left.

Overhead, the creak and rattle of washing-line pulleys sounded louder in the darkness, as did the scurrying of rats' feet scratching around rubbish bins. She knew the hospital wasn't far off. The familiar stench from the nearby manure works stung the insides of her nostrils. She was close; she recognized Bucks Row as she crossed it. Just a few more streets and she could hail a cab on Whitechapel Road.

In the quiet of Hope Lane, had she imagined the tap-tap of leather on the pavement behind her? She stopped and listened. Nothing. Probably just the echo of her boots against the brick walls of the narrow byway. Peering behind her, holding her breath, she strained to detect the sound of something in the darkness. Perhaps it was only her heartbeat or the thrum of tension pulsing against her eardrums. But she felt its presence.

Turning away, she drew a deep breath and walked on. Ahead, beyond the curve of the road, the yellow glow of the lamps lit up her destination. But she had to pick her way through thirty yards of pitch darkness before she reached it.

Then she heard it, a low whistling—scattered notes, at first, not a settled melody. Heart pounding, she gathered her skirts and moved faster. Still, the sound grew louder, finally resolving into a tune she recognized. Close behind her, she heard someone call her name and repeat it in an eerie singsong. She choked back a cry, stumbled forward, and, with the end of Hope Lane agonizingly near, she heard her pursuer laugh.

"You can't outrun me."

Hands seized her shoulders and jerked her back. Then a voice whispered in her ear.

"Pop. It's time to pay."

The duty sergeant held up an envelope, and Tennant spotted the purple ink from across the lobby.

"A constable found it late last night, propped against the door."

The inspector resisted the urge to tear it open on the spot. Instead, he hustled up the steps to his office, where he would examine it closely.

When Sergeant Graves arrived, he found his boss scrutinizing the envelope for any faint marks, looking for any clue to its origins. But the envelope was frustratingly pristine.

"Just heard the news. The arrogant bugger—dropping it on our doorstep."

Carefully, Tennant slit the envelope and extracted the letter. When he read the single line of script, his stomach dropped.

"What's he got to say this time, guv?"

In a rasping voice, Tennant read it. "I'm sorry, my dear Inspector, but the bitch got what was coming to her."

"Her?" Graves said. "But . . ."

Tennant stuck his head out the door and bellowed to a bobby down the hall. "Send a runner up. Now."

He scribbled a note and handed it to the boy. "Take a cab and deliver this to Doctor Julia Lewis at 17 Finsbury Circus. *Julia* Lewis, do you hear me, boy?" He nodded. Tennant fished in his pocket for a half crown to pay the fare. "If she's in, wait for an answer. If she's not, find out where she is and get back here as if your job depended on it."

A minute after the runner vanished, Tennant wished he'd gone himself.

"Something's off here, guv," Graves said. "If something's happened to the doc, or if she's gone missing, we'd have heard about it by now."

Boots pounded down the hallway. Constable O'Malley, white-faced, gasping for breath, leaned against the doorframe.

"A message came from H Division. Coppers found the body of a woman just off Whitechapel Road. They think it's our killer. They said . . . they think—" O'Malley swallowed hard. "They think she might have been a nurse."

"Why?" Tennant rasped. "Why do they think that?"

"She . . . she was found near the London. With a medical bag."

The next thirty minutes were some of the grimmest of Tennant's life. Far worse than the aftermath of his dismissal from the Grenadier Guards, infinitely more dreadful than the long walk back to his flat after Isobel broke their engagement.

The halting traffic between Whitehall and the East End gave him too much time to think. What would he find at the end of the journey? Julia, dead, mutilated, since the local police had already linked the victim to their killer. When the cab came to a dead stop at the corner of Court Street and Whitechapel Road, Tennant ordered Graves and O'Malley to follow him. He jumped from the four-wheeler, wincing when his left boot hit the ground, and paid off the cabbie. They ran the last six cross streets to Hope Lane, Tennant ignoring the stabbing pain in his leg. A stony-faced constable holding back a curious crowd nodded as they passed.

Tennant rounded the curve in the lane and stopped. Half a dozen constables stood between him and the body of a woman lying prone in the gutter. Her bare limbs were pitilessly exposed. Her attacker had violated her with a stick that protruded obscenely from between her legs. A wave of nausea rose in his throat, and he tasted bile in his mouth.

No. No. Tennant wasn't sure he hadn't groaned the words aloud. Then he felt a restraining hand on his arm. *O'Malley.*

"Wait, sir. Wait here a minute."

His men walked forward. As they drew closer, they exchanged glances. O'Malley returned, leaving Graves staring at the body.

" 'Tis someone else," he said quietly.

Tennant expelled the breath he held and followed O'Malley to the corpse. When the constables stood back to let the inspector through, he stared down at the body of a stranger.

Seconds ticked; O'Malley shifted and cleared his throat. Finally, Graves asked, "Should I send a constable to fetch Doctor Lewis?" Tennant said nothing. "Guv?"

"Not Doctor Lewis. Send for Abernathy. Or Doctor MacKay—anyone but her."

"Sir." O'Malley nodded down the lane.

Julia Lewis strode around the curving road, medical bag in hand.

In the morgue, Tennant fought the feeling of being swallowed whole as he waited for Julia to complete the autopsy.

When she'd arrived unexpectedly—drawn to the Yard by his puzzling note and then to the murder scene—he wanted to grab her arm and hustle her out of the lane. But with no legitimate reason to stop her from doing her job, he let her through. He wished to God he hadn't.

His arms folded, his hands jammed tightly into his armpits, Tennant tried to hold himself together. His hair felt damp at the scalp, and he fought against a vertiginous swirl in the pit of his stomach. Even after he'd threaded the labyrinth of narrow hallways and arrived at the examining room, there was no letup. Tennant choked on the stench of decay that the carbolic soap barely covered. But it wasn't only the place. It was his feeling of impotence, of being toyed with by a madman who enjoyed his twisted games. And then there was Julia.

The inspector barely registered her words as she reached the end of her examination.

"Cause of death was a stab wound to the heart. Approximate time of death, between four p.m. and midnight. She also sustained some cuts to her neck, similar to those I observed on Mister Atwater." Julia examined an object in her hand before placing it in an evidence bag. "The stick used to sodomize the victim looks like a length of joiner's trim, about eighteen inches long. Did the constables find anything like it in the lane?" When Tennant didn't answer, she looked up from the table. "Inspector?" He shook his head. "Well, he may have had it with him. It wouldn't have been difficult to conceal on his person."

The killer hadn't overlooked his finishing touch: the doctor had extracted a red balloon from inside the woman's mouth.

The postmortem over, Julia drew a sheet over the body of the late Patience Milhous. There had been no delay in identifying the victim. Julia recognized her at once: she was the nursing matron she'd battled at the London Hospital over Freddie's care.

Julia moved to a basin. Tennant watched her, sleeves rolled up, scrubbing her forearms, wrists, and hands—her clever, capable hands, with their long, tapering fingers. He pictured them cold and still, palms lying lifeless against a metal table. His eyes slid to the thin sheet that covered the mound of the victim's arm and suppressed a shudder. Tennant turned away, not wanting her to catch him staring at the corpse.

"Other than the sex of the victim, did you find any surprises?"

Julia nodded. "He cut out her tongue."

He looked down and stared at his boot tips. "I'll send some men back to the alley to look for it."

She slipped her arms into her sleeves, buttoned her jacket, and walked over to him. "This must have been terribly distressing for you and your officers—that appalling scene. And, now, to fit a *female* victim into the equation . . ."

Tennant pulled the killer's one-line letter from his coat's inner pocket and handed it to her. Julia read it and looked up.

"We thought it was you."

"But . . ."

"A murdered woman found with a medical bag by her side? He knew we'd make that mistake. He enjoyed it."

"Well, I don't know."

"The other day, Sir Harry Jackson drove you home from the London. Was he aware of your dispute with Nurse Milhous? And the reporter, Osborne—what about him?"

"Yes, they were there. But surely . . ."

"You think it's a coincidence? Of all the women in Whitechapel, this lunatic chooses her, someone with whom you quarreled only days ago? He's a hunter who has you in his crosshairs. Then he swings his barrel and picks off other prey."

Julia shook her head.

Tennant had been leaning against the tiled wall of the morgue.

Then, abruptly, he pulled his shoulders away and gripped her upper arms. He had to restrain himself from shaking her.

"Don't you see the danger you're in? Any time he pleases, he can have you in his sights. You must know that. You're not a fool. I've sent one innocent man to the gallows in this case. Damn it, Julia, do you think I want another death on my hands?"

The military order was on his lips: *stand down*. He nearly said the words. But the Met wasn't the army, and he wasn't her superior officer.

She pulled herself out of his grasp, wincing.

"I'm sorry," he said, stepping back.

Julia picked up her medical bag and turned. "Shall we go?"

Tennant wanted to put his fist through the door's glass. Instead, he pulled it open and waited for her to pass through, afraid his warning was too little too late.

The inspector's team had waited in his office for the autopsy results, and for Tennant to issue his orders. He wasted no time, starting with Graves.

"Johnny Osborne and Sir Harry Jackson were at the hospital and witnessed the quarrel between Doctor Lewis and the victim. Where were they last night? Pin them down."

"You think the killer's got the doc in his sights?"

"Get their statements, Sergeant. Lean on them if they're evasive. Interview anyone who can confirm their whereabouts between four and midnight."

Graves slid off the edge of the desk. "Right, guv."

"Take a constable with you to make careful notes. O'Malley, you're with me. We're heading to the London."

Sir Harry Jackson didn't hide his impatience from Sergeant Graves.

"I can spare five minutes. What do you want to know?"

"Nurse Patience Milhous of the London Hospital was murdered last night. Can you account for your movements between four and midnight?"

"What the blazes d'you mean by that question? Bloody hell, has Tennant lost his mind? Why would I murder some nurse?"

"Would you answer the question, Sir Harry?"

Jackson sprang from his chair, banging it against the wall. Brick-faced, he shouted, "I ought to throw you out on your arse."

"I wouldn't do that, sir. Laying hands on a police officer is a criminal offense. I'd have to charge you."

"You insolent bugger. I'll have your stripes."

"And I'll have your answer. Don't force me to shut your business down for the day to interview your workers."

Jackson balled his hands into fists and took a step closer.

Graves nodded at the constable taking notes. "I can have reinforcements here in an hour to help this officer record your men's statements. It will take some time." He paused. "So, Sir Harry, between four o'clock and midnight, where were you?"

The sergeant's interviews with the brewer's foreman and butler confirmed Jackson's account. The working day at the Black Falcon Brewery stretched from six to six. Between four and six in the evening, Sir Harry was on the factory floor or in his office. The foreman had spoken to Jackson at six o'clock about the next day's deliveries. After that, Sir Harry was alone in his brewery. Jackson said he'd worked another four hours, arriving home just after ten. His butler confirmed the hour. It was not unusual, he said, for Sir Harry to work late into the evening.

Graves and the constable eyed the traffic outside the brewery, hoping to flag a hansom to take them on to Fleet Street.

The constable grunted. "That leaves four unaccounted hours, Sarge."

"Yes, a bloke can get up to a lot in four hours."

*   *   *

At first, Johnny Osborne seemed amused to find he was a suspect in the murder of Nurse Milhous. He took a sip of his pint and wiped the foam from his grin.

"Getting desperate, your guv."

When Graves mentioned the hours in question and asked Osborne for his whereabouts, a ripple flickered across the reporter's face.

A shade less confidently, Osborne said, "Is there anything that compels me to answer that question, Sergeant?"

"Nothing at all. I take it you'd rather make your statement in a more official setting . . . at the Yard?"

The reporter's grip tightened on his pint. "Where did you say they found the body?"

"I didn't, but I'll tell you. She was found on Hope Lane, a street just north of the London Hospital. Early this morning."

Osborne's hand slipped from his glass into his lap. His eyes tracked a path from his ale to a pile of shillings and pence and back again.

"That's right," Graves said. "Take your time. No hurry. The constable here will take down your evidence. Whenever you're ready."

"Well, you see," Osborne cleared his throat. "The thing is, I was called away last night, by a tip."

"A tip, you say?"

"Yes, but it turned out to be a hoax."

"A hoax?"

"Yes, damn it, a hoax, a trick," he responded, somewhat loudly. Heads at nearby tables swiveled. "I thought it was some kind of ruddy joke."

"Can you give me the particulars of this hoax?"

Grudgingly, he told Graves his story. The day before, a boy had stopped him on Fleet Street and handed him a note. A glue factory in Mile End was dumping the offal of dead horses into the Regent's Canal. The writer directed him to a location and suggested a time. If the reporter showed up between nine and eleven, he'd catch the drays arriving in darkness to dump their loads. His source claimed some carts had the Black Falcon Brewery's insignia stamped on their sides.

"I thought it had the makings of a good story," Osborne said, "given the public's heightened interest in the safety of the water supply. Sir Harry bloody Jackson peddling his old dray horses to a glue factory is one thing. Dumping rotting horse entrails into the canal is another."

"And the location suggested by your tipster?"

The reporter looked cornered. He licked his lips. "Near Mile End Lock."

Graves nodded. "That would be—what—under a mile from the London Hospital?"

"You know it is, Sergeant."

"And you were there between nine and eleven, you say?"

"Yes, damn it, and I hung around until midnight to be sure I didn't miss anything. Couldn't stand it any longer; the stench from the glue factory was overpowering."

"On your own, were you?"

Osborne nodded.

"This boy who delivered the message. Did you recognize him? Was he one of the lads you employ?"

The reporter shook his head.

"The note you say you received—can you show it to me?"

"I tossed it. No reason to keep it."

"A pity that, Mister Osborne."

At the London Hospital, the first answers to Tennant's questions were brief, polite, and evasive.

Once he made it clear that the murder was linked to events away from the hospital, the orderlies and nurses unbent. Patience Milhous, they told him, was a "bit of a tartar." But she was no worse than most supervising nurses. Many of them believed that fear and a well-ordered ward went hand in hand. Several on the staff had witnessed the altercation between Patience Milhous and Dr. Lewis. And the orderly who had wheeled Freddie out of the ward remembered seeing Sir Harry Jackson and Johnny Osborne.

Tennant asked, "Did anyone else take notice—other patients in the ward or their visitors?"

"Didn't happen there. Matron stopped Doctor Lewis out in the hallway. That reporter chap was there, interviewing Sir Harry. Don't remember seeing anyone else hanging about."

Tennant interviewed the head matron of the London, who praised Nurse Milhous but knew little about her life outside the hospital.

"Very proud of her work with Miss Nightingale, and so she should have been."

"Where would I find her personal details?"

"There should be references on file in the administrative office," she said. "The hospital director's secretary should be able to help you."

The file the secretary gave Tennant included a letter written by Nurse Milhous summarizing her medical experience. She'd worked with her apothecary father as his assistant and nursed him until he died in 1851. After that, she went into private nursing. Finally, she'd served in the Crimea before applying for the post at the London.

The Milhous file held two testimonials, both of them glowing. The first was for the private nursing she'd done before leaving for the Crimea. From May 1851 to December 1853, she cared for an elderly invalid until he died. The gentleman's daughter was lavish in her praise.

The second reference would have opened any hospital door: a letter written by Florence Nightingale's secretary. With her private nursing duties at an end, Patience Milhous had sailed for the Crimea in February 1854 with the famous nurse. She served with her for the next two years. The secretary, Miss Millicent Grant, was pleased to provide a reference on Miss Nightingale's behalf.

A detail caught Tennant's eye. The timing was wrong. In the late winter of 1854, she couldn't have been there with Florence Nightingale. That summer, he'd languished in the squalid military hospital at Scutari, sweating and burning in the fever ward. Miss Nightingale had arrived months after his release. Was it a simple error, or was something wrong with the reference?

Tennant looked up from the letter. "Were her testimonials verified?"

The secretary shrugged. "It was ten years ago, before my time."

The inspector and his constable left the London with more questions than answers.

"She lied in her letter of application," Tennant said. "And she may have forged her references, as well. Shall we find out?"

The day after the murder, every news peddler wearing a sandwich board had some variation of the headline "NURSE MURDERED IN EAST LONDON ALLEY" plastered across their fronts and backs.

Fishing pennies from his pocket, Sergeant Graves purchased three different editions and carried them back to the Yard. Neither the inspector nor O'Malley had arrived, so he shoved the papers into a drawer and started writing his report. He'd just finished when he heard O'Malley's cheerful greetings precede him down the hallway.

Graves pulled out his pocket watch and grunted. "Nice work for some. Nobody told me we were on banker's hours."

"Been hard at it all morning, Sarge. The inspector asked me to run down an address—one of the nurse's references. Talked to the lady of the house."

"And?"

"Didn't know her from Adam."

The sergeant gave a low whistle. "Something dodgy about Patience Milhous then."

O'Malley pulled up a chair. "If the inspector's right, we're not knowing the half of it. Did you track down Osborne and Sir Harry?"

"Just finished my report. What do you reckon? Our favorite reporter has a hole bigger than the Thames Tunnel running through his alibi. And—wait for it—an anonymous tip placed him within shouting distance of the murder scene." The sergeant explained Osborne's story of the hoax.

"That's sounding like bollocks to me. What about Jackson?"

"Huffed and puffed and threatened to have my stripes. But Jackson can't bluster his way through four missing hours. Working in the brewery from six to ten. Alone, the blighter says." Graves laughed. "And my Aunt Fanny."

"Sod it, Sarge. What are you so cheerful about? Easier if we could eliminate one of the buggers."

A "Morning, sir" from a constable in the hallway alerted them that the inspector had arrived. Graves shoved his report into a folder, while O'Malley got to his feet. They followed the inspector into his office. Tennant shrugged off his coat, nodded to the chairs, and sat on the edge of his desk.

"So what have we got?"

When O'Malley and Graves finished their reports, the constable said, "I'm thinking about that note to Osborne. Something sounds off about it."

"Something?" Graves snorted. "How about the whole thing?"

"I mean, if it's the truth he's telling—if the killer wrote it. The tip mentioned carts from the Black Falcon Brewery."

Graves shrugged. "What of it?"

O'Malley tapped on a spot on the map. "The Lisbon Street Brewery's a stone's throw from the Regent's Canal. Why bring

Sir Harry's Black Falcon Brewery into it at all? It's miles away. The only thing that links Osborne and Sir Harry is—"

"Our suspicions," Tennant said. "I find it odd, as well."

"The killer is out there watching us," Graves said. "Doling out clues to implicate men under our investigation. Osborne's a clever bastard. If he's our killer and knows we have Sir Harry in our sights, he's using the note to throw dust in our eyes."

O'Malley crossed his arms. "Maybe."

"Killing the nurse has done one thing," Graves said. "It's blown a hole through Osborne's 'music-hall murders' bollocks."

"He'll be coming up with some other tripe to peddle in that rag of his," O'Malley said. "What about your letter, sir? On the up and up?"

"Almost certainly forged. I spoke to the director of Miss Nightingale's nursing school at St. Thomas' Hospital. She served with her in the Crimea and said she's never heard of a Patience Milhous. What's more, she was fairly certain Miss Nightingale never employed a secretary named Millicent Grant."

Graves cocked a brow.

"Miss Nightingale is ill and not receiving visitors. So the director will send an inquiry and forward her answer. But I think we can proceed on the assumption that Nurse Milhous was a fraud."

"Maybe not altogether," O'Malley said. "I'm thinking that head matron's a sharp one. Milhous must have had some nursing in her. I'd say she lied about a lot of things, but not that."

"Fair enough," Tennant said. "To her colleagues at the London, Patience Milhous was something of an enigma. But someone knows her. She lived in Stepney. Try her neighbors. Search for friends and acquaintances."

O'Malley looked at the map again. "She had the sound of an East Ender in her, the head matron said. They usually don't stray far from home." He tapped the location of the London Hospital. "I'll nose around here as well. See what I can turn up."

Tennant nodded. "Something in her past must connect her to our victims. And to our killer."

A name, dropped casually but known in a flash, had inspired him to alter the script and improvise.

He'd enclosed a pound note in the letter he'd sent her, certain the promise of more to come at the sick man's bedside would lure her. He'd been right. On cue, she'd arrived at the street he'd named in his note. He'd watched her walk up and down, looking for a house number that didn't exist.

The greedy bitch hadn't changed. Sacked for stealing from the infirmary, she was running true to form. He'd heard all about it when he went hunting for her. But she'd covered her tracks, and he'd lost her scent.

He tossed crumpled bits of newspaper into his fireplace. He was done with them, anyway. He lit a few corners of the sheets and flicked the match onto the grate. Tipping coal from his scuttle, he sat back on his haunches. It took a few minutes, but the flames glowed red, then orange, and finally white-hot. As the black fuel turned ash-gray along the edges, he remembered how he'd almost given up, written her off. But revenge, he thought, was like a well-laid fire: *Patience is rewarded.* He laughed at the joke in the cliché. Defiled, left in a filthy lane among the rubbish bins, she got what she deserved.

Reaching into his pocket, he dug them out, testing them between his thumb and forefinger, feeling the slick, rubbery stretch of the last two balloons.

One was for the porter. The last was for her.

The morning after the murder, Barney Dunlap unlocked the workhouse gates. A newspaper wedged between the doors fell to the ground. Without a glance, the old porter rolled it up and stuffed it into his jacket pocket.

He pushed the doors wide. A trickle of ragged, gray-faced men shuffled out—the "casuals" who sought temporary refuge rather than long-term residence. Each had done a day's labor on the workhouse rock pile in exchange for three meals and a bed. They wouldn't be back if they found employment and could afford a night in a three-penny doss-house.

A few minutes later, a second group passed through the gates. They wore the same gray trousers and jackets, their workhouse clothing marking them as pauper boys. To defray costs, the workhouse guardians farmed their children out. It kept the ratepayers happy. For a few pennies a day, they scraped their fingers raw in rag-picking shops or coughed their way through mountains of dust-yard ash, hunting for bits of unburned coal.

The porter spent the morning overseeing new arrivals and jumping at every whim of the workhouse master. At noon, Dunlap eased himself onto a favorite bench at his local. Over a pint and a cheese and pickle sandwich, he opened the newspaper. The story on page three made his stomach drop. MURDERED NURSE FOUND NEAR THE LONDON HOSPITAL. In the first line of the article was a name: Patience Milhous.

Months earlier, the porter had shrugged when he heard about Bertie Parker's death. *Not surprising.* The showman's sins had caught up with him. A few weeks back, he'd thought, *Funny that*, when he'd read that Mr. Atwater had been stabbed to death. Then, when he'd read that Willie Lomax had been shivved too, fear twisted in his bowels.

Now Milhous.

Hands shaking, he signaled the barman and asked for a whiskey. He tossed it back. *What are the odds?* He was a betting man, so he knew they weren't good. Furtively, he looked around the pub, searching the faces. From then on, he knew he'd be looking over his shoulder everywhere he went.

The porter reckoned he knew why, but *who* was harder to figure out.

Barney Dunlap had had a good run for over a decade. But once the new workhouse master and matron took charge, that old lark had ended. It forced him to sort out other ways to earn a quid or two on the side. Still, it lined his pockets while it lasted, all for unlocking a door. But the porter knew when it was time to fold. He was an old man, anyway, past it. It was time to retire to Brighton to live with his widowed sister. *That ought to be far enough.*

He'd tell the master in the morning. Work to the end of the month and collect his wages. If he left sooner, he'd be docked for it. No matter. He'd be careful.

Years of boys—one of them had decided it was time to pay.

That evening, in a very different part of London, another elderly man read a newspaper's account of the murder.

Andrew Lewis set the paper aside and reached for his glass. A tremor sent a few drops of sherry over the rim and onto the marble tabletop. He groped for his handkerchief and wiped away the spillage.

Thirty minutes earlier, he'd heard his granddaughter in the front hallway. For once, she was home in time for a drink before dinner. He hadn't much time to arrange his thoughts, to decide what he wanted to say or how to say it. He swirled the pale, golden liquid and watched it circle counterclockwise in his glass. The letter from the killer had infected his mind with a fear he couldn't shake.

From his window that morning, he'd watched his granddaughter close the gate and stride off, a solitary figure walking away from his protection. Then Julia stopped at the top of Circus Place and raised a hand to hail a cab. The doctor had craned his neck, looking up and down the curving roadway.

Days before, the killer had sent a lad to their door with the note. How long had he lurked, hidden behind the trees in the park across the street? Had he waited and watched until the letter was delivered? Dr. Lewis conjured him, a furtive creature melting into the shadows. For a doctor, he had too much imagination. His late wife had often told him so.

He hadn't felt so helpless since those weeks and months, years in the past, waiting for news of a ship overdue, fearing the worst, finally accepting the truth. On solitary walks or in waking hours before sleep released him, he had imagined the storm at sea, the clamor and confusion on deck, the howling wind and shredded sails. Boiling, surging waters rising to meet the lowering storm clouds, erasing the separation between sea and sky. And most terrible of all, his mind's eye showed him that moment when his beautiful boy, hollow-eyed and doomed, knew all was lost. So persistent were those fearful, waking images that Dr. Lewis had wondered if he were going mad.

But I'm not mad—not now. After that letter, he was right to be afraid.

Julia swept into the room. "Is that for me?" She picked up her glass and took a sip of sherry. "Lovely."

"How was your ride home?" Traffic and the state of the roads seemed a safe enough topic to start them off.

"The usual crush, with holiday shopping adding to the bedlam. I walked south and caught a cab along Little Alie Street. We rolled through fogs of steam drifting from the sugar refinery. Longer as the crow flies, but we avoided most of the traffic on Whitechapel High Street."

"Talking of the holidays, Mrs. Ogilvie asked if you'd see her about the menu for Christmas dinner, although I hardly know why she bothers to ask."

"Yes, it's the same every year. I suppose it's her sense of the fitness of things. I may be a doctor, but I am still the 'lady of the house.' It's my place to choose the sauce."

"Do you mind, my dear?"

"Not a bit." Leaning back, she lifted the toe of her right slipper to the fire grate and settled into her chair. "Hmm . . . this is nice."

"Julia."

She sat up. "What is it, Grandpa?"

"My dear, your involvement in this case, I'm very uneasy about it."

Inwardly, he cursed at the inadequacy of the word. Her gaze shifted to the newspaper at his elbow. He saw her read the headline from her chair.

"But my involvement is slight. I'm just the medical examiner, called on as doctors are in other cases."

"Why does it seem much more than that? The murder of this nurse you knew and that letter he wrote to you. Julie, he knows where you live."

"That wouldn't be hard. Our names are on the brass plate outside the door."

"He sent someone to our doorstep. Julia, I want you to listen to me. This man, this murderous lunatic . . ."

"Why are you and Richard so convinced I'm the object of his interest?"

"Richard?"

"Inspector Tennant."

"He wants you off the case as well?"

"I didn't say that."

"What does he say?"

Julia looked away. "That I should be careful." She got up and knelt at her grandfather's side. She put her hand over his. "Grandpa. These murders have nothing to do with me. Oh, he enjoys his games, all right, but I'm irrelevant to his deadly purpose. Something else is driving him."

His gaze fell away, lost in the flames of the fireplace. Her grandfather's voice caught when he said, "My dear, can we be sure of that?"

*   *   *

After dinner, Julia looked up from her copy of *Our Mutual Friend*. She bookmarked her place in the novel and set it aside.

Her grandfather had fallen asleep in his chair, his head tipped to the side, his spectacles in danger of slipping off his nose. Each time he exhaled, he pursed his lips and made a slight puffing sound. She glanced at the clock. *Only nine-thirty.* He seemed to be nodding off earlier and earlier.

Julia uncurled herself from her chair and stood over him. "Grandpa." She put her hand on the maroon velvet sleeve of his smoking jacket and gave him a gentle shake.

His eyes opened. "Hmm . . . what's that, my dear?"

"Time for bed, Grandpa." She slipped her other hand under his arm, helped him from the chair, and walked him up the staircase. When they reached the landing, he was leaning heavily on her arm.

"I can make it the rest of the way." He patted her cheek. "Go back to your Dickens, my dear."

She kissed him on the forehead. "Good night, Grandpa." She watched until his door closed.

Julia returned to the library and tugged the bell pull. When the housekeeper answered her summons, she asked her to sit.

"Mrs. Ogilvie, you're here all day with Grandfather. How does he seem to you?"

"Well, he's not the man he was two months ago. We both see that." Mrs. Ogilvie looked at her squarely. "And it's clear he frets about you, Doctor Julie. Every night close to seven, he's pacing the library, peering out the window. Looking for you."

"Has he always done that?"

The housekeeper shook her head. "Only the last few weeks. Since . . ." she nodded to the newspaper.

"I see. Thank you, Mrs. Ogilvie."

The housekeeper stood and wished her a good night.

Julia stared into the fire. *The case.*

She had been stung by Tennant's tone at the end of the nurse's autopsy, and her upper arms were still tender where he had grabbed her. *A female victim has thrown him off-balance*, she thought. Still, the coincidence of the nurse's murder so soon after their meeting was odd. Tennant was right about that. The amputation of the tongue was strange as well. *And the balloon in the victim's mouth.* She wondered about their placement in the other cases.

For Lomax, the killer had impaled it on the knife she'd extracted from his anus. She tried to remember the medical report about Bertie Parker—on the ground, she thought. They'd found the balloons for Atwater and Ball in their left breast pockets. *Placed over their hearts?* Well, the inspector would have to sort it out for himself. He'd made it clear he was interested in her medical opinions and nothing else.

Julia still didn't think she was in any danger. That was nonsense, and patronizing of him. *If Grandfather had been the doctor on the case . . .* She looked over at his empty chair.

But there was more at stake than professional pride and sparring with Richard Tennant.

Julia had to think.

CHAPTER 13

"She kept herself to herself." Constable O'Malley heard it again and again, a frustrating refrain.

He'd located Nurse Milhous's lodgings in Stepney in a once-grand town house off Arbour Square. At some point, the landlord had subdivided it into poky flats. The entire area exuded the shabby gentility of a formerly prosperous neighborhood going slowly to pot.

She'd rented a furnished flat but had added few personal touches. O'Malley found a hinged picture frame in the top drawer of her bedside table. It opened on the left to a faded drawing of an unsmiling young woman in an old-fashioned dress. The right side was empty, but a faint shadow had left its mark. Someone had removed the picture.

O'Malley searched a chest of drawers and peered under the bed. He pulled aside the counterpane and blankets and shifted the mattress. Underneath, he spotted a flat parcel tied with string, stuck between the webbing of the bedframe. In the package, he found a surprising number of pound notes.

Interviews with the nurse's landlady and fellow lodgers

elicited variations on a single theme. Nurse Milhous was a quiet woman of regular habits with no family or friends in evidence. Shopkeepers along the Commercial Road valued her as a customer. "Settled her account without a squeak," a grocer said. It was a tradesman's highest praise. Other than that, they had little of value to tell the constable.

He walked a few streets to St. Dunston's church and spoke to the verger. Patience Milhous was not a parishioner. The man had worked there for thirty years and knew no one with that surname. He suggested visiting Bow Church or St. Philip's near the London Hospital. O'Malley doggedly followed each lead, but Patience Milhous hadn't worshipped at either location. He wondered if she'd been R.C., like him. He'd check the local Catholic churches in the morning.

At day's end, O'Malley hauled himself up the ladder of an omnibus with nothing to show for his trouble. He settled onto a topside bench for the first stage of a slow, cold ride back to the Yard. Halfway along Whitechapel Road, the 'bus stopped in heavy traffic in front of the Blind Beggar public house. A preacher had erected a sign for the "East London Christian Mission" and called on the pub's patrons to forego "demon drink" and join his crusade.

Good luck with that, boy-o.

A woman wearing a Quaker-like cap and dress was handing leaflets to any who would take one. O'Malley sat bolt upright on the bench. *That first beat in Woolwich.* He remembered the girls with names like Amity and Charity and Patience who walked to the Friends Meeting House every Sunday morning.

He felt sure he wouldn't find the nurse's name on any Church of England parish register. Patience Milhous was a Quaker.

* * *

"That's an inspired guess, Constable," Tennant said the following morning. He leaned back in his chair. "It's a line of inquiry, at any rate."

"Especially since the guv and me came up dry," Graves said.

Tennant had visited every hospital in London, hoping to find some trace of Patience Milhous. For his part, the sergeant had flagged down all the cabbies and omnibus drivers he could find along the streets surrounding the Black Falcon Brewery. None remembered seeing Sir Harry Jackson on the night of the nurse's murder. And his coachman swore Sir Harry's carriage and horses had been stabled all day and evening.

"He could have hitched up one of the brewery nags and taken a cart." Graves shrugged. "But I doubt it—too risky. The night watchman might have seen him."

"The night watchman? What did he see? Anything?"

"Nothing much, guv. A light in Sir Harry's office, but he didn't see the brewer. Still, Jackson could have left a gas lamp burning."

"Too risky," O'Malley said. "What if the watchman knocked on the door to report something or ask a question?"

Tennant righted his chair. "All right. Drop Sir Harry for the moment, Sergeant. Switch your focus to Osborne. Someone must have seen him somewhere between Fleet Street and Mile End Lock. Constable, you'll need a list of all the Quaker meeting houses in London."

"East London, sir," he said. "I'll be starting there."

By late afternoon, Constable O'Malley's feet ached. He'd trudged across half of East London on a cold, overcast day in search of Patience Milhous. Wearily, he eyed a final stretch of road along a rusting iron fence. At the end, he'd probably find a locked gate, but he pressed on anyway. *Long odds*, he thought, but someone at his last stop had suggested he try the old Quaker cemetery on Thomas Street.

The Stepney Meeting House had closed its doors ten years earlier, but the burial ground was quiet and green and not overgrown. Through the bars, O'Malley spotted fresh flowers on scattered graves but no withered bouquets. Someone was looking after the dead. When he tried the gate, it swung smoothly on oiled hinges.

The cemetery was a small one. He walked up and down the rows of markers squinting at the fading inscriptions, looking for a name. He found it near the back. Milhous—a cluster of family graves dating back to the 1700s. Two names carved on the most recent headstone stood out clearly. Abigail, age thirty-three, the wife of William, died in 1826. Five years later, William Milhous, twelve years her senior, was buried in 1831.

The gate clanged, and O'Malley turned. An elderly lady carrying a basket of flowers looked at him curiously.

"Can I help you, luv? Looking for family?"

He removed his helmet and smiled. "Looking for *a* family, yes. And I think I found them." He pointed to the Milhous gravestone.

"Abigail was lovely. Consumption took her young."

"And William?"

The old lady pursed her lips. "They say you mustn't speak ill of the dead, but he was a hard man."

"The stone hasn't a child's name on it. Did they have children?"

"A daughter. Took her mum's death hard. Some do say she was a wild one, but he drove her to it. Him with his hard ways, that's my thinking. He was an apothecary; the girl worked with him in his shop until he died, sudden-like. Then she was off." She shook her head. "Money didn't last her long. Took to nursing after it was gone."

"Can you recall her name?"

"Patience. Patience Milhous."

O'Malley took a deep breath. "A last question, missus. D'you recollect where she nursed, by chance?"

She smiled a gap-toothed grin. "You're testing me, right and all, sonny. But I remember, all right. Patience didn't go far." She pointed to the hulking brick building on the other side of Thomas Street.

Whitechapel Workhouse.

Tennant held two letters. One he expected; the other was a surprise.

The nursing director at St. Thomas' wrote, "Miss Nightingale is in regular communication with all the nurses who served in her corps. A Patience Milhous never nursed with her in the Crimea. Furthermore, she never employed a secretary named Millicent Grant."

"Done and dusted," Tennant said, adding the letter to his file. *Patience Milhous, you were a clever fraud.*

Julia's grandfather had sent the second note: "If you can spare the time, would you join me for a drink at my club? I'll be at the Athenaeum this evening until six. If not today, pray suggest another day that might suit."

Tennant glanced at the clock. Twenty minutes to five, and he wasn't expecting his men to report until the following day.

He loosened his tie, opened the bottom drawer of his desk, and pulled out a fresh collar. When he popped the old one, his collar stud flew off, and he had to crawl around to find it. On his feet again, collar in place, he caught his reflection in the picture glass on the wall. Gray eyes stared back.

He straightened his tie and smoothed his hair. "Steady on," he said to his reflection. Then he grabbed his hat and overcoat and headed out the door.

Tennant hunched his shoulders against the bite of mid-December, pushing through the blasts of wintry wind. The traffic stopped him on the corner of Pall Mall and Waterloo Place just as the snow started falling. At the Athenaeum, he picked his way up the slippery steps of the portico and, looking around, knocked his boots against a Doric column. Inside the vestibule, he handed his damp hat and overcoat to a footman, confident they'd be returned to him brushed and dried. Then, pulling on his cuffs, he followed a servant into the smoking room.

Tennant nursed a second glass of a superb single malt, warmed by the glowing fire.

They'd talked about Dr. Lewis's medical school days in Edinburgh and touched lightly on Tennant's career in the Grenadier Guards. The doctor probed his views on modern policing. He canvassed the inspector's opinion on the likelihood of a general election and the prospects for a new reform bill in Parliament.

"Will the Lords try to block it, do you think?"

"Yes, but they'll probably fail," Tennant said.

Dr. Lewis held up his glass. "Another?"

"Thank you, sir, but no."

A few moments of silence followed. Tennant decided to help his host along.

"Doctor Lewis, it's many years since I sat in a comfortable chair at my late father's club and shared a drink with him. I thank you for the invitation; it's brought back happy memories. But I think you have something on your mind, sir, something you'd like to ask me."

Dr. Lewis put down his glass and sighed. "It's about Julia. I know I have no earthly right, and she'll be furious when she finds out I spoke to you."

"You'll tell her we met?"

"I'm not such a fool to mention it beforehand, but I won't

go behind her back." He smiled. "Well, that's not entirely true. I'd try saying I bumped into you on Whitehall Place if I thought she'd believe me." His smile faded. "I'm worried, Inspector, worried about Julia and her involvement in this case. I'm hoping you can reassure me."

"I'm not sure I can."

"That boy and the letter on our doorstep—she says it means nothing."

"I know that's her view. And she may be right. He enjoys his games."

"But you don't believe it."

"He's too dangerous for me to be sure of anything."

Tennant saw despair register on his host's face. His cheek muscles seemed to loosen and sag, and his shoulders slumped. "I was afraid you'd say that."

"I didn't tell your granddaughter, but the last time I was at the clinic, I pulled Jackie Archer aside. I gave him a constable's truncheon and told him to carry it whenever he walked her to a cabstand."

"Thank you, Inspector."

"It's not enough, sir. Jackie trains as a boxer. He's wiry and strong, but little more than a lad."

Dr. Lewis shook his head. "Julie refuses to take our carriage. Doesn't want to tie it up every evening. And she says it's too large and ostentatious for the backstreets of the East End. But enough is enough."

"Why not set up a contract with a hansom company? The London General is a sound one. Have a cabbie at the clinic door every evening at six sharp."

"It will be done tomorrow." The doctor pulled an agenda out of his breast pocket. He wrote down the name and tucked the notebook away. "One last thing, Inspector—two, actually." He cleared his throat. "About the examinations you ask

Julia to conduct . . . if the killer strikes again, perhaps you could call in another doctor? Consult with her on other cases?"

"I understand, sir. And the second thing?"

"Tomorrow evening, we're dining with a few family friends. Are you free to join us?"

Tennant thought about refusing. His long, unpredictable work hours provided an easy excuse.

"Thank you, Doctor. I'd be delighted."

The following day, Tennant listened to Constable O'Malley's report. For the first time in weeks, he felt a frisson of excitement. They were getting somewhere.

"Whitechapel Workhouse, that's where we'll be finding our answers, sir. Not the music hall. Mister Atwater was chaplain there and now the nurse."

"And let's not forget Sir Harry bleeding Jackson," Graves said. "When did Milhous start working there? Did the old girl know?"

O'Malley nodded. "Soon after the father died. His gravestone said 1831."

"That fits. Little Harry and his mum arrived in the cholera year—1832." Graves laughed. " 'Why would I kill a nurse?' he says to me." He slammed his fist into his palm. "While you and the constable go to the workhouse, what if I take another crack at Sir Harry? Ask him if he remembers a certain nurse from the old days. I'd enjoy that. What do you say, guv?"

"Yes . . . but be careful. And after you're done with Jackson, ask around at the *Illustrated London News*. Check the archives. See if the reporter has shown any interest in Whitechapel Workhouse."

Graves grinned. "Or maybe Osborne's another poor orphan laddie sent there to rot. I'll see what I can find out."

Tennant pulled out his pocket watch. "We'll meet back here at four."

*   *   *

Before the old porter let him in, the inspector had noticed the heavy oak doors stood slightly ajar.

"The gate isn't kept locked?"

The porter shrugged. "Not during the day. Why bother? The workhouse isn't a prison, is it? Paupers are free to go any time they like. Ratepayers would be glad if they left and never came back." He hitched up his trousers. A set of heavy keys jangled from a ring clipped to his belt. "Door's locked at night—nine o'clock sharp. Opens at six."

"I'd like to see the master of the workhouse."

"Who's asking?"

"Detective Inspector Tennant, Scotland Yard."

He hadn't noticed O'Malley standing behind him and hadn't guessed, Tennant thought. *And Barney Dunlap probably has a nose for a copper.*

The porter licked his lips. "I'll see if the master is in."

As Dunlap shuffled off, O'Malley said, "Shifty old creature."

A few minutes passed, and the porter returned. "The master will see you. Follow me."

He led them down a dark hallway lit by lamplights dimmed to the barest flame. All along the passageway, women in identical workhouse dresses knelt, scrubbing a floor that already looked clean. They passed a room where inmates, old women and a scattering of children, sat at rough, wooden tables, working at a task Tennant couldn't fathom. Lengths of fraying rope curled in piles at their feet. They picked it apart, separating it into strands by impaling it on long, narrow spikes and pulling. He could see the hands of the woman nearest the door. They were raw and bleeding.

"Oakum picking," the porter said. "They got to pick a pound a day. Bales of the stuff are sent off each week and rewoven into rope."

Halfway along the corridor, Tennant stopped between a pair of facing windows. They opened to courtyards on opposite sides of the hallway. Each space ended at a distant wing of the workhouse. Surrounded by forbidding brick walls, the courts reminded him of the exercise yard at Newgate Prison.

"Men's yard is on the right. Their ward is beyond. Women's wing is on the left. Kiddies are housed on the opposite side of the building."

"What about families that enter as a group?" O'Malley asked. "Mothers and their children, I'm thinking?"

"Eat separate, work separate, sleep separate. This is no bleedin' lodging house."

At his door, Mr. Withers, the workhouse master, curtly dismissed the porter. Dunlap shuffled out, leaving the door open a crack. Then he stopped to tie a bootlace. *Listening in*, Tennant thought.

"Close the door, if you will, Constable," the master said.

He doesn't miss much, Tennant thought. Windows in his office gave Withers a view of the empty courtyards and the dormitory wings beyond them. On that freezing morning, men and women shunned the outdoor spaces.

Withers gestured to a chair. "How can I help you, Inspector?"

"A few days ago, the body of a nurse was found not far from the London Hospital. I believe she once worked here."

"Patience Milhous. I saw the newspapers."

"You remember her."

"Oh, yes. Not long after I arrived, I fired her."

"May I know why, Mister Withers?"

"She was stealing from the infirmary's dispensary. After I took over as the master, I conducted an audit and found shortages in almost every category. After I dismissed her, one of the doctors on call told me he suspected she'd removed a vial of opium from his medical bag." He sniffed. "If I were in charge at the London, I'd check their supply cupboards."

"I'll make a note to tell them. But you didn't call in the police?"

"Left to me, I'd have had them arrest the woman, but the guardians didn't want a new scandal on their hands. Not long before we fired Milhous, the newspapers had splashed the story about Andover Workhouse all over their pages. The stories of the deplorable conditions there were still fresh in people's memories."

Tennant remembered: starving children stripping scraps of rotting meat and sucking the marrow from the animal bones they were supposed to be crushing up for fertilizer.

"I dismissed Milhous without a reference," Withers said, "thinking it would keep her from working again in a medical capacity. Instead, I was shocked to read that she was a nurse at the London Hospital at the time of her death."

"But not shocked by her murder?"

"By that as well, Inspector."

"Had she made enemies while she was here?"

"As far as I recall, not among the staff, but our turnover is considerable. You've met the only worker who would remember her—Dunlap, our porter."

"Did he know her well?"

"Thick as thieves, the two of them. But Dunlap has a feral cleverness about him. He covers his tracks well."

"Do you recall the year you dismissed her?"

He nodded. "Very well, indeed. It was 1854, not long after I arrived."

"What about the inmates? What did they think of her?"

Withers swung his chair around and gazed out a window. Tennant waited.

"Inspector, I'll tell you a hard truth. The ratepayers of Whitechapel and Spitalfields support this institution, but they want me to run it on a shoestring. As a result, I've never been able to hire and retain the staff I'd like. The guardians only agreed to sack Nurse Milhous because she was a thief. That she was a hard, uncaring woman interested them less. I was glad to have a reason to get rid of her."

"So a workhouse inmate mistreated by the nurse might have carried away a grudge."

"Murder seems an extreme response, Inspector, and a delayed one. She left twelve years ago. Still, Milhous worked here for several decades; that gives you a long list of suspects."

O'Malley looked up from his notebook. "Would she be nursing here in 1832, sir?"

"Possibly. I can check our records."

"I'd like the names of all those who worked with her," Tennant said. "I'll also need their last known addresses."

"That will take time, but it will be done. Before you go, you might want to talk to Dunlap. Our porter's last day of work is just before the New Year."

"Fired?"

"Retiring, and good riddance to him."

But Barney Dunlap couldn't help them—or wouldn't. He denied knowing Patience Milhous well, pleaded ignorance of her larcenies, and claimed he hadn't laid eyes on her since the day she walked out the gate. When Tennant demanded his new address, saying he might have questions for him later, Dunlap parted with it reluctantly.

Back at the Yard, Graves asked, "Do we believe the porter?"

"Something's off about him," O'Malley said. "Cold as a tomb, the workhouse was. And there he was, sweating like he'd plowed the lower field. And he kept jangling those fecking keys at his belt, all nervous-like."

Tennant, too, had noticed his unease. "Before he leaves, speak to him again, Constable. Nose around the neighborhood. Find his local; talk to anyone who shares a pint with him."

"Right, sir."

"And what did Sir Harry have to say, Sergeant?"

"Accused me of harassment. I ask you, guv, a peaceable bloke like me? When I pushed, he said he'd never been sick a day in his life. Never saw the inside of the workhouse infirmary. So 'how the bloody hell' would *he* know who worked there."

"Pretty thin," O'Malley said.

"Agreed, Constable. Sir Harry Jackson stays on our docket."

Kate decided that if Dr. Julie wouldn't give any thought to what she wore, she'd do her thinking for her. So she chose a silk gown in a deep russet that set off her chestnut hair and dark eyes. Kate spread it across the bed and stepped back, satisfied. She doubted she'd be overruled: the doctor usually breezed in with only minutes to spare and slipped into anything Kate handed her.

Avant-garde, the "artistic style," the dressmaker called it. The doctor's wardrobe had taken some getting used to, but she had to admit, it suited her.

The flowing silk fell from a high waist, without under-hoops or stiff crinolines. Kate placed a necklace and earrings next to the dress. Nodding, she scooped them up and moved them to the dressing table.

An hour later, Kate would have been pleased to know her choices had the desired effect. Tennant had just arrived and was handing Mrs. Ogilvie his top hat and cape when he looked up. Julia swept down the stairs; lamplight caught the flash of burnt-orange silk and the glow of garnets at her throat.

"Inspector." She extended her hand. He kissed it.

She stepped back, taking in his evening clothes. "My, don't you look a treat, as my old nanny would say."

Tennant made a mock bow. "Mine would return the compliment."

She laughed and took his arm. "In that case, let's repair to the drawing room and dazzle the guests."

At the end of dinner, Julia replaced her napkin and looked around the table. "Shall we?"

Tennant, seated at her right, rose to pull out her chair. Rather than go their separate ways—the men to brandy and cigars in the library, the women to tea in a sitting room—the company left for the drawing room in pairs. He offered Julia his arm and followed them.

Mrs. Ogilvie had set out glasses and decanters. She carried a tray of drinks to the guests on the other side of the room. Julia put her hand on the decanter and looked at him.

Tennant nodded. She handed him his port and said, "A peace offering."

He swirled the ruby liquid in his glass and breathed in. "It's a pleasure to declare a truce with such a fine vintage."

She poured herself a sherry. "My grandmother enjoyed a spot of something stronger after dinner. She was American, and my grandfather teased her about having a prejudice against our national drink—all that unpleasantness over the tea at Boston Harbor. And she objected to 'this English nonsense' of separating the sexes after dinner."

Tennant lifted his glass. "A toast to sage grandmothers. Mine was a source of boundless good advice at a time when I needed it badly. And when she died, she left me her house in town, along with a small income." He smiled. "Just enough to augment the Met's laughable pay; it keeps the creditors off my doorstep."

Julia hesitated. "What was the wisest counsel she gave you?"

"To ignore the world and take the job Sir Richard offered. I've never looked back."

"My grandmother gave me similar advice, and I sailed to Philadelphia." Julia's gaze dropped to the golden liquid in her glass. She waited until the catch in her throat eased. "I think she knew she was unwell, knew she'd never see me again. I remember her waving bravely from the dock at Southampton—my last memory of her."

"I'm sorry she didn't live to see you . . . triumph over the world."

"Is that what I've done? I'm not so sure. In the end, the world always seems to win." She smiled. "But that's much too somber for such a lovely evening."

She parted the drapes with her free hand and gestured to the trees on the other side of the curving roadway. "Look. Yesterday's snow is still clinging to the branches. Perhaps it will linger through Christmas." She let a moment pass. "Did you get caught in it on your way home from the Athenaeum?"

"Yes." He took a sip and eyed her over the rim of his glass.

"I want to talk to you about that."

She glanced over her shoulder and caught her Aunt Caroline watching them. Julia took his glass and set it down on the table next to hers. Then, taking his arm, she announced, "I'm going to show Inspector Tennant the library," and led him through the door.

After Julia closed the door behind them, he said, "I thought it wasn't polite to talk shop at a dinner party."

"My grandfather told me about your conversation, and what he asked you to do. You share his views, I know."

"I admit it. Are you angry?"

"Let's say I was annoyed that the two of you discussed my professional life without including me. And you met in a gentleman's club to do it."

"And now?"

She closed her eyes for a moment. "Even before this madman's killing spree, I knew my grandfather worried about me. He's had one attack, and I won't be the cause of another. He's been too good to me, loved me too unconditionally for stubborn ingratitude. And I won't risk his health by adding to his fears."

"He is afraid. That was clear to me."

"I know. Of course, had I been a grandson, he never would have sought you out. But I'm not going to argue the point or stand on some principle of supposed equality we both know doesn't exist."

"The world always wins." A moment passed. "What, then, are you saying?"

"Only this—if the killer strikes again, ask for another doctor." She looked away. "But if you want to consult me on other cases, I'm at your service."

He touched her lightly on the upper arm.

Julia smiled and took his hand. "Now let's return to the others before Aunt Caroline suspects an assignation."

She tried to lead him forward, but he wouldn't budge. When she turned, his face was inches away. He was so close she could see the dark rim and the tiny speckles of green in the gray of his eyes. For a moment, she thought he was going to kiss her. She held her breath as his gaze shifted to her hair. She followed his hand as it crossed her face.

"Let's give Lady Aldridge something to think about," he said.

A strand of her hair was coming loose from its clasp. Curling his finger around it, he released the lock from its clip. The tendril fell across her forehead.

She laughed and said, "Why not," sounding more collected than she felt. Then, pushing one side of his white tie askew, she stepped back. "There. That should do it."

As she passed through the door, she thought, *Well . . . a playful Richard Tennant. Who would have guessed?*

Julia assured Kate she'd had a lovely evening and had everything she needed. She bid her maid good night.

It hadn't taken her long to regret withdrawing from the case, but she wouldn't retract her decision. After a few desultory swipes with her hairbrush, she tossed it on her dressing table and stared at her reflection. Among her discontents was a dispiriting realization: she'd be seeing less of the inspector.

Julia liked him, even though he could be irritatingly taciturn and annoyingly opaque. Still, she found his equipoise a matter of fascination and a challenge. Wondering at its source, she took pleasure in prodding its edges, in shifting him slightly off-balance. That she rarely succeeded spiced the challenge.

She had enjoyed the evening more than she'd anticipated. He actually told her something about himself. *He had a grandmother.* Julia smiled into the mirror. *Fancy that.* And he showed he could join in a joke.

Still, she'd decided long ago that marriage and her profession, her calling, could never coexist. Over the years, Julia had tallied her sums, added and subtracted her gains and losses. On the whole, she'd been content with her bargain. But, just lately, she'd wondered if there was another way to live.

Some, she knew, ventured boldly outside the state of matrimony. It was rumored that Mr. Dickens had left his wife for a young actress. And Mary Ann Evans—Mrs. Lewes, as she styled herself, although the world knew she was nothing of the sort—lived openly with a married man. But Miss Evans, writing as George Eliot, was the author of *Silas Marner* and *The Mill on the Floss.* She was not the granddaughter of a respectable doctor.

But a marriage partnership—with someone who spurned the

rules, someone willing to invent new ones with her—was it possible?

Julia lowered the flame until the lamp went out. Then she opened her curtains to let the moonlight spill through the windows.

"Probably not," she said, slipping between the sheets.

CHAPTER 14

The day after the dinner party, Julia found herself humming "Pop Goes the Weasel" at odd hours of the day. She may have performed her last autopsy for the case, but she couldn't shake the murders or the song as she sorted instruments in the surgery and walked from ward to ward.

A lively tune is like an infection, she thought. *Once it's in your head, it's hard to shake.*

Julia was humming it when she stopped at a patient's bedside to watch Jackie change a bandage. He showed her the wound before wrapping the leg.

"It's healing nicely, I think," he said.

Nodding, Julia said to the patient, "You've been in good hands, Mister Evans."

He was the last of the omnibus accident patients still in their care. Julia had been worried about the bump on his head; four days earlier, it had been the size of a child's fist.

"Any headache this morning?" He shook his head. "Can you follow my finger from side to side?" Julia watched his eyes move left to right. "How about getting out of bed? Any dizziness?"

"Not a scrap, Doctor. I think I'm ready to be sprung. Twice, Jackie walked me to the loo and back. No worries—right, mate?"

Julia looked at her assistant. He nodded. "Shipshape and Bristol fashion, Doctor."

She thought, *Jackie's picked up his nautical slang from Q. Turns of phrase spread like infections, too.*

"Right," Julia said. "We'll send a message to your wife, lay on some transportation, and you can be on your way this afternoon."

She picked up the chart clipped to the foot of his bed, humming as she scanned the recent additions to the medical record. Then she added a notation and scrawled her signature at the bottom of the page. When she looked up, a pair of faded blue eyes squinted from across the room.

"Is that you, Doctor Lewis? Can't see you properly."

Julia walked over to his bed. "How are you today, Mister Watkins?"

"Better for your asking, Doctor. It's a tonic you are, and no mistake."

Benny Watkins was a charmer. The oldest patient in the ward, his recovery from pneumonia had been touch-and-go.

"Well, if that's true, another few days of my company are just what the doctor ordered." She patted his knee. "Don't worry. We'll have you home for Christmas."

"You know, Doctor, listening to you put me in mind of—"

"Excuse me," Nurse Clemmie said. "A messenger is here from the Inspector of Nuisances." She lowered her voice. "Another possible cholera outbreak."

"Tell him I'll be with him in a moment." Julia smiled at Benny. "Jackie and I have to leave you, Mister Watkins, but Nurse Emily will rub some liniment on your chest. And when I get back, I want to hear that you napped right through to teatime."

After Julia left, the nurse pulled up a chair and rubbed slow circles across Benny's chest.

"Took me back, didn't it?" he said. "Listening to the doctor humming that tune. I remember Little Jacko, a tiny tyke, popping out of that music box, his pa sweeping down on a trapeze, grabbing him up, balloons and all." Benny shook his head. "'Pop Goes the Weasel' and the old days at the Eagle. There's nothing like 'em now."

Nurse Emily nodded and smiled and rubbed.

At Scotland Yard, Tennant and his men tested the links that joined the victims. The inspector wrote six names on slips of paper and arranged them across his desk.

"Our killer marked all his victims with his signature balloons," Tennant said. "But there are differences, so let's start with the method of murder."

O'Malley dragged four slips out of the lineup. "Mister Atwater; our two music-hall fellas, Bertie Parker and Willie Lomax; and our latest victim, Patience Milhous. The killer mutilated them all."

"But not the banker or company director," Tennant said. "That leaves out Thomas Rigby and Sir Maxwell Ball."

"Our killer didn't slice up Sir Maxwell, but he shoved a handful of shite down his throat. Considering the cause of death, a knife thrust to the heart . . ." O'Malley moved Sir Maxwell Ball down with the others.

Tennant nodded. "That leaves Thomas Rigby as the outlier."

"Geography sets the banker apart too, sir," O'Malley said.

"Agreed. The killer tracked him to North London, well outside his East End hunting grounds."

O'Malley looked away. "Something . . . something about Rigby. 'Tis always nagging at me."

"You spotted that balloon, mate," Graves said. "That links him to all the other victims."

"I'm thinking, sir . . ."

"Yes, Constable?"

"We're looking for a single 'why' that links them all. Could the killer have more than one motive in him?"

Graves pulled his hand from his pocket and waved away the suggestion. "Never mind motive and the cause of death. Let's look at the victims who knew each other, see where that takes us. Bertie Parker and Willie Lomax, for example. They were friends. Both performed at the Eagle. And there's Sir Maxwell Ball; we know he fancied a bit of music-hall skirt." He moved the company director's name to join the pair of old performers.

O'Malley assembled a different trio. "We traced Willie Lomax and Mister Atwater to the molly house. And Bertie Parker was a sodomite, as well."

Tennant reached across and drew two names toward him. "Mister Atwater, the one-time chaplain, and Patience Milhous, the nurse—their time at Whitechapel Workhouse overlapped."

"It's a ruddy merry-go-round," Graves muttered. "And it still doesn't make sense."

Tennant tapped a slip of paper. "In a web of connections, the banker stands alone again."

"What about the suspects?" Graves elbowed O'Malley. "Do you fancy your pal Rollie Jakeways as the killer?"

The constable ignored his sergeant's jibe. "'Tis three of the victims that Jakeways knew, but he's got nothing else incriminating in him."

"Too bad. He sounds like a smug bastard."

"He isn't linked to the workhouse or connected to the nurse or the hospital—as far as we know," O'Malley said. "But Johnny Osborne and Sir Harry Jackson saw Patience Milhous at the London only days before her murder."

Tennant swept the papers into a pile. "And Sir Harry Jackson was a workhouse boy when Nurse Milhous ran the infirmary."

"According to the workhouse master, she was a hard woman," O'Malley said.

Tennant nodded. "And we have a theory—and it's just a theory, mind you—that Sir Harry nursed a slow-burning fury over the death of his mother in the cholera epidemic of 1832."

"And all the deaths this year could have set him off," O'Malley said.

Sir Harry's slip had ended up on the top of the pile. Graves drummed his fingers on it. "Jackson never saw the inside of the infirmary, or so he says. But his mother did. Sickened and died there, didn't she? So my money's on him, guv."

"What's happened to Osborne?" O'Malley said. "Last week, you were sizing him up for a noose."

Graves tapped his temple. "Got to keep an open mind, Constable. It's the secret of sound police work."

"Are you forgetting Doctor Lewis told us the reporter knew about the balloons? How is that possible, Sarge?"

"Paddy, we all know a bobby or two who can be bought for a pint. Osborne said as much when I questioned him."

"One part of his story checked out," O'Malley said. "I found those glue factories on the canal, just where he said they were."

Graves grunted. "Bet you smelled them a mile off. Before his business went pear-shaped, my old uncle had a warehouse along that canal. Stank to high heaven."

"What about our witnesses?" Tennant said. "We only have two—the night watchman who saw Atwater on the street and the doorman at Sir Maxwell's club who was the last to see him alive. Both saw the victims speaking to women."

"*Possibly* a woman in the doorman's case," Graves said.

"It could be a murderous pair we're looking at, a man and woman working together," O'Malley said.

There was a cough from the doorway. "Excuse me, Inspector."

"What is it, Constable?"

"I've been sent to fetch you, sir."

He sighed. "Chief Inspector Clark?"

"Higher." He pointed to the ceiling. "Sir Richard wants to see you."

"What now?" Graves muttered.

Twenty minutes later, Tennant returned to his office.

Graves was leaning forward in his chair, his right knee jumping like a piston. "Good news or bad, guv?"

"As it happens, Sergeant, *you* were Sir Richard's first topic of discussion. The commissioner had a visitor this morning: Sir Harry Jackson."

Graves stopped fidgeting. "Crikey."

"From what I can tell, Sir Richard sent him off with a flea in his ear. The commissioner had read your report. He called it 'a solid interview of a possible suspect.' Sir Richard asked me to tell you so."

The sergeant let out a long breath, but Tennant wasn't surprised. Sir Richard had been the head of Scotland Yard for thirty-seven years. Tennant had seen politicians rise and fall, but his godfather remained at his post, unassailable and immune to outside interference.

"Sir Richard complimented you as well, Constable. Tracing Nurse Milhous back to Whitechapel Workhouse was 'a fine piece of work,' he said. The commissioner is putting your name on the promotion list. Congratulations—it's sergeant stripes for you, Paddy."

"Thank you, sir. My sister, now, she'll be the happiest one to hear it. With two kiddies and another one on the way, it's glad she'll be to have me out of her back bedroom."

Graves punched his shoulder. "Perfect timing, mate."

Two days after the dinner party, Julia Lewis knelt beside a body in the shadow of a railway viaduct. She had received a note from Tennant that honored her offer and her grand-father's request. He had a corpse, a victim not connected to the case, that needed a medical examiner.

The girl had jumped from the pedestrian walkway or had been pushed. Julia couldn't tell. She'd landed at the shallow edge of the canal, striking her head on a pillar along the embankment.

Someone had thrown a tarp over the girl's body. Julia pulled it aside. Her emaciated arms and legs showed no evidence of bloating, so she hadn't been dead for long. Her thinness emphasized the rounded mound at her waist. If she'd jumped, two lives ended that morning in one terrible act of despair. Julia lifted the girl's left hand out of the shallow water. She had no wedding ring on her finger.

The spray of freckles across the bridge of the girl's nose and the way they stood out against the lifeless alabaster of her skin made Julia's hand tremble. And the long, auburn tresses—she closed her eyes, tried to switch off the memory. Then she stood up too quickly, took a step back, and lost her balance. Tennant grabbed her under the elbow, supporting her against his upper arm and shoulder until she regained her footing.

"Thank you," Julia said. "I skipped breakfast this morning."

"Do you see anything inconsistent with suicide, Doctor?"

"No." She picked up her bag and turned away.

"You're finished?"

She nodded. Tennant watched her make her way up the bank. She reached the top quickly and strode away, disappearing around a corner.

"What the blazes?" he said through gritted teeth.

The inspector left Graves to supervise the removal of the body and scrambled awkwardly up the incline. By the time he reached the road, Julia was thirty yards away. He swore under his breath when his left boot skidded on loose gravel, twisting his knee.

Tennant struggled to close the gap between them. When he finally caught up to her, he grabbed her by the elbow.

"What in God's name was that back there?" He jerked his thumb over his shoulder. "You said you wanted to continue consulting for the Yard. If I wanted a doctor who'd give two minutes to that poor wretch, I'd have asked for Abernathy."

Julia pulled her arm from his grasp and looked away.

"If you're too busy, Doctor, or if a case like this isn't interesting enough for you, I'll call in someone else next time."

Julia's head snapped up. "Her name was Helen."

Tennant looked back over his shoulder. "You knew her?"

"Not the girl by the canal. Someone else."

"I don't understand."

"Of course, you don't. A chance resemblance to someone I failed utterly, someone important to me." She looked him up and down. "The iron Inspector Tennant wouldn't know what that feels like; I doubt such a person exists for you. But I'll tell you what it's like. It's hell."

Tears slid down her cheeks. Roughly, with the sleeve of her jacket, she tried to rub them away. "I assure you, Inspector, that 'poor wretch' will have my full attention during her postmortem."

He stopped her when she turned to walk away, took her arm, and pushed open a coffeehouse door.

Tennant returned to their booth, balancing two steaming cups. A waiter followed with a plate of rolls and butter.

"You said you hadn't eaten any breakfast."

"Thank you."

He sat on the bench across from her and nodded to her coffee. "Drink it slowly. I asked the owner to put a little brandy in it."

Julia took a sip and sat back in her seat. "Hmm. It's off-license for serving alcohol. Someone may report you to the police."

He cleared his throat. "I'm sorry. Will you accept my apology?"

She nodded and nibbled at a piece of her buttered roll. Tennant waited until the waiter poured a second cup.

"Can you tell me about that girl?"

At first, he thought she wasn't going to answer him. Then she looked up from her plate.

"She reminded me of Helen, my friend in Philadelphia. We were in medical school together."

"I see."

Julia leaned back on the bench. "It never leaves you—what you could have done. What you should have done goes 'round and 'round in your head. Helen came to me, wanting to talk. The night she jumped to her death."

"And you believe you could have stopped her?"

"I saw she was upset, but I was busy. I had a final paper to finish." Julia stopped. "No. That's a lie. I'd finished the thing, reviewed it countless times." She pushed herself back from the table. "Pride." She spit out the word. "I wanted it to be perfect, to deny my professor the pleasure of finding fault with it."

Tennant stayed silent. Julia picked at the remains of her roll, tearing off bits.

"All autumn, Helen had been unhappy. She spent hours in my room, questioning her calling as a doctor, talking late into the night while I tried to hide my impatience. Then, after Christmas, she changed. Helen became quiet. Secretive. Several nights a week, she returned home late—working in the laboratory, she told me."

Julia pushed the plate away, her roll in fragments.

Dully, she said, "I never asked her what was wrong. I was happy, you see, happy to be left alone to get on with my work. But that night, for the first time in months, Helen wanted to talk. And I didn't have time for my friend." She balled her hand into a fist and struck the table, rattling the cups. "That bloody paper—what does it matter now?"

"Is it possible you're too hard on yourself? You said your friend had been unhappy for nearly a year. Often, there's little one can do to—"

"She was pregnant," Julia said. "The postmortem revealed it. Two weeks left of medical school . . ." She shook her head. "Had I known, I could have taken her home with me to London. Grandfather could have arranged for her to give birth at a clinic on the Continent. He's done it often enough. Helen had a practical problem. I could have provided a solution . . . if only I'd put the paper aside and listened to my friend."

Julia closed her eyes. "I dream about it. Often."

Tennant said nothing at first. She had asked if he knew what it was like to fail someone. He thought about his mother, remembered her contempt for his new profession. How, after his father's disgrace, she withheld her small stores of sympathy and support. And Tennant's father—he died knowing he'd failed as a lawyer, believing he'd failed as a husband. He thought of Isobel and the speed at which she cut her losses and traded up for the son of an earl. As far as he knew, neither his mother nor Isobel ever betrayed a moment's regret.

Then Tennant thought of his own life of deliberate solitude. Still, he hesitated; reticence was a habit hard to break.

Finally, he cleared his throat. "You've made me recall times in my life when others failed me and ways I've stumbled, as well. But I was lucky; those experiences ended in heartache, not tragedy. You weren't as fortunate. But to take the blame . . ." He shook his head.

"If only." Julia slumped back on the bench. "They're the saddest words in the language."

"Absent without leave," he said gruffly.

She looked up. "Sorry?"

"That's your self-accusation, but even our military code recognizes gradations of guilt. You condemn yourself for not being there when you were needed. You've forgotten you hid your impatience and listened to your friend all those months. And had she confided in you the day *after* you turned in your paper, you would have moved heaven and earth to help her. Isn't that true?"

A few seconds ticked by before Julia nodded.

"Others in your position might have turned their backs." He shook his head. "We both know how cruel the world can be to 'fallen women.' That pathetic creature in the canal is proof of that. Still, words mean little unless *you* feel the truth of them."

She looked down at the crumbled remains on her plate. "To feel a different truth." She said it slowly. "It's a hard lesson, but I thank you for your words." She smiled uncertainly. "And for listening. Sometimes, one needs to peel the plaster back, expose a wound to the air."

He nodded gravely. "You would know best about that, Doctor."

On Christmas Eve, Julia's cab pulled up to her house on Finsbury Circus just as a group of carolers began the final verse of "We Wish You a Merry Christmas."

In keeping with tradition, when they sang, "We won't go until we've got some," Mrs. Ogilvie and a kitchen maid appeared with a tray of Christmas cookies. Julia exchanged good wishes with them as she ascended the steps, and they headed off. The lead singer, his lantern swinging from a pole, lighted their way to the town house next door.

In the foyer, Julia pulled off her gloves and touched her cheek to the housekeeper.

"You're freezing, Doctor Julie." Mrs. Ogilvie took her cape. "Emma lit the fire in the library an hour ago. Go straight in and warm yourself."

Julia rubbed her hands together. "Is the tree up?"

"Yes. And Lady Aldridge is adding some final touches."

"Rearranging all the ornaments, you mean."

Mrs. Ogilvie smiled. "I'll send Emma in to set out the sherry."

In the library, Julia kissed her aunt and wished her a happy Christmas Eve. Then she stood back to assess the tree.

"Well?" Aunt Caroline said. "What do you think, my dear?"

"Perfect."

She knew by heart what her aunt's next words would be. With a firm nod, Lady Aldridge gave her yearly verdict. "A German tradition, but a good one. Of course, Prince Albert gets all the credit. But, as a girl, I remember Christmas trees from Queen Charlotte's time, a half century before the prince consort came along."

"Yes, Aunt. But you must admit, he made them a fixture in every home."

"And very festive they are. All over London, you can see candlelights on branches winking between the curtains."

Julia took two glasses of sherry from the tray, passed one to her aunt, and took a sip.

"Hmm. Lovely."

When Julia sank into a chair by the fire, her Aunt Caroline wasted no time. She sat next to her niece and fixed her with a direct gaze.

"That was a pleasant evening on Wednesday. The guests were so congenial."

Let the interrogation begin, Julia thought. She'd been expecting it.

"Anyone in particular, Aunt?"

"Don't be coy, my dear. It doesn't suit you. I want to know all about this policeman. Who is Richard Tennant?"

Julia lifted an eyebrow. "I'd like to know, too, but I can give you the bare facts."

"Well, it's a start. Proceed."

Julia recited his biographical details, as far as she knew them, and explained their professional association.

Her aunt nodded. "His choice of profession is odd, certainly. On the other hand, he is quite presentable; his manners are impeccable, and he is handsome in a forbidding sort of way." She flicked her hand dismissively. "But none of this is to the point. I want to know how you feel about him."

"Well . . . at first, I wasn't sure I liked him at all, but I find I do. And you're right, he's quite attractive. But you understand the difficulties. Before I left for Philadelphia, you spelled them out for me, in this very room, if my memory serves."

"You resented my interference?"

Julia got up and kneeled by her aunt's chair. "No. What you said was true, and you spoke from the heart."

Aunt Caroline drew a breath. "At that moment, it was full of the loss of your uncle, I think. That your pursuit of a medical career might rob you of the kind of happiness we had; it seemed a steep price to pay."

"All the sacrifices you mentioned—of marriage and children—none of that has changed." Julia rose and returned to her chair. "I think the girl of twenty who left for America didn't fully understand the costs. They are clearer to me at twenty-eight."

"My dear, if the woman could speak to the girl, would she advise her to change her life's course?"

Julia shook her head. "It's difficult to explain—not to myself, but to others. To be a doctor means everything to me. It is who I am, although many would say the feeling is unseemly in a woman. In marriage, we both know that one partner must always give way. We know who that person is; it will never change."

"Well, *this* woman of nearly seventy may have been wrong all those years ago. You must make the change you want. If you care for this man, seize your chance."

"I barely know him, Aunt, and he's not an easy man to understand." She folded her arms. "And you realize, as a married woman, I would have no independent legal identity. It's absurd, but the law would declare me a 'feme covert,' covered by the full protection—and authority—of my husband. My property would be his to command."

"My father used the Court of Chancery to protect my fortune, Julia. Your grandfather would do the same for you."

"Yes, and the court would appoint a guardian to oversee how I spent every penny. It's absurd. And while my inherited wealth would be protected from my husband, any wages I earn as a doctor would be his by law."

"But he might not—"

She held up her hand. "Even if he leaves my money untouched, there is the practical matter of contracts. The law doesn't allow wives to sign them. Aunt, I run a clinic. I engage all manner of men to provide services for it. But as a married woman, I couldn't hire the dustman who carts away the rubbish."

Lady Aldridge waved away her objection. "I'm sure that's easily arranged."

Julia frowned into the fire. "And there's another thing, although one is never supposed to speak of it." She looked up. "Aunt, allow me to be frank with you. Richard Tennant is a man well into his thirties. He's unmarried and a former army officer. Do you know that a full third of all men treated in military hospitals suffer from venereal diseases?"

Lady Aldridge shook her head. "Are you serious, my dear? Is this really an argument against matrimony?"

"More and more, I see the illness in the wedded women I treat. The danger increases when they marry a mature husband; one hardly expects celibacy from such a man. In marriage, a woman risks more than her heart. She risks her health, as well."

"If so, I suppose no one should marry." Her aunt sighed. "Life is full of risks. You must choose the ones that are worth taking."

Julia stood and gave the coals a few sharp thrusts with the

poker. "I wish things were different, but it's not in my power to remake the world. No, Aunt, I'm afraid I'm destined for spinsterhood." She turned from the fire. "Perhaps I'll keep cats for company."

"Don't be so certain about it. And don't underestimate Richard Tennant. He might be just the sort of man to marry an unconventional partner. For someone of his class, his choice of profession makes him almost as unusual as you."

"You forget one thing. Even if I *were* interested in the inspector, you may be overestimating his regard for me."

"Perhaps." Lady Aldridge took a sip of her sherry. "But I observed him closely when you were together. Elderly aunts have a fine eye for this sort of thing."

Julia smiled. "I've seen more of him than you have, Aunt. I think I bemuse him more than anything else—or amuse him. It's hard to tell. And more than once, he's made it clear to me that he's utterly conventional in his thinking about women. No, it's not possible. Marriage with him would not be a companionable union of equals."

On Christmas Eve, Richard Tennant boarded the five o'clock train to Adisham. Two nights before, he'd felt a powerful desire to wake up in Kent on Christmas morning. The following day, he sent a telegram to his old housekeeper; Hannah would have his room waiting for him.

For Tennant, summers on the lake were his happiest times. While his reasons for visiting in the dead of winter were clear to him, where he was headed was cloudier. That, somehow, Julia was at the root of it, he understood. He wanted to walk for miles across the windswept downs and think.

On the platform, he waved away the stationmaster's offer of a pony trap. He had only his carpetbag and would cover the two miles to the lodge on foot. His left leg had been bothering him less lately, and the exercise would do him good if he took it easy.

Walking along the road at night intensified his sense of leaving one world behind and entering another. He'd exchanged the acrid odors of London town for breaths of air that carried scents of pine and hints of hayfields lately mown. And the stars: in the city, they were invisible beyond the smoke, but in Kent, they exploded like frozen fireworks across the black dome of the sky.

Rounding the curve, he spotted the glow of candles framed in the diamond windowpanes of the house. Hannah would be on the lookout for him. He unlatched the gate that separated the garden from the apple orchard beyond. *Home*—the word surprised him. The house was not the one he had lived in as a boy. But with each visit to his aging father, the sensation had grown; it only deepened during the summer holidays after his death.

Five years before his father died, he sold the great house, severing the lodge and orchard from the sale. He lived there, content, for the final years of his life. The family finances, already strained by the scandal, were made worse by his wife's living away from him in town. Tennant remembered her repressed fury when the lawyer read his father's will. He'd deeded Hannah the lodge and left her a modest annuity. Tennant would inherit both after she died—a father's sole legacy to his son.

It was clear to Tennant what those bequests had meant— clear to his mother, as well. At last, near the end of his life, his father had found joy with a warm and loving companion. Tennant's only wish—no, he was wrong about that, foolish to regret it came late for the old man. His father had the wisdom to take the happiness life presented him. Tennant hoped he would do the same if it were ever offered. Perhaps that example was his father's final and most valuable gift.

The following day, after services at the village church and a meal of Christmas turkey and apple tart, Tennant left the lodge and logged miles across the Kentish downs. He arrived home pleasantly exhausted but no surer than when he left. Still, as he watched Hannah heat a poker in the fire, plunge it sizzling into a cup of cider, and pass it along to him, he understood the simple riches of his father's final days and the poverty of his own last years.

On Boxing Day, his brief holiday was at an end. As the train gathered speed and pulled away from the station, Tennant knew he wanted something that, likely, was beyond his reach.

CHAPTER 15

Two days after Christmas, the knocker-up had nearly finished his rounds.

For sixpence a week, he woke his clients by rapping on ground-floor shutters or tapping with his stick at second-story windows. His service was the only way many laboring men on early shifts could get up in time for work. He'd rarely give some huddled figure a second glance in the early hours before daybreak. Someone drunk or sleeping rough, he'd think. But tired as he was and longing for his bed, he couldn't mistake what he'd seen.

A constable heard the pounding of boot leather ricocheting off the brick walls of the workhouse. He swung his bull's-eye lantern until he caught a running, stumbling figure in its beam. The man halted a few steps from the bobbie. Doubled over, gasping, his breath thick in the cold air, the knocker-up dropped his long, narrow pole and tried to catch his breath.

He pointed over his shoulder. "On Thomas Street. He's dead."

The constable rounded the corner and found a man curled

on his side, facing away, trousers pulled to the ankles. As he raked his light over the body, the policeman caught a flash of something protruding from his buttocks.

Reluctantly, the knocker-up agreed to stay with the victim while the constable sought help. As the policeman turned the corner and passed the oak gates of Whitechapel Workhouse, he thought of its porter. He'd send the man to the police station at Bethnal Green and return to the corpse.

The constable knocked. No answer. He pounded again, and the heavy door opened a crack under the force of his hammering. Surprised, he pushed, and it creaked open. The constable swung his lantern around the entryway and spotted the open door of a small bedchamber.

The policeman called out. "Dunlap? You there, mate?"

The room was empty, the covers on the bed thrown back. The flickering light of a candle moved along a hallway toward the constable. The master of the workhouse appeared in his nightshirt and slippers.

"What's going on, Constable?" He looked around. "Where is Dunlap?"

"I'll thank you to dress, sir, and accompany me around the corner. I'll need you to identify a body."

"What the devil do you mean?"

"I think it's your porter. He's dead."

Sergeant Graves volunteered to oversee the street-by-street search for witnesses while Tennant and O'Malley focused on the workhouse.

They questioned both the knocker-up and the constable on the beat. Neither man had seen anything unusual before the discovery of the body. Next the inspector interviewed the orderlies on duty in the workhouse infirmary. Its windows overlooked Thomas Street, where the porter's body was found. No one had heard a thing.

They turned their attention to Dunlap's room. "It won't be taking us long," O'Malley said, looking at the bare space. "He's made it easy for us."

Barney Dunlap had packed up before he died. He'd filled a crate with his few household items: a cooking pot, some chipped, brown crockery, a tankard—items that testified to an impoverished life. But a carpetbag stuffed with clothing told a different story.

O'Malley tossed the shirts and other garments onto the bed and felt around at the bottom of the bag. A panel of dark, stiffened felt yielded to the constable's fingers. Underneath the false bottom was a flat package wrapped in newspaper. It held twenty gold sovereigns and a thick wad of pound notes. Next to it, he found an agenda.

O'Malley whistled. He handed Tennant the notebook and started counting.

"A hundred, a hundred and ten—over a hundred and twenty quid in paper, sir."

Tennant paged through the notebook. "He's listed names, dates, and small money amounts going back two years."

"Not likely on the up-and-up," O'Malley said. "Or why hide it away? Some kind of shakedown, most like."

"Let's find the workhouse master. Perhaps Mister Withers can shed some light."

The inspector spotted a girl sweeping the hallway and gave her a penny to fetch the master. When Withers arrived, Tennant passed him the agenda. With each turn of a page, the master's expression soured.

"It's a list of local merchants and artisans," he said. "Men who provide supplies and services to the workhouse. It's part of the porter's duties to oversee deliveries and arrange all needful repairs. Clearly, Dunlap made arrangements with these men that lined his pocket at the expense of the ratepayers." Withers handed the notebook back to the inspector.

"You suspected nothing?"

"I knew Dunlap was a villain. What I lacked was proof. Is this behind his murder—a falling-out among thieves?"

"I don't think so. Something else, entirely."

The master nodded to the notebook. "When you're done with it, I'd like the agenda back. The workhouse guardians will be interested to see that list."

"Of course. Had the porter been behaving oddly of late? This retirement, for instance, was it long-planned or a sudden decision?"

"Sudden. Dunlap wanted to leave before his two-week notice was up. He only stayed because I threatened to dock his pay." His face paled. "Good God. He'd be alive today if I'd let him go."

"You couldn't have known that. Was the man angry about your decision?"

"Oh, yes. And he seemed . . ."

"Yes, Mister Withers?"

"Now that I think of it, he seemed shiftier than usual. Nervous. Edgy."

"Sir?" O'Malley had spread out the newspaper Dunlap used to wrap the parcel. "Look at the headline—MURDERED NURSE FOUND NEAR THE LONDON HOSPITAL."

"I think we know why he was in a hurry to leave," Tennant said. "He was afraid he was next on the killer's list."

O'Malley nodded. "Desperate to scarper, but too greedy to leave money on the table. Left it too late, in the end."

It all began here, Tennant thought. The links they'd turned up to the music hall and the water scandal were secondary, at best. Something seeded itself at Whitechapel Workhouse. It festered and grew into an obsession, something that involved the porter and the nurse.

"How long was Nurse Milhous here, Mister Withers?"

"I checked our records. She arrived in 1832. I dismissed her in 1854."

"What about the porter? Do those years overlap his tenure?"

"He was here before the Poor Law reorganization in '34, so yes."

"It's a lot of ground to cover, but I'll see your record books, if I may," Tennant said. "How are they arranged?"

"We keep biennial ledgers of all admissions, departures, and deaths."

"We'll begin with the last years the nurse was here. Let's start with the record books covering 1842 to '54. We'll work backward from there, if we must."

"I'll send them to you. Do you plan to use this room, Inspector?" When Tennant nodded, the master looked up at the single oil lamp. "You'll need more light and a place to work. I'll make the arrangements."

After Withers left, Tennant turned up the light, and O'Malley packed away the evidence of Dunlap's larcenies. Ten minutes later, four inmates carried in a table and two chairs, a box of candles, and six heavy volumes. They'd start reading the books, back to front, beginning with 1854.

Tennant handed O'Malley that volume. "Let's see if anyone connected to this investigation turns up."

It was slow reading because the entries listed everyone, the long-term residents and the "casuals" admitted to the workhouse for a day at a time. They'd barely started when the constable posted at the workhouse gate interrupted with a message for the inspector.

"A runner from the Yard says the chief wants to see you, sir."

Bloody hell, what now? Tennant closed the volume for 1851–52. "Thank you, Constable. Find Sergeant Graves and ask him to report here. He can take over for me, Paddy."

Then the inspector followed the constable out the door. A few minutes later, Graves showed up.

O'Malley looked up from a ledger. "Canvass turn up any witnesses, Sarge?"

"Not yet. I left a pair of coppers to finish the job. What's the drill?"

"Find yourself a volume and start reading."

"So we divide and conquer." Graves picked up the two ledgers that covered 1849 to 1852. "I'll get started on these."

They read through line after line of neat, copperplate script, pages of it, until their eyes itched and watered. After an hour, Graves looked up.

"Paddy . . . mate, will you give those bleeding knuckles a rest?"

"Sorry, Sarge, bad habit."

They read on. Finally, O'Malley was the first to surrender. "That's it, back through 1848. Let's throw in the towel."

"I'm almost through with 1849," Graves said without looking up. "One more page."

"If you don't quit soon, 'tis a blind man you'll be, Sarge."

"Done." The sergeant closed his volume. "If we go back another ten years, we'll both be cross-eyed. Could you do with a pint, Paddy?"

"That I would. I could murder a Guinness now."

"Then let's find a pub." Graves picked up the completed volumes and passed them to an inmate to return to the master.

Outside the workhouse, O'Malley said, "At the end of the day, do you ever wish you had a wife and kiddies to go home to?"

"Not me, Paddy; free and easy, that's my motto. 'Trouble and strife' rhymes with wife—ask any Cockney." Graves pointed to a pub at the end of Charles Street. "Let's try that one."

"We're closing in, Sarge," O'Malley said as they crossed the road. "The answer is in those ledgers somewhere. I feel it."

"I think you're right, Paddy." He clapped him on the back. "Now let's have that pint. We've earned it."

The next day, Graves and O'Malley resumed their search through the ledgers while Inspector Tennant returned to the brewery to question Sir Harry Jackson. He waited twenty minutes while the secretary looked for him on the factory floor. Finally, the brewer arrived coatless and cross, his sleeves unbuttoned and rolled above his muscular forearms.

"Good morning, Sir Harry."

"It's not."

He pointed at a chair and sat behind his desk. The inspector settled into it, taking his time before he asked his first question. Jackson leaned his right elbow and forearm on the desk and drummed his fingers impatiently.

"Well, Tennant? What is it this time?"

"Do you remember the old porter at Whitechapel Workhouse? A man named Barney Dunlap?"

"What of it?"

"He's dead. Murdered in circumstances that mirror the earlier deaths. We suspect the workhouse is the key to the killings."

The brewer snorted. "Key or not, it doesn't make me your locksmith. Yes, I was a workhouse lad; I've never made a secret of it. One of the thousands sent to Whitechapel over the past thirty years."

"We know your mother died there."

"What the hell does that have to—"

"She died in misery. In agony, most likely, if cholera was the cause, as we suspect."

The muscles of Jackson's jaws tightened. "If you know she died of cholera, you know more 'n I do. I'd like to see your evidence."

"You were angry with Sir Maxwell Ball. Furious and in a

mood for vengeance, if the testimony of the man's secretary is accurate."

"You're clutching at straws, Tennant. Wisps. Sir Maxwell had no hand in my mother's death, as I had none in his."

"What about the hands that did play a role? Cruel neglect of the sick is common in workhouse infirmaries. It's mentioned in every newspaper exposé and parliamentary report. Do you expect me to believe you don't remember Nurse Milhous, perhaps the last person to see your mother alive?"

"Believe it or not, as you like—and be damned!"

"Not long ago, you followed the trail of your mother's corpse and realized, enraged, that they'd sold her for a pittance like scrap. Peddled her off to a medical college to be sliced on a dissecting table. Did you imagine the crowd in the operating theater? Do they haunt you still, those doctors in training? Do you see them, their necks craning for a better view, others yawning, bored and indifferent, and some gagging, afraid they'll lose their breakfasts all over their boots? What happened to her remains, Sir Harry? I doubt that monument you erected in place of a missing grave is solace enough."

Jackson lurched to his feet, knocking over his chair. "You bastard. Arrest me or get the hell out."

"Not before I search this office and see your agenda—with your permission, of course."

Sir Harry fished in his pocket and slammed down the keys. He pulled an appointment book out of his top drawer and flung it on the desk.

"Search all you like. I'll be on the brewery floor. The next time we talk, it will be at Scotland Yard or my solicitor's office."

Tennant searched thoroughly but found nothing. Jackson's agenda was equally unrevealing. He found no evidence that Sir Harry had been out of town on the dates in question, nothing that eliminated him as a suspect or incriminated him.

But back at the workhouse, O'Malley had turned up a familiar name in a ledger. In December 1847, Whitechapel welcomed a family of four: Joe Archer, Ida, his wife, and their two children, Jackie and Ellen.

After many nights spent watching from the trees of Finsbury Circus, he knew the timing of the constable's rounds by heart.

It took the policeman twenty minutes to make his slow circuit around the curving pavement. At each address, the copper rattled the gates and raked his bull's-eye beam across the bushes and walkways. Luckily, the bobby ignored the park in the center, intent on securing the valuable properties around the ring. And it took the constable another half hour to patrol the four streets that enclosed the circus in a box. For long, convenient stretches, 17 Finsbury Circus was out of the policeman's sight.

Plenty of time, he thought.

He knew the evenings the grandfather entertained—every Wednesday, regular as clockwork. But he was surprised the night a cab dropped the inspector at the door. *Well, well. Even better*, he'd thought. Another heart to rip open?

He'd grown familiar with the household's routine. He knew the hour when the kitchen door opened and the coachman emerged, dog in tow. He could predict the order in which the lights winked out, leaving the house asleep. He'd wait for the window of the southwest bedroom to go dark. Usually, it was the last. And on moonlit nights, when her light dimmed and the curtains parted, he'd see the flash of her nightdress appear and vanish.

And then, one night, a surprise: a man dressed in the tweeds and gaiters of the countryside stepped out from the shadows of the portico.

The watcher smiled. *Reinforcements.*

The guard shouldered his shotgun, paced to the end of the property, and returned to his post at the front door.

No matter. The house was too risky, anyway.

He'd find another place.

Julia arrived at the clinic just before noon and found Johnny Osborne waiting at her door. She wasn't surprised; she'd read about the porter's murder in the morning newspaper.

She held up her hand. "Before you ask, the answer is no. I haven't the time for an interview, and I have nothing to say about the latest victim." She brushed by him, but he followed her into the hallway.

"You should find the time, Doctor. I'm here to suggest an arrangement advantageous to us both."

"Why do I doubt that?"

He lifted his shoulders and smiled. "I can't figure it out either. I awoke this morning with a feeling of good fellowship. How, I wondered, could I use the power of the press to do some good? In a flash, the answer came to me. Take the good doctor's advice and write a story about the Whitechapel Clinic and the miracles of healing she performs here. Only . . ."

"I thought there'd be an 'only.'"

He nodded. "The old quid pro quo. You scratch my back, and I'll scratch yours."

"I can't think of anything I'd enjoy less."

"Come, now. Doctor, you know how the world works. With the story I write, you'll have every reader with sixpence to spare sending you money. But, first, my editor would like a story about the porter's murder, an inside look from the medical examiner's perspective."

"I can't help you there. I wasn't called in." The words slipped out before she had time to consider them.

"Oh? Why is that, Doctor? Unless I'm misinformed, you examined most of the earlier victims. It seems strange that— "

"Mister Osborne, you are wasting my time and interfering

with the work of this clinic. In the future, write to request an interview. Can I make myself any clearer?"

"If not, let me translate it for you." Q walked into the hallway, his considerable bulk filling the passage, his hands balled into fists. "Maybe I can help him understand, Doctor."

The reporter raised his hands in surrender. Then, with his back to the wall, he edged around the quartermaster.

"There's no need to parse the doctor's meaning, Q. Words are my business. It is Q, isn't it, the celebrated pugilist-philanthropist?" From the safety of the doorway, Osborne fired off a parting shot. "I've often wondered: Are you the Good Samaritan or the Pied Piper of East End rent boys?"

When Q took a step toward him, Julia laid a restraining hand on his arm. "Let him go," she said. "He isn't worth the trouble, and you've had enough of that."

"You're right. And I promised Mister Tennant I'd behave myself."

"In Osborne's case, the inspector might overlook a lapse." Julia hooked her arm around his and led him into her office. She pointed to a chair. "I hope you've been giving Joe Archer a wide berth. The world's full of petty tyrants and injustice, but there's only so much anyone can do about it."

"You're right on both counts, Doctor."

"So what brings you here today?"

He pulled a blue bottle out of his coat pocket. "You said I should bring this back when it was empty."

Julia carried the bottle to her dispensary cabinet, unlocked the glass-paneled door, and refilled the container with mercury tablets. "I'll drop in before the New Year and take a look at the boys."

He took the bottle and touched it to his forehead in a salute. With his hand on the doorknob, he stopped. "That workhouse porter . . ."

"What about him? What is it, Q? Have your lads been talking about him?"

The quartermaster shook his head. "I was thinking, the music hall might not be the answer after all."

Julia sighed. "One person knows."

The inspector didn't believe that Jackie Archer or his father was the killer. Still, O'Malley had discovered their names in the record book, so he had to follow up. But he was honest enough to admit to himself he that wanted to see Julia.

Their last communication had been a brief, cheerful reply to his thank-you note for dinner. It included her good wishes for a happy Christmas. But its postscript stayed with him. "So, in advance of New Year's resolutions, I'm remembering your words and your kindness that morning in the coffeehouse. To believe a different truth—it's a hard but healing way forward."

When Tennant arrived at the clinic in the late afternoon, he registered the presence of a hansom cab waiting at the door. Julia flashed him a signal from inside her office, to wait while she finished up some business with her head nurse. Three patients needed special attention in the handoff of care from Nurse Clemmie to Emily.

Julia finished, then smiled and gestured to a chair. "To what do I owe the pleasure?"

"Two things, really. I wanted to know how you were—you and your grandfather." He cocked his thumb over his shoulder. "I noticed the cab waiting at the curb."

She nodded. "And I can't walk out the door without Fred or Jackie stuck to me like a plaster—your doing, I understand."

"Julia . . ."

She waved away his reply. "I'm not complaining. I understand. And if it eases my grandfather's fears, I'm happy. The caretaker from our house in Surrey patrols the town house every night with a shotgun in his hands." She grimaced. "I'm guarded more closely than the queen."

"I'm glad to hear it. Still, four would-be assassins have taken potshots at Victoria over the years."

"Thank you. That's very reassuring." She leaned back in her chair. "You said two things brought you here?"

"Something's come up in connection with the murder of the porter."

"May I ask who examined the body?"

"Doctor MacKay. Nothing wrong with his report, but he's a dour and cautious Scot. Not a doctor who is willing to . . . theorize beyond the barest facts."

"That sounds dangerously close to an admission that you've missed me, Inspector."

He half-smiled. "Dangerously close, Doctor."

"Do you need a second opinion on the medical report?"

"No, something else. We think Whitechapel Workhouse may be at the heart of things. From its records, Constable O'Malley discovered that Jackie Archer and his family were admitted there. It overlaps the time Nurse Milhous and the porter were on the staff. So I need to speak with Jackie."

"Surely you don't think . . ."

"No, he was just a baby. And that father of his is a drunken brute; he's no murderous mastermind. But I'll track him down as well. In any investigation, even unlikely boxes must be ticked."

Frowning, Julia looked past him to the doorway.

Tennant glanced over his shoulder at Nurse Emily, waiting at the door. "Time for the changing of the guard?"

"Yes." Julia stood. "Jackie must be somewhere about, talking to Fred." At the door, she said, "I suppose this means you're no longer looking at the music hall. So much pointed to the Eagle Tavern." She sighed. "That song—'Pop Goes the

Weasel.' And the balloons. Somehow I don't connect them with the workhouse."

"I agree. It doesn't make sense." Tennant nodded to Emily. "She's all yours, Nurse."

Emily watched him walk away and turned to Julia.

"Funny, mentioning that. Just the other day, Benny Watkins talked all about the Eagle and 'Pop Goes the Weasel.' He heard you humming it in the ward." She smiled. "He entertained us with his memories of an act at the music hall—sang all the lyrics, too." Emily scrunched her eyebrows. "Little, Little . . ." She snapped her fingers. "Can't quite remember the name of the boy with the balloons."

Julia gripped the nurse's upper arms. "Stay here. Don't move. I'll be right back."

She ran down the corridor and dragged Tennant back to her office. "Emily, tell the inspector the story you just told me."

They'd discharged Benny Watkins just before Christmas, but Nurse Emily found his address in the clinic's records. He lived with his son only a few streets away on Chapel Place. When Julia suggested she accompany him, Tennant answered with a firm no. Instead, he escorted her to her hansom and instructed the cabbie to drive the lady to number 17 Finsbury Circus.

Tennant located Jackie, and they went off to find Benny.

A gentleman appearing at her door startled Benny's daughter-in-law. When he turned out to be a copper, she refused to open it more than a crack.

Jackie said, "Missus, the inspector here just wants to ask Benny a few questions—about something he remembered from years ago in the music halls. He's in no trouble."

She looked over her shoulder. "Is it all right, Alf?"

"Let 'em in."

Five faces looked up at Tennant from around a kitchen table.

The middle-aged man at the head of it asked, "What's this all about?"

"Mister and Mrs. Watkins, I apologize for interrupting your meal, but I need to speak to Benny. The information I seek is a matter of some urgency."

His son pointed his fork over his shoulder. "Dad's in the back bedroom." He stood up. "I'll take you."

The old man had been dozing on his bed, a tray of food resting on the counterpane. Benny stirred and squinted at them. "Who's this, then, Alf?"

"It's me, Mister Watkins—Jackie Archer. I've got someone here who'd like to ask you a few questions about a story you told Nurse Emily."

"It's a police officer, Dad. This is . . ." Alf Watkins looked at him.

"Detective Inspector Tennant from Scotland Yard. How are you this evening, Mister Watkins? Are you well enough to answer a few questions?"

Benny Watkins stared back at him from a face as crackled as a piece of old china. "Blimey—a 'tec from the Yard." Benny pushed back his covers. "Don't just stand there, Alf. Move this here tray and get me sitting up. Pull up a chair for the inspector."

It turned out Benny Watkins—his eyesight failing, but his mind razor-sharp—remembered them all. Little Jacko Fratelli was "a tiny tyke in a sailor's cap," his sister, "cute as a button," and their parents, the Flying Fratellis—Carlo and his wife. Benny couldn't recall her Christian name.

"Any idea what happened to them, Mister Watkins? Are they still performing?"

Benny shook his head. "Died. At least the parents are dead. The 'King' got 'em. Died of the cholera a ways back."

"And the boy and girl?"

"Nothing for it, poor little blighters. Heard they sent 'em to the workhouse."

Tennant spent a mostly sleepless night, his mind racing, impatient for the morning.

He arrived at the Yard at dawn for what would turn out to be a dank and sunless day. They were in for several days of a "London Particular"—when fog made morning, noon, and night almost indistinguishable. He'd sent runners into the gloom to summon his officers early to his office.

When the inspector finished telling Benny's story, Graves smacked his palm on Tennant's desk. "We've got him, guv. With a name, I can get somewhere with those ruddy workhouse records. Shall I go back and hit the books again?"

"Yes. Benny thought the parents died fifteen or twenty years ago. Go back over 1844 to 1852. See if you can find a John, a Jack, or a Jacko Fratelli entered in one of the ledgers. And find out what happened to him."

"Right, guv, I'm on it."

"I'll head over to Somerset House," Tennant said.

O'Malley nodded. "You'll find something there, sure. A marriage license or birth certificate, death notices for the parents and the like. But you'll be needing to know the parish."

Since the 1830s, all public records for England and Wales could be found at Somerset House. But wading through them could be tricky: documents were stored separately by parish neighborhood.

"We can make some likely guesses," Tennant said. "I'll start with Whitechapel, Spitalfields, and Hackney. O'Malley, you go back to the Eagle. Rollie Jakeways is probably too young, but question all the old stagehands—the Eagle's manager, as well. See if anyone remembers the Fratellis and where they lived. If anyone can tell you a neighborhood, let me know immediately."

O'Malley said, "Should we tell the chief?"

Tennant checked his pocket watch. "It will be an hour before he's in. I'll leave a message."

Graves smiled. "Won't be long now, guv. This is it—the endgame. You'll find what you're looking for at Somerset House. I know it."

Tennant's hansom crawled through the fog-shrouded streets. A bobbie with a torch was stationed at every intersection, trying to keep the traffic moving and avert collisions. When his cab finally pulled up at Somerset House, the inspector paid the cabby and raced up the steps, ignoring the ache in his left thigh. His rapid pace along the west corridor of the stately building drew stares.

At the General Records desk, Tennant gave his name and rank to the clerk and asked to speak to the department's director. After he explained his errand and its urgency, the director sent three clerks to examine the relevant parochial files, looking for anyone named Fratelli. The surname was unusual in England; the inspector hoped it would facilitate the search. Still, he waited an hour.

Then, one by one, documents arrived in quick succession. The clerks handed him a marriage certificate from the parish of Hackney. Two minutes later, a birth certificate and two death certificates from Whitechapel dropped on his table. A clerk added the fifth parchment to the pile—an adoption certificate.

A marriage license recorded the union of Carlo Fratelli, born in the village of San Martino in Tuscany, and Amelia, "a spinster of this parish." It included the usual seals, the signature of the Anglican clergyman who presided over the wedding, and the two persons who witnessed the marriage. At the bottom of the document, Carlo and his wife had signed the license as well.

Tennant stared at the signature of the bride. His hand shaking, the inspector placed three other documents side by side. Then he looked up from two birth certificates and a document of adoption, gathered the papers, and dashed out the door.

Constable O'Malley had headed to a destination a mile or so east of Somerset House. At ten in the morning, the Eagle Tavern seemed deserted, but he followed the banging noises until they brought him to the stage. It would be hours until the performers arrived. The theater manager and the stagehands were hard at it, rebuilding a set.

The manager rolled his eyes at the sight of the constable. "What, you again, mate?"

When O'Malley explained what he wanted, the man shook his head. "Before my time, but let's see what this lot knows." He let out a shrill whistle, and the stagehands dropped their hammers and ambled over.

Two old-timers remembered the Fratellis, their children, and the balloons, the entire act. They confirmed the parents' deaths, thought the son and daughter had ended up in the workhouse, but had no idea what happened to him after that.

O'Malley decided to head back to the Yard. Maybe the inspector or Sergeant Graves had had better luck. They were close. *A matter of time.*

Outside the theater, O'Malley cursed his bad luck as he watched an omnibus disappear into the fog. He headed south on foot, hoping to hail a hansom or spot another 'bus passing by. As he crossed Cowper Street, O'Malley thought of Willie Lomax and his empty rooms. It was a filthy morning, and the last time he'd seen Willie's lodgings, they were covered in blood. *Why not*, he thought. *It'll only take a few minutes, and I'm not squeamish.*

He spotted a notice on the door: "For Rent: Two Flats." It listed the name and address of the agent, Benny Kane, at 123

Willow Street. The constable flagged a crossing lad and asked for directions.

"Around the bend, second turn on the left. Can't miss it."

O'Malley feared he might pass the street in the fog, so he offered the boy thruppence to light the way with his torch. At the door of Kane's office, the lad pocketed his money and melted into the mist.

CHAPTER 16

Years later, Jacko still carried his first day at the workhouse inside him. The memory was a scar and a spur. He thought about it as he dodged the ghostly figures that loomed out of the mists along Whitechapel Road and disappeared behind him.

His first day, abandoned and frightened, he'd jumped at the sound of the slamming doors. With a hollow bang, they closed on a tiny boy and girl, holding hands, forsaken by the world. He looked around wildly and stumbled when the porter prodded him in the back. Whimpering, he dropped the sack he'd been clutching to his chest.

"Leave it and walk on," the gatekeeper told him.

He passed from the porter's indifferent shove into other hands that separated him from his sister. Cold, efficient fingers stripped off his clothes and pointed him to a washing tub. He stood in the basin, its water gray from the bodies that had preceded him. He swayed in the fug of sweat and steam, submitting mutely to the swipes of a rough cloth. Dripping, he was directed to a cupboard and handed a pair of yellowing underdrawers and a shirt. Then he dragged the rough garments over his damp skin. He shivered while he waited for the matron to pass him a pair of ill-fitting trousers and a jacket.

His eyes followed her hands as she carried away the clothing he came in, wanting to cry out for the penknife and prized marbles tucked away in the pockets of his trousers. But he was too frightened to utter a word. Ordered to move along to the records room, he waited, dwarfed by the high desk and the looming figure of the master. He nodded at his name. He whispered those of his parents, his sister, and their parish, louder when the master growled, "Speak up, boy," as the man scratched the bare details of his life into a thick ledger. When the man shut it with a thud, the boy felt as if it had closed over him, as well. Little Jacko no longer existed. He was just another pauper child, invisible, forgotten.

Not so long ago, he'd been someone. Lit by limelight, soaring across the stage to wild applause, he was Little Jacko Fratelli, the boy with the balloons. And Jillie.

Their parents had been the aerialist act at the Eagle, and during school holidays, they added the children to their show. His father had built a jack-in-the-box big enough to hold his boy and the balloons. While the orchestra played and the audience sang along, Jacko hid in his box. Just in time, he'd release the catch and "pop"—he'd leap up, right on cue, puncturing the balloon. Hands in the air, Jacko waited for his father to swoop down on his trapeze. Then Carlo Fratelli seized his son by the wrists and delivered him to his mother and sister, who waited on a perch high above the stage.

Little Jacko missed it all. The wardrobe ladies who cooed over his blue eyes and golden curls, the glow of the footlights as the velvet curtain rose, the cascades of love flowing from the audience, reaching him in the rafters—gone.

He and Jillie had been at school the afternoon they took his parents away. Water and the scant supply of it figured in his memory of that last day. The slop pail from their morning wash sat by the door. His papa at his shaving mirror had bowls of hot and cold at the ready, the hot to lather his soap to a snowy peak. With long strokes, he stropped his cutthroat razor and curved the blade carefully around his handlebar mustache, scraping paths through the creamy froth. Jacko's mum poured steaming water from the kettle and let him stir an extra lump of sugar in his cup.

When he left with Jillie for the walk to school, his mother had readied the jugs for a water day. For a few short hours, the company would pump the precious supply into their parched neighborhood. Then the water would trickle off, with nothing flowing for days. Jacko's parents would lug as much as they could from the standpipe at the end of their street. But when he and Jillie returned in the evening, their mum and papa were gone. They'd been taken to the fever hospital, where they died the next day, two cholera victims among thousands that year. The great epidemic of 1849 had begun.

Jacko never saw their bodies. The Inspector of Nuisances greeted the children at the door, his men already stripping the flat of everything they could haul away. They were allowed to keep the clothes they wore to school and the small sack Jacko had carried that day. The vicar's wife was there to take them away for the night.

The next day, the parish relieving officer questioned the little boy. But Jacko could name no relative who might take over the children's care. His father had left his homeland years before. "And your mother?" She never spoke of it to him, but in hushed conversations between his parents, Jacko pieced together the story. When his mother defied her family and married a music hall "dago," her father had cut her off.

The relieving officer searched through papers but found no clue to anyone who might take charge of the children. For another night, he left Little Jacko and his sister at the vicarage while he questioned neighbors and interviewed colleagues at the music hall.

Two days after their parents died, the relieving officer wrote up the order that admitted Little Jacko and his sister Jillie to Whitechapel Workhouse. He did it reluctantly, for the children's sake and the ratepayers' pocketbooks.

Workdays inside the institution were wearying and long. Jacko hated the oakum picking that left his hands bloody, but it was the one task boys and girls performed together. As miserable as it was, it was a rare chance to see Jillie and exchange a few whispered words. He'd see her across the dining hall; boys and girls ate their meals apart.

A day's labor outside the building offered a glimpse of a world beyond the walls. Three months after he'd arrived at the workhouse, Jacko was told he would be "farmed out" to a dustheap after breakfast.

That morning, he joined a group of ragged boys outside the gate. Together, they walked a mile from the workhouse to their employment site, passing a line of gray-caked horses and dustmen inching their way forward. The men waited to dump the coal ash they had scraped from the fire grates of East London. Lines of filth etched their cheeks, muddy rivulets of dirt and sweat that had dried in the freezing February morning. The whites of their eyes, bright in their sooty faces, gave them a ghostly aura.

At the entrance to the heap, the gatekeeper handed the boy in front of him a shovel. He pressed two baskets and a sieve into Jacko's arms and pointed to the mountain of dust on the left. The boys would work as a team—one shoveling, the other picking through the pile. They tossed fragments of unburned coal into one basket; anything else of value landed in the other. By the day's end, Jacko's hands were red-raw and bloody from the freezing cold and the scraping sieve. Then he joined the line of shuffling, exhausted dust pickers who hauled their loads to the accounting desk. Pennies changed hands, but not for Little Jacko. His wages went on the workhouse account.

He would learn to be grateful for the sinking light of a winter evening. It made it easy for an ash-covered boy in a workhouse uniform to cling to the shadows as he walked down the street. In the bright of high summer, he'd have to endure the jeers and taunts of other children as they shouted, "Pauper boy" or "Workhouse brat." Sometimes they pelted him with clods of mud or stones.

Outside the oaken gates, darkness was his ally. Inside, it brought new terrors.

Life in the workhouse—its days of numbing routine and gnawing hunger, of barked commands and the back of matron's hand—had chipped away at him, a slight boy made smaller by the day. But the nights . . . nights were a bottomless chute of fear.

It had happened to others before the porter finally came for him. On many nights, Jacko woke to the sound of jangling keys and the door swinging open. A lantern's beam would pick out a boy, and the porter would lead him away. On some evenings, the clinking keys passed them by and stopped at the girls' dormitory door.

None of the lads spoke of it. Jacko had no idea what was happening, but he knew it was something bad. Finally, one night, it was his turn.

Years later, it was a point of sharp fury that he didn't know the name of that first man. He'd dearly love to know it . . . take his time with him . . . find a fat, jagged stick and ram it home. *Pop.*

But the porter, the chaplain, and the nurse—he knew them. The nurse who saw the hollowed-eyed girls and the bent-over boys and ignored their bloody underdrawers. She had it coming. And that pair of buggers—Bertie and Willie, they called each other—one on top of him, rutting and grunting, the other watching with his hand in his trousers.

Jacko had a moment of hope the night he recognized the chaplain. Gently, Mr. Atwater pushed him down by his shoulders until he was kneeling. The chaplain rested a hand on his head—a blessing, he thought. But with his other one, Mr. Atwater opened his buttons and pulled Jacko's face into him, telling the boy what he wanted him to do.

Two years after he arrived at the workhouse, Little Jacko spent his last day toiling on the dustheap. When he returned in the evening, the matron met him at the gate. She hurried him to the washroom, cleaned him up, and dressed him in a new set of workhouse clothes.

The master was waiting in his office. At his side was a stranger, a tall, cadaverous man who beat a battered hat impatiently against his leg. His thinning hair hung in wispy strings that touched the frayed collar of his black coat.

The stranger looked Jacko up and down. "I trust the workhouse has been true to its godly purpose, that it's taught the hard lesson of life. Since Adam's fall, toil from dawn to dusk is what the Lord ordained. It's what the boy can expect from me."

"You'll not be disappointed, sir," the master said.

"Well, boy?" The stranger barked. "Speak up. What's your name?"

"Jacko, sir," he whispered. "Jacko Fratelli."

"Not anymore, it's not." His bony hand darted out and clutched him above the elbow. "My sister named you Jonathan after me. From now on, you're Jonathan Graves."

It amused Graves that Paddy O'Malley had been right all along: the banker didn't fit.

When Inspector Tennant asked his sergeant to fetch the evidence box from the storage room, he'd slipped the balloon inside. It was his way of having some fun, a little sleight of hand at the investigation's expense. And he'd enjoyed tormenting Tennant with pangs of guilt. Poor innocent Meyer—what a joke. He was as guilty as sin.

He'd made sure Paddy discovered the balloon in the banker's box. Nothing was easier. He always kept one or two on him, tucked in a pocket in the lining of his coat. In idle moments at his desk, he'd reach inside and finger them, wrapping their rubbery smoothness around his forefinger and thumb. He'd fantasize about where he'd put them next. With his heart beating and his breaths coming quickly, he'd press them deeper into their secret pouch and get on with his work.

Sometimes he thought it was all too easy. He preened when he recalled how he dodged the jobs at the music hall and the workhouse. Before Tennant handed out assignments, he jumped in and volunteered for something else—looking for the street-sweeping lad, questioning Sir Harry Jackson, or grilling Johnny Osborne. Not that he thought he'd be recognized, but it paid to be careful. And he was happy to lead the investigation down any wrong garden path or to change the subject deftly whenever sodding Paddy O'Malley was on to something.

The riskiest part of the plot was topping Willie Lomax in his lodgings. Stupid, pathetic Willie; he was so willing to do his bidding for a rent-free flat, not knowing what was going on. With that pox-addled brain of his, the old fool hadn't a clue. But on command, he'd dress up in that flaming wig and play his part.

He had one or two close calls. After Willie's murder, Graves made sure he was the one who interviewed the rent collector, never dreaming the bugger would show up at the Yard. Benny Kane was the only person who knew he was Willie's landlord, that he'd inherited the house from his uncle. Still, Kane was a worry; he'd have to do something about him.

In the end, he'd slipped through that noose nimbly. The second one, those ruddy workhouse ledger books—he'd handled that just as deftly, made sure to grab the telltale editions before O'Malley saw them. The volume for 1849 recorded his arrival with his sister. And the 1851 edition listed the departure of one Jacko Fratelli, aged twelve, released into the care of his uncle, Mr. Jonathan Graves, residing at 165 Cowper Street in Hoxton. It also recorded a death two months earlier: Jillian Fratelli, aged nine, died of fever.

He'd turned the page, closed the book, and announced to Paddy, "Nothing in this one, mate."

He paid them back with a stick, all except Sir Maxwell Ball. With his knife at their throats, frenzied, hate-filled, he felt sated—at least, for a while.

No, he didn't sodomize Sir Maxwell or slice him up. The man never visited Little Jacko or his sister on those nights at the workhouse. But it was time he paid for all the mothers he'd poisoned, for the children he'd left fatherless and homeless over the years. For all he knew, it was Ball's filthy water that his parents drank that terrible day, the day that changed everything.

Graves had an earlier tick mark on his tally sheet: his first kill. Such a tragedy—a cask of slippery molasses leaking across the warehouse platform and a nasty fall. He looked down at the broken body of his uncle and curled a length of rope artfully around his ankles.

It was past time the bastard paid. He'd cast off his own sister, hadn't he? With a little help, Jacko's family needn't have rotted in a cholera-ridden slum. And for two years, he'd condemned his nephew and niece to the hell of the workhouse. *He came too late to save Jillie.* No. He wouldn't think about her now. He wouldn't think about how he'd failed her.

His uncle only looked for Jacko after the death of his son. He wanted a Graves to inherit and carry on the business, failing as it was. Jonathan granted his uncle's wish a little sooner than he'd planned.

Still, one thing worried him: How would he entertain himself once it was over? Of course, he wasn't ruling out a return engagement. Strolling through a park or waiting on a station platform, he might spot another monster from his past. But, for the moment, he was nearly done.

Only one scene left to play.

CHAPTER 17

O'Malley pounded along the pavement and skidded to a stop in front of the entrance to the Yard. He scrambled through the doors and doubled over at the duty sergeant's desk.

"Inspector Tennant," he gasped. "Is he back from Somerset House?"

"Back and gone twenty minutes ago." The sergeant's face was a mask of stone. "Left a message for you, but I'm guessing you've heard."

"Tennant knows?"

The sergeant nodded. "Found the records at Somerset House."

"Where is he? Where's the inspector?"

"Took three constables with him and left for Whitechapel Workhouse. He's hunting for Graves."

Outside the Yard, O'Malley cut in front of an outraged passenger. "Sorry, sir. I'm taking this cab. Official business." He shouted directions at the cabbie and slammed his back against the seat, cursing his blindness for the hundredth time.

At the end of his conversation with the rent collector, after he'd written his name and address, O'Malley had gaped like a fish.

"*Detective*-Constable O'Malley," Kane had said. "You work at Scotland Yard?" When he nodded, the man exploded his bomb: "Then you must know the landlord—Sergeant Graves. Generous bloke. Let Willie live rent-free. Maybe he'll give you a discount—brothers in blue and all."

His mind was like a child's kaleidoscope: every time he shook his head, images and memories reformed into a different pattern. The sergeant—his sergeant—was the murderer. It beggared the imagination. Quickly, disbelief changed shape and settled into realization. *It was so easy*, simple for him to use his closeness to the case to manipulate and deceive. "I'll start with these ledgers, mate." Graves said it with his usual cheer, no doubt taking charge of the guilty volumes.

O'Malley stared out into the murk of the gray morning. *This fecking cab.* Its crawling pace through the smoke-shrouded streets added to his frustration. *Smoke and mirrors*—the sergeant had them all stumbling in the dark.

Still, O'Malley saw one thing as clear and bright as a summer morning: Jonathan Graves had taken up lodging in his head. It would be a long time before he was evicted.

Tennant reread the Somerset House documents on the ride from the Yard to Whitechapel Workhouse. The lanterns the driver had hung to avoid collisions provided just enough light. A clerk had added a last-minute document from the Probate Registry Office: the uncle's will. It named his adopted son, Jonathan Graves—born Jonathan Fratelli—as his heir, listing the properties he inherited.

Tennant looked up at the grim faces of the constables who shared the four-wheeler cab with him. They would all feel it, bottom to top, from the Yard's newest bobby to Sir Richard Mayne; all would feel tainted by the treachery of one of their own. For the inspector, there was an added layer of humiliation. To be so deceived by a member of your team was a galling realization.

They were on their way to the workhouse, but would Graves be such a fool as to wait around for them to pick him up? He must realize the evidence was there, at Somerset House, enough to send him to the gallows. Tennant doubted he'd find him paging through the ledger books, but that was his last known destination. He'd have to pick up his trail from there.

What would be his next move? Would he flee to the Channel, try to hide somewhere on the Continent? Or South America, perhaps; the inspector had ordered telegrams with his description sent to all the ports.

What would he do if he couldn't get away and knew he was cornered? In a sickening flash, Tennant knew the answer. He'd add a final victim to his ledger, and the aftermath be damned.

He pounded on the roof of the carriage. When the cabbie pulled over, Tennant shouted out the window. "Turn right in front of the London Hospital, then right again on Charlotte Street. Fast as you can, man—take us to the Whitechapel Clinic at Fieldgate and New streets."

Julia smiled at the sight of Sergeant Graves. Through her doorway, she watched him exercise his considerable charm on the stoic Nurse Clemmie. Then the clinic's cook appeared and handed him a cup of tea and a biscuit. When he looked up, Julia waved him into her office.

"You have my whole staff eating out of your hand, Sergeant."

He put his cup on the edge of her desk. "Can't explain it, Doc. Ladies of a certain age all want to mother me. It's the younger ones who won't give me the time of day."

"Well, I have a little time today. What can I do for you?"

"We've got a body on our hands, down Mile End way. It's a young woman, nothing to do with our murders. The guv wants to know if you can give it a squint."

"Give me a few minutes to finish this report and check on the wards. Then I'm all yours."

Graves wandered around her office. He stopped in front of a life-size drawing of the interior organs of the human body and muttered, "Blimey," and moved on. He peered through the glass of Julia's medicine cupboard. Then, over his shoulder, he said, "You could polish off half of East London with what you've got in here. Hope you keep it locked." He rattled the door to check.

Julia signed a document with a flourish, blotted her signature, and looked up. "Five minutes, Sergeant, to speak to Nurse Clemmie in the wards, and then we can be off. I'll ask Fred to whistle up a cab."

Idly, he picked up the letter opener on her desk. "Plenty of time, Doc. No worries."

Fred opened the door of the hansom and handed Jonathan his bull's-eye lantern.

"Here you are, Sarge, though it won't do you much good in this murk. Where are you headed?" he asked.

Graves gave Fred the address of a warehouse on Canal Road in Mile End. The porter repeated it to the cabbie, and the hansom rattled off.

After Julia had settled into her seat, she turned to Graves. "I was thinking. You might try your luck with Emily—she's half Nurse Clemmie's age."

"Are you playing matchmaker, Doc?" She nodded. "Right, then. Put in a good word for me."

They trundled along for a while until he broke a companionable silence. "I remember the day I first met you. Surprised, I was. I can't deny it—a lady doctor. You made a joke about showing us your medical license."

"You looked as if you wanted to see some evidence."

He grinned. "You got me there, Doc. Never can hide what I'm thinking. It's a disadvantage for a copper."

"So, tell me a little about the victim."

"Some lads playing in an empty warehouse along Regent's

Canal found her on the second floor. Throat cut ear to ear. That's about all I've got."

They made slow progress in the fog. Julia peered into the gloom, trying to make out some landmarks. "I think we just passed Mile End Green, but it's hard to tell in this dreadful smoke."

"The canal's just ahead. We'll cross a footbridge to the other side. The warehouse is right on the water."

At the end of the road, the cab shuddered to a stop. Jonathan hopped out and helped Julia down. "Careful, now, Doc. Watch your step on the bridge. Take my hand; some of the planks are a bit wobbly."

The fog hovered low along the water's surface, but the warehouse was clear enough. It was a hulking edifice built right to the bank of the canal. From three shuttered windows, drawbridge platforms jutted out like petulant lower lips. The hoists above the windows had been used in more prosperous times to lower heavy loads into barges below. From a spot just south of the building, one such derelict vessel sagged at its stern, taking on water.

Graves flashed his beam on the steps to the warehouse. Pushing the doors open, he waited while Julia passed him. Inside, they paused in the gloom to get their bearings. Speckles of floating dust glittered in the lamp beam. Turning his head to cough, Graves pulled out his handkerchief and pointed his light toward the staircase.

"That's the way, Doc. One floor up." At the top of the stairs, he said. "First door on the right."

It was open a crack, so she gave it a push. Graves shone the light over her shoulder to show her the way. He followed her into the room and put the lantern down the floor.

Julia looked around. "Where is the victim?"

His left arm came around her shoulder and pulled her against him in a crushing grip. She felt the tip of a blade touch her neck.

"She's right here, Doctor."

He jammed a cloth against her nose and mouth, and the room went dark.

Tennant slammed through the clinic's doors and walked rapidly along the hallway, looking left and right. He spotted the head nurse and the porter standing at an open cupboard in Julia's office.

Nurse Clemmie rattled the broken latch. "But who, Fred? One of the patients?"

"Where is Doctor Lewis?"

The heads of the nurse and porter snapped around. Fred said, "Didn't they turn up? They were supposed to be meeting you down Mile End way."

The inspector knew the answer, but he asked anyway. "When you say 'they,' who do you mean?"

"Doctor Lewis and your sergeant, of course. Sergeant Graves."

Stiff-armed, he gripped the back of a chair and barked, "When?"

"Just after morning rounds."

"How long ago, exactly."

"Forty-five minutes, give or take."

Nurse Clemmie looked back at the broken cabinet. "Is something wrong, Inspector?"

"I'm not sure. Fred, you said Mile End. How do you know that?"

He scratched his head. "Well, Doctor Lewis asked me to whistle up a hansom, and Sergeant Graves gave me the address. I repeated it to the cabbie."

Tennant took him by the shoulders. "Do you remember it?"

Fred bit his lip, trying to recall.

"Think hard, Fred. I need that address."

"Canal Road, the sergeant said. Number—"

Tennant released the porter. "Canal Road. That's . . ."

He reached into the breast pocket of his coat and pulled out a bundle of papers. Selecting a document, he unfolded a will's stiff parchment, scanning the text until he found what he wanted.

"Did Graves say 187 Canal Road?"

"That's it. I told the cabbie to drive to 187 Canal Road."

Outside, Tennant gave the cab driver the address. "White-chapel Road will be too slow. Take Charlotte to Oxford Street. In Stepney, we'll cut over to Mile End Road. As fast as you can, man." The inspector slammed the door and thumped on the roof for the cabbie to get moving.

He eyed the grim faces of the three constables sitting around him. "He has Doctor Lewis."

"Bloody hell," his seatmate muttered.

"On the way to the warehouse, we'll stop at the Bethnal Green station and round up some reinforcements."

Another constable said, "You gave the cabbie an exact address. How's that, sir?"

"He made no secret of his destination. Graves made a point of telling the porter."

"He's leading us right to him, then."

"Yes." Tennant looked out the window, then back at his officers. "It's a filthy day; visibility is compromised. But check your weapons. One of you may have to take him down." The inspector held the eye of Constable Hawkins, the Yard's crack shot.

"Understood, sir," he said.

"We'll leave the carriage a street away and walk the distance. Two of you—Robbins and Smythe—will survey the perimeter and report back to me. I'll make a final assessment on the spot before we proceed. Any questions?"

The men shook their heads.

"Remember, he knows his cover is blown. He's armed, dangerous, and has nothing to lose."

* * *

Julia woke up stiff and cold, lying on her side, her cheek pressed against a bare, wooden floor. She groaned as she propped herself on her elbow and tried to sit up. As the room swirled and her head spun, a surge she couldn't suppress flooded her mouth. She turned her head and vomited.

"Sorry about that, Doc."

Sergeant Graves. She remembered.

"Use this." He tossed a piece of rough sacking across the room. "I'd give you my handkerchief, but I'm afraid it's saturated with your chloroform, and it's time to wake up. Hadn't planned to use it, but there it was, sitting in your medicine cabinet."

Julia's eyes adjusted to the dim light. He had opened one side of the window's shutters, but the day was so dark it did little to relieve the gloom. What little light there was came from his lantern. But she could see him across the room, see why he didn't need to tie her up to subdue her. Graves leaned against the closed half of the shutter, pointing a gun in her direction.

"Why . . ." She cleared her throat. "Why am I here?"

"We're waiting, Doc, for your rescuers to arrive."

"But why, Sergeant? Why have you brought *me* here?"

"First, it's to hear my story. After that? We'll see."

He shoved a crate over to the window with the heel of his boot and sat. He directed an occasional glance outside while he told Julia everything about the workhouse from his first day to his last. He spared no detail.

"I sent my story to Johnny Osborne, so the world will hear it. It should drop on his desk with the afternoon mail."

Julia was silent.

"Well, doctor? Cat got your tongue?"

"You suffered as no child deserves to suffer. Anyone who hears your story will understand your fury at the monsters who abused you. But why have you chosen me?"

"It's your grandfather. Don't you remember that day, the

morning you explained it all to the inspector? I was sitting at my desk right outside the door, and I heard every word." His grin twisted. "How *shattered* your grandfather was, how wracked with guilt he was for not believing Doctor Snow."

"But it wasn't his . . ."

"I had no idea he was one of those bastards on the sanitary board. You told me that. You said he ignored the evidence Snow put under his nose and allowed the poison to flow unchecked."

"Yes, but in the end, my grandfather realized he was wrong and worked to change the minds of others, the minds of those in power."

"Sorry, Doc. 'In the end' was too late to save my parents. Too late to save Jillie."

"Jillie?"

"My sister. She was nine years old when she died in the workhouse."

Something outside caught his attention. Screened by the left shutter, he stood and peered into the gloom. But the distance to the window was too great to take advantage of his distraction. And he had a gun. He turned back to her and resumed his seat.

"False alarm—no rescue just yet. We'll have to wait a while. Now, where was I? Oh, yes. At first, I thought about killing your grandfather the way I took care of Sir Maxwell Ball. I planned to tell him what he'd done to people like me, drive my knife into his guilty heart, and fill his throat with the shit he condemned others to drink."

Ask him questions, Julia thought. There was nothing else she could do. She tried to steady her voice.

"But you changed your mind and chose me. Why?"

He gave her a sad smile. "I like you, Doc. I do. But killing you will be the perfect revenge. The person he loves the most in the world will be dead. That's just what happened to me when I lost my parents." His smile vanished. "He'll pay for all the men like him—those blind and arrogant doctors, so smug and stubborn."

"But—"

"What do they care? It means nothing to them. Water flows clear and pure into *their* neighborhoods. I'd see them all dead if I could," he snarled, "choking on the white vomit of cholera. Think of the thousands who died. You've seen it many times, Doctor. Their faces, sunken and blue, knickers filled with runny shit, bodies wrapped and carried away in vomit-splattered bedding. That's the way my mother and father died."

"You said we were waiting for rescuers. How will they find us?"

"I expect Inspector Tennant to appear any minute now. As soon as he starts hunting and can't find me, I think he'll run to the clinic." He tipped his head and looked at her through narrowed eyes. "He's been worried about you. Dear Inspector Tennant, and you are dear to him, aren't you? Your grandfather won't be the only one haunted by regrets."

"He knows that you're the one who . . ."

"Oh, didn't I mention it, Doc? He went to Somerset House this morning. Guessed the right parish records to check. He'll find it all. Then he'll come looking for me. Your porter will give him the address. In fact . . ."

His head swung around. Graves jumped up and shoved the crate away from the window. He pressed himself against the shutter. "I think he's here now." He laughed. "Right on cue. Curtain up, Doc. It's time for the final act."

Tennant crouched behind a stack of abandoned crates, watching the side of the warehouse that faced the canal. The whole neighborhood looked derelict, a corner of East London left to rot. The only living soul he spotted was the canal's lockkeeper drowsing at his post just south of the warehouse.

He squinted at the mist rising from the canal and thought he detected a faint glow behind a half-open shutter. Barely breathing out his instructions, Tennant sent constables Robbins and Smythe across the canal's footbridge to confirm the house number. Then, as stealthily as possible, they were to round the warehouse, looking for exits. He kept Hawkins with his revolver by his side. The four other coppers he'd rounded up at Bethnal Green waited behind an abandoned cart for his signal.

Five minutes passed, and Robbins returned.

"It's the warehouse, all right—187 Canal Road. On the street side, there's a main entrance and a cellar door to the left of it. I left Smythe behind to keep an eye on both exits. The front door is standing open."

The inspector nodded. "An invitation."

He held up two fingers. A pair of bobbies from Putney Green crept up to him. "All right, constables. Cross over with Robbins and wait for my signal. If you hear a shot, enter the building at speed. I think Graves is holed up in the southwest upstairs room. Use your weapons if you must. But remember, he has a hostage."

Robbins and the constables scrambled off, keeping low to the ground.

Tennant wondered if Graves knew they were there. Had he spotted them, watched him as he made his preparations? To Constable Hawkins, he said, "Keep your eye and your revolver trained on that corner window."

It was time for Tennant to reach a decision. The element of surprise wasn't working in his favor, leaving him two choices, neither of them good. He could lead his men into the house in a sudden show of force. Storm up the staircase and hope Graves hadn't already done the worst. They could overwhelm him, certainly, killing or capturing him in the process. But Julia could die. Graves might kill her, or a policeman's stray bullet could strike her. Or Tennant could try another way. Surround the warehouse, bring his men into the open, and show Graves that escape was impossible. Call on him to surrender and release Julia unharmed.

What would he do, trapped like an animal with no way out? With the gallows his fate, would Graves decide that another death made little difference? Whatever choice Tennant made, the risk to Julia was severe.

"Sir," Hawkins whispered, "I thought I saw movement in the window."

Tennant made up his mind.

From his post behind the shutter, Graves watched a pair of policemen cross the canal. He trained his revolver on Julia and moved to the door. He listened.

"Our company isn't joining us just yet," he said. "Reconnoitering, I expect. So, what do you reckon, Doc, a full-on assault with guns blazing? I'd say the inspector judges that to be too risky. But what other choice does he have?"

"Jonathan, it's not too late to . . . to pull back from the brink. You can—"

"Shut your mouth, Doctor, and think about a little boy. Imagine him crying himself to sleep. Softly, so the other lads won't hear. Asking God why he took his parents away. Why the Lord brought him to that hellish place. Think about a boy who was *happy* when the porter passed his door and stopped at the other room. The room where Jillie . . . ."

"Jonathan, I am so sorry."

"Imagine one last thing, Doctor. A little boy on the night the porter first takes him to Mister Atwater. I started shaking, crying because I was so relieved. I ran to Atwater, thinking God had answered my prayers. That He had heard me at last. What a joke." He waved the gun across the room.

"Jonathan, any judge or jury who hears your story will find that you committed these acts while . . . ."

"While the 'balance of my mind was disturbed'?" He took a

step toward her. "Are you saying *I'm* insane? After what those devils did to me? A clergyman, others, more than I can count. Night after night." The last words came out in a sob.

"Jonathan, that's not what I'm saying. I'm saying the fathers on the jury will consider what was done to you and Jillie. When they hear your story, they'll think of their own sons and daughters, and what might happen if they're left alone in the world one day."

"No one can imagine. No one."

"I was orphaned, too, Jonathan, at an early age. My parents, like yours, died because of a company's criminal negligence."

She waited. After a little while, he said, "Is that true, Doc?"

"Yes. They were lost at sea, victims of greed and a poorly de-signed ship overloaded with cargo. All hands and passengers vanished."

"Bastards. They're all bastards." He shook his head. "But a jury won't spare me the rope. Even if I wanted to rot for years with the loonies in Broadmoor, they'd never swallow it—too well planned to be out of my mind. And a criminal copper must pay the full price. It's a matter of the fitness of things. No, it won't wash, Doc."

Graves pushed the shutter open a fraction. For a moment, a faint light caught his fair hair and lit the side of his face before he turned back to her. In the darkness, she couldn't see his blue eyes, but they were looking at her.

"Jonathan, do you remember you told me why you wanted to be a policeman in the first place? How I gave the same an-swer about being a doctor? We both wanted to do some good in the world."

He grunted.

"I'd like to tell a jury all about *that*, Jonathan. We both see so much of the world's ugliness, you and I. We're enraged at the world's indifference to sickness, suffering, and evil. We chose helping professions, the pair of us. Jonathan, we wanted to make a difference."

"We wasted our time, Doc."

Julia nodded. "I sometimes feel that way, too. But you? You righted the terrible wrongs done to you. And you explained yourself to the world; the *Illustrated* will print your story. Readers will understand your actions. Some will think they would have done the same in your place."

In the darkness, Julia couldn't read Jonathan's expression. Was she getting through to him? *Keep talking.*

"Jonathan, those monsters who hurt you—they'll get no sympathy when Johnny Osborne tells your story. But to kill me . . ." Julia shook her head. "To kill me as an act of revenge against another . . . you'll have an innocent person's blood on your hands. That will undo everything you've done."

Julia heard his quickening breaths.

"Do you remember that day in my office, Jonathan, when you picked up that wooden stethoscope from my desk? If you harm me now, you won't be Gabriel blowing your horn on Judgment Day. Instead, the world will think you are as evil as the men who abused you. Its judgment will be on you, not where it belongs—on them."

"The spotlight . . ."

"Yes, the limelight's glare. Shine it on center stage and expose the monsters. Don't dim it now."

The lantern light glinted off the metal of his gun. Julia saw the barrel waver and drop.

"Doc, I—"

"Come out, Graves!"

"Well, well," Graves said. "Tennant, at last."

"The building is surrounded by constables, front and back. Release Doctor Lewis and show yourself. My men will hold their fire."

Graves leveled his gun at her. "It's too late, Doc. Too late to rewrite the script." He smiled. "You almost had me, but Tennant's called time." He waggled the pistol. "On your feet."

Stiff and cramped, Julia knelt and then pushed herself up

from the floor. She stood for a moment with her back against the far wall.

"Jonathan, please. Don't do this."

He pointed with his gun. "Push the shutter open—all the way, mind—and stand in front of the window. I want the inspector to get a good look."

She walked as slowly as she dared, hoping all the time that an assault would begin, hoping for anything that might alter the course of the next few moments. When she reached the window, she looked to her left.

"Jonathan—"

"That's enough. Open the shutter and stand in the window frame so he can see you."

Julia pushed the shutter back and looked out. Everything was gray. She'd lost track of time, and with the smoky sky and swirling mists, it might have been any hour. The loading platform that jutted from the window blocked her view of the canal below. But she could make out the shapes of things along the bank on the other side—abandoned carts, barrels, and boxes. Yet, strain as she might against the mist, she detected no movement.

Julia felt the barrel of his gun against the center of her back. In her ear, he whispered, "Go forward. Step onto the platform. Slowly, now, I'm right behind you."

She lifted her foot over the low threshold and stepped onto the loading bridge. It creaked under her weight, and she wondered if the chains would hold. Something clattered across the floor behind her. Graves locked his left arm around her upper arms and chest. Once again, she felt the tip of a blade against her neck. He'd exchanged his revolver for the knife.

"Tennant!" Graves shouted. He didn't answer. "Come out, Tennant. Show yourself." The inspector stood from behind the crates. "Let me see your hands." Tennant raised his arms. "Good. Now order your company to do the same."

Tennant nodded to Hawkins. "Put the revolver in your pocket. It's no use anyway."

When the constable stood up and raised his hands, Graves laughed. "Hawkins, of course. Sorry, mate. Even you haven't got a shot at me today."

With his hands still in the air, Tennant took several steps toward the canal's edge. "You don't have to do this, Jonathan. There's nothing to be gained by more bloodshed."

"Now that's where you're wrong, guv. And you're here to witness it—the final act of justice. After Hawkins finally blows my brains out, you can read all about it in the *Illustrated*. I mailed my statement to Johnny Osborne this morning."

Tennant took another step forward.

"That's far enough," Graves shouted. "Stop right there."

With their attention fixed on each other, neither Tennant nor Graves had noticed the ancient lockkeeper. He'd abandoned his post and slowly picked his way along the far side of the canal while Julia stared into the dark water below.

"What's all the bleeding shouting about?" the old man yelled.

Graves jerked his head to the left, and the tip of his knife came away from her throat.

Jump. Julia hurled herself forward with all her strength, pulling her captor with her. Graves flailed his arms in a desperate attempt to regain his balance. The blade sliced into her neck before it flew into the mist, and they plunged headlong into the dark canal.

Julia had managed a breath before she hit the water. She sank deeper and deeper before the tip of her boot scraped the bottom. She tried to get a firm footing on the canal floor, to plant her foot and propel her body upward. But imprisoned in the folds of her skirt and petticoat, she couldn't find the bottom. She struggled to use her arms to reach the surface, but the weight of her boots and the shroud of her clothing held her suspended underwater. Her lungs were bursting. Her movements slowed, and she felt pins and needles prick at the backs of her eyes. She took a breath, and her lungs began to fill with water. A moment later, she went limp and floated upward, drifting into darkness.

Tennant had torn off his coat, ripped off his boots, and plunged into the black water of the narrow canal. With a few strokes, he arrived at the spot where Julia went under. He dove once, then again, kicking his way to the bottom. Each scissoring thrust sent stabs of searing pain down his leg. Finally, on his third try, his left hand felt something—long tresses floating in the water. Then both hands found her shoulders. He wrapped his arms around her and kicked his way to the surface. Two coppers were in the canal to help him pull Julia to the edge. Two others helped drag her out of the water.

He hoisted himself up and fell on his knees beside her. She didn't seem to be breathing, but as a boy in Kent, he'd watched a French doctor revive a child pulled from the lake. Everyone else had given him up for dead.

Tennant rolled Julia onto her stomach. He positioned her head to the side and forced her mouth open. He tried to ignore the blood seeping from her neck, straddled her at the hips, and started pushing and pounding on her back. After a few moments, her torso jerked, and a gush of canal water flowed from her mouth. He fell back at her side, exhausted, listening to the sound of her retching.

When he opened his eyes, Paddy O'Malley was staring down at him. Tennant extended his hand, and the constable pulled him to his feet. He'd found Tennant's coat on the ground and tugged it around his shoulders.

Two constables lifted Julia onto a stretcher. She turned her head to the side, coughed, and opened her eyes. Tennant stood there. She tried to prop herself up by her elbow and fell back. "Where . . . what's happened to—"

"It's all right, Doctor. You're safe now," Tennant said. "Graves is dead."

"No, no," she moaned. "I'd nearly . . . he was about to . . ." Her head fell to the side. "If only you'd waited, damn it! Why didn't you . . ." Her eyes closed again. The constables picked up her stretcher and carried her away.

O'Malley looked at the inspector. "She'll be all right?"

"Oh, I think so. Barely conscious, and she's second-guessing my decisions." He found his hat on the ground and picked it up. A constable held his sodden boots. "Let's go."

O'Malley looked like he'd just witnessed a train wreck. "I saw Kane, the rent collector. He told me Graves was the landlord, so I came looking for you."

"It was all there—at Somerset House."

They followed Julia's stretcher to the police wagon. Tennant said, "I'm going with her to the hospital. Take charge of the search for the body. Set up torches and guards around the perimeter, although I believe he's dead. I'll send the wagon on to the Bethnal Green station for reinforcements. And send a runner with a message for her grandfather."

Tennant climbed in. He folded a blanket on his lap to make a pillow for her. The constables laid Julia across the bench and handed him a towel to press against the wound on her neck. A bobbie piled two more blankets over her. Another dropped Tennant's boots on the wagon floor and banged the door shut. Then, with a forward tug, the horses pulled away. They headed for the Royal London Hospital at Mile End, only a few streets from the canal. He looked down at Julia and felt the light puff of her breath against his wrist.

While Tennant slumped in a chair outside her door, Andrew Lewis was inside, conferring with the doctors. Someone had brought the inspector a change of clothes, the trousers and heavy cotton tunic of a hospital orderly. He'd finally stopped shivering.

Tennant waved away medical care, but a nurse said, "Nonsense," and dragged him off to a treatment room. A doctor listened to his chest and left the nurse to administer the eyewash. She tut-tutted. "Bathing in the Regent's Canal, were you?" She pushed his head backward over a sink and poured a liquid into each of his eyes.

An hour passed. Dr. Lewis finally emerged, gray-faced but managing a smile. He reached for Tennant's hand and gripped it in both of his.

"Inspector, I . . ." Blinking, he looked away.

"Yes."

"She'll recover. She's sleeping now, but would you like to see her?"

"Yes."

Dr. Lewis opened the door for him, then closed it gently.

The following morning, Tennant arrived early at the hospital, but his constable had beaten him there. Julia was propped up in bed, awake but groggy. Her scrapes and bruises were turning green and purple, a vivid contrast against her pale skin and the white bandage at her neck.

"Constable O'Malley was here with the birds," she said. "He dropped in on his way to the canal. He told me what happened. That I have you to thank for my life."

"Thank me by being a good patient. I'm told doctors make the worst."

"You're right about that." She shifted in her bed and winced. "And I also have you to thank for these bruises on my back, I'm told. Where did you learn the technique?"

"I saw it done years ago. I'll tell you about it when you're stronger."

Julia's head fell back against her pillow. "It's unbelievable. Jonathan."

"I'll ask you to tell me everything that happened, everything he said to you, but not now." He smiled. "I don't presume to advise a doctor, but it's best not to think about it just yet."

"Hmm—probably right . . ." she nodded, her eyes closing.

Tennant watched her drift into sleep.

At the canal, the inspector found two lines of constables thrusting poles into the water, hoping to hit their mark. O'Malley waved to him from the lock and made his way along the bank.

"Nothing yet, sir. The lockkeeper is saying it can take twenty-four hours—or more—for the canal to give up its dead."

They didn't find him until late in the day. Then, at dusk, torchlight caught the white, bobbing face of Jonathan Graves, bumping against the gate of the lock. When they hauled him out, he was hard to recognize. Bloated, his fair hair black with muck, his eyes open, blue and staring. Tennant reached down and closed them. Two constables moved him to a stretcher and carried him away.

O'Malley looked past the inspector. "Mother of God. Here's that gobshite Johnny Osborne."

Tennant turned. The reporter was hailing them from the footbridge.

"The man's timing is diabolical." Tennant walked toward him. "I'll thank you to keep your distance, Mister Osborne."

The reporter craned his neck to see what the constables were carrying away, but he made no move to follow them. "I'll tell you, Inspector. It's one thing to write about a monster you've never met, but a man you shared a pint with? And the blighter was so bloody cheerful all the time."

Tennant seized Osborne by the shoulders and turned him around. Then he walked him across the bridge with a hand on the reporter's back.

"I can confirm we found the body of Sergeant Graves, but that is all I have to say for now."

Osborne flashed his cocky grin. "Tell me one thing, Inspector. Did you really suspect me?"

"Had your name turned up in the workhouse records, I wouldn't have been surprised. Let's leave it at that."

"And here I am, extending a professional courtesy." The reporter handed Tennant a copy of the *Illustrated London News*. "Hot off the press, as we say on Fleet Street. Tomorrow, it'll be on all the streets of London."

Tennant unfolded the copy and read the headline: A MURDERER'S LAST TESTAMENT.

"It arrived yesterday in the afternoon mail," Osborne said. "We worked on it all night."

Graves would be pleased he made the front page, Tennant thought.

"Well, Inspector, I'm off . . . for now." Osborne flicked a two-fingered salute and sauntered away.

O'Malley joined Tennant, eying the reporter's retreating back. "What did the creature want?"

The inspector showed him the headline.

The constable nodded. "The keeper said the canal always gives up its secrets. So did the sergeant in the end."

Aunt Caroline leaned over Julia's bed and kissed her niece.

"Try not to dwell on things, my dear. It can't be good for your recovery." She rested her hand on Julia's cheek. "I'll be back tomorrow. Kate will bring your travel things, and we'll take you home. Rest now."

"Thank you, Aunt. I am a little tired."

Lady Aldridge nodded and closed the door behind her.

It was exhausting, being told to rest and not to think. *Might as well tell me not to breathe.*

The sensation of falling, the shock of hitting the water, reaching with her hands, her feet, floating as she drifted into darkness. Julia doubted the memory of those sensations would ever leave her.

Still, her leap into the water had taught her some things she didn't want to forget. She better understood that the world's dangers were like the layers of clothing that nearly dragged her to her death: they ensnared women and men unequally. That was a reality she would have been wiser not to minimize. *But for those damnable skirts, I could have made it to the bank on my own.*

Clothing might be a trivial example of women's limitations, but her confining garments seemed more emblematic than ever. Julia would start there. She resolved to write to the *Times* in support of the dress reform movement. *Much good that will do.*

Still, Julia had learned something about herself, as well. At the moment of maximum peril, she didn't wait for rescue. She jumped. She freed herself from Jonathan's grasp. Before that, she'd kept her wits about her, had nearly persuaded him to release her. *Before Tennant blundered in.* Women were capable of so much more than they realized. Both women and men needed schooling in what the "weaker sex" could do, starting with the inspector.

Still, Tennant had saved her life, and she was grateful. She remembered the first time they'd met, how he'd struggled in and out of the sewage ditch with that bad leg. Diving in, pulling her to safety—he'd probably been in great pain. *The stronger sex.* Perhaps that was why he went to such trouble to hide his limp. Society's expectations imprisoned men and women.

There were moments when Julia felt angrier with Tennant than with Jonathan, even though she knew it wasn't reasonable or fair. *Impossible*, she thought, *to stand on the precipice with someone and not feel a kind of kinship.* Her empathy for the sergeant had been genuine, even though he wished her the worst sort of harm. Perhaps that was why she'd nearly changed his mind.

She had tried to explain it all to her Aunt Caroline, wanting her to see the damaged child and not the monster.

Julia saw a boy filled with relief and then consumed with

self-loathing when men with other tastes passed his room to prey on the little girls. And she knew what it was to live with guilt and shame. Julia also remembered the man whose hand wavered near the end. It didn't erase the memory of his knife at her neck, but it balanced it.

There was one thing more. Although Julia had no choice and would do it again, there was something terrible in knowing she had caused the death of another human being. She closed her eyes. While rest wouldn't come, tears she couldn't stop arrived in sleep's place.

The day faded to dusk. Outside her window, a gaslight blinked on, the lamplighter making his rounds.

What do you do after you nearly die? She knew the answer. It was both simple and infinitely complicated.

You live, but not as you lived before.

CHAPTER 18

That evening, Tennant drove to Finsbury Circus to deliver the news that his team had recovered the body. He brought the copy of the *Illustrated* with him as well.

When he arrived, Julia's grandfather was upstairs, changing. Mrs. Ogilvie invited the inspector to wait for him in the library, where he'd find a warm fire, Julia's aunt, and a glass of sherry—or whiskey, if he preferred.

The housekeeper opened the door. "Inspector Tennant, my lady," she said, and withdrew.

Lady Aldridge rose and extended her hand. "Words are . . . impossible. Inadequate. But for you, it would have been the end of my poor brother as well as his granddaughter."

"It's what Graves wanted." Tennant laid the *Illustrated* on the table. "It will all be here, in tomorrow's edition."

"When my brother left the room to speak to Julia's doctors, she told me the things that madman said. It will crush Andrew to hear that Graves planned to kill her as vengeance against him. It's only been two months since his attack. Thank God, the shock didn't produce a second crisis." She folded the paper. "I'll put this aside and speak to him tomorrow morning."

She put her hand on the whiskey decanter and looked at him. When Tennant nodded, she poured him a drink and handed it to him.

"Thank you, Lady Aldridge." He took a sip. "The *Illustrated* is not always reliable, but the story appears to be a verbatim account of Graves's life."

"Julia told me that the man's childhood was a nightmare. Pitiable, I suppose, but I'm afraid I cannot summon up that emotion."

"I agree with you. His narrative included two surprises for our investigation. To my relief, Graves confessed he'd laid a false trail to include Thomas Rigby as his supposed first victim. That we hanged the banker's real killer is one less burden for my conscience. We also learned that he harbored a murderous rage against the uncle who adopted him, blaming him for all his tragedies and for arriving too late to save his little sister. Graves killed him."

"The police never suspected?"

Tennant shook his head. "I also came to tell you that we retrieved the sergeant's body. Julia doesn't know it yet. I saw her earlier today, before our search party recovered the corpse."

"My niece told me you visited." She gestured to a chair. "Shall we sit?"

"Thank you." He took another sip of his drink. "She looked better than I expected."

"An hour ago, Andrew and I left her sitting up in bed. Two days in the hospital will be enough. My brother thinks there's no point in keeping her there beyond tomorrow."

"I'm sure she agrees—and who can stand up against two doctors named Lewis?"

When Tennant arrived at the hospital the following morning, he thought he detected some change for the better. Julia seemed more alert. But she was still pale, and her voice sounded scratchy.

She waved at her throat. "The result of some God-awful muck I swallowed. But I'm feeling stronger."

There was a pot of tea on the table next to her bed. "Would you like some of that?"

She nodded, and he poured her a cup. "It feels good — laced with honey." She took a sip. "Better." She shifted under her blankets. "Although I've slept on more comfortable mattresses; this one seems made of iron." She took a few more sips and handed him the cup. "Have you any news?"

"We recovered the body late yesterday afternoon. And there's something else I wanted you to know. Johnny Osborne turned up with a copy of the *Illustrated*. They printed Graves's life story in today's edition, written by him."

Julia closed her eyes. "Dear God, my grandfather."

"I gave Lady Aldridge a copy last night. She planned to speak to him this morning before he saw it. Break it to him as gently as possible."

"Despite the happy ending, it will take its toll on him."

"Yes, but he'll have you back, safe and sound. This afternoon, I understand."

"Home again. Back to normal."

Julia didn't sound convinced. Despite her improvement, she seemed different to him, not so quick to smile, more somber.

As if she read his mind, she sighed. "Normal. When you think you're about to die, but instead you live, it changes you. As if you returned to the womb, reborn as a different person in an unfamiliar world. I — I feel I don't have my bearings, that I don't quite know who I am." With a ghost of her old smile, she said, "Perhaps it will pass."

"I had a similar experience in the Crimea. But like a stubborn gambler, I doubled down. Buried my feelings, desperate to get back to normal. It wasn't a winning strategy."

"I'll try to be patient with myself."

"In time, I think most of the old Julia will be back."

"Who knows?" she shrugged. "There may be something about the new one I'll want to keep."

"Perhaps." He smiled. "Although I hope you'll hold on to your old instincts. You were right from the beginning, you know."

"What do you mean?"

"That the crimes grew out of a lacerating childhood experience that haunted the killer through life. I believe those were your words."

"About one thing, I was wrong—the danger to me. I'm sorry I was so dismissive."

He stood and offered his hand. "So that makes us all square, Doctor?"

She took it. "Yes. All square, Inspector."

With Mrs. Ogilvie on one side and Kate on the other, Julia climbed slowly up the stairs. Her Aunt Caroline and her grandfather watched from the foot of the staircase.

"Andrew? She looks as if she's struggling. Were we too hasty? Is she well enough to be home?"

He patted her arm. "My dear sister, she's all right. She's been in bed for two days. She's a little weak, that's all."

"She can hear you," Julia said from the top of the stairs. "And she's fine."

Mrs. Ogilvie pushed open her bedroom door and stood back. When Kate walked her to the chair at her dressing table, Julia sat with a thud.

"That was harder than I thought. Don't tell Aunt Caroline I said that."

Kate looked past her to something on the dressing table.

Julia turned. "What's this?" It was a bouquet nestled in a rose bowl. "Who sent these, Kate?"

"They arrived early in the afternoon. There's a card."

Julia opened the tiny envelope. "They're from Inspector Tennant. How kind of him." She put the card aside. "Let me walk to my wardrobe without your arm, see how I do." She stood and took a few unsteady steps.

The maid looked down at the note. "*Hothouse roses sent in winter with my good wishes. 'Can spring be far behind?' Tennant.*"

When Tennant's hansom pulled up to Julia's town house, he spotted her rounding the curve on Kate's arm. He paid off the cabbie and strode after them.

At the sound of his footsteps, Kate glanced over her shoulder and slowed. "Inspector Tennant, good evening, sir. Can you take over for me?"

"A pleasure, Miss Connolly." He took Julia's arm.

As the maid walked away, Julia sighed. "Kate fusses. I'm well enough, but she won't let me walk even the shortest distance on my own." When he moved to release her, she held on to his arm. "I'm not complaining."

"You *are* better. I had to stretch my legs to catch up to you."

"On the mend." They walked a few paces. "How are things at the Yard?"

"In turmoil, as you'd expect. As for me . . ."

"They blame you?"

"I failed to detect that my immediate junior was a homicidal lunatic—not helpful to the career of a detective inspector."

Julia stopped and looked at him. "How worried are you?"

He shrugged. "Sir Richard Mayne is a fair-minded man. And as for the chief—Clark pushed Graves forward, recommended him for sergeant. And he served under the chief inspector's overall command."

"Inconvenient for the old boy."

"Quite. And there's another thing that makes this disastrous case less . . . it's awkward to put it into words."

She looked at him. "What?"

"The public's reaction would be different if the victims had been a string of innocent schoolgirls. After we failed to unmask that killer quickly, the heartbreak and the outrage would have been severe. It's not that people approve of murder, but . . ."

"There's not much sympathy for his targets."

He pressed her arm. "For all except the last one, no."

"The account in the *Illustrated* . . . Jonathan told me his story in more lurid, more hideous detail. Such depravity visited on a little boy; some of the images may never fade from my memory."

"I'm sorry for that. It's part of why I wanted to see you, to ask how you are."

"How am I?" She looked at the sky and followed the flight of a pigeon as it flew past them and alighted on a fence post. "I'm happy. I'm happy to see that most ordinary bird—and all his friends of a feather. I'm blessed with this lovely evening and to be on my feet, walking around the circus." Her voice grew husky. "And I'm grateful—everlastingly grateful—to you for my life. But you know that. I've told you often enough the past few days."

The shake of his head was imperceptible. He pointed to a bench. "Shall we sit a while? Or are you cold?"

"Not a bit."

Once they'd settled in their seats, Julia said, "What's the other part?"

"Sorry?"

"You said, to ask how I was feeling was *part* of why you wanted to see me."

He turned to face her. Her dark eyes held tiny flames, reflections from the lamplight behind him. "Well . . . I wanted to put a proposition to you."

"A proposition, Inspector?"

He cleared his throat. "I understand from Lady Aldridge that your grandfather is retiring from medicine."

"That's true."

"So he'll no longer be on the Yard's list of medical examiners."

"That's also true."

He looked down, fiddling with his gloves. "Well . . . Johnny Osborne informed me he's writing a second article about the case. It will appear in the next edition of the *Illustrated*. 'Police bungle arrest of a killer; lady doctor wrestles with a madman and rescues herself.' That seems to be the gist of it."

"What has this to do with my grandfather's retirement?"

"I persuaded Sir Richard to add your name to the list of medical examiners, in place of your grandfather."

Julia stared at him.

"If you agree, of course."

"That's about the last thing I expected you to say."

He watched her closely, wanting to make out her expression, but she'd tilted her head away.

Finally, she looked back at him. "Why would you ask the commissioner to do that?"

"Well, I thought . . . that is to say . . . it seems to me that we work well together. I also told him that it was one way to get ahead of the story. By next week, you'll be famous, and we'll look like idiots. Bringing you onboard will make lemonade out of lemons."

"I see." She let a few seconds tick by. "So, in your discussion with Sir Richard, I was the lemon?"

"I may have employed an unfortunate metaphor. I apologize."

"How far are you willing to go?"

"Hmm?"

"With your apologies. Are you willing to admit you've been

wrong all along? That you've underestimated the capabilities of women? That we're smarter, stronger, and more enterprising than you thought?"

"Yes, damn it. I admit it. Are you satisfied?"

"Not yet. But it's a start."

Dusk was sinking fast into darkness, the faint light of early winter vanishing from the sky. Julia stood and offered Tennant her arm. They made one last turn around the circus, guided home by a ring of glowing lamplights.

ACKNOWLEDGMENTS

I'll begin by thanking my first reader and sister, Carol McDonough. She told me to stop reading and start writing.

Next is my "beta team," Kathy Sandt and Ginny Quain. Kathy's multiple readings and our afternoons mulling motivation and character strengthened the writing and the story immeasurably. I'll say it now: when we disagreed, Kathy was right in the end—nearly always. And Ginny's keen eye for too-obvious clues kept the mystery mysterious.

Murder by Lamplight would be just a file on my laptop without the support of so many others. Wendy McCurdy at Kensington took a chance on a first-time author. Thank you, Wendy. Elizabeth Trout got back to me in a flash whenever I had questions, which was often. I'm grateful to all the talented people at Kensington Publishing, especially Seth Lerner, for his fantastic cover design, production editor Robin Cook, publicist Jesse Cruz, and copy editor Pat Fogarty. Pat's eagle eye caught many mistakes. (Who knew that "bonkers" wasn't used until 1945?) I thank you all.

But my most heartfelt gratitude is reserved for my agent, Jim Donovan. His efforts and editorial advice made the final version of *Murder by Lamplight* much better than the manuscript I sent him. And Jim's confidence that the novel would find a publisher and an audience made me believe it, too.